D1029890

THE SHORT STORIES OF FRANK HARRIS

A Selection

Edited, with an Afterword by
Elmer Gertz

Southern Illinois University Press
CARBONDALE AND EDWARDSVILLE

Feffer & Simons, Inc.
LONDON AND AMSTERDAM

H3142ᴀ

Library of Congress Cataloging in Publication Data

Harris, Frank, 1855–1931.
    The short stories of Frank Harris.

    CONTENTS: Eatin' crow.—The best man in Garotte.—
The sheriff and his partner.—Montes: the matador.
[etc.]
    I. Title.
PZ3.H2412Sh4   [PR4759.H37]   823'.9'12   75-6883
ISBN 0-8093-0721-9

DEDICATORY EPISTLE

WHEN I WAS a very young man, even before I was graduated from college, I became acquainted with Arthur Leonard Ross, a distinguished New York attorney who seemed to devote as much time to befriending writers and public figures as to earning professional fees. I got to know him because of his close attachment to Frank Harris, whose writings and personality were absorbing my attention to so great a degree that I wrote the first serious book about him, in collaboration with Dr. A. I. Tobin, while I was still in law school.

Naturally, we turned to Ross to find a publisher for us. He devoted an extraordinary amount of time until the book was finally published in 1931, and he would take no compensation for his work.

During the years I kept in touch with him I observed his self-sacrificial efforts in behalf of the famous anarchist, Emma Goldman, a friend of the Frank Harrises and of all mankind. He did more than anyone to protect the interests of Frank Harris and subsequently of his widow, the glamorous Nellie Harris. He saw to it that Harris's books received at least some of the attention that they deserved after his death. Thus it was that he and I worked with Barney Rosset, years later, in the effort which led to the open publication of Frank Harris's *My Life and Loves* by Grove Press.

Much to our surprise, in the shadow of the suppression in the past, no effort was made to censor the book or prosecute anyone in connection with its distribution. Indeed, in England, which once had looked upon Harris with troubled eyes, *My Life and Loves* became a best seller. I seem to recall that more was paid for the paperback edition of the onetime shocker than for any other paperback in recent history.

I think of these things and more as I see this collection of some of Frank Harris's better short stories through the press. I am indebted to Arthur Leonard Ross for the necessary permission in his role as Executor of the Frank Harris Estate. Advanced in years, but still a charmer and still a man of bright intellect and many interests, I am proud to call him my friend for almost half a century. To me, he is the prototype of what a lawyer should be— devoted to his profession, but still a complete man and citizen, loving the best in life and the arts.

I take great pleasure in dedicating this book to Arthur Leonard Ross.

Elmer Gertz

CONTENTS

page v   Dedicatory Epistle

ix   Preface

1   Eatin' Crow

7   The Best Man in Garotte

14   The Sheriff and His Partner

36   Montes: The Matador

79   The Miracle of the Stigmata

95   The Magic Glasses

128   The Holy Man

138   The King of the Jews

144   A Daughter of Eve

187   Akbar: "The Mightiest"

207   St. Peter's Difficulty

210   The Extra Eight Days

215   A Mad Love

258   A Chinese Story

287   The Tom Cat—An Apologue

291   Afterword: The Legend of Frank Harris

PREFACE

FRANK HARRIS, the cowboy from the plains of Kansas and points west, devoted his first published stories to the special world he had known as a youth while on the trail of cattle and rough men. Now, a little more than a decade after his great American adventures, he was the editor of the prestigious *Fortnightly Review* in London, which numbered the greatest writers of England and the European continent among its contributors. Almost as if inviting comparison, he published in its pages "A Modern Idyll" and others of the western tales ultimately included in the volume known as *Elder Conklin and Other Stories*, his first book. Because Harris later wrote better stories of the same genre, I have not included "A Modern Idyll" here. It might have cost Harris the editorship of the *Fortnightly*, because of its amoral treatment of love, had not George Meredith, a giant of English literature in the nineteenth century, intervened in his behalf. Meredith remained one of the great admirers of Harris's stories. Later, he pronounced "Montes" one of the supreme tales of our language. Those who reviewed the first volume by Harris, issued in England and America in 1894, were extraordinary men by any standards—among them, Edward Dowden, the Shakespearean scholar, and Coventry Patmore, the poet-mystic. They compared Harris with Bret Harte, whose stories of the West, like "The Outcasts of Poker Flat," had become classics. Harris's stories, they said, had economy and distinction of phrasing and incident. "Eatin' Crow," included in this volume, was a superb example of what Harris could do in a few deft pages. Its stark essence would linger forever in the minds of all who read it.

Restless as always, Harris did not seek to capitalize on this American mood. He ventured immediately into other experiences and depicted persons and places having little resemblance to the nation he had visualized in his maiden venture, if one can use so prissy a phrase in discussing the robust cowboy-editor. True, "Profit and Loss" had an American setting, but it was not typical of the book which followed.

Montes the Matador and Other Stories was published only a few years after *Elder Conklin*. Indeed, the title story was written in 1891, even before the publication of the first book, and all save one of the stories were composed before the dawn of the new century. If Harris had written only "Montes," he would have deserved high place in the history of the short story. As Meredith pointed out, Harris gave life not only to the people in his tale, but even more to the bulls. He gave them personality, character. One expected them to speak, to act, to react. No story of bull-fighting has so much of the peculiar spirit of the great Spanish pursuit as this one. It is as nearly perfect as anything Harris ever wrote. He had a gift for great impressionistic dabs of paint. In this story, he dwells upon each detail, and not simply the overall effect. It is carefully wrought from first to last word. There is an inevitability about it which is overwhelming.

The book *Montes the Matador* closes with "Sonia," the story of the Russian anarchists who slew a czar and won martyrdom. It was a theme to which Harris returned in his first novel, *The Bomb*, changing only the scene but not the essential sympathy for those who were prepared to throw away their very lives for a principle. Bernard Shaw referred to him as the Homer of this cause.

Preoccupied with Shakespearean criticism, the editing of a succession of nondescript magazines, and the pursuit of dollars and superexcitation, Harris did not publish another book of short stories until 1913, when one of his most important works, *Unpath'd Waters*, appeared. In essence, it is utterly different from earlier volumes, but with at least one story, "An English Saint," reminiscent of the amorality of "A Modern Idyll." The longest story in the book, it tells of a man who gained sanctity by being seduced by the right women at the right times. This is representative of a particular Harrisian mood of cynicism. "Mr. Jacob's Philosophy" and "The Ring" have a similar aura of skepticism and contempt for some classes of mankind. "The Irony of Chance" and "The Magic Glasses" rise several notches above the cheapness that disfigures "Mr. Jacob." But it is in the stories of Jesus, in *Unpath'd Waters*, especially "The Miracle of the Stigmata," that Harris exhibits a spiritual quality that makes one forget the seedier and more sordid side of his personality and style. Occasionally, later, as in "St. Peter's Difficulty" (*Undream'd of Shores*), Harris recaptured the elevated religiosity of a true mystic.

Harris's stories, like everything he has written, bear witness to the combination of diverse qualities that has always distinguished his work at its best and at its worst— an irresistible attraction for all sorts and conditions of men and women, striking and diversified scenes and situations, variety almost for its own sake, always dramatic and sometimes shocking changes and chances, conversation from the most naturalistic to the poetic and unreal, a preoccupation with the most primitive passion no less than the most suble nuances of action and contemplation so intertwined as to be indistinguishable.

These traits were illustrated in all of the stories by

Harris which followed. When Harris first became an exile from England and resided again in America, *The Yellow Ticket and Other Stories* was published in England and *The Veils of Isis and Other Stories* in the United States. The content of both volumes is largely the same, except for the tender "In the Vale of Tears" which appears only in the British volume and "Within the Shadow" and "The Kiss," in the American volume.

The great story of these two books is "A Daughter of Eve," a tremendous tragic tale of passion. It is better, I think, than anything in Harris's autobiography, *My Life and Loves,* despite the latter's advertised sexuality. Harris should have learned from this simple story that one can arouse the senses to the utmost without trafficking in explicitness of action or language. Harris was an anatomist and chronicler of love. In story after story, he turned to the greatest of human passions, never wholly satisfied with the results, because he had a zealot's faith that someday, somehow, he was going to achieve a perfect story in that realm. Harris felt that restraint, inhibition, was the great enemy. Yet, that very quality of reticence made "A Daughter of Eve" a great story, and "A Mad Love," in his last book of stories, *Undream'd of Shores,* published in 1924, possibly more subtle and overpowering.

In some respects, *Undream'd of Shores* is Harris's literary testament. In it he tried to include everything that gave power and sometimes distinction to his work. There are stories of New York, Vienna, Paris, Scotland, England, China, India, Africa, many of the colorful spots of this kaleidoscopic world, not to mention heaven. There are stories of musicians, warriors, rulers, prizefighters, cannibals; stories of intellect, feeling, action. There are moods and fancies, realized and unrealized. There is much striving, some stridancy, and sometimes success.

Harris's output of stories is not as voluminous as some masters. He has written enough, however, to recapture the reputation that he once had in this area. This selection of his most representative and some of his best stories points to a kind of pathetic grandeur. Because Harris yearned for goals that he could not reach, what he accomplished in one field, the tale, has been too long ignored, if not forgotten.

NOTE: My sources for the individual stories reprinted in this volume have been varied. Three stories were taken from the volume *Elder Conklin, and Other Stories;* four from *Undream'd of Shores;* seven stories from the E. Haldeman-Julius, ed., Little Blue Book editions; and one story was privately printed in a limited edition. It has, therefore, been necessary to regularize the few instances of British spelling and punctuation and to correct an occasional typographic error so as to conform to modern American practices.

E. G.

Chicago, Illinois
March 1, 1975

THE SHORT STORIES OF FRANK HARRIS

EATIN' CROW

The evening on which Charley Muirhead made his first appearance at Doolan's was a memorable one; the camp was in wonderful spirits. Whitman was said to have struck it rich. Garotte, therefore, might yet become popular in the larger world, and its evil reputation be removed. Besides, what Whitman had done any one might do, for by common consent he was a "derned fool." Good-humor accordingly reigned at Doolan's, and the saloon was filled with an excited, hopeful crowd. Bill Bent, however, was anything but pleased; he generally was in a bad temper, and this evening, as Crocker remarked carelessly, he was "more ornery than ever." The rest seemed to pay no attention to the lanky, dark man with the narrow head, round, black eyes, and rasping voice. But Bent would croak: "Whitman's struck nothin'; thar ain't no gold in Garotte; it's all work and no dust." In this strain he went on, offending local sentiment and making every one uncomfortable.

Muirhead's first appearance created a certain sensation. He was a fine upstanding fellow of six feet or over, well-made, and good-looking. But Garotte had too much experience of life to be won by a stranger's handsome looks. Muirhead's fair moustache and large blue eyes counted for little there. Crocker and others, masters in the art of judging men, noticed that his eyes were unsteady, and his manner, though genial, seemed hasty. Reggitt summed up their opinion in the phrase, "looks as if he'd bite off more'n he could chaw." Unconscious of the criticism, Muirhead talked, offered drinks, and made himself agreeable.

At length in answer to Bent's continued grumbling, Muirhead said pleasantly: " 'Tain't so bad as that in Garotte, is it? This bar don't look like poverty, and if I set up drinks for the crowd, it's because I'm glad to be in this camp."

"P'r'aps you found the last place you was in jes' a leetle too warm, eh?" was Bent's retort.

Muirhead's face flushed, and for a second he stood as if he had been struck. Then, while the crowd moved aside, he sprang toward Bent, exclaiming, "Take that back—right off! Take it back!"

"What?" asked Bent coolly, as if surprised; at the same time, however, retreating a pace or two, he slipped his right hand behind him.

Instantly Muirhead threw himself upon him, rushed him with what seemed demoniac strength to the open door and flung him away out on his back into the muddy ditch that served as a street. For a moment there was a hush of expectation, then Bent was seen to gather himself up painfully and move out of the square of light into the darkness. But Muirhead did not wait for this; hastily, with hot face and hands still working with excitement, he returned to the bar with:

"That's how I act. No one can jump me. No one, by God!" and he glared round the room defiantly. Reggitt, Harrison, and some of the others looked at him as if on the point of retorting, but the cheerfulness was general, and Bent's grumbling before a stranger had irritated them almost as much as his unexpected cowardice. Muirhead's challenge was not taken up, therefore, though Harrison did remark, half sarcastically:

"That may be so. You jump them, I guess."

"Well, boys, let's have the drink," Charley Muirhead went on, his manner suddenly changing to that of friendly greeting, just as if he had not heard Harrison's words.

The men moved up to the bar and drank, and before the liquor was consumed, Charley's geniality, acting on the universal good-humor, seemed to have done away with the discontent which his violence and Bent's cowardice had created. This was the greater tribute to his personal charm, as the refugees of Garotte usually hung together, and were inclined to resent promptly any insult offered to one of their number by a stranger. But in the present case harmony seemed to be completely re-established, and it would have taken a keener observer than Muirhead to have understood his own position and the general opinion. It was felt that the stranger had bluffed for all he was worth, and that Garotte had come out "at the little end of the horn."

A day or two later Charley Muirhead, walking about the camp, came upon Dave Crocker's claim, and offered to buy half of it and work as a partner, but the other would not sell; "the claim was worth nothin'; not good enough for two, anyhow"; and there the matter would have ended, had not the young man proposed to work for a spell just to keep his hand in. By noon Crocker was won; nobody could resist Charley's hard work and laughing high spirits. Shortly afterwards the older man proposed to knock off; a day's work, he reckoned, had been done, and evidently considering it impossible to accept a stranger's labor without acknowledgment, he pressed Charley to come up to his shanty and eat. The simple meal was soon dispatched, and Crocker, feeling the obvious deficiencies of his larder, produced a bottle of Bourbon, and the two began to drink. Glass succeeded glass, and at length Crocker's reserve seemed to thaw; his manner became almost easy, and he spoke half frankly.

"I guess you're strong," he remarked. "You threw Bent out of the saloon the other night like as if he was nothin'; strength's good, but 'tain't everythin'. I mean," he added, in answer to the other's questioning look, "Samson wouldn't have a show with a man quick on the draw who meant bizness. Bent didn't pan out worth a cent, and the boys didn't like him, but—them things don't happen often." So in his own way he tried to warn the man to whom he had taken a liking.

Charley felt that a warning was intended, for he replied decisively: "It don't matter. I guess he wanted to jump me, and I won't be jumped, not if Samson wanted to, and all the revolvers in Garotte were on me."

"Wall," Crocker went on quietly, but with a certain curiosity in his eyes, "that's all right, but I reckon you were mistaken. Bent didn't want to rush ye; 'twas only his cussed way, and he'd had mighty bad luck. You might hev waited to see if he meant anythin', mightn't ye?" And he looked his listener in the face as he spoke.

"That's it," Charley replied, after a long pause, "that's just it. I couldn't wait, d'ye see!" and then continued hurriedly, as if driven to relieve himself by a full confession: "Maybe you don't *sabe*. It's plain enough, though I'd have to begin far back to make you understand. But I don't mind if you want to hear. I was raised in the East, in Rhode Island, and I guess I was liked by everybody. I never had trouble with any one, and I was a sort of favorite. . . . I fell in love with a girl, and as I hadn't much money, I came West to make some, as quick as I knew how. The first place I struck was Laramie—you don't know it? 'Twas a hard place; cowboys, liquor saloons, cursin' and swearin', poker and shootin' nearly every night. At the beginning I seemed to get along all right,

and I liked the boys, and thought they liked me. One
night a little Irishman was rough on me; first of all I didn't
notice, thought he meant nothin', and then, all at once, I
saw he meant it—and more.

"Well, I got a kind of scare—I don't know why—and I
took what he said and did nothin'. Next day the boys sort
of held off from me, didn't talk; thought me no account, I
guess, and that little Irishman just rode me round the
place with spurs on. I never kicked once. I thought I'd get
the money—I had done well with the stock I had
bought—and go back East and marry, and no one would
be any the wiser. But the Irishman kept right on, and first
one and then another of the boys went for me, and I took
it all. I just," and here his voice rose, and his manner
became feverishly excited, "I just ate crow right along for
months—and tried to look as if 'twas quail.

"One day I got a letter from home. She wanted me to
hurry up and come back. She thought a lot of me, I could
see; more than ever, because I had got along—I had written and told her my best news. And then, what had been
hard grew impossible right off. I made up my mind to sell
the stock and strike for new diggings. I couldn't stand it
any longer—not after her letter. I sold out and cleared.
. . . I ought to hev stayed in Laramie, p'r'aps, and gone
for the Irishman, but I just couldn't. Every one there was
against me."

"I guess you oughter hev stayed. . . . Besides, if you
had wiped up the floor with that Irishman the boys would
hev let up on you."

"P'r'aps so," Charley resumed, "but I was sick of the
whole crowd. I sold off, and lit out. When I got on the
new stagecoach, fifty miles from Laramie, and didn't
know the driver or any one, I made up my mind to start
fresh. Then and there I resolved that I had eaten all the
crow I was going to eat; the others should eat crow now,
and if there was any jumpin' to be done, I'd do it, what-

ever it cost. And so I went for Bent right off. I didn't want to wait. 'Here's more crow,' I thought, 'but I won't eat it; he shall, if I die for it,' and I just threw him out quick."

"I see," said Crocker, with a certain sympathy in his voice, "but you oughter hev waited. You oughter make up to wait from this on, Charley. 'Tain't hard. You don't need to take anythin' and set under it. I'm not advisin' that, but it's stronger to wait before you go fer any one. The boys," he added significantly, "don't like a man to bounce, and what they don't like is pretty hard to do."

"Damn the boys," exclaimed Charley vehemently, "they're all alike out here. I can't act different. If I waited, I might wait too long—too long, d'you *sabe?* I just can't trust myself," he added in a subdued tone.

"No," replied Crocker meditatively. "No, p'r'aps not. But see here, Charley, I kinder like you, and so I tell you, no one can bounce the crowd here in Garotte. They're the worst crowd you ever struck in your life. Garotte's known for hard cases. Why," he went on earnestly, as if he had suddenly become conscious of the fact, "the other night Reggitt and a lot came mighty near goin' fer you—and Harrison, Harrison took up what you said. You didn't notice, I guess; and p'r'aps 'twas well you didn't; but you hadn't much to spare. You won by the odd card.

"No one can bounce this camp. They've come from everywhere, and can only jes' get a livin' here—no more. And when luck's bad they're"—and he paused as if no adjective were strong enough. "If a man was steel, and the best and quickest on the draw ever seen, I guess they'd bury him if he played your way."

"Then they may bury me," retorted Charley bitterly, "but I've eaten my share of crow. I ain't goin' to eat any more. Can't go East now with the taste of it in my mouth. I'd rather they buried me."

And they did bury him—about a fortnight after.

THE
BEST MAN
IN GAROTTE

LAWYER RABLAY had come from nobody knew where. He was a small man, almost as round as a billiard ball. His body was round, his head was round; his blue eyes and even his mouth and chin were round; his nose was a perky snub; he was florid and prematurely bald—a picture of good-humor. And yet he was a power in Garotte. When he came to the camp, a row was the only form of recreation known to the miners. A "fuss" took men out of themselves, and was accordingly hailed as an amusement; besides, it afforded a subject of conversation. But after Lawyer Rablay's arrival fights became comparatively infrequent. Would-be students of human nature declared at first that his flow of spirits was merely animal, and that his wit was thin; but even these envious ones had to admit later that his wit told, and that his good-humor was catching.

Crocker and Harrison had nearly got to loggerheads one night for no reason apparently, save that each had a high reputation for courage, and neither could find a worthier antagonist. In the nick of time Rablay appeared; he seemed to understand the situation at a glance, and broke in:

"See here, boys. I'll settle this. They're disputin'—I know they are. Want to decide with bullets whether

'Frisco or Denver's the finest city. 'Frisco's bigger and older, says Crocker; Harrison maintains Denver's better laid out. Crocker replies in his quiet way that 'Frisco ain't dead yet." Good temper being now re-established, Rablay went on: "I'll decide this matter right off. Crocker and Harrison shall set up drinks for the crowd till we're all laid out. And I'll tell a story," and he began a tale which cannot be retold here, but which delighted the boys as much by its salaciousness as by its vivacity.

Lawyer Rablay was to Garotte what novels, theatres, churches, concerts are to more favored cities; in fact, for some six months, he and his stories constituted the chief humanizing influence in the camp. Deputations were often despatched from Doolan's to bring Rablay to the bar. The miners got up "cases" in order to give him work. More than once both parties in a dispute, real or imaginary, engaged him, despite his protestations, as attorney, and afterwards the boys insisted that, being advocate for both sides, he was well fitted to decide the issue as judge. He had not been a month in Garotte before he was christened Judge, and every question, whether of claim-boundaries, the suitability of a nickname, or the value of "dust," was submitted for his decision. It cannot be asserted that his enviable position was due either to perfect impartiality or to infallible wisdom. But everyone knew that his judgments would be informed by shrewd sense and good-humor, and would be followed by a story, and woe betide the disputant whose perversity deferred that pleasure. So Garotte became a sort of theocracy, with Judge Rablay as ruler. And yet he was, perhaps, the only man in the community whose courage had never been tested or even considered.

One afternoon a man came to Garotte, who had a widespread reputation. His name was Bill Hitchcock. A marvelous shot, a first-rate poker player, a good rider—these virtues were outweighed by his desperate temper. Though not more than five-and-twenty years of age his courage and ferocity had made him a marked man. He was said to have killed half-a-dozen men; and it was known that he had generally provoked his victims. No one could imagine why he had come to Garotte, but he had not been half an hour in the place before he was recognized. It was difficult to forget him, once seen. He was tall and broad-shouldered; his face long, with well-cut features; a brown moustache drooped negligently over his mouth; his heavy eyelids were usually half-closed, but when in moments of excitement they were suddenly updrawn, one was startled by a naked hardness of grey-green eyes.

Hitchcock spent the whole afternoon in Doolan's, scarcely speaking a word. As night drew down, the throng of miners increased. Luck had been bad for weeks; the camp was in a state of savage ill-humor. Not a few came to the saloon that night intending to show, if an opportunity offered, that neither Hitchcock nor any one else on earth could scare them. As minute after minute passed the tension increased. Yet Hitchcock stood in the midst of them, drinking and smoking in silence, seemingly unconcerned.

Presently the Judge came in with a smile on his round face and shot off a merry remark. But the quip didn't take as it should have done. He was received with quiet nods and not with smiles and loud greetings as usual. Nothing daunted, he made his way to the bar, and, standing next to Hitchcock, called for a drink.

"Come, Doolan, a Bourbon; our only monarch!"

Beyond a smile from Doolan the remark elicited no applause. Astonished, the Judge looked about him; never in his experience had the camp been in that temper. But still he had conquered too often to doubt his powers now. Again and again he tried to break the spell—in vain. As a last resort he resolved to use his infallible receipt against ill-temper.

"Boys! I've just come in to tell you one little story; then I'll have to go."

From force of habit the crowd drew toward him, and

faces relaxed. Cheered by this he picked up his glass from the bar and turned toward his audience. Unluckily, as he moved, his right arm brushed against Hitchcock, who was looking at him with half-opened eyes. The next moment Hitchcock had picked up his glass and dashed it in the Judge's face. Startled, confounded by the unexpected suddenness of the attack, Rablay backed two or three paces, and, blinded by the rush of blood from his forehead, drew out his handkerchief. No one stirred. It was part of the unwritten law in Garotte to let every man in such circumstances play his game as he pleased. For a moment or two the Judge mopped his face, and then he started toward his assailant with his round face puckered up and outthrust hands. He had scarcely moved, however, when Hitchcock leveled a long Navy Colt against his breast:

"Git back, you —— —— —— ——"

The Judge stopped. He was unarmed but not cowed. All of a sudden those wary, long eyes of Hitchcock took in the fact that a score of revolvers covered him.

With lazy deliberation Dave Crocker moved out of the throng toward the combatants, and standing between them, with his revolver pointing to the ground, said sympathetically:

"Jedge, we're sorry you've been jumped, here in Garotte. Now, what would you like?"

"A fair fight," replied Rablay, beginning again to use his handkerchief.

"Wall," Crocker went on, after a pause for thought. "A square fight's good but hard to get. This man," and his head made a motion toward Hitchcock as he spoke, "is one of the best shots there is, and I reckon you're not as good at shootin' as at—other things." Again he paused to think, and then continued with the same deliberate air of careful reflection, "We all cotton to you, Jedge; you know that. Suppose you pick a man who kin shoot, and leave it to him. That'd be fair, an' you kin jes' choose any of us, or one after the other. We're all willin'."

"No," replied the Judge, taking away the handkerchief, and showing a jagged, red line on his forehead. "No! he struck *me*. I don't want any one to help me, or take my place."

"That's right," said Crocker, approvingly; "that's right, Jedge, we all like that, but 'tain't square, and this camp means to hev it square. You bet!" And, in the difficult circumstances, he looked round for the approval which was manifest on every one of the serious faces. Again he began: "I guess, Jedge, you'd better take my plan, 'twould be surer. No! Wall, suppose I take two six-shooters, one loaded, the other empty, and put them under a *capote* on the table in the next room. You could both go in and draw for weapons; that'd be square, I reckon?" and he waited for the Judge's reply.

"Yes," replied Rablay, "that'd be fair. I agree to that."

"Hell!" exclaimed Hitchcock, "I don't. If he wants to fight, I'm here; but I ain't goin' to take a hand in no sich derned game—with the cards stocked agen me."

"Ain't you?" retorted Crocker, facing him, and beginning slowly. "I reckon *you'll* play any game we say. *See!* any damned game *we* like. D'ye understand?"

As no response was forthcoming to this defiance, he went into the other room to arrange the preliminaries of the duel. A few moments passed in silence, and then he came back through the lane of men to the two combatants.

"Jedge," he began, "the six-shooters are there, all ready. Would you like to hev first draw, or throw for it with him?" contemptuously indicating Hitchcock with a movement of his head as he concluded.

"Let us throw," replied Rablay, quietly.

In silence the three dice and the box were placed by Doolan on the bar. In response to Crocker's gesture the Judge took up the box and rolled out two fives and a three—thirteen. Every one felt that he had lost the draw, but his face did not change any more than that of his adversary. In silence Hitchcock replaced the dice in the box and threw a three, a four, and a two—nine; he put down the box emphatically.

"Wall," Crocker decided impassively, "I guess that gives you the draw, Jedge; we throw fer high in Garotte—sometimes," he went on, turning as if to explain to Hitchcock, but with insult in his voice, and then, "after you, Jedge!"

Rablay passed through the crowd into the next room. There, on a table, was a small heap covered with a cloak. Silently the men pressed round, leaving Crocker between the two adversaries in the full light of the swinging lamp.

"Now, Jedge," said Crocker, with a motion toward the table.

"No!" returned the Judge, with white, fixed face, "he won; let him draw first. I only want a square deal."

A low hum of surprise went round the room. Garotte was more than satisfied with its champion. Crocker looked at Hitchcock, and said:

"It's your draw, then." The words were careless, but the tone and face spoke clearly enough.

A quick glance round the room and Hitchcock saw that he was trapped. These men would show him no mercy. At once the wild beast in him appeared. He stepped to the table, put his hand under the cloak, drew out a revolver, dropped it, pointing toward Rablay's face, and pulled the trigger. A sharp click. That revolver, at any rate, was unloaded. Quick as thought Crocker stepped between Hitchcock and the table. Then he said:

"It's your turn now, Jedge!"

As he spoke a sound, half of relief and half of content came from the throats of the onlookers. The Judge did not move. He had not quivered when the revolver was leveled within a foot of his head; he did not appear to have seen it. With set eyes and pale face, and the jagged wound on his forehead whence the blood still trickled, he had waited, and now he did not seem to hear. Again Crocker spoke:

"Come, Jedge, it's your turn."

The sharp, loud words seemed to break the spell which

had paralyzed the man. He moved to the table, and slowly drew the revolver from under the cloak. His hesitation was too much for the crowd.

"Throw it through him, Jedge! Now's your chance. Wade in, Jedge!"

The desperate ferocity of the curt phrases seemed to move him. He raised the revolver. Then came in tones of triumph:

"I'll bet high on the Jedge!"

He dropped the revolver on the floor, and fled from the room.

The first feeling of the crowd of men was utter astonishment, but in a moment or two this gave place to half-contemptuous sympathy. What expression this sentiment would have found it is impossible to say, for just then Bill Hitchcock observed with a sneer:

"As he's run, I may as well walk"; and he stepped toward the barroom.

Instantly Crocker threw himself in front of him with his face on fire.

"Walk—will ye?" he burst out, the long-repressed rage flaming up—"walk! when you've jumped the best man in Garotte—walk! No, by God, you'll crawl, d'ye hear? crawl—right out of this camp, right now!" and he dropped his revolver on Hitchcock's breast.

Then came a wild chorus of shouts.

"That's right! That's the talk! Crawl, will ye! Down on yer hands and knees. Crawl, damn ye! Crawl!" and a score of revolvers covered the stranger.

For a moment he stood defiant, looking his assailants in the eyes. His face seemed to have grown thinner, and his moustache twitched with the snarling movement of a brute at bay. Then he was tripped up and thrown forwards amid a storm of, "Crawl, damn ye—crawl!" And so Hitchcock crawled, on hands and knees, out of Doolan's.

Lawyer Rablay, too, was never afterwards seen in Garotte. Men said his nerves had "give out."

THE SHERIFF
AND
HIS PARTNER

ONE AFTERNOON in July, 1869, I was seated at my desk in Locock's law office in the town of Kiota, Kansas. I had landed in New York from Liverpool nearly a year before, and had drifted westwards seeking in vain for some steady employment. Lawyer Locock, however, had promised to let me study law with him, and to give me a few dollars a month besides, for my services as a clerk. I was fairly satisfied with the prospect, and the little town interested me. An outpost of civilization, it was situated on the border of the great plains, which were still looked upon as the natural possession of the nomadic Indian tribes. It owed its importance to the fact that it lay on the cattle trail which led from the prairies of Texas through this no man's land to the railway system, and that it was the first place where the cowboys coming north could find a bed to sleep in, a bar to drink at, and a table to gamble on. For some years they had made of Kiota a hell upon earth. But gradually the land in the neighborhood was taken up by farmers, emigrants chiefly from New England, who were determined to put an end to the reign of violence. A man named Johnson was their leader in establishing order and tranquillity. Elected, almost as soon as he came to the town, to the dangerous post of City Marshal, he organized a vigilance committee of the younger and more daring settlers, backed by whom he resolutely suppressed the drunken rioting of the cowboys. After the ruffians had been taught to behave themselves, Johnson was made Sheriff of the County, a post which gave him a house and permanent position. Though married now, and apparently "settled down," the Sheriff was a sort of hero in Kiota. I had listened to many tales about him, showing desperate determination veined with a sense of humor, and I often regretted that I had reached the place too late to see him in action. I had little or nothing to do in the office. The tedium of the long days was almost unbroken, and Stephen's *Commentaries* had become as monotonous and unattractive as the bare uncarpeted floor. The heat was tropical, and I was dozing when a knock startled me. A Negro boy slouched in with a bundle of newspapers:

"This yer is Jedge Locock's, I guess?"

"I guess so," was my answer as I lazily opened the third or fourth number of the *Kiota Weekly Tribune*. Glancing over the sheet my eye caught the following paragraph:

HIGHWAY ROBBERY WITH VIOLENCE
JUDGE SHANNON STOPPED
THE OUTLAW ESCAPES
HE KNOWS SHERIFF JOHNSON

Information has just reached us of an outrage perpetrated on the person of one of our most respected fellow-citizens. The crime was committed in daylight, on the public highway within four miles of this city; a crime, therefore, without parallel in this vicinity for the last two years. Fortunately our County and State authorities can be fully trusted, and we have no sort of doubt that they can command, if necessary, the succor and aid of each and every citizen of this locality in order to bring the offending miscreant to justice.

We now place the plain recital of this outrage before our readers.

Yesterday afternoon, as Ex-Judge Shannon was riding from his law office in Kiota toward his home on Sumach Bluff, he was stopped about four miles from this town by a man who drew a revolver on him, telling him at the same time to pull up. The Judge, being completely unarmed and unprepared, obeyed, and was told to get down from the buckboard, which he did. He was then ordered to put his watch and whatever money he had, in the road, and to retreat three paces.

The robber pocketed the watch and money, and told him he might tell Sheriff Johnson that Tom Williams had "gone through him," and that he (Williams) could be found at the saloon in Osawotamie at any time. The Judge now hoped for release, but Tom Williams (if that be the robber's real name) seemed to get an afterthought, which he at once proceeded to carry into effect. Drawing a knife he cut the traces, and took out of the shafts the Judge's famous trotting mare, Lizzie D., which he mounted with the remark:

"Sheriff Johnson, I reckon, would come after the money anyway, but the hoss'll fetch him—sure pop."

These words have just been given to us by Judge Shannon himself, who tells us also that the outrage took place on the North Section Line, bounding Bray's farm.

After this speech the highway robber Williams rode toward the township of Osawotamie, while Judge Shannon, after drawing the buckboard to the edge of the track, was compelled to proceed homewards on foot.

The outrage, as we have said, took place late last evening, and Judge Shannon, we understand, did not trouble to inform the County authorites of the circumstance till today at noon, after leaving our office. What the motive of the crime may have been we do not worry ourselves to inquire; a crime, an outrage upon justice and order, has been committed; that is all we care to know. If anything fresh happens in this connection we propose to issue a second edition of this paper. Our fellow-citizens may rely upon our energy and watchfulness to keep them posted.

Just before going to press we learn that Sheriff Johnson was out of town attending to business when Judge Shannon called; but Sub-Sheriff Jarvis informs us that he expects the Sheriff back shortly. It is necessary to add, by way of explanation, that Mr. Jarvis cannot leave the jail unguarded, even for a few hours.

As may be imagined this item of news awakened my keenest interest. It fitted in with some things that I knew already, and I was curious to learn more. I felt that this was the first act in a drama. Vaguely I remembered some-one telling in disconnected phrases why the Sheriff had left Missouri, and come to Kansas:

" 'Twas after a quor'll with a pardner of his, named Williams, who kicked out."

Bit by bit the story, to which I had not given much attention when I heard it, so casually, carelessly was it told, recurred to my memory.

"They say as how Williams cut up rough with Johnson, and drawed a knife on him, which Johnson gripped with his left while he pulled trigger. Williams, I heerd, was in the wrong; I hain't perhaps got the right end of it; anyhow, you might hev noticed the Sheriff hes lost the little finger off his left hand. Johnson, they say, got right up and lit out from Pleasant Hill. Perhaps the fold in Mizzoori kinder liked Williams the best of the two; I don't know. Anyway, Sheriff Johnson's a square man; his record here proves it. An' real grit, you bet your life."

The narrative had made but a slight impression on me at the time; I didn't know the persons concerned, and had no reason to interest myself in their fortunes. In those early days, moreover, I was often homesick, and gave myself up readily to dreaming of English scenes and faces. Now the words and drawling intonation came back to me distinctly, and with them the question: Was the robber of Judge Shannon the same Williams who had once been the Sheriff's partner? My first impulse was to hurry into the street and try to find out; but it was the chief part of my duty to stay in the office till six o'clock; besides, the Sheriff was "out of town," and perhaps would not be back that day. The hours dragged to an end at last; my supper was soon finished, and, as night drew down, I hastened along the wooden sidewalk of Washington Street toward the Carvell House. This hotel was much too large for the needs of the little town; it contained some fifty bedrooms, of which perhaps half-a-dozen were permanently occupied by "high-toned" citizens, and a billiard room of gigantic size, in which stood nine tables, as well as the famous bar. The space between the bar, which ran across one end of the room, and the billiard tables, was the favorite nightly resort of the prominent politicians and gamblers. There, if anywhere, my questions would be answered.

On entering the billiard room I was struck by the number of men who had come together. Usually only some twenty or thirty were present, half of whom sat smoking and chewing about the bar, while the rest watched a game of billiards or took a "life" in pool. This evening, however, the billiard tables were covered with their slate-colored "wraps," while at least a hundred and fifty men were gathered about the open space of glaring light near the bar. I hurried up the room, but as I approached the crowd my steps grew slower, and I became half ashamed of my eager, obtrusive curiosity and excitement. There was a kind of reproof in the lazy, cool glance which one man after another cast upon me, as I went by. Assuming an air of indecision I threaded my way through the chairs uptilted against the sides of the billiard tables. I had drained a glass of Bourbon whisky before I realized that these apparently careless men were stirred by some emotion which made them more cautious, more silent, more warily on their guard than usual. The gamblers and loafers, too, had taken "back seats" this evening, whilst hard-working men of the farmer class who did not frequent the expensive bar of the Carvell House were to be seen in front. It dawned upon me that the matter was serious and was being taken seriously.

The silence was broken from time to time by some casual remark of no interest, drawled out in a monotone; every now and then a man invited the "crowd" to drink with him, and that was all. Yet the moral atmosphere was oppressive, and a vague feeling of discomfort grew upon me. These men "meant business."

Presently the door on my left opened—Sheriff Johnson came into the room.

"Good evenin'," he said; and a dozen voices, one after another, answered with "Good evenin'! good evenin', Sheriff!" A big frontiersman, however, a horse-dealer called Martin, who, I knew, had been on the old vigilance committee, walked from the center of the group in front of the bar to the Sheriff, and held out his hand with:

"Shake, old man, and name the drink." The Sheriff took the proffered hand as if mechanically, and turned to the bar with "Whisky—straight."

Sheriff Johnson was a man of medium height, sturdily built. A broad forehead, and clear, grey-blue eyes, that met everything fairly, testified in his favor. The nose, however, was fleshy and snub. The mouth was not to be seen, nor its shape guessed at, so thickly did the brown moustache and beard grow; but the short beard seemed rather to exaggerate than conceal an extravagant outjutting of the lower jaw, that gave a peculiar expression of energy and determination to the face. His manner was unobtrusively quiet and deliberate.

It was an unusual occurrence for Johnson to come at night to the bar-lounge, which was beginning to fall into disrepute among the puritanical or middle-class section of the community. No one, however, seemed to pay any further attention to him or to remark the unusual cordiality of Martin's greeting. A quarter of an hour elapsed before anything of note occurred. Then, an elderly man whom I did not know, a farmer, by his dress, drew a copy of the *Kiota Tribune* from his pocket, and stretching it toward Johnson, asked with a very marked Yankee twang:

"Sheriff, hev yeou read this *Tribune?*"

Wheeling half around toward his questioner, the Sheriff replied:

"Yes, sir, I hev." A pause ensued, which was made significant to me by the fact that the barkeeper suspended his hand and did not pour out the whisky he had just been asked to supply—a pause during which the two faced each other; it was broken by the farmer saying:

"Ez yeou wer out of town today, I allowed yeou might hev missed seein' it. I reckoned yeou'd come straight hyar before yeou went to hum."

"No, Crosskey," rejoined the Sheriff, with slow emphasis; "I went home first and came on hyar to see the boys."

"Wall," said Mr. Crosskey, as it seemed to me, half apologetically, "knowin' yeou I guessed yeou ought to hear the facks," then, with some suddenness, stretching out his hand, he added, "I hev some way to go, an' my old woman 'ull be waitin' up fer me. Good night, Sheriff." The hands met while the Sheriff nodded: "Good night, Jim."

After a few greetings to right and left Mr. Crosskey left the bar. The crowd went on smoking, chewing, and drinking, but the sense of expectancy was still in the air, and the seriousness seemed, if anything, to have increased. Five or ten minutes may have passed when a man named Reid, who had run for the post of Sub-Sheriff the year before, and had failed to beat Johnson's nominee Jarvis, rose from his chair and asked abruptly:

"Sheriff, do you reckon to take any of us uns with you tomorrow?"

With an indefinable ring of sarcasm in his negligent tone, the Sheriff answered:

"I guess not, Mr. Reid."

Quickly Reid replied: "Then I reckon there's no use in us stayin' "; and turning to a small knot of men among whom he had been sitting, he added, "let's go, boys!"

The men got up and filed out after their leader without greeting the Sheriff in any way. With the departure of this group the shadow lifted. Those who still remained showed in manner a marked relief, and a moment or two later a man named Morris, whom I knew to be a gambler by profession, called out lightly:

"The crowd and you'll drink with me, Sheriff, I hope? I want another glass, and then we won't keep you up any longer, for you ought to have a night's rest with tomorrow's work before you."

The Sheriff smiled assent. Every one moved toward the bar, and conversation became general. Morris was the center of the company, and he directed the talk jokingly to the account in the *Tribune*, making fun, as it seemed to me, though I did not understand all his allusions, of the editor's timidity and pretentiousness. Morris interested and amused me even more than he amused the others; he talked like a man of some intelligence and reading, and listening to him I grew lighthearted and careless, perhaps more careless than usual, for my spirits had been icebound in the earlier gloom of the evening.

"Fortunately our County and State authorities can be fully trusted," someone said.

"Mark that 'fortunately,' Sheriff," laughed Morris. "The editor was afraid to mention you alone, so he hitched the State on with you to lighten the load."

"Ay!" chimed in another of the gamblers, "and the 'aid and succor of each and every citizen,' eh, Sheriff, as if you'd take the whole town with you. I guess two or three'll be enough fer Williams."

This annoyed me. It appeared to me that Williams had addressed a personal challenge to the Sheriff, and I thought that Johnson should so consider it. Without waiting for the Sheriff to answer, whether in protest or acquiescence, I broke in:

"Two or three would be cowardly. One should go, and one only." At once I felt rather than saw the Sheriff free himself from the group of men; the next moment he stood opposite to me.

"What was that?" he asked sharply, holding me with keen eye and outthrust chin—repressed passion in voice and look.

The antagonism of his bearing excited and angered me not a little. I replied:

"I think it would be cowardly to take two or three against a single man. I said one should go, and I say so still."

"Do you?" he sneered. "I guess you'd go alone, wouldn't you? to bring Williams in?"

"If I were paid for it I should," was my heedless retort. As I spoke his face grew white with such passion that I instinctively put up my hands to defend myself, thinking he was about to attack me. The involuntary movement may have seemed boyish to him, for thought came into his eyes, and his face relaxed; moving away he said quietly:

"I'll set up drinks, boys."

They grouped themselves about him and drank, leaving me isolated. But this, now my blood was up, only added to the exasperation I felt at his contemptuous treatment, and accordingly I walked to the bar, and as the only unoccupied place was by Johnson's side I went there and said, speaking as coolly as I could:

"Though no one asks me to drink I guess I'll take some whisky, barkeeper, if you please."

Johnson was standing with his back to me, but when I spoke he looked round, and I saw, or thought I saw, a sort of curiosity in his gaze. I met his eye defiantly. He turned to the others and said, in his ordinary, slow way:

"Wall, good night, boys; I've got to go. It's gittin' late, an' I've had about as much as I want."

Whether he alluded to the drink or to my impertinence I was unable to divine. Without adding a word he left the room amid a chorus of "Good night, Sheriff!" With him went Martin and half-a-dozen more.

I thought I had come out of the matter fairly well until I

spoke to some of the men standing near. They answered me, it is true, but in monosyllables, and evidently with unwillingness. In silence I finished my whisky, feeling that everyone was against me for some inexplicable cause. I resented this and stayed on. In a quarter of an hour the rest of the crowd had departed, with the exception of Morris and a few of the same kidney.

When I noticed that these gamblers, outlaws by public opinion, held away from me, I became indignant. Addressing myself to Morris, I asked:

"Can you tell me, sir, for you seem to be an educated man, what I have said or done to make you all shun me?"

"I guess so," he answered indifferently. "You took a hand in a game where you weren't wanted. And you tried to come in without ever having paid the *ante*, which is not allowed in any game—at least not in any game played about here."

The allusion seemed plain; I was not only a stranger, but a foreigner; that must be my offense. With a "Good night, sir; good night, barkeeper!" I left the room.

The next morning I went as usual to the office. I may have been seated there about an hour—it was almost eight o'clock—when I heard a knock at the door.

"Come in," I said, swinging round in the American chair, to find myself face to face with Sheriff Johnson.

"Why, Sheriff, come in!" I exclaimed cheerfully, for I was relieved at seeing him, and so realized more clearly than ever that the unpleasantness of the previous evening had left in me a certain uneasiness. I was eager to show that the incident had no importance.

"Won't you take a seat? and you'll have a cigar?—these are not bad."

"No, thank you," he answered. "No, I guess I won't sit nor smoke jest now." After a pause, he added, "I see you're studyin'; p'r'aps you're busy today; I won't disturb you."

"You don't disturb me, Sheriff," I rejoined. "As for studying, there's not much in it. I seem to prefer dreaming."

"Wall," he said, letting his eyes range round the walls furnished with Law Reports bound in yellow calf, "I don't know, I guess there's a big lot of readin' to do before a man gets through with all those."

"Oh," I laughed, "the more I read the more clearly I see that law is only a sermon on various texts supplied by common sense."

"Wall," he went on slowly, coming a pace or two nearer and speaking with increased seriousness, "I reckon you've got all Locock's business to see after: his clients to talk to; letters to answer, and all that; and when he's on the drunk I guess he don't do much. I won't worry you any more."

"You don't worry me," I replied. "I've not had a letter to answer in three days, and not a soul comes here to talk about business or anything else. I sit and dream, and wish I had something to do out there in the sunshine. Your work is better than reading words, words—nothing but words."

"You ain't busy; hain't got anything to do here that might keep you? Nothin'?"

"Not a thing. I'm sick of Blackstone and all Commentaries."

Suddenly I felt his hand on my shoulder (moving half round in the chair, I had for the moment turned sideways to him), and his voice was surprisingly hard and quick:

"Then I swear you in as a Deputy-Sheriff of the United States, and of this State of Kansas; and I charge you to bring in and deliver at the Sheriff's house, in this county of Elwood, Tom Williams, alive or dead, and—there's your fee, five dollars and twenty-five cents!" and he laid the money on the table.

Before the singular speech was half ended I had swung round facing him, with a fairly accurate understanding of what he meant. But the moment for decision had come with such sharp abruptness, that I still did not realize my position, though I replied defiantly as if accepting the charge:

"I've not got a weapon."

"The boys allowed you mightn't hev, and so I brought some along. You ken suit your hand." While speaking he produced two or three revolvers of different sizes, and laid them before me.

Dazed by the rapid progress of the plot, indignant, too, at the trick played upon me, I took up the nearest revolver and looked at it almost without seeing it. The Sheriff seemed to take my gaze for that of an expert's curiosity.

"It shoots true," he said meditatively, "plumb true; but it's too small to drop a man. I guess it wouldn't stop any-one with grit in him."

My anger would not allow me to consider his advice; I thrust the weapon in my pocket:

"I haven't got a buggy. How am I to get to Osawo-tamie?"

"Mine's hitched up outside. You ken hev it."

Rising to my feet I said: "Then we can go."

We had nearly reached the door of the office, when the Sheriff stopped, turned his back upon the door, and look-ing straight into my eyes said:

"Don't play foolish. You've no call to go. Ef you're busy, ef you've got letters to write, anythin' to do—I'll tell the boys you sed so, and that'll be all; that'll let you out."

Half-humorously, as it seemed to me, he added:

"You're young and a tenderfoot. You'd better stick to what you've begun upon. That's the way to do somethin'. I often think it's the work chooses us, and we've just got to get down and do it."

"I've told you I had nothing to do," I retorted angrily; "that's the truth. Perhaps" (sarcastically) "this work chooses me."

The Sheriff moved away from the door.

On reaching the street I stopped for a moment in utter wonder. At that hour in the morning Washington Street was usually deserted, but now it seemed as if half the men in the town had taken up places round the entrance to Locock's office stairs. Some sat on barrels or boxes tipped up against the shop-front (the next store was kept by a German, who sold fruit and eatables); others stood about in groups or singly; a few were seated on the edge of the sidewalk, with their feet in the dust of the street. Right before me and most conspicuous was the gigantic figure of Martin. He was sitting on a small barrel in front of the Sheriff's buggy.

"Good morning," I said in the air, but no one answered me. Mastering my irritation, I went forward to undo the hitching-strap, but Martin, divining my intention, rose and loosened the buckle. As I reached him, he spoke in a low whisper, keeping his back turned to me:

"Shoot off a joke quick. The boys'll let up on you then. It'll be all right. Say somethin', for God's sake!"

The rough sympathy did me good, relaxed the tightness round my heart; the resentment natural to one entrapped left me, and some of my self-confidence returned:

"I never felt less like joking in my life, Martin, and humor can't be produced to order."

He fastened up the hitching-strap, while I gathered the reins together and got into the buggy. When I was fairly seated he stepped to the side of the open vehicle, and, holding out his hand, said, "Good day," adding, as our hands clasped, "wade in, young un; wade in."

"Good day, Martin. Good day, Sheriff. Good day, boys!"

To my surprise there came a chorus of answering "Good days!" as I drove up the street.

A few hundred yards I went, and then wheeled to the right past the post office, and so on for a quarter of a mile, till I reached the descent from the higher ground, on which the town was built, to the river. There, on my left, on the verge of the slope, stood the Sheriff's house in a lot by itself, with the long, low jail attached to it. Down the hill I went, and across the bridge and out into the open country. I drove rapidly for about five miles—more than halfway to Osawotamie—and then I pulled up, in order to think quietly and make up my mind.

I grasped the situation now in all its details. Courage was the one virtue which these men understood, the only one upon which they prided themselves. I, a stranger, a "tenderfoot," had questioned the courage of the boldest among them, and this mission was their answer to my insolence. The "boys" had planned the plot; Johnson was not to blame; clearly he wanted to let me out of it; he would have been satisfied there in the office if I had said that I was busy; he did not like to put his work on anyone else. And yet he must profit by my going. Were I killed, the whole country would rise against Williams; whereas if I shot Williams, the Sheriff would be relieved of the task. I wondered whether the fact of his having married made any difference to the Sheriff. Possibly—and yet it was not the Sheriff; it was the "boys" who had insisted on giving me the lesson. Public opinion was dead against me. I had come into a game where I was not wanted, and I had never even "paid the *ante*"—that was Morris's phrase. Of course it was all clear now. I had never given any proof of courage, as most likely all the rest had at some time or other. That was the *ante* Morris meant. . . .

My willfulness had got me into the scrape; I had only myself to thank. Not alone the Sheriff but Martin would have saved me had I profited by the door of escape which he had tried to open for me. Neither of them wished to push the malice to the point of making me assume the Sheriff's risk, and Martin at least, and probably the Sheriff also, had taken my quick, half-unconscious words and acts as evidence of reckless determination. If I intended to live in the West I must go through with the matter.

But what nonsense it all was! Why should I chuck away my life in the attempt to bring a desperate ruffian to justice? And who could say that Williams was a ruffian? It was plain that his quarrel with the Sheriff was one of old date and purely personal. He had "stopped" Judge Shannon in order to bring about a duel with the Sheriff. Why should I fight the Sheriff's duels? Justice, indeed! justice had nothing to do with this affair; I did not even know which man was in the right. Reason led directly to the conclusion that I had better turn the horse's head northward, drive as fast and as far as I could, and take the train as soon as possible out of the country. But while I recognized that this was the only sensible decision, I felt that I could not carry it into action. To run away was impossible; my cheeks burned with shame at the thought.

Was I to give my life for a stupid practical joke? "Yes!" a voice within me answered sharply. "It would be well if a man could always choose the cause for which he risks his life, but it may happen that he ought to throw it away for a reason that seems inadequate."

"What ought I to do?" I questioned.

"Go on to Osawotamie, arrest Williams, and bring him into Kiota," replied my other self.

"And if he won't come?"

"Shoot him—you are charged to deliver him 'alive or dead' at the Sheriff's house. No more thinking, drive straight ahead and act as if you were a representative of the law and Williams a criminal. It has to be done."

The resolution excited me, I picked up the reins and proceeded. At the next section line I turned to the right, and ten or fifteen minutes later saw Osawotamie in the distance.

I drew up, laid the reins on the dashboard, and examined the revolver. It was a small four-shooter, with a large bore. To make sure of its efficiency I took out a cartridge; it was quite new. While weighing it in my hand, the Sheriff's words recurred to me, "It wouldn't stop anyone with grit in him." What did he mean? I didn't want to think, so I put the cartridge in again, cocked and replaced the pistol in my right-side jacket pocket, and drove on. Osawotamie consisted of a single street of straggling frame buildings. After passing half-a-dozen of them I saw, on the right, one which looked to me like a saloon. It was evidently a stopping place. There were several hitching-posts, and the house boasted instead of a door two green Venetian blinds put upon rollers—the usual sign of a drinking-saloon in the West.

I got out of the buggy slowly and carefully, so as not to shift the position of the revolver, and after hitching up the horse, entered the saloon. Coming out of the glare of the sunshine I could hardly see in the darkened room. In a moment or two my eyes grew accustomed to the dim light, and I went over to the bar, which was on my left. The barkeeper was sitting down; his head and shoulders alone were visible; I asked him for a lemon squash.

"Anythin' in it?" he replied, without lifting his eyes.

"No; I'm thirsty and hot."

"I guessed that was about the figger," he remarked, getting up leisurely and beginning to mix the drink with his back to me.

I used the opportunity to look round the room. Three steps from me stood a tall man, lazily leaning with his right arm on the bar, his fingers touching a half-filled glass. He seemed to be gazing past me into the void, and thus allowed me to take note of his appearance. In shirt sleeves, like the barkeeper, he had a belt on in which were two large revolvers with white ivory handles. His face was prepossessing, with large but not irregular features, bronzed fair skin, hazel eyes, and long brown moustache.

He looked strong and was lithe of form, as if he had not done much hard bodily work. There was no one else in the room except a man who appeared to be sleeping at a table in the far corner with his head pillowed on his arms.

As I completed this hasty scrutiny of the room and its inmates, the barkeeper gave me my squash, and I drank eagerly. The excitement had made me thirsty, for I knew that the crisis must be at hand, but I experienced no other sensation save that my heart was thumping and my throat was dry. Yawning as a sign of indifference (I had resolved to be as deliberate as the Sheriff) I put my hand in my pocket on the revolver. I felt that I could draw it out at once.

I addressed the barkeeper:

"Say, do you know the folk here in Osawotamie?"

After a pause he replied:

"Most on 'em, I guess."

Another pause and a second question:

"Do you know Tom Williams?"

The eyes looked at me with a faint light of surprise in them; they looked away again, and came back with short, half-suspicious, half-curious glances.

"Maybe you're a friend of his'n?"

"I don't know him, but I'd like to meet him."

"Would you, though?" Turning half around, the barkeeper took down a bottle and glass, and poured out some whisky, seemingly for his own consumption. Then: "I guess he's not hard to meet, isn't Williams, ef you and me mean the same man."

"I guess we do," I replied; "Tom Williams is the name."

"That's me," said the tall man who was leaning on the bar near me, "that's my name."

"Are you the Williams that stopped Judge Shannon yesterday?"

"I don't know his name," came the careless reply, "but I stopped a man in a buckboard."

Plucking out my revolver, and pointing it low down on his breast, I said:

"I'm sent to arrest you; you must come with me to Kiota."

Without changing his easy posture, or a muscle of his face, he asked in the same quiet voice:

"What does this mean, anyway? Who sent you to arrest me?"

"Sheriff Johnson," I answered.

The man started upright, and said, as if amazed, in a quick, loud voice:

"Sheriff Johnson sent *you* to arrest me?"

"Yes," I retorted, "Sheriff Samuel Johnson swore me in this morning as his deputy, and charged me to bring you into Kiota."

In a tone of utter astonishment he repeated my words, "Sheriff Samuel Johnson!"

"Yes," I replied, "Samuel Johnson, Sheriff of Elwood County."

"See here," he asked suddenly, fixing me with a look of angry suspicion, "what sort of a man is he? What does he figger like?"

"He's a little shorter than I am," I replied curtly, "with a brown beard and bluish eyes—a square-built sort of man."

"Hell!" There was savage rage and menace in the exclamation.

"You kin put that up!" he added, absorbed once more in thought. I paid no attention to this; I was not going to put the revolver away at his bidding. Presently he asked in his ordinary voice:

"What age man might this Johnson be?"

"About forty or forty-five, I should think."

"And right off Sam Johnson swore you in and sent you to bring me into Kiota—an' him Sheriff?"

"Yes," I replied impatiently, "that's so."

"Great God!" he exclaimed, bringing his clenched right hand heavily down on the bar. "Here, Zeke!" turning to the man asleep in the corner, and again he shouted "Zeke!" Then, with a rapid change of manner, and speaking irritably, he said to me:

"Put that thing up, I say."

The barkeeper now spoke too: "I guess when Tom sez you kin put it up, you kin. You hain't got no use fur it."

The changes of Williams' tone from wonder to wrath and then to quick resolution showed me that the doubt in him had been laid, and that I had but little to do with the decision at which he had arrived, whatever that decision might be. I understood, too, enough of the Western spirit to know that he would take no unfair advantage of me. I therefore uncocked the revolver and put it back into my pocket. In the meantime Zeke had got up from his resting place in the corner and had made his way sleepily to the bar. He had taken more to drink than was good for him, though he was not now really drunk.

"Give me and Zeke a glass, Joe," said Williams; "and this gentleman, too, if he'll drink with me, and take one yourself with us."

"No," replied the barkeeper sullenly, "I'll not drink to any damned foolishness. An' Zeke won't neither."

"Oh, yes, he will," Williams returned persuasively, "and so'll you, Joe. You aren't goin' back on me."

"No, I'll be just damned if I am," said the barkeeper, half-conquered.

"What'll you take, sir" Williams asked me.

"The barkeeper knows my figger," I answered, half-jestingly, not yet understanding the situation, but convinced that it was turning out better than I had expected.

"And you, Zeke?" he went on.

"The old pizen," Zeke replied.

"And now, Joe, whisky for you and me—the square bottle," he continued, with brisk cheerfulness.

In silence the barkeeper placed the drinks before us. As soon as the glasses were empty Williams spoke again, putting out his hand to Zeke at the same time:

"Good-bye, old man, so long, but saddle up in two hours. Ef I don't come then, you kin clear; but I guess I'll be with you."

"Good-bye, Joe."

"Good-bye, Tom," replied the barkeeper, taking the proffered hand, still half-unwillingly, "if you're stuck on it; but the game is to wait for 'em here—anyway that's how I'd play it."

A laugh and shake of the head and Williams addressed me:

"Now, sir, I'm ready if you are." We were walking toward the door, when Zeke broke in:

"Say, Tom, ain't I to come along?"

"No, Zeke, I'll play this hand alone," replied Williams, and two minutes later he and I were seated in the buggy, driving toward Kiota.

We had gone more than a mile before he spoke again. He began very quietly, as if confiding his thoughts to me:

"I don't want to make no mistake about this business—it ain't worth while. I'm sure you're right, and Sheriff Samuel Johnson sent you, but, maybe, ef you was to think you could kinder bring him before me. There might be two of the name, the age, the looks—though it ain't likely." Then, as if a sudden inspiration moved him:

"Where did he come from, this Sam Johnson, do you know?"

"I believe he came from Pleasant Hill, Missouri. I've heard that he left after a row with his partner, and it seems to me that his partner's name was Williams. But that you ought to know better than I do. By-the-bye, there is one sign by which Sheriff Johnson can always be recognized; he has lost the little finger of his left hand. They say he caught Williams' bowie with that hand and shot him with the right. But why he had to leave Missouri I don't know, if Williams drew first."

"I'm satisfied now," said my companion, "but I guess you hain't got that story correct; maybe you don't know the cause of it nor how it began; maybe Williams didn't draw fust; maybe he was in the right all the way through; maybe—but thar!—the first hand don't decide everythin'. Your Sheriff's the man—that's enough for me."

After this no word was spoken for miles. As we drew near the bridge leading into the town of Kiota I remarked half-a-dozen men standing about. Generally the place was deserted, so the fact astonished me a little. But I said nothing. We had scarcely passed over half the length of the bridge, however, when I saw that there were quite twenty men lounging around the Kiota end of it. Before I had time to explain the matter to myself, Williams spoke: "I guess he's got out all the vigilantes"; and then bitterly: "the boys in old Mizzouri wouldn't believe this ef I told it on him, the doggoned mean cuss."

We crossed the bridge at a walk (it was forbidden to drive faster over the rickety structure), and toiled up the hill through the bystanders, who did not seem to see us, though I knew several of them. When we turned to the right to reach the gate of the Sheriff's house, there were groups of men on both sides. No one moved from his place; here and there, indeed, one of them went on whittling. I drew up at the sidewalk, threw down the reins, and jumped out of the buggy to hitch up the horse. My task was done.

I had the hitching-rein loose in my hand, when I became conscious of something unusual behind me. I looked round—it was the stillness that foreruns the storm.

Williams was standing on the sidewalk facing the low wooden fence, a revolver in each hand, but both pointing negligently to the ground; the Sheriff had just come down the steps of his house; in his hands also were revolvers; his deputy, Jarvis, was behind him on the stoop.

Williams spoke first:

"Sam Johnson, you sent for me, and I've come."

The Sheriff answered firmly, "I did!"

Their hands went up, and crack! crack! crack! in quick succession, three or four or five reports—I don't know how many. At the first shots the Sheriff fell forward on his face. Williams started to run along the sidewalk; the groups of men at the corner, through whom he must pass, closed together; then came another report, and at the same moment he stopped, turned slowly half around, and sank down in a heap like an empty sack.

I hurried to him; he had fallen almost as a tailor sits, but his head was between his knees. I lifted it gently; blood was oozing from a hole in the forehead. The men were about me; I heard them say:

"A derned good shot! Took him in the back of the head. Jarvis kin shoot!"

I rose to my feet. Jarvis was standing inside the fence supported by someone; blood was welling from his bared left shoulder.

"I ain't much hurt," he said, "but I guess the Sheriff's got it bad."

The men moved on, drawing me with them, through the gate to where the Sheriff lay. Martin turned him over on his back. They opened his shirt, and there on the broad chest were two little blue marks, each in the center of a small mound of pink flesh.

MONTES: THE MATADOR

"YES! I'M BETTER, and the doctor tells me I've escaped once more—as if I cared! . . . And all through the fever you came every day to see me, so my niece says, and brought me the cool drink that drove the heat away and gave me sleep. You thought, I suppose, like the doctor, that I'd escape you, too. Ha! ha! And that you'd never hear old Montes tell what he knows of bullfighting and you don't. . . . Or perhaps it was kindness; though, why you, a foreigner and a heretic, should be kind to me, God knows. . . . The doctor says I've not got much more life in me, and you're going to leave Spain within the week—within the week, you said didn't you? . . . Well, then, I don't mind telling you the story.

"Thirty years ago I wanted to tell it often enough, but I knew no one I could trust. After that fit passed, I said to myself I'd never tell it; but as you're going away, I'll tell it to you, if you swear by the Virgin you'll never tell it to anyone, at least until I'm dead. You'll swear, will you? Easily enough! they all will; but as you're going away, it's much the same. Besides, you can do nothing now; no one can do anything now; no one can do anything; they never could have done anything. Why, they wouldn't believe you if you told it to them, the fools! . . . My story will teach you more about bullfighting than Frascuelo or Mazzantini, or—yes, Lagartijo knows. Weren't there Frascuelos and Mazzantinis in my day? Dozens of them. You could pick one Frascuelo out of every thousand laborers if you gave him the training and the practice, and could keep him away from wine and women. But a Montes is not to be found every day, if you searched all Spain for one. . . . What's the good of bragging? I never bragged when I was at work; the deed talks—louder than any words. Yet I think, no one has ever done the things I used to; for I read in a paper once an account of a thing I often did, and the writer said 'twas incredible. Ha! ha! incredible to the Frascuelos and Mazzantinis and the rest, who can kill bulls and are called *espadas*. Oh, yes! bulls so tired out they can't lift their heads. You didn't guess when you were telling me about Frascuelo and Mazzantini that I knew them. I knew all about both of them before you told me. I know their work, though I've not been within sight of a ring for more than thirty years. . . . Well, I'll tell you my story: I'll tell you my story—if I can."

The old man said the last words, as if to himself, in a low voice, then sank back in the armchair, and for a time was silent.

Let me say a word or two about myself and the circumstances which led me to seek out Montes.

I had been in Spain off and on a good deal, and from the first had taken a great liking to the people and country; and no one can love Spain and the Spaniards without becoming interested in the bull ring—the sport is so characteristic of the people, and in itself so enthralling. I set myself to study it in earnest, and when I came to know the best bullfighters, Frascuelo, Mazzantini, and Lagartijo, and heard them talk of their trade, I began to understand what skill and courage, what qualities of eye and hand and heart, this game demands. Through my love of the sport, I came to hear of Montes. He had left so great a name that thirty years after he had disappeared from the scene of his triumphs, he was still spoken of not infrequently. He would perhaps have been better remembered, had the feats attributed to him been less astounding. It was Frascuelo who told me that Montes was still alive:

"Montes," he cried out in answer to me; "I can tell you about Montes. You mean the old *espada* who, they say, used to kill the bull in its first rush into the ring—as if anyone could do that! I can tell you about him. He must have been clever; for an old *aficionado* I know, swears no one of us is fit to be in his *caudrilla*. Those old fellows are all like that, and I don't believe half they tell me about Montes. I dare say he was good enough in his day, but there are just as good men now as ever there were. When I was in Ronda, four years ago, I went to see Montes. He lives out of the town in a nice, little house all alone, with one woman to attend to him, a niece of his, they say. You know he was born in Ronda; but he would not talk to me; he only looked at me and laughed—the little, lame, conceited one!"

"You don't believe then, in spite of what they say, that he was better than Lagartijo or Mazzantini?" I asked.

"No, I don't," Frascuelo replied. "Of course, he may have known more than they do; that wouldn't be difficult, for neither of them knows much. Mazzantini is a good *matador* because he's very tall and strong—that's his advantage. For that, too, the women like him, and when he makes a mistake and has to try again, he gets forgiven. It wasn't so when I began. There were *aficionados* then, and if you made a mistake they began to jeer, and you were soon pelted out of the ring. Now the crowd knows nothing and is no longer content to follow those who do know. Lagartijo? Oh, he's very quick and daring, and the women and boys like that too. But he's ignorant: he knows nothing about a bull. Why, he's been wounded oftener in his five years than I in my twenty. And that's a pretty good test. Montes must have been clever; for he's very small, and I shouldn't think he was ever very strong, and then he was lame almost from the beginning, I've heard. I've no doubt he could teach the business to Mazzantini or Lagartijo, but that's not saying much. . . . He must have made a lot of money, too, to be able to live on it ever since. And they didn't pay as high then or even when I began as they do now."

So much I knew about Montes when, in the spring of 188—, I rode from Seville to Ronda, fell in love with the place at first sight, and resolved to stop at Polos' inn for some time. Ronda is built, so to speak, upon an island tableland high above the sea level, and is ringed about by still higher mountain ranges. It is one of the most peculiar and picturesque places in the world. A river runs almost all around it; and the sheer cliffs fall in many places three or four hundred feet, from the tableland to the water, like a wall. No wonder that the Moors held Ronda after they had lost every other foot of ground in Spain. Taking Ronda as my headquarters I made almost daily excursions, chiefly. on foot, into the surrounding mountains. On one of these I heard again of Montes. A peasant with whom I had been talking and who was showing me a short cut back to the town, suddenly stopped and said, pointing to a little hut perched on the mountain shoulder in front of us, "From that house you can see Ronda. That's the house where Montes, the great *matador*, was born," he added, evidently with some pride. Then and there the conversation with Frascuelo came back to my memory, and I made up my mind to find Montes out and have a talk with him. I went to his house, which lay just outside the town, next day with the *alcalde*, who introduced me to him and then left us. The first sight of the man interested me. He was short—about five feet three or four, I should think—of well-knit, muscular frame. He seemed to me to have Moorish blood in him. His complexion was very dark and tanned; the features clean-cut; the nose sharp and inquisitive; the nostrils astonishingly mobile, the chin and jaws square, bony—resolute. His hair and thick moustache were snow white, and this, together with the deep wrinkles on the forehead and round the eyes and mouth, gave him an appearance of great age. He seemed to move, too, with extreme difficulty, his lameness, as he afterwards told me, being complicated with rheumatism. But when one looked at his eyes, the appearance of age vanished. They were large and brown, usually inexpressive, or rather impenetrable, brooding wells of unknown depths. But when anything excited him, the eyes would suddenly flash to life and become intensely luminous. The effect was startling. It seemed as if all the vast vitality of the man had been transmuted into those wonderful gleaming orbs: they radiated courage, energy, intellect. Then as his mood changed, the light would die out of the eyes; and the old, wizened wrinkled face would settle down into its ordinary ill-tempered, wearied expression. There was evidently so much in the man—courage, melancholy, keen intelligence—that in spite of an anything but flattering reception I returned again and again to the house. One day his niece told me that Montes was in bed, and from her description I inferred that he was suffering from an attack of malarial fever. The doctor who attended him, and whom I knew, confirmed this. Naturally enough, I did what I could for the sufferer, and so it came about that after his recovery he received me with kindness, and at last made up his mind to tell me the story of his life.

"I may as well begin at the beginning," Montes went on. "I was born near here about sixty years ago. You thought I was older. Don't deny it. I saw the surprise in your face. But it's true: in fact, I am not yet, I think, quite sixty. My father was a peasant with a few acres of land of his own and a cottage."

"I know it," I said. "I saw it the other day."

"Then you may have seen on the further side of the hill

the pasture-ground for cattle which was my father's chief possession. It was good pasture; very good. . . . My mother was of a better class than my father; she was the daughter of the chemist in Ronda; she could read and write, and she did read, I remember, whenever she could get the chance, which wasn't often, with her four children to take care of—three girls and a boy—and the house to look after. We all loved her, she was so gentle besides, she told us wonderful stories; but I think I was her favorite. You see I was the youngest and a boy, and women are like that. My father was hard—at least, I thought him so, and feared rather than loved him; but the girls got on better with him. He never talked to me as he did to them. My mother wanted me to go to school and become a priest; she had taught me to read and write by the time I was six. But my father would not hear of it. 'If you had had three boys and one girl,' I remember him saying to her once, 'you could have done what you liked with this one. But as there is only one boy, he must work and help me.' So by the time I was nine I used to go off down to the pasture and watch the bulls all day long. For though the herd was a small one—only about twenty head—it required to be constantly watched. The cows were attended to in an enclosure close to the house. It was my task to mind the bulls in the lower pasture. Of course I had a pony, for such bulls in Spain are seldom approached, and cannot be driven by a man on foot. I see you don't understand. But it's simple enough. My father's bulls were of good stock, savage and strong; they were always taken for the ring, and he got high prices for them. He generally managed to sell three *novillos* and two bulls of four years old each year. And there was no bargaining, no trouble; the money was always ready for that class of animals. All day long I sat on my pony, or stood near it, minding the bulls. If any of them strayed too far, I had to go and get him back again. But in the heat of the day they never moved about much, and that time I turned to use by learning the lessons my mother gave me. So a couple of years passed. Of course in that time I got to know our bulls pretty well; but it was a remark of my father's which first taught me that each bull had an individual character and first set me to watch them closely. I must have been then about twelve years old; and in that summer I learned more than in the two previous years. My father, though he said nothing to me, must have noticed that I had gained confidence in dealing with the bulls; for one night, when I was in bed, I heard him say to my mother—'The little fellow is as good as a man now.' I was proud of his praise, and from that time on, I set to work to learn everything I could about the bulls.

"By degrees I came to know every one of them—better far than I ever got to know men or women later. Bulls, I found, were just like men, only simpler and kinder; some were good-tempered and honest, others were sulky and cunning. There was a black one which was wild and hot-tempered, but at bottom, good, while there was one almost as black, with light horns and flanks, which I never trusted. The other bulls didn't like him. I could see they didn't; they were all afraid of him. He was cunning and suspicious, and never made friends with any of them; he would always eat by himself far away from the others—but he had courage, too; I knew that as well as they did. He was sold that very summer with the black one for the ring in Ronda. One Sunday night, when my father and eldest sister (my mother would never go to *los toros)* came back from seeing the game in Ronda, they were wild with excitement, and began to tell the mother how one of our bulls had caught the *matador* and tossed him, and how the *chulos* could scarcely get the *matador* away. Then I cried out—'I know; 'twas Judas' (so I had christened him), and as I saw my father's look of surprise I went on confusedly, 'the bull with the white horns I mean. Juan, the black one, wouldn't have been clever enough.' My father only said,

'The boy's right'; but my mother drew me to her and kissed me, as if she were afraid. . . . Poor mother! I think even then she knew or divined something of what came to pass later. . . .

"It was the next summer, I think, that my father first found out how much I knew about the bulls. It happened in this way. There hadn't been much rain in the spring; the pasture, therefore, was thin, and that, of course, made the bulls restless. In the summer the weather was unsettled—spells of heat and then thunderstorms—till the animals became very excitable. One day, there was thunder in the air, I remember, they gave me a great deal of trouble and that annoyed me, for I wanted to read. I had got to a very interesting tale in the storybook my mother had given me on the day our bulls were sold. The story was about Cervantes—ah, you know who I mean, the great writer. Well, he was a great man, too. The story told how he escaped from the prison over there in Algiers and got back to Cadiz, and how a widow came to him to find out if he knew her son, who was also a slave of the Moors. And when she heard that Cervantes had seen her son working in chains, she bemoaned her wretchedness and ill-fortune, till the heart of the great man melted with pity, and he said to her, 'Come, mother, be hopeful, in one month your son shall be here with you.' And then the book told how Cervantes went back to slavery, and how glad the Bey was to get him again, for he was very clever; and how he asked the Bey, as he had returned of his free will, to send the widow's son home in his stead; and the Bey consented. That Cervantes was a man! . . . Well, I was reading the story, and I believed every word of it, as I do still, for no ordinary person could invent that sort of tale; and I grew very much excited and wanted to know all about Cervantes. But as I could only read slowly and with difficulty, I was afraid the sun would go down before I could get to the end. While I was reading as hard as ever I could, my father came down on foot and caught me. He hated to see me reading—I don't know why; and he was angry and struck at me. As I avoided the blow and got away from him, he pulled up the picket line, and got on my pony to drive one of the bulls back to the herd. I have thought since, he must have been very much annoyed before he came down and caught me. For though he knew a good deal about bulls, he didn't show it then. My pony was too weak to carry him easily, yet he acted as if he had been well mounted. For as I said, the bulls were hungry and excited, and my father should have seen this and driven the bull back quietly and with great patience. But no; he wouldn't let him feed even for a moment. At last the bull turned on him. My father held the goad fairly against his neck, but the bull came on just the same, and the pony could scarcely get out of the way in time. In a moment the bull turned and prepared to rush at him again. My father sat still on the little pony and held the goad; but I knew that was no use; he knew it, too; but he was angry and wouldn't give in. At once I ran in between him and the bull, and then called to the bull, and went slowly up to him where he was shaking his head and pawing the ground. He was very angry, but he knew the difference between us quite well, and he let me come close to him without rushing at me, and then just shook his head to show me he was still angry, and soon began to feed quietly. In a moment or two I left him and went back to my father. He had got off the pony and was white and trembling, and he said:

" 'Are you hurt?'

"And I said laughing, 'No: he didn't want to hurt me. He was only showing off his temper.'

"And my father said, 'There's not a man in all Spain that could have done that! You know more than I do—more than anybody.'

"After that he let me do as I liked, and the next two

years were very happy ones. First came the marriage of
my second sister, then the eldest one was married, and
they were both good matches. And the bulls were sold
well, and my father had less to do, as I could attend to the
whole herd by myself. Those were two good years. My
mother seemed to love me more and more every day, or I
suppose I noticed it more, and she praised me for doing
the lessons she gave me; and I had more and more time to
study as the herd got to know me better and better.

"My only trouble was that I had never seen the bulls in
the ring. But when I found my father was willing to take
me, and 'twas mother who wanted me not to go, I put up
with that, too, and said nothing, for I loved her greatly.
Then of a sudden came the sorrow. It was in the late winter, just before my fifteenth birthday. I was born in
March, I think. In January my mother caught cold, and as
she grew worse my father fetched the doctor, and then her
father and mother came to see her, but nothing did any
good. In April she died. I wanted to die, too.

"After her death my father took to grumbling about the
food and house and everything. Nothing my sister could
do was right. I believe she only married in the summer
because she couldn't stand his constant blame. At any rate
she married badly, a good-for-nothing who had twice her
years, and who ill-treated her continually. A month or
two later my father, who must have been fifty, married
again, a young woman, a laborer's daughter without a
duro. He told me he was going to do it, for the house
needed a woman. I suppose he was right. But I was too
young then to take such things into consideration, and I
had loved my mother. When I saw his new wife I did not
like her, and we did not get on well together.

"Before this, however, early in the summer that followed the death of my mother, I went for the first time to
see a bullfight. My father wanted me to go, and my sister,
too; so I went. I shall never forget that day. The *chulos*

made me laugh, they skipped about so and took such extra good care of themselves; but the *banderilleros* interested me. Their work required skill and courage, that I saw at once; but after they had planted the *banderillas* twice, I knew how it was done, and felt I could do it just as well or better. For the third or fourth *banderillero* made a mistake! He didn't even know with which horn the bull was going to strike; so he got frightened, and did not plant the *banderillas* fairly—in fact, one was on the side of the shoulder and the other didn't even stick in. As for the *picadores*, they didn't interest me at all. There was no skill or knowledge in their work. It was for the crowd, who liked to see blood and who understand nothing. Then came the turn of the *espada*. Ah! that seemed splendid to me. He knew his work I thought at first, and his work evidently required knowledge, skill, courage, strength—everything. I was intensely excited, and when the bull, struck to the heart, fell prone on his knees, and the blood gushed from his nose and mouth, I cheered and cheered till I was hoarse. But before the games were over, that very first day, I saw more than one *matador* make a mistake. At first I thought I must be wrong, but soon the event showed I was right. For the *matador* hadn't even got the bull to stand square when he tried his stroke and failed. You don't know what that means—'to stand square.' "

"I do partly," I replied, "but I don't see the reason of it. Will you explain?"

"It's very simple," Montes answered. "So long as the bull's standing with one hoof in front of the other, his shoulder blades almost meet, just as when you throw your arms back and your chest out; they don't meet, of course, but the space between them is not as regular, and, therefore, not as large as it is when their front hooves are square. The space between the shoulder blades is none too large at any time, for you have to strike with force to drive the sword through the inch-thick hide, and through a foot of muscle, sinew, and flesh besides, to the heart. Nor is the stroke a straight one. Then, too, there's always the backbone to avoid. And the space between the backbone and the nearest thick gristle of the shoulder blade is never more than an inch and a half. So if you narrow this space by even half an inch you increase your difficulty immensely. And that's not your object. Well, all this I've been telling you, I divined at once. Therefore, when I saw the bull wasn't standing quite square I knew the *matador* was either a bungler or else very clever and strong indeed. In a moment he proved himself to be a bungler, for his sword turned on the shoulder blade, and the bull, throwing up his head, almost caught him on his horns. Then I hissed and cried, 'Shame!' And the people stared at me. That butcher tried five times before he killed the bull, and at last even the most ignorant of the spectators knew I had been right in hissing him. He was one of your Mazzantinis, I suppose."

"Oh, no!" I replied, "I've seen Mazzantini try twice, but never five times. That's too much!"

"Well," Montes continued quietly, "the man who tries once and fails ought never to be allowed in a ring again. But to go on. That first day taught me I could be an *espada*. The only doubt in my mind was in regard to the nature of the bulls. Should I be able to understand new bulls—bulls, too, from different herds and of different race, as well as I understood our bulls? Going home that evening I tried to talk to my father, but he thought the sport had been very good, and when I wanted to show him the mistakes the *matadores* had made, he laughed at me, and, taking hold of my arm, he said, 'Here's where you need the gristle before you could kill a bull with a sword, even if he were tied for you.' My father was very proud of his size and strength, but what he said had reason in it, and made me doubt myself. Then he talked about the gains of the *matadores*. A fortune, he said, was given for a single day's work. Even the pay of the *chulos* seemed to me to be extravagant, and a *banderillero* got enough to make one rich for life. That night I thought over all I had seen and heard, and fell asleep and dreamt I was an *espada*, the best in Spain and rich, and married to a lovely girl with golden hair—as boys do dream.

"Next day I set myself to practice with our bulls. First I teased one till he grew angry and rushed at me; then, as a *chulo*, I stepped aside. And after I had practiced this several times, I began to try to move aside as late as possible and only just as far as was needful; for I soon found out the play of horn of every bull we had. The older the bull the heavier his neck and shoulders become, and, therefore, the sweep of horns in an old bull is much smaller than a young one's. Before the first morning's sport was over I knew that with our bulls at any rate I could beat any *chulo* I had seen the day before. Then I set myself to quiet the bulls, which was a little difficult, and after I had succeeded I went back to my pony to read and dream. Next day I played at being a *banderillero*, and found out at once that my knowledge of the animal was all important. For I knew always on which side to move to avoid the bull's rush. I knew how he meant to strike by the way he put his head down. To plant the *banderillas* perfectly would have been child's play to me, at least with our bulls. The *matador's* work was harder to practice. I had no sword; besides, the bull I wished to pretend to kill, was not tired and wouldn't keep quiet. Yet I went on trying. The game had a fascination to me. A few days later, provided with a makeshift red *capa*, I got a bull far away from the others. Then I played with him till he was tired out. First I played as a *chulo*, and avoided his rushes by an inch or two only; then, as *banderillero*, I escaped his stroke, and, as I did so, struck his neck with two sticks. When he was tired I approached him with the *capa* and found I could make him do what I pleased, stand crooked or square in a moment, just as I liked. For I learned at once that as a rule the bull rushes at the *capa* and not at the man who holds it. Some bulls, however, are clever enough to charge the man. For weeks I kept up this game, till one day my father expressed his surprise at the thin and wretched appearance of the bulls. No wonder! The pasture ground had been a ring to them and me for many a week.

"After this I had to play *matador*—the only part which had any interest for me—without first tiring them. Then came a long series of new experiences, which in time made me what I was, a real *espada*, but which I can scarcely describe to you.

"For power over wild animals comes to a man, as it were, by leaps and bounds. Of a sudden one finds he can make a bull do something which the day before he could not make him do. It is all a matter of intimate knowledge of the nature of the animal. Just as the shepherd, as I've been told, knows the face of each sheep in a flock of a thousand, though I can see no difference between the faces of sheep, which are all alike stupid to me, so I came to know bulls, with a complete understanding of the nature and temper of each one. It's just because I can't tell you how I acquired this part of my knowledge that I was so long-winded in explaining to you my first steps. That I knew more than I have told you, will appear as I go on with my story, and that you must believe or disbelieve as you think best."

"Oh," I cried, "you've explained everything so clearly, and thrown light on so many things I didn't understand, that I shall believe whatever you tell me."

Old Montes went on as if he hadn't heard my protestation:

"The next three years were intolerable to me: my stepmother repaid my dislike with interest and found a hundred ways of making me uncomfortable, without doing anything I could complain of and get altered. In the

spring of my nineteenth year I told my father I intended
to go to Madrid and become an *espada*. When he found he
couldn't induce me to stay, he said I might go. We parted,
and I walked to Seville; there I did odd jobs for a few
weeks in connection with the bull ring, such as feeding the
bulls, helping to separate them, and so forth; and there I
made an acquaintance who was afterwards a friend. Juan
Valdera was one of the *cuadrilla* of Girvalda, a *matador* of
the ordinary type. Juan was from Estramadura, and we
could scarcely understand each other at first; but he was
kindly and careless and I took a great liking to him. He
was a fine man; tall, strong and handsome, with short,
dark, wavy hair and dark moustache, and great black eyes.
He liked me, I suppose, because I admired him and because I never wearied of hearing him tell of his conquests
among women and even great ladies. Of course I told him
I wished to enter the ring, and he promised to help me to
get a place in Madrid where he knew many of the officials.
'You may do well with the *capa*,' I remember he said con-
descendingly, 'or even as a *banderillero*, but you'll never go
further. You see, to be an *espada*, as I intend to be, you
must have height and strength,' and he stretched his fine
figure as he spoke. I acquiesced humbly enough. I felt that
perhaps he and my father were right, and I didn't know
whether I should even have strength enough for the task of
an *espada*. To be brief, I saved a little money, and managed
to get to Madrid late in the year, too late for the bull ring.
Thinking over the matter I resolved to get work in a blacksmith's shop, and at length succeeded. As I had thought,
the labor strengthened me greatly, and in the spring of my
twentieth year, by Juan's help, I got employed on trial one
Sunday as a *chulo*.

"I suppose," Montes went on, after a pause. "I ought to
have been excited and nervous on that first Sunday—but I
wasn't; I was only eager to do well in order to get engaged
for the season. The blacksmith, Antonio, whom I had

worked with, had advanced me the money for my costume, and Juan had taken me to a tailor and got the things made, and what I owed Antonio and the tailor weighed on me. Well, on that Sunday I was a failure at first. I went in the procession with the rest, then with the others I fluttered my *capa;* but when the bull rushed at me, instead of running away, like the rest, I wrapped my *capa* about me and, just as his horns were touching me, moved aside— not half a pace. The spectators cheered me, it is true, and I thought I had done very well, until Juan came over to me and said:

" 'You mustn't show off like that. First of all, you'll get killed if you play that game; and then you fellows with the *capa* are there to make the bull run about to tire him out so that we *matadores* may kill him.'

"That was my first lesson in professional jealousy. After that I ran about like the rest, but without much heart in the sport. It seemed to me stupid. Besides, from Juan's anger and contempt, I felt sure I shouldn't get a permanent engagement. Bit by bit, however, my spirits rose again with the exercise, and when the fifth or sixth bull came in, I resolved to make him run. It was a good, honest bull; I saw that at once; he stood in the middle of the ring, excited, but not angry, in spite of the waving of the *capas* all round him. As soon as my turn came, I ran forward, nearer to him than the others had considered safe, and waved the challenge with my *capa*. At once he rushed at it, and I gave him a long run, half around the circle and ended it by stopping and letting him toss the *capa* which I held not quite at arm's length from my body. As I did this I didn't turn round to face him. I knew he'd toss the *capa* and not me, but the crowd rose and cheered as if the thing were extraordinary. Then I felt sure I should be engaged, and I was perfectly happy. Only Juan said to me a few minutes later:

" 'You'll be killed, my boy, one of these fine days if you

try those games. Your life will be a short one if you begin by trusting a bull.'

"But I didn't mind what he said. I thought he meant it as a friendly warning, and I was anxious only to get permanently engaged. And sure enough, as soon as the games were over, I was sent for by the director. He was kind to me, and asked me where I had played before. I told him that was my first trial.

" 'Ah!' he said, turning to a gentleman who was with him, 'I knew it, Señor Duque; such courage always comes from—want of experience, let me call it.'

" 'No,' replied the gentleman, whom I afterwards knew as the Duke of Medina Celi, the best *aficionado*, and one of the noblest men in Spain; 'I'm not so sure of that. Why,' he went on, speaking now to me, 'did you keep your back turned to the bull?'

" 'Señor,' I answered, ' 'twas an honest bull, and not angry, and I knew he'd toss the *capa* without paying any attention to me.'

" 'Well,' said the Duke, 'if you know that much, and aren't afraid to risk your life on your knowledge, you'll go far. I must have a talk with you some day, when I've more time; you can come and see me. Send in your name; I shall remember.' And as he said this, he nodded to me and waved his hand to the director, and went away.

"Then and there the director made me sign an engagement for the season, and gave me one hundred *duros* as earnest money in advance of my pay. What an evening we had after that! Juan, the tailor, Antonio, the blacksmith, and I. How glad and proud I was to be able to pay my debts and still have sixty *duros* in my pocket after entertaining my friends. If Juan had not hurt me every now and then by the way he talked of my foolhardiness, I should have told them all I knew; but I didn't. I only said I was engaged at a salary of a hundred *duros* a month.

" 'What!' said Juan, 'Come, tell the truth; make it fifty.'

" 'No,' I said; 'it was a hundred,' and I pulled out the money.

" 'Well,' he said, 'that only shows what it is to be small and young and foolhardy! Here am I, after six years' experience, second, too, in the *cuadrilla* of Girvalda, and I'm not getting much more than that.'

"Still, in spite of such little drawbacks, in spite, too, of the fact that Juan had to go away early, to meet 'a lovely creature,' as he said, that evening was one of the happiest I ever spent.

"All that summer through I worked every Sunday, and grew in favor with the Madrileñas, though not with these in Juan's way. I was timid and young; besides, I had a picture of a woman in my mind, and I saw no one like it. So I went on studying the bulls, learning all I could about the different breeds, and watching them in the ring. Then I sent money to my sister and to my father, and was happy.

"In the winter I was a good deal with Antonio; every day I did a spell of work in his shop to strengthen myself, and he, I think, got to know that I intended to become an *espada*. At any rate, after my first performance with the *capa*, he believed I could do whatever I wished. He used often to say God had given him strength and me brains, and he only wished he could exchange some of his muscle for some of my wits. Antonio was not very bright, but he was good-tempered, kind, and hardworking, the only friend I ever had. May Our Lady give his soul rest!

"Next spring when the director sent for me, I said that I wanted to work as a *banderillero*. He seemed to be surprised, told me I was a favorite with the *capa*, and had better stick to that for another season at least. But I was firm. Then he asked me whether I had ever used the *banderillas* and where? The director always believed I had been employed in some other ring before I came to Madrid. I told him I was confident I could do the work. 'Besides,' I added, 'I want more pay,' which was an untruth; but the argument seemed to him decisive, and he engaged me at two hundred *duros* a month, under the condition that, if the spectators wished it, I should work now and then with the *capa* as well. It didn't take me long to show the *aficionados* in Madrid that I was as good with the *banderillas* as I was with the *capa*. I could plant them when and where I liked. For in this season I found I could make the bull do almost anything. You know how the *banderillero* has to excite the bull to charge him before he can plant the darts. He does that to make the bull lower his head well, and he runs toward the bull partly so that the bull may not know when to toss his head up, partly because he can throw himself aside more easily when he's running fairly fast. Well, again and again I made the bull lower his head and then walked to him, planted the *banderillas*, and as he struck upwards swayed aside just enough to avoid the blow. That was an infinitely more difficult feat than anything I had ever done with the *capa*, and it gave me reputation among the *aficionados* and also with the *espadas;* but the ignorant herd of spectators preferred my trick with the *capa*. So the season came and went. I had many a carouse with Juan, and gave him money from time to time, because women always made him spend more than he got. From that time, too, I gave my sister fifty *duros* a month, and my father fifty. For before the season was half over my pay was raised to four hundred *duros* a month, and my name was always put on the bills. In fact I was rich and a favorite of the public.

"So time went on, and my third season in Madrid began, and with it came the beginning of the end. Never was anyone more absolutely content than I when we were told *los toros* would begin in a fortnight. On the first Sunday I was walking carelessly in the procession beside Juan, though I could have been next to the *espadas*, had I wished, when he suddenly nudged me, saying:

" 'Look up! there on the second tier; there's a face for you.'

"I looked up, and saw a girl with the face of my dreams, only much more beautiful. I suppose I must have stopped, for Juan pulled me by the arm crying: 'You're moon-struck, man; come on!' and on I went—love-struck in heart and body. What a face it was! The golden hair framed it like a picture, but the great eyes were hazel, and the lips scarlet, and she wore the *mantilla* like a queen. I moved forward like a man in a dream, conscious of nothing that went on round me, till I heard Juan say:

" 'She's looking at us. She knows we've noticed her. All right, pretty one! We'll make friends afterwards.'

" 'But how?' I asked, stupidly.

" 'How!' he replied, mockingly. 'I'll just send someone to find out who she is, and then you can send her a box for next Sunday, and pray for her acquaintance, and the thing's done. I suppose that's her mother sitting behind her,' he went on. 'I wonder if the other girl next to her is her sister. She's as good-looking as the fair-haired one, and easier to win, I'd bet. Strange how all the timid ones take to me.' And again he looked up.

"I said nothing; nor did I look up at the place where she was sitting; but I worked that day as I had never worked before. Then, for the first time, I did something that has never been done since by anyone. The first bull was honest and kindly: I knew the sort. So, when the people began to call for *El Pequeño* (the little fellow)—that was the nickname they had given me—I took up a *capa*, and, when the bull chased me, I stopped suddenly, faced him, and threw the *capa* round me. He was within ten paces of me before he saw I had stopped, and he began to stop; but before he came to a standstill his horns were within a foot of me. He tossed his head once or twice as if he would strike me, and then went off. The people cheered and cheered as if they would never cease. Then I looked up at her. She must have been watching me, for she took the red rose from her hair and threw it into the ring toward me, crying, 'Bien! Muy bien! El Pequeño!'

"As I picked up the rose, pressed it to my lips, and hid it in my breast, I realized all that life holds of triumphant joy! . . . Then I made up my mind to show what I could do, and everything I did that day seemed to delight the public. At last, as I planted the *banderillas*, standing in front of the bull, and he tried twice in quick succession to strike me and failed, the crowd cheered and cheered and cheered, so that, even when I went away, after bowing and stood among my fellows, ten minutes passed before they would let the game go on. I didn't look up again. No! I wanted to keep the memory of what she looked like when she threw me the rose.

"After the games were over, I met her, that same evening. Juan had brought it about, and he talked easily enough to the mother and daughter and niece, while I listened. We all went, I remember, to a restaurant in the Puerta del Sol, and ate and drank together. I said little or nothing the whole evening. The mother told us they had just come from the north: Alvareda was the family name; her daughter was Clemencia, the niece, Liberata. I heard everything in a sort of fever of hot pulses and cold fits of humility, while Juan told them all about himself, and what he meant to do and be. While Clemencia listened to him, I took my fill of gazing at her. At last Juan invited them all to *los toros* on the following Sunday, and promised them the best *palco* in the ring. He found out, too, where they lived, in a little street running parallel to the Alcala, and assured them of our visit within the week. Then they left, and as they went out of the door Liberata looked at Juan, while Clemencia chatted with him and teased him.

" 'That's all right,' said Juan, turning to me when they were gone, 'and I don't know which is the more taking, the niece or Clemencia. Perhaps the niece; she looks at one so appealingly; and those who talk so with their eyes are always the best. I wonder have they any money? One might do worse than either with a good portion.'

" 'Is that your real opinion?' I asked hesitatingly.

" 'Yes,' he answered; 'why?'

" 'Because, in that case leave Clemencia to me. Of course you could win her if you wanted to. But it makes no difference to you, and to me all the difference. If I cannot marry her, I shall never marry.'

" 'Jesu!' he cried, 'how fast you go, but I'd do more than that for you, Montes; and besides, the niece really pleases me better.'

"So the matter was settled between us.

"Now, if I could tell you all that happened, I would. But much escaped me at the time that I afterwards remembered, and many things that then seemed to me to be as sure as a straight stroke, have since grown confused. I only know that Juan and I met them often, and that Juan paid court to the niece, while I from time to time talked timidly to Clemencia.

"One Sunday after another came and went, and we grew to know each other well. Clemencia did not chatter like other women: I liked her the better for it, and when I came to know she was very proud, I liked that, too. She charmed me; why? I can scarcely tell. I saw her faults gradually, but even her faults appeared to me fascinating. Her pride was insensate. I remember one Sunday afternoon after the games, I happened to go into a restaurant, and found her sitting there with her mother. I was in costume and carried in my hand a great nosegay of roses that a lady had thrown me in the ring. Of course as soon as I saw Clemencia I went over to her and—you know it is the privilege of the *matadores* in Spain, even if they do not know the lady—taking a rose from the bunch I presented it to her as the fairest of the fair. Coming from the cold

North, she didn't know the custom and scarcely seemed pleased. When I explained it to her, she exclaimed that it was monstrous; she'd never allow a mere *matador* to take such a liberty unless she knew and liked him. Juan expostulated with her laughingly; I said nothing; I knew what qualities our work required, and didn't think it needed any defense. I believed in that first season, I came to see that her name Clemencia wasn't very appropriate. At any rate she had courage and pride, that was certain. Very early in our friendship she wanted to know why I didn't become an *espada*.

" 'A man without ambition,' she said, 'is like a woman without beauty.'

"I laughed at this and told her my ambition was to do my work well, and advancement was sure to follow in due course. Love of her seemed to have killed ambition in me. But no. She wouldn't rest content in spite of Juan's telling her my position already was more brilliant than that of most of the *espadas*.

" 'He does things with the *capa* and the *banderillas* which no *espada* in all Spain would care to imitate. And that's position enough. Besides, to be an *espada* requires height and strength.

"As he said this she seemed to be convinced, but it annoyed me a little, and afterwards as we walked together, I said to her,

" 'If you want to see me work as an *espada*, you shall.'

" 'Oh, no!' she answered half carelessly; 'if you can't do it, as Juan says, why should you try? To fail is worse than to lack ambition.'

" 'Well,' I answered, 'you shall see.'

"And then I took my courage in both hands and went on:

" 'If you cared for me I should be the first *espada* in the world next season.'

"She turned and looked at me curiously and said,

" 'Of course I'd wish it if you could do it.'

"And I said, 'See, I love you as the priest loves the Virgin; tell me to be an *espada* and I shall be one for the sake of your love.'

" 'That's what all men say, but love doesn't make a man tall and strong.'

" 'No; nor do size and strength take the place of heart and head. Do you love me? That's the question.'

" 'I like you, yes. But love—love, they say, comes after marriage.'

" 'Will you marry me?'

" 'Become an *espada* and then ask me again,' she answered coquettishly.

"The very next day I went to see the Duke of Medina Celi; the servants would scarcely let me pass till they heard my name and that the Duke had asked me to come. He received me kindly. I told him what I wanted.

" 'Have you ever used the sword?' he asked in surprise. 'Can you do it? You see we don't want to lose the best man with *capa* and *banderillas* ever known, to get another second-class *espada*.'

" 'Señor Duque, I have done better with the *banderillas* than I could with the *capa*. I shall do better with the *espada* than with the *banderillas*.'

" 'You little fiend!' he laughed, 'I believe you will, though it is unheard-of to become an *espada* without training; but now for the means. All the *espadas* are engaged; it'll be difficult. Let me see. . . . The Queen has asked me to superintend the sports early in July, and then I shall give you your chance. Will that do? In the meantime, astonish us all with *capa* and *banderillas*, so that men may not think me mad when I put your name first on the bill.'

"I thanked him from my heart, as was his due, and after a little more talk I went away to tell Clemencia the news. She only said:

" 'I'm glad. Now you'll get Juan to help you.'

"I stared at her.

" 'Yes!' she went on, a little impatiently; 'he has been taught the work; he's sure to be able to show you a great deal.'

"I said not a word. She was sincere, I saw, but then she came from the North and knew nothing. I said to myself, 'That's how women are!'

"She continued, 'Of course you're clever with the *capa* and *banderillas*, and now you must do more than ever, as the Duke said, to deserve your chance.' And then she asked carelessly, 'Couldn't you bring the Duke and introduce him to us some time or other? I should like to thank him.'

"And I, thinking it meant our betrothal, was glad, and promised. And I remember I did bring him once to the box and he was kind in a way, but not cordial as he always was when alone with me, and he told Clemencia that I'd go very far, and that any woman would be lucky to get me for a husband, and so on. After a little while he went away. But Clemencia was angry with him and said he put on airs; and, indeed, I had never seen him so cold and reserved; I could say little or nothing in his defense.

"Well, all that May I worked as I had never done. The director told me he knew I was to use the *espada* on the first Sunday in July, and he seemed to be glad; and one or two of the best *espadas* came to me and said they'd heard the news and should be glad to welcome me among them. All this excited me, and I did better and better. I used to pick out the old prints of Goya, the great painter—you know his works are in the Prado—and do everything the old *matadores* did, and invent new things. But nothing 'took' like my trick with the *capa*. One Sunday, I remember, I had done it with six bulls, one after another, and the people cheered and cheered. But the seventh was a bad bull, and, of course I didn't do it. And afterwards Clemencia asked me why I didn't, and I told her. For you see

I didn't know then that women rate high what they don't understand. Mystery is everything to them. As if the explanation of such a thing makes it any easier! A man wins great battles by seizing the right moment and using it—the explanation is simple. One must be great in order to know the moment, that's all. But women don't see that it is only small men who exaggerate the difficulties of their work. Great men find their work easy and say so, and, therefore, you'll find that women underrate great men and overpraise small ones. Clemencia really thought I ought to learn the *espada's* work from Juan. Ah! women are strange creatures. . . . Well, after that Sunday she was always bothering me to do the *capa* trick with every bull.

" 'If you don't,' she used to say, 'you won't get the chance of being an *espada*.' And when she saw I laughed and paid no attention to her talk, she became more and more obstinate.

" 'If the people get to know you can only do it with some bulls, they won't think much of you. Do it with every bull, then they can't say anything.'

"And I said 'No! and I shouldn't be able to say anything either.'

" 'If you love me you will do as I say!'

"And when I didn't do as she wished—it was madness—she grew cold to me, and sneered at me, and then urged me again, till I half yielded. Really, by that time I hardly knew what I couldn't do, for each day I seemed to get greater power over the bulls. At length a Sunday came, the first, I think in June, or the last in May. Clemencia sat with her mother and cousin in the best *palco;* I had got it from the director, who now refused me nothing. I had done my *capa* trick with three bulls, one after the other, then the fourth came in. As soon as I saw him, I knew he was bad, cunning I mean, and with black rage in the heart of him. The other men stood aside to let me do the trick, but I wouldn't. I ran away like the rest, and let him toss the *capa*. The people liked me, and so they cheered just the same, thinking I was tired; but suddenly Clemencia called out: 'The *capa* round the shoulders; the *capa* trick!' and I looked up at her; and she leaned over the front of the *palco*, and called out the words again.

"Then rage came into me, rage at her folly and cold heart; I took off my cap to her, and turned and challenged the bull with the *capa*, and, as he put down his head and rushed, I threw the *capa* round me and stood still. I did not even look at him. I knew it was no use. He struck me here in the thigh, and I went up into the air. The shock took away my senses. As I came to myself they were carrying me out of the ring, and the people were all standing up; but, as I looked toward the *palco*, I saw she wasn't standing up; she had a handkerchief before her face. At first I thought she was crying, and I felt well, and longed to say to her, 'It doesn't matter, I'm content'; then she put down the handkerchief and I saw she wasn't crying; there wasn't a tear in her eyes. She seemed surprised merely, and shocked. I suppose she thought I could work miracles, or rather she didn't care much whether I was hurt or not. That turned me faint again. I came to myself in my bed, where I spent the next month. The doctor told the Duke of Medina Celi—he had come to see me the same afternoon—that the shock hadn't injured me, but I should be lame always, as the bull's horn had torn the muscle of my thigh from the bone. 'How he didn't bleed to death,' he said, 'is a wonder; now he'll pull through, but no more play with the bulls for him.' I knew better than the doctor, but I said nothing to him, only to the Duke I said:

" 'Señor, a promise is a promise; I shall use the *espada* in your show in July.'

"And he said, 'Yes, my poor boy, if you wish it, and are able to; but how came you to make such a mistake?'

" 'I made no mistake, Señor.'

" 'You knew you'd be struck?'

"I nodded. He looked at me for a moment, and then held out his hand. He understood everything, I'm sure; but he said nothing to me then.

"Juan came to see me in the evening, and next day Clemencia and her mother. Clemencia was sorry, that I could see, and wanted me to forgive her. As if I had anything to forgive when she stood there so lithe and straight, with her flower-like face and the appealing eyes. Then came days of pain while the doctors forced the muscles back into their places. Soon I was able to get up, with a crutch, and limp about. As I grew better, Clemencia came seldomer, and when she came, her mother never left the room. I knew what that meant. She had told her mother not to go away; for, though the mother thought no one good enough for her daughter, yet she pitied me, and would have left us alone—sometimes. She had a woman's heart. But no, not once. Then I set myself to get well soon. I would show them all, I said to myself, that a lame Montes was worth more than other men. And I got better, so the doctor said, with surprising speed. . . . One day, toward the end of June, I said to the servant of the Duke—he sent a servant every day to me with fruit and flowers—that I wished greatly to see his master. And the Duke came to see me, the very same day.

"I thanked him first for his kindness to me, and then asked:

" 'Señor, have you put my name on the bills as *espada?*'

" 'No,' he replied; 'you must get well first, and, indeed, if I were in your place, I should not try anything more till next season.'

"And I said, 'Señor Duque, it presses. Believe me, weak as I am, I can use the sword.'

"And he answered my very thought: 'Ah! She thinks you can't. And you want to prove the contrary. I shouldn't take the trouble, if I were you; but there! Don't deceive yourself or me; there is time yet for three or four

days: I'll come again to see you, and if you wish to have
your chance you shall. I give you my word.' As he left the
room I had tears in my eyes; but I was glad, too, and confident: I'd teach the false friends a lesson. Save Antonio,
the blacksmith, and some strangers, and the Duke's servant, no one had come near me for more than a week.
Three days afterwards I wrote to the Duke asking him to
fulfil his promise, and the very next day Juan, Clemencia,
and her mother all came to see me together. They all
wanted to know what it meant. My name as *espada* for the
next Sunday, they said, was first on the bills placarded all
over Madrid, and the Duke had put underneath it—'By
special request of H.M. the Queen.' I said nothing but
that I was going to work; and I noticed that Clemencia
couldn't meet my eyes.

"What a day that was! That Sunday I mean. The
Queen was in her box with the Duke beside her as our
procession saluted them, and the great ring was crowded
tier on tier, and she was in the best box I could get. But I
tried not to think about her. My heart seemed to be frozen. Still I know now that I worked for her even then.
When the first bull came in and the *capa* men played him,
the people began to shout for me—'El Pequeño! El
Pequeño! El Pequeño'—and wouldn't let the games go on.
So I limped forward in my *espada's* dress and took a *capa*
from a man and challenged the bull, and he rushed at
me—the honest one; I caught his look and knew it was all
right, so I threw the *capa* round me and turned my back
upon him. In one flash I saw the people rise in their
places, and the Duke lean over the front of the *palco;* then,
as the bull hesitated and stopped, and they began to cheer,
I handed back the *capa*, and, after bowing, went again
among the *espadas*. Then the people christened me afresh—
'El Cojo' (The Cripple!)—and I had to come forward and
bow again and again, and the Queen threw me a gold cigarette case. I have it still. There it is. . . . I never looked

up at Clemencia, though I could see her always. She threw no rose to me that day. . . . Then the time came when I should kill the bull. I took the *muleta* in my left hand and went toward him with the sword uncovered in my right. I needed no trick. I held him with my will, and he looked up at me. 'Poor brute,' I thought, 'you are happier than I am.' And he bowed his head with the great, wondering, kindly eyes, and I struck straight to the heart. On his knees he fell at my feet, and rolled over dead, almost without a quiver. As I hid my sword in the *muleta* and turned away, the people found their voices, 'Well done, The Cripple! Well done!' When I left the ring that day I left it as the first *espada* in Spain. So the Duke said, and he knew—none better. After one more Sunday the sports were over for the year, but that second Sunday I did better than the first, and I was engaged for the next season as first *espada*, with fifty thousand *duros* salary. Forty thousand I invested as the Duke advised—I have lived on the interest ever since—the other ten thousand I kept by me.

"I had resolved never to go near Clemencia again, and I kept my resolve for weeks. One day Juan came and told me Clemencia was suffering because of my absence. He said:

" 'She's proud, you know, proud as the devil, and she won't come and see you or send to you, but she loves you. There's no doubt of that: she loves you. I know them, and I never saw a girl so gone on a man. Besides they're poor now, she and her mother; they've eaten up nearly all they had, and you're rich and could help them.'

"That made me think. I felt sure she didn't love me. That was plain enough. She hadn't even a good heart, or she would have come and cheered me up when I lay wounded—because of her obstinate folly. No! It wasn't worthwhile suffering any more on her account. That was clear. But if she needed me, if she were really poor? Oh, that I couldn't stand. I'd go to her. 'Are you sure?' I asked Juan, and when he said he was, I said:

" 'Then I'll visit them tomorrow.'

"And on the next day I went. Clemencia received me, as usual; she was too proud to notice my long absence, but the mother wanted to know why I had kept away from them so long. From that time on the mother seemed to like me greatly. I told her I was still sore—which was the truth—and I had had much to do.

" 'Some lady fallen in love with you, I suppose,' said Clemencia half-scoffingly—so that I could hardly believe she had wanted to see me.

" 'No,' I answered, looking at her, 'one doesn't get love without seeking for it, sometimes not even then—when one's small and lame as I am.'

"Gradually the old relations established themselves again. But I had grown wiser, and watched her now with keen eyes as I had never done formerly. I found she had changed—in some subtle way had become different. She seemed kinder to me, but at the same time her character appeared to be even stronger than it had been. I remember noticing one peculiarity in her I had not remarked before. Her admiration of the physique of men was now keen and outspoken. When we went to the theatre (as we often did) I saw that the better-looking and more finely formed actors had a great attraction for her. I had never noticed this in her before. In fact, she had seemed to me to know nothing about virile beauty, beyond a girl's vague liking for men who were tall and strong. But now she looked at men critically. She had changed; that was certain. What was the cause? . . . I could not divine. Poor fool that I was! I didn't know then that good women seldom or never care much for mere bodily qualities in a man; the women who do are generally worthless. Now, too, she spoke well of the men of Southern Spain; when I first met her she professed to admire the women of the South, but to think little of the men. Now she admired the men, too; they were warmer-hearted, she said; had more love and passion in them, and were gentler with women than those of the North. Somehow I hoped that she referred to me, that her heart was beginning to plead for me, and I was very glad and proud, though it all seemed too good to be true.

"One day in October, when I called with Juan, we found them packing their things. They had to leave, they said, and take cheaper lodgings. Juan looked at me, and some way or other I got him to take Clemencia into another room. Then I spoke to the mother: Clemencia, I hoped would soon be my wife; in any case I couldn't allow her to want for anything; I would bring a thousand *duros* the next day, and they must not think of leaving their comfortable apartments. The mother cried and said, I was good: 'God makes few such men,' and so forth. The next day I gave her the money, and it was arranged between us without saying anything to Clemencia. I remember about this time, in the early winter of that year, I began to see her faults more clear, and I noticed that she had altered in many ways. Her temper had changed. It used to be equable though passionate. It had become uncertain and irritable. She had changed greatly. For now, she would let me kiss her without remonstrance, and sometimes almost as if she didn't notice the kiss, whereas before it used always to be a matter of importance. And when I asked her when she would marry me, she would answer half-carelessly, 'Some time, I suppose,' as she used to do, but her manner was quite different. She even sighed once as she spoke. Certainly she had changed. What was the cause? I couldn't make it out, therefore I watched, not suspiciously but she had grown a little strange to me—a sort of puzzle, since she had been so unkind when I lay wounded. And partly from this feeling, partly from my great love for her, I noticed everything. Still I urged her to marry me. I thought as soon as we were married, and she had a child to take care of and to love, it would be all right with both of us. Fool that I was!

"In April, which was fine, I remember, that year in Madrid—you know how cold it is away up there, and how keen the wind is; as the Madrileños say, ' 'twon't blow out a candle, but it'll kill a man'—Clemencia began to grow pale and nervous. I couldn't make her out; and so, more than ever, pity strengthening love in me, I urged her to tell me when she would marry me; and one day she turned to me, and I saw she was quite white as she said:

" 'After the season, perhaps.'

"Then I was happy, and ceased to press her. Early in May the games began—my golden time. I had grown quite strong again, and was surer of myself than ever. Besides, I wanted to do something to deserve my great happiness. Therefore, on one of the first days when the Queen and the Duke and Clemencia were looking on, I killed the bull with the sword immediately after he entered the ring, and before he had been tired at all. From that day on the people seemed crazy about me. I couldn't walk in the streets without being cheered; a crowd followed me wherever I went; great nobles asked me to their houses, and their ladies made much of me. But I didn't care, for all the time Clemencia was kind, and so I was happy.

"One day suddenly she asked me why I didn't make Juan an *espada*. I told her I had offered him the first place in my *cuadrilla*; but he wouldn't accept it. She declared that it was natural of him to refuse when I had passed him in the race; but why didn't I go to the Duke and get him made an *espada*? I replied laughingly that the Duke didn't make men *espadas*, but God or their parents. Then her brows drew down, and she said she hadn't thought to find such mean jealousy in me. So I answered her seriously that I didn't believe Juan would succeed as an *espada*, or else I should do what I could to get him appointed. At once she came and put her arms on my shoulders, and said 'twas like me, and she would tell Juan; and after that I could do nothing but kiss her. A little later I asked Juan about it, and he told me he thought he could do the work at least as well as Girvalda, and if I got him the place, he would never forget my kindness. So I went to the director and told him what I wished. At first he refused, saying Juan had no talent, he would only get killed. When I pressed him he said all the *espadas* were engaged, and made other such excuses. So at last I said I'd work no more unless he gave Juan a chance. Then he yielded after grumbling a great deal.

"Two Sundays later Juan entered the ring for the first time as as *espada*. He looked the part to perfection. Never was there a more splendid figure of a man, and he was radiant in silver and blue. His mother was in the box that day with Clemencia and her mother. Just before we all parted as the sports were about to begin, Clemencia drew me on one side, and said, 'You'll see that he succeeds, won't you?' And I replied, 'Yes, of course, I will. Trust me; it'll be all right.' And it was, though I don't think it would have been, if she hadn't spoken. I remembered my promise to her, and when I saw that the bull which Juan ought to kill was vicious, I told another *espada* to kill him, and so got Juan an easy bull, which I took care to have tired out before I told him the moment had come. Juan wasn't a coward—no! but he hadn't the peculiar nerve needed for the business. The *matador's* spirit should rise to the danger, and Juan's didn't rise. He was white, but determined to do his best. That I could see. So I said to him, 'Go on, man! Don't lose time, or he'll get his wind again. You're all right; I shall be near you as one of your *cuadrilla*.' And so I was, and if I hadn't been, Juan would have come to grief. Yes, he'd have come to grief that very first day.

"Naturally enough we spent the evening together. It

was a real *tertulia*, Señora Alvareda said; but Clemencia sat silent with the great, dark eyes turned in upon her thoughts, and the niece and myself were nearly as quiet, while Juan talked for every one, not forgetting himself. As he had been depressed before the trial so now he was unduly exultant, forgetting altogether, as it seemed to me, not only his nervousness but also that it had taken him two strokes to kill the bull. His first attempt was a failure, and the second one, though it brought the bull to his knees, never reached his heart. But Juan was delighted and seemed never to weary of describing the bull and how he had struck him, his mother listening to him the while adoringly. It was past midnight when we parted from our friends; and Juan, as we returned to my rooms, would talk of nothing but the salary he expected to get. I was out of sorts; he had bragged so incessantly I had scarcely got a word with Clemencia, who could hardly find time to tell me she had a bad headache. Juan would come up with me; he wanted to know whether I'd go on the morrow to the director to get him a permanent engagement. I got rid of him, at last, by saying I was tired to death, and it would look better to let the director come and ask for his services. So at length we parted. After he left me I sat for some time wondering at Clemencia's paleness. She was growing thin too! And what thoughts had induced that rapt expression of face?

"Next morning I awoke late and had so much to do that I resolved to put off my visit to Clemencia till the afternoon, but in the meantime the director spoke to me of Juan as rather a bungler, and when I defended him, agreed at last to engage him for the next four Sundays. This was a better result than I had expected, so as soon as I was free I made off to tell Juan the good news. I met his mother at the street door where she was talking with some women; she followed me into the *patio* saying Juan was not at home.

" 'Never mind,' I replied carelessly, 'I have good news for him, so I'll go upstairs to his room and wait.'

" 'Oh!' she said, 'you can't do that; you mustn't; Juan wouldn't like it.'

"Then I laughed outright. Juan wouldn't like it—oh no! It was amusing to say that when we had lived together like brothers for years, and had had no secrets from one another. But she persisted and grew strangely hot and excited. Then I thought to myself—there you are again; these women understand nothing. So I went away, telling her to send Juan to me as soon as he came in. At this she seemed hugely relieved and became voluble in excuses. In fact her manner altered so entirely that before I had gone fifty yards down the street, it forced me to wonder. Suddenly my wonder changed to suspicion. Juan wasn't out! Who was with him I mustn't see?

"As I stopped involuntarily, I saw a man on the other side of the street who bowed to me. I went across and said:

" 'Friend, I am Montes, the matador. Do you own this house?'

"He answered that he did, and that every one in Madrid knew me.

"So I said, 'Lend me a room on your first floor for an hour; *cosa de mujer* (A lady's in the case); you understand.'

"At once he led me upstairs and showed me a room from the windows of which I could see the entrance to Juan's lodging. I thanked him, and when he left me I stood near the window and smoked and thought. What could it all mean? . . . Had Clemencia anything to do with Juan? She made me get him his trial as *espada;* charged me to take care of him. He was from the South, too, and she had grown to like Southern men; 'they were passionate and gentle with women.' Curses on her! Her paleness occurred to me, her fits of abstraction. As I thought, every memory fitted into its place, and what had been mysterious grew plain to me; but I wouldn't accept the evidence of reason No! I'd wait and see. Then at once I grew quiet. But again the thoughts came—like the flies that plague the cattle in summertime—and again I brushed them aside, and again they returned.

"Suddenly I saw Juan's mother come into the street wearing altogether too careless an expression. She looked about at haphazard as if she expected someone. After a moment or two of this she slipped back into the *patio* with mystery in her sudden decision and haste. Then out came a form I knew well, and, with stately, even step, looking neither to the right hand nor the left, walked down the street. It was Clemencia, as my heart had told me it would be. I should have known her anywhere even had she not— just below the window where I was watching—put back her *mantilla* with a certain proud grace of movement which I had admired a hundred times. As she moved her head to feel that the *mantilla* draped her properly I saw her face; it was drawn and set like one fighting against pain. That made me smile with pleasure.

"Five minutes later Juan swung out of the doorway in the full costume of an *espada*—he seemed to sleep in it now—with a cigarette between his teeth. Then I grew sad and pitiful. We had been such friends. I had meant only good to him always. And he was such a fool! I understood it all now; knew, as if I had been told, that the intimacy between them dated from the time when I lay suffering in bed. Thinking me useless and never having had any real affection for me, Clemencia had then followed her inclination and tried to win Juan. She had succeeded easily enough, no doubt, but not in getting him to marry her. Later, she induced me to make Juan an *espada*, hoping against hope that he'd marry her when his new position had made him rich. On the other hand he had set himself to cheat me because of the money I had given her mother, which relieved him from the necessity of helping them;

and secondly, because it was only through my influence that he could hope to become an *espada*. Ignoble beasts! And then jealousy seized me as I thought of her admiration of handsome men, and at once I saw her in his arms. Forthwith pity, and sadness and anger left me, and, as I thought of him swaggering past the window, I laughed aloud. Poor weak fools! I, too, could cheat.

"He had passed out of the street. I went downstairs and thanked the landlord for his kindness to me. 'For your good-nature,' I said, 'you must come and see me work from a box next Sunday. Ask for me, I won't forget.' And he thanked me with many words and said he had never missed a Sunday since he had first seen me play with the *capa* three years before. I laughed and nodded to him and went my way homewards, whither I knew Juan had gone before me.

"As I entered my room, he rose to meet me with a shadow as of doubt or fear upon him. But I laughed cheerfully, gaily enough to deceive even so finished an actor as he was, and told him the good news. 'Engaged,' I cried, slapping him on the shoulder. 'The director engages you for four Sundays certain.' And that word 'certain' made me laugh louder still—jubilantly. Then afraid of overdoing my part, I sat quietly for some time and listened to his expressions of fatuous self-satisfaction. As he left me to go and trumpet the news from *café* to *café*, I had to choke down my contempt for him by recalling that picture, by forcing myself to see them in each other's arms. Then I grew quiet again and went to call upon my betrothed.

"She was at home and received me as usual, but with more kindness than was her wont. 'She feels a little remorse at deceiving me,' I said to myself, reading her now as if her soul were an open book. I told her of Juan's engagement and she let slip 'I wish I had known that sooner!' But I did not appear to notice anything. It amused me now to see how shallow she was and how blind I had

been. And then I played with her as she had often, doubtless, played with me. 'He will go far, will Juan,' I said,
'now that he has begun—very far, in a short time.' And
within me I laughed at the double meaning as she turned
startled eyes upon me. And then, 'His old loves will
mourn for the distance which must soon separate him
from them. Oh, yes, Juan will go far and leave them behind.' I saw a shade come upon her face, and, therefore,
added: 'But no one will grudge him his success. He's so
good-looking and good-tempered, and kind and true.' And
then she burst into tears, and I went to her and asked as if
suspicious, 'Why, what's the matter, Clemencia?' Amid
her sobs, she told me she didn't know, but she felt upset,
out of sorts, nervous; she had a headache. 'Heartache,' I
laughed to myself, and bade her go and lie down; rest
would do her good; I'd come again on the morrow. As I
turned to leave the room she called me back and put her
arms round my neck and asked me to be patient with her;
she was foolish, but she'd make it up to me yet. . . . And
I comforted her, the poor, shallow fool, and went away.

"In some such fashion as this the days passed; each
hour—now my eyes were opened—bringing me some
fresh entertainment; for, in spite of their acting, I saw that
none of them were happy. I knew everything. I guessed
that Juan, loving his liberty, was advising Clemencia to
make up to me, and I saw how badly she played her part.
And all this had escaped me a few days before; I laughed
at myself more contemptuously than at them. It interested
me, too, to see that Liberata had grown suspicious. She no
longer trusted Juan's protestations implicitly. Every now
and then, with feminine bitterness, she thrust the knife of
her own doubt and fear into Clemencia's wound. 'Don't
you think, Montes, Clemencia is getting pale and thin?'
she'd ask; 'it is for love of you, you know. She should
marry soon.' And all the while she cursed me in her heart
for a fool, while I laughed to myself. The comedy was in-

finitely amusing to me, for now I held the cords in my hand, and knew I could drop the curtain and cut short the acting just when I liked. Clemencia's mother, too, would sometimes set to work to amuse me as she went about with eyes troubled, as if anxious for the future, and yet stomach-satisfied with the comforts of the present. She, too, thought it worthwhile, now and then, to befool me, when fear came upon her—between meals. That did not please me! When she tried to play with me, the inconceivable stupidity of my former blind trust became a torture to me. Juan's mother I saw but little of; yet I liked her. She was honest at least, and deceit was difficult to her. Juan was her idol; all he did was right in her eyes; it was not her fault that she couldn't see he was like a poisoned well. All these days Juan was friendly to me as usual, with scarcely a shade of the old condescension in his manner. He no longer showed envy by remarking upon my luck. Since he himself had been tested, he seemed to give me as much respect as his self-love could spare. Nor did he now boast, as he used to do, of his height and strength. Once, however, on the Friday evening, I think it was, he congratulated Clemencia on my love for her, and joked about our marriage. The time had come to drop the curtain and make an end.

"On the Saturday I went to the ring and ordered my *palco* to be filled with flowers. From there I went to the Duke of Medina Celi. He received me as always, with kindness, thought I looked ill, and asked me whether I felt the old wound still. 'No,' I replied, 'no Señor Duque, and if I come to you now it is only to thank you once more for all your goodness to me.'

"And he said after a pause—I remember each word; for he meant well:

" 'Montes, there's something very wrong.' And then, 'Montes, one should never adore a woman; they all want a master. My hairs have grown gray in learning that. . . .

A woman, you see, may look well and yet be cold-hearted and—not good. But a man would be a fool to refuse nuts because one that looked all right was hollow.'

" 'You are wise,' I said 'Señor Duque! and I have been foolish. I hope it may be well with you always; but wisdom and folly come to the same end at last.'

"After I left him I went to Antonio and thanked him, and gave him a letter to be opened in a week. There were three enclosures in it—one for himself, one for the mother of Juan, and one for the mother of Clemencia, and each held three thousand *duros*. As they had cheated me for money, money they should have—with my contempt. Then I went back to the ring, and as I looked up to my *palco* and saw that the front of it was one bed of white and scarlet blossoms, I smiled. 'White for purity,' I said, 'and scarlet for blood—a fit show!' And I went home and slept like a child.

"Next day in the ring I killed two bulls, one on his first rush, and the other after the usual play. Then another *espada* worked, and then came the turn of Juan. As the bull stood panting I looked up at the *palco*. There they all were, Clemencia with hands clasped on the flowers and fixed, dilated eyes, her mother half asleep behind her. Next to Clemencia, the niece with flushed cheeks, and leaning on her shoulder his mother. Juan was much more nervous than he had been on the previous Sunday. As his bull came into the ring he asked me hurriedly: 'Do you think it's an easy one?' I told him carelessly that all bulls were easy and he seemed to grow more and more nervous. When the bull was ready for him he turned to me, passing his tongue feverishly over his dry lips.

" 'You'll stand by me, won't you, Montes?'

"And I asked with a smile:

" 'Shall I stand by you as you've stood by me?'

" 'Yes, of course, we've always been friends.'

" 'I shall be as true to you as you have been to me!' I

said. And I moved to his right hand and looked at the bull. It was a good one; I couldn't have picked a better. In his eyes I saw courage that would never yield and hate that would strike in the death throe, and I exulted and held his eyes with mine, and promised him revenge. While he bowed his horns to the *muleta*, he still looked at me and I at him; and as I felt that Juan had leveled his sword and was on the point of striking, I raised my head with a sweep to the side, as if I had been the bull; and as I swung, so the brave bull swung too. And then—then all the ring swam round with me, and yet I had heard the shouting and seen the spectators spring to their feet. . . .

"I was in the street close to the Alvaredas'. The mother met me at the door; she was crying and the tears were running down her fat, greasy cheeks. She told me Clemencia had fainted and had been carried home, and Juan was dead—ripped open—and his mother distracted, and 'twas a pity, for he was so handsome and kind and good-natured, and her best dress was ruined, and *los toros* shouldn't be allowed, and—as I brushed past her in disgust—that Clemencia was in her room crying.

"I went upstairs and entered the room. There she sat with her elbows on the table and her hair all round her face and down her back, and her fixed eyes stared at me. As I closed the door and folded my arms and looked at her, she rose, and her stare grew wild with surprise and horror, and then, almost without moving her lips, she said:

" 'Holy Virgin! You did it! I see it in your face!'

"And my heart jumped against my arms for joy, and I said in the same slow whisper, imitating her:

" 'Yes, I did it.'

"As I spoke she sprang forward with hate in her face, and poured out a stream of loathing and contempt on me. She vomited abuse as from her very soul: I was low and base and cowardly; I was—God knows what all. And he was handsome and kind, with a face like a king. . . . And I had thought she could love me, me, the ugly, little, lame cur, while he was there. And she laughed. She'd never have let my lips touch her if it hadn't been that her mother liked me and to please him. And now I had killed him, the best friend I had. Oh, 'twas horrible. Then she struck her head with her fists and asked how God, God, God, could allow me to kill a man whose finger was worth a thousand lives such as mine!

"Then I laughed and said:

" 'You mistake. You killed him. You made him an *espada*—you!'

"As I spoke her eyes grew fixed and her mouth opened, and she seemed to struggle to speak, but she only groaned—and fell face forward on the floor.

"I turned and left the room as her mother entered it." After a long pause Montes went on:

"I heard afterwards that she died next morning in premature childbirth. I left Madrid that night and came here, where I have lived ever since, if this can be called living. . . . Yet at times, now fairly content, save for one thing— 'Remorse?' Yes!"—and the old man rose to his feet, while his great eyes blazing with passion held me "Remorse! That I let the bull kill him. I should have torn his throat out with my own hands."

THE MIRACLE
OF THE
STIGMATA

IT WAS after the troubles in Jerusalem that a man called
Joshua, a carpenter and smith, came to Caesarea. Almost
before the neighbors were aware of it, he had settled down
in a little hut opposite the house of Simon the image-
maker, and was working quietly at his trade. He was a
Jew, to all appearances: a middle-aged Jew, with features
sharpened by suffering, or possibly by illness, and yet in
many ways he was not like a Jew: he never went near a
synagogue, he never argued about religion or anything
else, and he took what people gave him for his work without bargaining.

To his loud, high-colored, grasping compatriots he
seemed to be rather a poor creature; but a certain liking
softened their contempt of him, for his shrinking self-
effacement flattered their vanity and disposed them in his
favor. And yet, now and then, when they talked with
most assurance and he lifted his eyes to them, they grew a
little uneasy: his look was more one of pity than of admiration. He was a queer fellow, they decided, and not easy to
understand; but, as he was peculiarly retiring and silent,
the less agreeable impression wore away, and they finally
took the view of him that was most pleasing to themselves,
and regarded him as unimportant.

Joshua seemed to accept their indifference with humble

gratitude. He hardly ever left his room, and made no friends, except Simon who modeled in clay and wax the little figures of the Phoenician gods. Simon had the name of a rich man and he was very clever; he used to paint some of his wax gods with rosy cheeks, black hair and gilded lips till they looked alive and their robes were green and purple and saffron with dark shadows in the folds so that they seemed to move. Simon took a great liking to Joshua from the beginning, and did his best to break down his reserve and make an intimate of him. But even Simon had to content himself with moderate success. Joshua was always sympathetic, and would listen to him for hours at a time; but he spoke very little and never about himself. Simon, however, used to maintain that Joshua's silence was more stimulating than the speech of other men.

Simon's wife, Tabitha, did not take to Joshua at first; she never felt at ease with him, she said, and his great eyes made her flesh creep. But, as she got to know him, she could not help seeing his industry and his love of home and a quiet life, and, in a month or so, she sent to Joppa for her sister's daughter, Judith, who was twenty-five years old, and still unmarried. It was poverty, Tabitha knew, and not choice that had kept Judith single. The very first night after the girl reached Caesarea the two had a long talk, and Judith drank in all her aunt had to tell of Joshua and his peculiarities and accepted the cunning advice of the older woman with complete submission.

"The girl is no fool," Tabitha said to herself, and began to take a liking to her pupil; while Judith felt that Tabitha was really clever in managing men, or how could she have contrived to keep her husband's affection, in spite of her age and barrenness, a thing which seemed to the girl wonderful? Tabitha's advice to Judith was not to hold off and thus excite Joshua's desire; but to show him that she liked him.

"He has been disappointed in life," Tabitha said, "and

wants comforting. Anyone can see he's soft and affectionate by nature, like a girl: he will be grateful to you for loving him. Trust me, I know the kind of man: there was Jonas when I was young; I might have had him ten times over, if I had wanted to; and James as well, the rich tanner of Joppa who married the Levite's daughter. You take my advice, Judith, make up to him, and you'll get him. Joshua has a lot of the woman in him or I'm a fool."

Tabitha turned out to be right, though Judith did not succeed as quickly as they had expected, for it was hard to persuade Joshua that he was loved by anyone.

"I am old," he said, "and broken, and my house is empty of hope."

But the women were patient, and, one afternoon, Simon put in a warm word for Judith, and a little later the wedding took place.

The marriage was not unhappy; indeed, the union of the two seemed to grow intimate as time went on, and nothing occurred to trouble the peace of the household, except the fact that the marriage of Judith, too, was barren, like the marriage of Tabitha. Now and again Judith took this to heart and blamed her husband, but her anger never lasted very long. Joshua had a way of doing kind little things, even while he was being scolded, which was hard to resist. Still Judith always felt she would have thought more of him if he had turned on her and mastered her, as she had seen her father master her mother.

In the third year of the marriage, one Philip, a deacon, came from Jerusalem, and created a good deal of excitement and curiosity in the Jewish community. He talked of miracles and a Messiah; but no one believed much in him. And, as soon as he had left the town, the effect of his words disappeared, as hot vapor disappears in air. A little later, another wandering preacher, called Peter, came to Caesarea, and with his coming the new doctrine began to be understood. Peter taught that one Jesus had been born in Bethlehem from the seed of David, and that He was the Messiah foretold by the prophets. But when it became known that this supposed Messiah had been crucified in Jerusalem as a sedition-monger, the more devout among the Jews grew indignant, and Peter often found it difficult to get a hearing. Still, he was a man of such passionate conviction that his teaching lent the subject an interest which, strangely enough, did not die out or even greatly diminish after he had gone away. From time to time, too, curiosity was excited anew by all sorts of rumors; so when it was told about that another apostle, Paul, had landed at Caesarea and was going to speak, the Jews ran together to hear him.

Judith had heard the news at Tabitha's. As soon as she had made arrangements to go to the place of meeting, she hurried across to her own house to dress and to tell Joshua. Joshua listened to her patiently as usual, but with a troubled brow, and when his wife told him to get ready to accompany them, to her amazement he said that he could not go, and, when she pressed him and insisted, he shook his head. In the years they had lived together, he had hardly refused her anything, and he had never gone against her wishes at any time without explaining and pleading as if he were in fault; so Judith was doubly determined to get her own way now. After asking once more for his reasons, she declared that he must go with her:

"It's seldom I ask you anything, and it is very dull here. You must come."

It pained him to refuse her, and, seeing this, she talked about the wretched loneliness of her life, and, at last, wept aloud over her poverty and childlessness. Joshua comforted her and wiped her eyes, but did not yield, and, in this plight, Simon and Tabitha found them, much to Judith's annoyance. Simon took in the position at once, and, in his good-humored way, soon settled the difficulty.

"Come on, Judith," he said; "you know you would not

like him so much if he were not a stay-at-home, and it is not flattering to cry when you have me and Tabitha for company"; and without further ado he took the women away with him.

When they returned that evening, Judith seemed like a new creature; her cheeks were red and her eyes glowed, and she was excited, as one is excited with the new wine. For hours she talked to Joshua about Paul and all he had said:

"He is the most wonderful man in the world," she declared; "not big, nor handsome; small, indeed, and ordinary-looking, but, as soon as he begins to speak, he seems to grow before your eyes. I never heard anyone talk as he talks: you cannot help believing him; he is like one inspired."

So she went on, while Joshua, from time to time, raised his eyes to her in surprise. In spite of her excitement she answered his mute questioning:

"If you once heard him, you would have to believe him. He began by saying that he came to preach Christ and Him crucified. You know how everyone is ashamed to speak of the crucifixion. Paul began with it; it was the crowning proof, he said (what beautiful words!) that Jesus was indeed the Messiah. For Jesus was crucified, and lay three days in the grave, and then came to life again and was seen of many. This is the chief doctrine of the new creed; we shall all have to die with Jesus to the things of the flesh, Paul says, in order to rise again with Him to everlasting life."

She spoke slowly, but with much feeling, and then, clasping her hands, she cried:

"Oh, it is true; I feel it is all true!"

"But did Jesus die?" Joshua asked. "I mean," he went on hesitatingly, "did Paul try to prove that?"

"No, indeed," replied Judith. "Everyone knows that a man is not crucified by the Romans and allowed to live."

"But Jesus was not a criminal to the Romans," Joshua remarked quietly; "perhaps they took less care in his case."

"Oh, that's foolish," Judith retorted. "Of course, He was dead; they don't bury men who are alive."

"But sometimes," Joshua went on, "men are thought to be dead who have only fainted. Jesus is said to have died on the Cross in a few hours; and that, you know, is very strange; the crucified generally live for two or three days."

"I've no patience with you!" cried Judith. "All your doubts come from your dislike of religion. If you had more piety, you would not go on like that; and, if you once heard Paul preach, you would know, you would feel in your heart, that he was filled with the very Spirit of God. He talks of Jesus beautifully."

"Did he know Jesus?" asked Joshua. "He was not one of the disciples, was he?"

"Oh, no," she said. "He made himself famous by persecuting the followers of Jesus. For a long time, he went everywhere, informing against them and throwing them into prison. He told us all about it: it is a wonderful story. He was going up to Damascus once to persecute the Christians—that's what they are called now—when suddenly, in the road, a great light shone upon him, and he fell to the ground, while a voice from heaven cried:

" 'Saul, Saul, why persecutest thou me?'

"The voice was the voice of Jesus. Paul was blind for three days in Damascus, and only got his sight again through the prayers of one of the Christians. Isn't it all—beautiful?"

"It may have been the sun," said Joshua slowly, "the noonday sun; his blindness afterwards seems to show that it was sunstroke."

"But the voice," said Judith, "the voice which came from heaven, and which the others didn't hear, that wasn't sunstroke, I suppose?"

"The others didn't hear the voice," repeated Joshua, as if he were speaking to himself; "perhaps then it was the voice of his own soul, wounded by those persecutions."

"Oh, you're hateful," cried Judith, "with your stupid explanations. I can't see what pleasure you find in them, myself. Besides, they hurt me, for I believe in Paul. Yes, I do," she added passionately; "he is as God to me"; and, after a pause, she said:

"I'm going with Tabitha tomorrow, to see Paul: I want to be baptised and to become a Christian, as Paul is."

Joshua shook his head and cast down his eyes in doubt and sorrow, but Judith turned from him: she had said what she wanted to say.

The next morning, Simon and Tabitha came over early, and they all talked of the effect of Paul's preaching: half the Jews in Caesarea had been converted already, Judith said, and hundreds were going to be baptised at once. Tabitha confirmed this, and hoped that Simon, too, would follow the good example. Simon, however, said that, for his part, he meant to wait: he would hear more, and do nothing rashly; but he did not wonder that the women were persuaded, for Paul was very eloquent.

"He's ugly," he went on. ("Oh, no!" cried Judith, "he's glorious!") "I think him very ugly," Simon persisted; "but his face gets hold of you: he's nearly bald, with a long beaked nose and thick black beard; but his eyes are wonderful; they blaze and grow soft and weep and his voice changes with his eyes till your very soul is taken out of you. His teaching, too, is astonishing.

"You see," he continued, "Paul's idea that the kingdom promised to us Jews is to be a spiritual kingdom, a kingdom of righteousness, and not a material kingdom, seems to me good. It is practicable at least, and that's something. And this Jesus of whom Paul preaches must have been an extraordinary being, greater than the prophets, greater even than Elias. He used to say, 'My kingdom is not of this world,' and he went about with the poor and the prostitutes and the afflicted. Did you ever happen to see him in Jerusalem?"

Joshua kept his eyes on the ground, and after a time replied in a low voice:

"He wasn't much in Jerusalem."

Day by day, the agitation spread and spread, like a pool in the rains, till it looked as if there were no limit to Paul's power of persuading the Jews. Conversion followed conversion; the meetings grew larger and larger, the interest in what he said more and more intense, till, at length, nearly all the Jews in Caesarea had become followers of the Nazarene. The excitement caught in the other quarters of the city. The Phoenician fishermen and some landsfolk began to come to the meetings, and, every now and then, some Roman soldiers, and here and there a centurion; but these more out of curiosity than emotion.

As Tabitha and Judith had been among the earliest converts, it was only natural that their zeal should grow when they found their example followed by the priests and Levites and other leaders of the people. It was natural, too, that Judith should continue to press Joshua to give the new doctrine at least a fair hearing, as Simon had done, to his soul's salvation, but Joshua remained obstinate. One evening, however, Judith's patience was rewarded. They were all talking at Simon's house, and, at length, Judith quoted some words of Paul on Charity:

"Charity suffereth long, and is kind; is not easily provoked; thinketh no evil . . . beareth all things, believeth all things, hopeth all things, endureth all things."

As she paused, Joshua looked at her for a moment and then said, simply:

"I will go with you tomorrow to hear Paul."

And they were all glad, and gave thanks unto God.

On the morrow, when they drew near the meeting

place, they found themselves in a great crowd of Jews, for the doors of the building had been closed by reason of the multitude. Everyone was talking about the new doctrine.

"I like Paul," said one, "because he is a Hebrew of the Hebrews, and aforetime a Pharisee."

"Ah!" cried another. "Do you remember that splendid thing he said yesterday, 'If thine enemy hunger, feed him; if he thirst, give him drink, for so thou shalt heap coals of fire on his head.' Ha! ha! ha! 'Coals of fire'! That was great, eh?"

"And true, too" exclaimed a friend.

"And new!" cried another.

And the men embraced each other, while their faces shone with conquering enthusiasm. Joshua plucked Simon by the garment:

"Do you hear?"

"Yes," said Simon impatiently, for the prevailing excitement was exciting him, and he didn't like the interruption; "of course, I hear."

Then a red Jew, with head of flame and beard of gold, started forward, and, uplifting his hand, cried:

"What I liked best in his last speech was what he said against backsliders and those who excite doubt by vain disputations; and, above all, that great word of the Messiah: 'He that is not with me is against me, and he that gathereth not with me, scattereth abroad.' " *

The man thundered out the words as if he were defying the world.

Again Joshua plucked Simon by the garment, and, when Simon turned to him, he saw that the carpenter's face was pale, and tears stood in his eyes.

"What is it, Joshua?" he asked.

Joshua tried to speak, but could not for a moment, and, when at length he had drawn Simon a little apart, all that he was able to say was:

* Matthew xii. 30.

"Do you hear what they say?"

"Of course, I hear," said Simon crossly, for he had enjoyed the vivid, impassioned talk; "but what of that? What is the matter with you?"

And Joshua asked:

"Are these men true witnesses? Does Paul indeed teach these things?"

Simon answered shortly:

"Yes: I suppose so."

Joshua looked at him regretfully, and said:

"I must go, Simon; I could not listen to Paul. He does not speak as Jesus spoke; I must go."

But Simon was impatient.

"Nonsense," he cried; "what do you know of Jesus that you should contradict His apostle?"

And Joshua made answer:

"I know what Jesus taught; and this is not his teaching. I remember his very words once: 'He that is not against us is on our part.' * He always preached love, Simon; and this man—I must go!"

Simon shrugged his shoulders and threw out by way of warning:

"Judith will be very angry!"

But, at that moment, the doors were opened, and, as Joshua turned to go, he saw Simon carried away by the rush of the human tide that swept past and in a moment filled the building.

From that day on, Judith took no pains to hide her coolness toward her husband. And even to Simon, Joshua seemed unreasonable; he would not listen now to any talk about Paul; the mere mention of Paul's name seemed to pain and distress him; and, as Judith went oftener and oftener to Paul's preaching, the rift between her and her husband widened from day to day.

At last the disagreement came to speech. One after-

* Mark ix. 40.

noon, after sitting still for a long time watching her husband at work fashioning a cattle-yoke, Judith said:

"I want to speak to you; I must speak to you."

Joshua leant on the tool he was using and paused to hear what she had to say, and she began:

"It is very hard for me to say it, but I must. You are the only Jew in Caesarea who has hardened his heart and refused even to listen to the teaching of Jesus, and that has hurt me. Now Paul is going away, and—and—he asked us before he left to write down any question we wished to have answered; so that his absence might not be so much felt."

She paused here, and seemed to grow a little confused, but, gathering courage, went on:

"I—I asked him something. I asked him," and she lifted her eyes to her husband boldly, "I asked him whether it was right to live with an unbeliever, one who would not even listen to the truth or hear it; and he answered me—"

She paused, looking down, and Joshua gazed at her with wistful eyes, but said nothing, and at length she began again:

"He answered me yesterday, and I remember every word he said: 'Be ye not unequally yoked together with unbelievers, for what fellowship hath righteousness with unrighteousness, and what communion hath light with darkness—' "

She recited the words with a certain exaltation, and, as her voice rose defiantly over the last syllables, she looked up at her husband as if she expected to meet his anger; but she was mistaken. His eyes were full of unshed tears, and, resenting his want of spirit, she rang out:

" '—and what concord hath Christ with Belial?' "

After a long pause, Joshua spoke:

"Can this indeed be Paul," he asked, with a sort of sorrowful wonder, "who calls himself the follower of Jesus; yet denies his teaching?

" 'Be ye not unequally yoked together with unbelievers,'
Paul says; but Jesus would have said, 'Be ye unequally
yoked together with unbelievers,' for faith is stronger than
doubt, as light is stronger than darkness."

"Oh, no," cried Judith, starting up; "it is not true. Paul
says, 'Be ye separate and touch not the unclean thing, and
I will receive you.' "

As she spoke, Joshua stretched out his hands to her
beseechingly.

"Ah, Judith, that is not the teaching of love; and Jesus
came into the world to teach love, and nothing else. Paul
has made doctrines of belief and rules of conduct; but
Jesus wanted nothing but love: love that is more than righteousness. . . . He may have been mistaken," he went on
in a voice broken by extreme emotion; "He trusted God,
cried to Him in his extremity, hoping for instant help—in
vain. . . . He was forsaken, cruelly forsaken, and all his
life's work undone. But he was not wrong, surely, in
preaching love to men—love that is the life of the soul."

He spoke with an impassioned tenderness; but Judith
broke in, her eyes narrowing with question and suspicion:

"What do you know of Jesus and what He said? You
never spoke to me about Him before. Did you know Him
in Jerusalem?"

Joshua hesitated, and his eyes fell; then he said:

"I know his teaching," and he went on hurriedly: "but
all this is only words, isn't it, Judith? Surely," and his
voice trembled, "you would not leave me after all these
years of happiness for what a stranger says?"

"What Paul says is always right," she retorted coolly.

Joshua stretched out his hands to her in hopeless appeal:
"Ah, Judith, why give pain; why add to that mist of
human tears that already veils the beauty of the world?"

Judith replied solemnly: "Paul says that we only come
to peace by leaving the lower for the higher way; no

earthly ties should fetter us who are called to the service of
the divine Master: I shall find a nobler satisfaction in the
new life."

As she spoke, Joshua's face grew drawn and pale, and in
alarm she cried:

"What is it? Are you ill?"

"No," he replied, "I am not ill."

But he sat down and covered his face with his hands.
After a while she touched him, and he looked up with
unutterable sadness in his eyes.

"How can I blame you—how?" and he sighed deeply.
"I, too, left my mother and my brethren, in obedience to
what I thought was the higher bidding; but, oh, Judith, if
I had my life to live over again, I don't think I should act
in the same way. I must have hurt my mother, and it
seems to me now that the higher love ought to include the
lower and not exclude it. I should be more—"

Again she interrupted him:

"Paul says hesitation is itself a fault; but I had no idea
that you felt so much or cared for me so much."

Her tone was gentler, and he replied, with a brave attempt at smiling:

"I have had no life, Judith, so peaceful and happy as my
life here with you."

Judith answered:

"You never say anything, so it is hard to believe you
feel much."

This brought the talk to sympathy and intimacy, and,
for a while, there was peace between them.

A little later, Paul held his last meeting. Before taking
ship, he preached once in the open air, on the foreshore
where water and land meet; and, of course, Judith was by
his side. He spoke with heavy sadness of the parting, and
with pride of those, his brothers and sisters, who would,
he knew, remain faithful until the present coming of

Christ. His words moved the people to tears and new resolutions; for they all sorrowed bitterly, fearing to lose him forever. . . .

The next day, when Joshua got up in the morning, Judith was nowhere to be found. He called her, but she did not answer; she was not in the house; he went across to Tabitha, and Tabitha could only tell him that Judith had resolved not to live with him any more and that she had gone back for a time to Joppa.

Joshua returned to his empty house and as soon as he had closed the door his loneliness and misery came over him in a flood and he stretched forth his hands crying in bitterness of soul:

"But why this cup, oh, Lord? why?"

Months passed. Judith returned to Caesarea and dwelt again with Tabitha; but, in spite of the reproaches of Simon, she refused to cross the road to see Joshua, and, as Joshua scarcely ever left his house, some time elapsed before they met. One morning, however, as Joshua was returning home from the market, Judith hurried out of Simon's house on her way to a meeting, and the two came face to face. They both stopped for a moment, and then Joshua, in divine pity and tenderness, forgiving everything, went toward his wife with outstretched hands; but Judith put her hands before her face, and turned her head aside, as if she didn't want to see him; and, when he still came toward her, she hastened back into the house without a word. After waiting a while in the road, Joshua went slowly into his house with downcast eyes. Neither of them then knew that they had seen each other in life for the last time.

After many days, Paul came again to Caesarea, on his way to Jerusalem; and, once again, all Caesarea thronged to hear the man whom everyone now recognized as the greatest of the apostles. As before, both Tabitha and Judith were diligent at the meetings, and Judith in especial was treated by Paul with great tenderness, as one who had suffered much for the faith.

One morning, Simon came in and told the women to go and see what had happened to Joshua; for he had not opened his door for two days, and was probably ill. The women went across and found Joshua. He had fallen by his bench, and was already cold; they could not lift him, and they came back to Simon, crying. Simon was angry with them, and said to Judith:

"He was too good for you, and so you left him. Paul says: 'Our faithful Judith,' and that's enough for you. Pish!"

Simon was too rich, Judith felt, ever to be a good Christian; but this time she bore his rebuke, for she needed his assistance. Simon went over with them, and helped to lift Joshua and lay him out straight on his bed, and there he left him to the care of the women.

Tabitha and Judith got clean linen and began to wash the body. Suddenly, Tabitha cried out:

"Judith, look! What are these marks on his hands?"

And she turned the palm of the right hand to Judith, and the whole palm was drawn together to a puckered white cicatrix in the middle.

"Oh, that is nothing," Judith replied; "an accident that happened to him in Jerusalem."

Tabitha repeated:

"An accident? How strange!"

A moment later, she cried again:

"Judith! The same marks are in his feet."

Judith started.

"Feet?" And then: "I never knew that. They used not to be there, I am sure, or—oh!" she cried, as a new thought struck her, "perhaps they were covered by the sandal-strap; he never could walk far, you know."

As she spoke, staring and puzzled, Tabitha snatched the sheet from the body, and, pointing, said:

"Look! in his side as well," and then, in an awed whisper: "the Stigmata—the Holy Stigmata!"

Judith's lips framed the words, too, but she was unable to speak. When she came to herself, she said:

"Oh, Tabitha, let us go and tell Paul," and they hurried to the house where Paul dwelt, and, in a few words, told him the whole matter; and at once Paul set off, with all those who were with him, to the house of Joshua.

When he had come to the house and had entered in, and had seen the marks on Joshua's hands and in his feet and in his side, Paul turned swiftly to those standing by, and holding up his hands, cried:

"Lo, a great work has been wrought today in Israel!"

And all who were with him shouted:

"A miracle! A miracle!"

And Paul began to speak, and, while he spoke, the Jews in Caesarea gathered about the house, and convinced themselves of the miracle that had been wrought on their behalf. And Paul went on preaching as one filled with the Spirit and with triumph in his voice, and soon the news spread to the port, and the Phoenician fishermen came and saw the wonder, and the Roman soldiers, and all listened now to Paul's words and were converted by him. For everyone knew that this Joshua, though a Jew, had not followed the new teaching, and that he had been as Paul said he was, the last unbeliever in Caesarea, and because of his unbelief, as Paul declared, and for a sign to the whole world, the Stigmata of Jesus the Crucified had been put upon him, and, indeed, the Stigmata were there, plain to be seen by everyone, in his hands and feet and side. And all the inhabitants of Caesarea, and of the parts round about, were converted and turned to the Lord through the preaching of Paul, and through the miracle of the Stigmata that had been wrought on the body of the last unbeliever in Caesarea.

THE
MAGIC
GLASSES

Oɴᴇ ʀᴀᴡ ɴᴏᴠᴇᴍʙᴇʀ morning, I left my rooms near the British Museum and walked along Oxford Street. It was cold and misty: the air like shredded cotton-wool. Before I reached the Quadrant, the mist thickened to fog, with the color of muddied water, and walking became difficult. As I had no particular object in view, I got into talk with a policeman, and, by his advice, went into the Vine Street Police Court, to pass an hour or two before lunch. Inside the court, the atmosphere was comparatively clear, and I took my seat on one of the oak benches with a feeling of vague curiosity. There was a case going on as I entered: an old man, who pretended to be an optician, had been taken up by the police for obstructing the traffic by selling glasses. His green tray, with leathern shoulder straps, was on the solicitors' table. The charge of obstruction could not be sustained; the old man had moved on as soon as the police told him to, and the inspector had substituted a charge of fraud, on the complaint of a workman and a shopkeeper. A constable had just finished his evidence when I came into the court. He left the box with a self-satisfied air and the muttered remark that the culprit was "a rare bad 'un."

I glanced about for the supposed criminal and found that he was seated near me on a cross-bench in the charge of a sturdy policeman. He did not look like a criminal: he was tall, thin and badly dressed in a suit of rusty black, which seemed to float about his meager person; his complexion was tallowy-white, like the sprouts of potatoes which have been kept a long time in a dark celler; he seemed about sixty years old. But he had none of the furtive glances of the criminal; none of the uneasiness: his eye rested on mine and passed aside with calm indifference, contemplative and not alarmed.

The workman who was produced by the police in support of the charge of fraud amused me. He was a young man, about middle height, and dressed in corduroys with a rough jacket of dark tweed. He was a bad witness: he hesitated, stopped and corrected himself, as if he didn't know the meaning of any words except the commonest phrases of everyday use. But he was evidently honest: his brown eyes looked out on the world fairly enough. His faltering came from the fact that he was only half-articulate. Disentangled from the mist of inappropriate words, his meaning was sufficiently clear.

He had been asked by the accused, whom he persisted in calling "the old gentleman," to buy a pair of spectacles: they would show him things truer-like than he could see 'em; and so he "went a bob on 'em." Questioned by the magistrate as to whether he could see things more plainly through the glasses, he shook his head:

"No; about the same."

Then came the question: Had he been deceived? Apparently he didn't know the meaning of the word "deceived."

"Cheated," the magistrate substituted.

No; he hadn't been cheated.

Well, disappointed then?

No; he couldn't say that.

Would he spend another shilling on a similar pair of glasses?

"No," he would not; "one bob was enough to lose."

When told he might go, he shuffled out of the witness box, and on his way to the door attempted more than once to nod to the accused. Evidently there was no malice in him.

The second police witness had fluency and self-possession enough for a lawyer: a middle-aged man, tall, florid and inclined to be stout; he was over-dressed, like a spruce shopman, in black frock coat, grey trousers and light-colored tie. He talked volubly, with a hot indignation which seemed to match his full red cheeks. If the workman was an undecided and weak witness, Mr. Hallett, of High Holborn, was a most convinced and determined witness. He had been induced to buy the glasses, he declared, by the "old party," who told him that they would show him things exactly as they were—the truth of everything. You'd only have to look through 'em at a man to see whether he was trying to "do" you or not. That was why he bought them. He was not asked a shilling for them, but a sovereign and he gave it—twenty shillings. When he put the glasses on, he could see nothing with them, nothing at all; it was a "plant": and so he wanted the "old party" to take 'em back and return his sovereign; that might have caused the obstruction that the policeman had objected to. The "old man" refused to give him his money back; said he had not cheated him; had the impudence to pretend that he (Hallett) had no eyes for truth, and, therefore, could see nothing with the glasses. "A blamed lie," he called it, and a "do," and the "old man" ought to get six months for it.

Once or twice, the magistrate had to direct the stream of emphatic words. But the accusation was formal and precise. The question now was: How would the magistrate deal with the case? At first sight, Mr. Brown, the magistrate, made a good impression on me. He was getting on in life: the dark hair was growing thin on top and a little grey at the sides. The head was well shaped; the forehead notably broad; the chin and jaw firm. The only unpleasant feature in the face was the hard line of mouth, with thin, unsympathetic lips. Mr. Brown was reputed to be a great scholar, and was just the type of man who would have made a pedant; a man of good intellect and thin blood, who would find books and words more interesting than men and deeds.

At first, Mr. Brown had seemed to be on the side of the accused: he tried to soften Mr. Hallett's anger. One or two of his questions, indeed, were pointed and sensible:

"You wouldn't take goods back after you had sold them, would you, Mr. Hallett?" he asked.

"Of course I would," replied Mr. Hallett stoutly; "I'd take any of my stock back at a twenty percent reduction; my goods are honest goods: prices marked plain on 'em. But 'e would not give me fifteen shillings back out of my sovereign; not 'e; 'e meant stickin' to it all."

The magistrate looked into the body of the court and, addressing the accused, said:

"Will you reserve your defense, Mr. Henry."

"Penry, your worship: Matthew Penry," corrected the old man in a quiet, low-pitched voice, as he rose to his feet. "If I may say so: the charge of fraud is absurd. Mr. Hallett seems to be angry because I sold one pair of glasses for a shilling and another pair to him for a sovereign. But they were not the same glasses and, if they had been, I am surely allowed to ask for my wares what I please."

"That is true," interrupted the magistrate; "but he says that you told him he would see the truth through them. I suppose you meant that he would see more truly through them than with his own eyes?"

"Yes," replied Mr. Penry, with a certain hesitation.

"But he did not see more truly through them," continued the magistrate, "or he would not have wanted you to take them back."

"No," Mr. Penry acknowledged; "but that is his fault, not the fault of the glasses. They would show the truth, if he had any faculty for seeing it: glasses are no good to the blind."

"Come, come," said the magistrate; "now you are beginning to confuse me. You don't really pretend that your glasses will show the truth of things, the reality; you mean that they will improve one's sight, don't you?"

"Yes," replied Mr. Penry, "one's sight for truth, for reality."

"Well," retorted the magistrate smiling, "that seems rather metaphysical than practical, doesn't it? If your spectacles enable one to discern the truth, I'd buy a pair myself: they might be useful in this court sometimes," and he looked about him with a smile, as if expecting applause.

With eager haste, the old man took him at his word, threw open his case, selected a pair of glasses and passed them to the clerk, who handed them up to Mr. Brown.

The magistrate put the glasses on; looked round the court for a minute or two, and then broke out:

"Dear me! Dear me! How extraordinary! These glasses alter everyone in the court. It's really astonishing. They don't improve the looks of people; on the contrary, a more villainous set of countenances it would be difficult to imagine. If these glasses are to be trusted, men are more like wild animals than human beings, and the worst of all are the solicitors; really a terrible set of faces. But this may be the truth of things; these spectacles do show one more than one's ordinary eyes can perceive. Dear me! Dear me! It is most astonishing; but I feel inclined to accept Mr. Penry's statement about them," and he peered over the spectacles at the court.

"Would you like to look in a glass, your worship?" asked one of the solicitors drily, rising, however, to his feet with an attitude of respect at the same time. "Perhaps that would be the best test."

Mr. Brown appeared to be a little surprised, but replied: "If I had a glass, I would willingly."

Before the words were out of his mouth, his clerk had tripped round the bench, gone into the magistrate's private room, and returned with a small looking glass, which he handed up to his worship.

As Mr. Brown looked in the glass, the smile of expectancy left his face. In a moment or two, he put down the glass gravely, took off the spectacles and handed them to the clerk, who returned them to Mr. Penry. After a pause, he said shortly:

"It is well, perhaps, to leave all these matters of fact to a jury. I will accept a small bail, Mr. Penry," he went on; "but I think you must be bound over to answer this charge at the sessions."

I caught the words, " £50 apiece in two sureties and his own recognizances in £100," and then Mr. Penry was told by the policeman to go and wait in the body of the court till the required sureties were forthcoming. By chance, the old man came and sat beside me and I was able to examine him closely. His moustache and beard must have been auburn at one time, but now the reddish tinge seemed only to discolor the grey. The beard was thin and long and unkempt, and added to the forlorn untidiness of his appearance. He carried his head bent forward, as if the neck were too weak to support it. He seemed feeble and old and neglected. He caught me looking at him, and I noticed that his eyes were a clear blue, as if he were younger than I had thought. His gentle, scholarly manner and refined voice had won my sympathy; and, when our eyes met, I introduced myself and told him I should be glad to be one of his sureties, if that would save him time or trouble. He thanked me with a sort of detached courtesy: he would gladly accept my offer.

"You stated your case," I remarked, "so that you confused the magistrate. You almost said that your glasses were—magic glasses," I went on, smiling and hesitating, because I did not wish to offend him, and yet hardly knew how to convey the impression his words had left upon me.

"Magic glasses," he repeated gravely, as if weighing the words; "yes, you might call them magic glasses."

To say that I was astonished only gives a faint idea of my surprise and wonder:

"Surely, you don't mean that they show things as they are," I asked: "the truth of things?"

"That is what I mean," he replied quietly.

"Then they are not ordinary glasses?" I remarked inanely.

"No," he repeated gravely; "not ordinary glasses."

He had a curious trick, I noticed, of peering at one very intently with narrowed eyes and then blinking rapidly several times in succession as if the strain were too great to be borne.

He had made me extremely curious, and yet I did not like to ask outright to be allowed to try a pair of his glasses; so I went on with my questions:

"But, if they show truth, how was it that Mr. Hallett could see nothing through them?"

"Simply because he has no sense of reality; he has killed the innate faculty for truth. It was probably at no time very great," went on this strange merchant, smiling; "but his trader's habits have utterly destroyed it; he has so steeped himself in lies that he is now blind to the truth, incapable of perceiving it. The workman, you remember, could see fairly well through his spectacles."

"Yes," I replied laughing; "and the magistrate evidently saw a good deal more through his than he cared to acknowledge."

The old man laughed, too, in an ingenuous, youthful way that I found charming.

At last I got to the Rubicon.

"Would you let me buy a pair of your glasses?" I asked.

"I shall be delighted to give you a pair, if you will accept them," he replied, with eager courtesy; "my surety
ought certainly to have a pair"; and then he peered at me
in his curious, intent way. A moment later, he turned
round, and, opening his tray, picked out a pair of spectacles and handed them to me.

I put them on with trembling eagerness and stared
about me. The magistrate had told the truth; they altered
everything: the people were the same and yet not the
same; this face was coarsened past all description; that face
sharpened and made hideous with greed; while another
was brutalized with lust. One recognized, so to speak, the
dominant passion in each person. Something moved me to
turn my glasses on the merchant; if I was astounded before, I was now lost in wonder: the glasses transfigured
him. The grey beard tinged with gold, the blue eyes luminous with intelligence; all the features ennobled; the coun-
tenance irradiated sincerity and kindliness. I pulled off the
glasses hastily and the vision passed away. Mr. Penry was
looking at me with a curious little pleased smile of antici-
pation: involuntarily, I put out my hand to him with a sort
of reverence:

"Wonderful," I exclaimed; "your face is wonderful and
all the others grotesque and hideous. What does it mean?
Tell me! Won't you?"

"You must come with me to my room," he said, "where
we can talk freely, and I think you will not regret having
helped me. I should like to explain everything to you.
There are so few men," he added, "who proffer help to
another man in difficulty. I should like to show you that I
am grateful."

"There is no cause for gratitude," I said hastily; "I have
done nothing."

His voice now seemed to me to be curiously refined and
impressive, and recalled to me the vision of his face, made
beautiful by the strange glasses. . . .

I have been particular to put down how Mr. Penry first appeared to me, because after I had once seen him through his spectacles, I never saw him again as I had seen him at first. Remembering my earliest impressions of him, I used to wonder how I could have been so mistaken. His face had refinement and gentleness in every line; a certain courage, too, that was wholly spiritual. Already I was keenly interested in Mr. Penry; eager to know more about him; to help him, if that were possible, in any and every way.

Some time elapsed before the formalities for his bail were arranged, and then I persuaded him to come out with me to lunch. He got up quietly, put the leathern straps over his shoulders, tucked the big case under his arm and walked into the street with perfect self-possession; and I was not now in any way ashamed of his appearance, as I should have been an hour or two before: I was too excited even to feel pride; I was simply glad and curious.

And this favorable impression grew with everything Mr. Penry said and did, till at last nothing but service would content me; so, after lunch, I put him into a cab and drove him off to my own solicitor. I found Mr. Morris, of Messrs. Morris, Coote, and Co., quite willing to take up his case at the sessions; willing, too, to believe that the charge was "trumped up" by the police and without serious foundation. But, when I drew Mr. Morris aside and tried to persuade him that his new client was a man of extraordinary powers, he smiled incredulously.

"You are enthusiastic, Mr. Winter," he said half reproachfully; "but we solicitors are compelled to see things in the cold light of reason. Why should you undertake to defend this Mr. Penry? Of course if you have made up your mind," he went on, passing over my interruption, "I shall do my best for him; but if I were you, I'd keep my eyes open and do nothing rashly."

In order to impress him, I put on a similar cold tone and declared that Mr. Penry was a friend of mine and that he must leave no stone unturned to vindicate his honesty. And with this I went back to Mr. Penry, and we left the office together.

Mr. Penry's lodging disappointed me; my expectations, I am afraid, were now tuned far above the ordinary. It was in Chelsea, high up, in a rickety old house overlooking a dingy road and barges drawn up on the slimy, fetid mudbanks. And yet, even here, romance was present for the romantic; the fog-wreaths curling over the river clothed the houses opposite in soft mystery, as if they had been draped in blue samite, and through the water-laden air the sun glowed round and red as a fiery wheel of Phaëthon's chariot. The room was very bare; by the broad low window stood a large deal table crowded with instruments and glasses; strong electric lamps on the right and left testified to the prolonged labors of the optician. The roof of the garret ran up toward the center, and by the wall there was a low truckle bed, fenced off by a cheap Japanese paper screen. The whole of the wall between the bed and the window was furnished with plain pine shelves, filled with books; everything was neat, but the room seemed friendless and cold in the thick, damp air.

There we sat and talked together, till the sun slid out of sight and the fog thickened and night came on: there our acquaintance, so strangely begun, grew to friendship. Before we went to dinner, the old man had shown me the portraits of his two daughters and a little miniature of his wife, who had died fifteen years before.

It was the first of many talks in that room, the first of many confidences. Bit by bit, I heard the whole of Mr. Penry's history. It was told to me piecemeal and inconsequently, as a friend talks to a friend in growing intimacy; and, if I now let Mr. Penry tell his tale in regular sequence and at one stretch, it is mainly in order to spare

the reader the tedium of interrupted narration and need-
less repetitions.

"My father was an optician," Mr. Penry began, "and a
maker of spectacles in Chelsea. We lived over the shop in
the Kings Road, and my childhood was happy enough,
but not in any way particular. Like other healthy children,
I liked play much better than lessons; but my school days
were too uneventful, too empty of love to be happy. My
mother died when I was too young to know or regret her;
my father was kind, in spite of his precise, puritanical
ways. I was the only boy, which perhaps made him kinder
to me, and very much younger than my two sisters, who
were grown up when I was in short clothes and who married and left my father's house before I had got to know
them, or to feel much affection for them.

"When I was about sixteen, my father took me from
school and began teaching me his own trade. He had been
an admirable workman in his time, of the old English
sort—careful and capable, though somewhat slow. The
desire was always present in him to grind and polish each
glass as well as he could, and this practice had given him a
certain repute with a circle of good customers. He taught
me every part of his craft as he had learnt it; and, in the
next five or six years, imbued me with his own wish to do
each piece of work as perfectly as possible. But this period
of initiation did not last long. Before I reached manhood, I
began to draw apart from my father, to live my own life
and to show a love of reading and thinking foreign to his
habit. It was religion which separated us. At school I had
learnt some French and German, and in both languages I
came across sceptical opinions which slowly grew in my
mind, and in time led me to discard and almost dislike the
religion of my father. I mention this simply because any
little originality in me seemed to spring from this inquiry
and from the mental struggle that convulsed three or four
years of my youth. For months and months I read fe-

verishly to conquer my doubts, and then I read almost as
eagerly to confirm my scepticism.

"I still remember the glow of surprise and hope which
came over me the first time I read that Spinoza, one of the
heroes of my thought, had also made his living by polish-
ing glasses. He was the best workman of his time, it appeared, and I determined to become the best workman of
my time; from that moment, I took to my trade seriously,
strenuously.

"I learned everything I could about glass, and began to
make my own material, after the best recipes. I got books
on optics, too, and studied them, and so, bit by bit, mastered the science of my craft.

"I was not more than nineteen or twenty when my father found out that I was a much better workman than his
assistant Thompson. Some glasses had been sent to us
from a great oculist in Harley Street, with a multitude of
minute directions. They had been made by Thompson,
and were brought back to us one afternoon by a very fid-
gety old gentleman who declared that they did not suit
him at all. The letter which he showed from Sir William
Creighton, the oculist, hinted that the glasses were not
carefully made. My father was out and, in his absence, I
opened the letter. As soon as I had looked at the glasses, I
saw that the complaint was justified, and I told the old
gentleman so. He turned out to be the famous parliamen-
tary speaker, Lord B. He said to me testily:

" 'All right, young man; you make my glasses correctly
and I shall be satisfied; but not till then; you understand,
not till then.'

"I smiled at him and told him I would do the work
myself, and he went out of the shop muttering, as if only
half reassured by my promises. Then I determined to
show what I could do. When my father returned, I told
him what had happened, and asked him to leave the work
to me. He consented, and I went off at once to the little

workshop I had made in our backyard and settled down to the task. I made my glass and polished it, and then ground the spectacles according to the directions. When I had finished, I sent them to Sir William Creighton with a note, and a few days afterwards we had another visit from Lord B., who told my father that he had never had such glasses and that I was a 'perfect treasure.' Like many very crotchety people, he was hard to satisfy, but once satisfied he was as lavish in praise as in blame. Lord B. made my reputation as a maker of spectacles and for years I was content with this little triumph.

"I married when I was about two or three-and-twenty and seven or eight years afterwards my father died. The gap caused by his death, the void of loss and loneliness, was more than filled up by my young children. I had two little girls who, at this time, were a source of perpetual interest to me. How one grows to love the little creatures, with their laughter and tears, their hopes and questions and make-believe! And how one's love for them is intensified by all the trouble one takes to win their love and by all the plans one weaves for their future! But all this is common human experience and will only bore you. A man's happiness is not interesting to other people, and I don't know that much happiness is good for a man himself; at any rate, during the ten or fifteen years in which I was happiest, I did least; made least progress, I mean, as a workman and the least intellectual advance as a man. But when my girls began to grow up and detach themselves from me and the home, my intellectual nature began to stir again. One must have some interests in life, and, if the heart is empty, the head becomes busier, I often think.

"One day I had a notable visit. A man came in to get a pair of spectacles made: a remarkable man. He was young, gay and enthusiastic, with an astonishing flow of words, an astonishing brightness of speech and manner. He seemed to light up the dingy old shop with his vivacity and happy frankness. He wanted spectacles to correct a slight dissimilarity between his right eye and his left, and he had been advised to come to me by Sir William Creighton, as the glasses would have to be particularly well-made. I promised to work at them myself, and on that he burst out:

" 'I shall be very curious to see whether perfect eyes help or hurt my art. You know I am a painter,' he went on, throwing his hair back from his forehead, 'and each of us painters sees life in his own way, and beauty with certain peculiarities. It would be curious, wouldn't it, if talent came from a difference between one's eyes!'

"I smiled at his eagerness, and took down his name, then altogether unknown to me; but soon to become known and memorable above all other names: Dante Gabriel Rossetti. I made the glasses and he was enthusiastic about them, and brought me a little painting of himself by way of gratitude.

"There it is," said Penry, pointing to a little panel that hung by his bedside; "the likeness of an extraordinary man—a genius, if ever there was one. I don't know why he took to me, except that I admired him intensely; my shop, too, was near his house in Chelsea, and he used often to drop in and pass an hour in my back parlor and talk—such talk as I had never heard before and have never heard since. His words were food and drink to me, and more than that. Either his thoughts or the magic of his personality supplied my mind with the essence of growth and vigor which had hitherto been lacking to it; in a very real sense, Rossetti became my spiritual father. He taught me things about art that I had never imagined; opened to me a new heaven and a new earth and, above all, showed me that my craft, too, had artistic possibilities in it that I had never dreamed of before.

"I shall never forget the moment when he first planted the seed in me that has since grown and grown till it has filled my life. It was in my parlor behind the shop. He had been talking in his eager, vivid way, pouring out truths and thoughts, epigrams and poetry, as a great jeweler sometimes pours gems from hand to hand. I had sat listening openmouthed, trying to remember as much as I could, to assimilate some small part of all that word-wealth. He suddenly stopped, and we smoked on for a few minutes in silence; then he broke out again:

" 'Do you know, my solemn friend,' he said abruptly, 'that I struck an idea the other day which might suit you. I was reading one of Walter Scott's novels: that romantic stuff of his amuses me, you know, though it isn't as deep as the sea. Well, I found out that, about a hundred years ago, a man like you made what they called Claude-glasses. I suppose they were merely rose-tinted,' he laughed, 'but at any rate, they were supposed to make everything beautiful in a Claude-like way. Now, why shouldn't you make such glasses? It would do Englishmen a lot of good to see things rose-tinted for a while. Then, too, you might make Rossetti-glasses,' he went on laughingly, 'and, if these dull Saxons could only get a glimpse of the passion that possesses him, it would wake them up, I know. Why not go to work, my friend, at something worth doing? Do you know,' he continued seriously, 'there might be something in it. I don't believe, if I had had your glasses at the beginning, I should ever have been the artist I am. I mean,' he said, talking half to himself, 'if my eyes had been all right from the beginning, I might perhaps have been contented with what I saw. But as my eyes were imperfect I tried to see things as my soul saw them, and so invented looks and gestures that the real world could never give.'

"I scarcely understood what he meant," said Mr. Penry, "but his words dwelt with me: the ground had been prepared for them; he had prepared it; and at once they took root in me and began to grow. I could not get the idea of the Claude-glasses and the Rossetti-glasses out of my head, and at last I àdvertised for a pair of those old Claude-glasses, and in a month or so a pair turned up.

"You may imagine that, while I was waiting, time hung heavy on my hands. I longed to be at work; I wanted to realize the idea that had come to me while Rossetti was talking. During my acquaintance with him, I had been to his studio a dozen times, and had got to know and admire that type of woman's beauty which is now connected with his name; the woman, I mean, with swanlike throat, languid air and heavy-lidded eyes, who conveys to all of us now something of Rossetti's insatiable desire. But, while I was studying his work and going about steeped in the emotion of it, I noticed one day a lovely girl whom Rossetti could have taken as a model. I had begun, in fact, to see the world as Rossetti saw it; and this talk of his about the Claude-glasses put the idea into my head that I might, indeed, be able to make a pair of spectacles which would enable people to see the world as Rossetti saw it and as I saw it when Rossetti's influence had entire possession of me. This would be a great deal easier to do, I said to myself, than to make a pair of Claude-glasses; for, after all, I did not know what Claude's eyes were really like and I did know the peculiarity of Rossetti's eyes. I accordingly began to study the disparate quality in Rossetti's eyes and, after making a pair of spectacles that made my eyes see unequally to the same degree, I found that the Rossettian vision of things was sharpened and intensified to me. From that moment on, my task was easy. I had only to study any given pair of eyes and then to alter them so that they possessed the disparity of Rossetti's eyes and the work was half done. I found, too, that I could increase this disparity a little and, in proportion as I increased it, I increased also the peculiarity of what I called the Rossettian view of things; but, if I made the disparity too great, everything became blurred again.

"My researches had reached this point, when the pair of old Claude-glasses came into my hands. I saw at a glance that the optician of the eighteenth century had no knowledge of my work. He had contented himself, as Rossetti had guessed, with coloring the glasses very delicately and in several tints; in fact, he had studied the color peculiarities of the eye as I had studied its form-peculiarities. With this hint, I completed my work. It took me only a few days to learn that Rossetti's view of color was just as limited, or, I should say, just as peculiar, as his view of form; and, when I once understood the peculiarities of his color-sight, I could reproduce them as easily as I could reproduce the peculiarities of his vision of form. I then set to work to get both these peculiarities into half-a-dozen different sets of glasses.

"The work took me some six or eight months; and, when I had done my best, I sent a little note round to Rossetti and awaited his coming with painful eagerness, hope and fear swaying me in turn. When he came, I gave him a pair of the spectacles; and, when he put them on and looked out into the street, I watched him. He was surprised—that I could see—and more than a little puzzled. While he sat thinking I explained to him what the old Claude-glasses were like and how I had developed his suggestion into this present discovery.

" 'You are an artist, my friend,' he cried at last, 'and a new kind of artist. If you can make people see the world as Claude saw it and as I see it, you can go on to make them see it as Rembrandt saw it, and Velásquez. You can make the dullards understand life as the greatest have understood it. But that is impossible,' he added, his face falling: 'that is only a dream. You have got my real eyes, therefore you can force others to see as I see; but you have not the real eyes of Rembrandt, or Velásquez, or Titian; you have not the physical key to the souls of the great masters of the past; and so your work can only apply to the present and

to the future. But that is enough, and more than enough,'
he added quickly. 'Go on: there are Whistler's eyes to get;
and Carot's in France, and half-a-dozen others; and glad I
shall be to put you on the scent. You will do wonderful
things, my friend, wonderful things.'

"I was mightily uplifted by his praise and heart-glad,
too, in my own way; but resolved at the same time not to
give up the idea of making Velásquez-glasses and Rem-
brandt-glasses; for I had come to know and to admire
these masters through Rossetti's talk. He was always refer-
ring to them, quoting them, so to say; and, for a long time
past, I had accustomed myself to spend a couple of after-
noons each week in our National Gallery, in order to get
some knowledge of the men who were the companions of
his spirit.

"For nearly a year after this, I spent every hour of my
spare time studying in the National; and at last it seemed
to me that I had got Titian's range of color quite as exactly
as the old glasses had got Claude's. But it was extraordinarily difficult to get his vision of form. However, I was
determined to succeed; and, with infinite patience and
after numberless attempts, success began slowly to come
to me. To cut a long story short, I was able, in eight or
ten years, to construct these four or five different sorts of
glasses. Claude-glasses and Rossetti-glasses, of course; and
also Titian-glasses, Velásquez-glasses and Rembrandt-
glasses; and again my mind came to anchor in the work accomplished. Not that I stopped thinking altogether; but
that for some time my thoughts took no new flight, but
hovered round and about the known. As soon as I had
made the first pair of Rossetti-glasses, I began to teach my
assistant, Williams, how to make them too, in order to put
them before the public. We soon got a large sale for them.
Chelsea, you know—old Chelsea, I mean—is almost peo-
pled with artists, and many of them came about me and
began to make my shop a rendezvous, where they met and

brought their friends and talked; for Rossetti had a certain following, even in his own lifetime. But my real success came with the Titian-glasses. The great Venetian's romantic view of life and beauty seemed to exercise an irresistible seduction upon everyone, and the trade in his glasses soon became important.

"My home life at this time was not as happy as it had been. In those long years of endless experiment, my daughters had grown up and married, and my wife, I suppose, widowed of her children, wanted more of my time and attention, just when I was taken away by my new work and began to give her less. She used to complain at first; but, when she saw that compliants did not alter me, she retired into herself, as it were; and I saw less and less of her. And then, when my work was done and my new trade established, my shop, as I have told you, became the rendezvous for artists, and I grew interested in the frank, bright faces and the youthful, eager voices, and renewed my youth in the company of the young painters and writers who used to seek me out. Suddenly, I awoke to the fact that my wife was ill, very ill, and almost before I had fully realized how weak she was, she died. The loss was greater than I would have believed possible. She was gentle and kind, and I missed her every day and every hour. I think that was the beginning of my dislike for the shop, the shop that had made me neglect her. The associations of it reminded me of my fault; the daily requirements of it grew irksome to me.

"About this time, too, I began to miss Rossetti and the vivifying influences of his mind and talk. He went into the country a great deal and for long periods I did not see him, and, when at length we met, I found that the virtue was going out of him: he had become moody and irritable, a neuropath. Of course, the intellectual richness in him could not be hidden altogether: now and then, he would break out and talk in the old magical way:

And conjure wonder out of emptiness,
Till mean things put on beauty like a dress
And all the world was an enchanted place.

But, more often, he was gloomy and harassed, and it sad-
dened and oppressed me to meet him. The young artists
who came to my shop did not fill his place; they chattered
gaily enough, but none of them was a magician as he had
been, and I began to realize that genius such as his is one
of the rarest gifts in the world.

"I am trying, with all brevity, to explain to you the
cause of my melancholy and my dissatisfaction: but I don't
think I have done it very convincingly; and yet, about this
time, I had grown dissatisfied, ill at ease, restless. And
once again my heart-emptiness drove me to work and
think. The next step forward came inevitably from the last
one I had taken.

"While studying the great painters, I had begun to notice that there was a certain quality common to all of
them, a certain power they all possessed when working at
highest pressure; the power of seeing things as they are—
the vital and essential truth of things. I don't mean to say
that all of them possessed this faculty to the same degree.
Far from it. The truth of things to Titian is overlaid with
romance: he is memorable mainly for his magic of color
and beauty; while Holbein is just as memorable for his
grasp of reality. But compare Titian with Giorgione or
Tintoretto, and you will see that his apprehension of the
reality of things is much greater than theirs. It is that
which distinguishes him from the other great colorists of
Venice. And, as my own view of life grew sadder and
clearer, it came to me gradually as a purpose that I should
try to make glasses that would show the reality, the essential truth of things, as all the great masters had seen it; and
so I set to work again on a new quest.

"About this time, I found out that, though I had many

more customers in my shop, I had not made money out of my artistic enterprises. My old trade as a spectacle-maker was really the most profitable branch of my business. The sale of the Rossetti-glasses and the Titian-glasses, which at first had been very great, fell off quickly as the novelty passed away, and it was soon apparent that I had lost more than I had gained by my artistic inventions. But whether I made £1,500 a year, or £1,000 a year, was a matter of indifference to me. I had doubled that cape of forty which to me marks the end of youth in a man, and my desires were shrinking as my years increased. As long as I had enough to satisfy my wants, I was not greedy of money.

"This new-born desire of mine to make glasses which would show the vital truth of things soon began to possess me; and, gradually, I left the shop to take care of itself, left it in the hands of my assistant, Williams, and spent more and more time in the little workshop at the back, which had been the theatre of all my achievements. I could not tell you how long I worked at the problem; I only know that it cost me years and years, and that, as I gave more time and labor to it and more and more of the passion of my soul, so I came to love it more intensely and to think less of the ordinary business of life. At length, I began to live in a sort of dream, possessed by the one purpose. I used to get up at night and go on with the work and rest in the day. For months together, I scarcely ate anything, in the hope that hunger might sharpen my faculties; at another time, I lived almost wholly on coffee, hoping that this would have the same effect; and, at length, bit by bit, and slowly, I got nearer to the goal of my desire. But, when I reached it, when I had constructed glasses that would reveal the naked truth, show things as they are and men and women as they are, I found that circumstances about me had changed lamentably.

"In the midst of my work, I had known without realiz-

ing it that Williams had left me and started a shop opposite, with the object of selling the artistic glasses, of
which he declared himself the inventor; but I paid no attention to this at the time, and when, two or three years
afterwards, I woke again to the ordinary facts of life, I
found that my business had almost deserted me. I am not
sure, but I think it was a notice to pay some debt which I
hadn't the money to pay, that first recalled me completely
to the realities of everyday life. What irony there is in the
world! Here was I, who had been laboring for years and
years with the one object of making men see things as they
are and men and women as they are, persecuted now and
undone by the same reality which I was trying to reveal.

"My latest invention, too, was a commercial failure: the
new glasses did not sell at all. Nine people out of ten in
England are truth-blind, and could make nothing of the
glasses; and the small minority, who have the sense of real
things, kept complaining that the view of life which my
glasses showed them, was not pleasant: as if that were any
fault of mine. Williams, too, my former assistant, did me a
great deal of harm. He devoted himself merely to selling
my spectacles; and the tradesman succeeded where the artist and thinker starved. As soon as he found out what my
new glasses were, he began to treat me contemptuously;
talked of me at times as a sort of half-madman, whose
brain was turned by the importance given to his inventions, and at other times declared that I had never invented anything at all, for the idea of the artistic glasses
had been suggested by Rossetti. The young painters who
frequented his shop took pleasure in spreading this legend
and attributing to Rossetti what Rossetti would have been
the first to disclaim. I found myself abandoned, and hours
used to pass without anyone coming into my shop. The
worst of it was that, when chance gave me a customer, I
soon lost him: the new glasses pleased no one.

"At this point, I suppose, if I had been gifted with ordinary prudence, I should have begun to retrace my steps; but either we grow more obstinate as we grow older, or else the soul's passion grows by the sacrifices we make for it. Whatever the motives of my obstinacy may have been, the disappointment, the humiliation I went through seemed only to nerve me to a higher resolution. I knew I had done good work, and the disdain shown to me drove me in upon myself and my own thoughts."

So much I learned from Mr. Penry in the first few days of our acquaintance, and then for weeks and weeks he did not tell me any more. He seemed to regard the rest of his story as too fantastic and improbable for belief, and he was nervously apprehensive lest he should turn me against him by telling it. Again and again, however, he hinted at further knowledge, more difficult experiments, a more arduous seeking, till my curiosity was all aflame, and I pressed him, perhaps unduly, for the whole truth.

In those weeks of constant companionship, our friendship had grown with almost every meeting. It was impossible to escape the charm of Penry's personality! He was so absorbed in his work, so heedless of the ordinary vanities and greeds of men, so simple and kindly and sympathetic, that I grew to love him. He had his little faults, of course, his little peculiarities; surface irritabilities of temper; moments of undue depression, in which he depreciated himself and his work; moments of undue elation, in which he overestimated the importance of what he had done. He would have struck most people as a little flighty and uncertain, I think; but his passionate devotion to his work lifted the soul and his faults were, after all, insignificant in comparison with his noble and rare qualities. I had met no one in life who aroused the higher impulses in me as he did. It seemed probable that his latest experiments would be the most daring and the most instructive, and, accordingly, I pressed him to tell me about them with some insistence, and, after a time, he consented:

"I don't know how it came about," he began, "but the contempt of men for my researches exercised a certain influence on me, and at length I took myself seriously to task: was there any reason for their disdain and dislike? Did these glasses of mine really show things as they are, or was I offering but a new caricature of truth, which people were justified in rejecting as unpleasant? I took up again my books on optics and studied the whole subject anew from the beginning. Even as I worked, a fear grew upon me: I felt that there was another height before me to climb, and that the last bit of road would probably be the steepest of all. . . . In the Gospels," he went on, in a low, reverent voice, "many things are symbolic and of universal application, and it always seemed to me significant that the Hill of Calvary came at the end of the long journey. I shrank from another prolonged effort; I said to myself I couldn't face another task like the last. But, all the while, I had a sort of uncomfortable prescience that the hardest part of my life's work lay before me.

"One day, a casual statement stirred me profoundly. The primary colors, you know, are red, yellow and blue. The colors shown in the rainbow vary from red to blue and violet; and the vibrations, or lengths, of the light-waves that give us violet grow shorter and shorter and, at length, give us red. These vibrations can be measured. One day, quite by chance, I came across the statement that there were innumerable light-waves longer than those which give violet. At once the question sprang: were these longer waves represented by colors which we don't see, colors for which we have no name, colors of which we can form no conception? And was the same thing true to the waves which, growing shorter and shorter, give us the sensation of red? There is room, of course, for myriads of colors beyond this other extremity of our vision. A little study convinced me that my guess was right; for all the colors which we see are represented to our sense of feeling in degrees of heat: that is, blue shows one reading on the thermometer and red a higher reading; and, by means of this new standard, I discovered that man's range of vision is not even placed in the middle of the register of heat, but occupies a little space far up toward the warmer extremity of it. There are thousands of degrees of cold lower than blue and hundreds of degrees of heat above red. All these gradations are doubtless represented by colors which no human eye can perceive, no human mind imagine. It is with sight as with hearing. There are noises louder than thunder which we cannot hear, the roar that lies on the other side of silence. We men are poor restless prisoners, hemmed in by our senses as by the walls of a cell, hearing only a part of nature's orchestra and that part imperfectly; seeing only a thousandth part of the color marvels about us and seeing that infinitesimal part incorrectly and partially. Here was new knowledge with a vengeance! Knowledge that altered all my work! How was I to make glasses to show all this? Glasses that would reveal things as they are and must be to higher beings—the ultimate reality. At once, the new quest became the object of my life, and, somehow or other I knew before I began the work that the little scraps of comfort or of happiness which I had preserved up to this time, I should now forfeit. I realized with shrinking and fear, that this new enquiry would still further remove me from the sympathy of my fellows.

"My prevision was justified. I had hardly got well to work—that is, I had only spent a couple of years in vain and torturing experiments—when I was one day arrested for debt. I had paid no attention to the writ; the day of trial came and went without my knowing anything about it; and there was a man in possession of my few belongings before I understood what was going on. Then I was taught by experience that to owe money is the one unforgivable sin in the nation of shopkeepers. My goods were sold up and I was brought to utter destitution"—the old man paused—"and then sent to prison because I could not pay."

"But," I asked, "did your daughters do nothing? Surely, they could have come to your help!"

"Oh! they were more than kind," he replied simply, "the eldest especially, perhaps because she was childless herself. I called her Gabrielle," he added, lingering over the name; "she was very good to me. As soon as she heard the news, she paid my debt and set me free. She bought things, too, and fitted out two nice rooms for me and arranged everything again quite comfortably; but you see," he went on with a timid, deprecating smile, "I tired out even her patience: I could not work at anything that brought in money and I was continually spending money for my researches. The nice furniture went first; the pretty tables and chairs and then the bed. I should have wearied an angel. Again and again Gabrielle bought me furniture and made me tidy and comfortable, as she said, and again and again, like a spendthrift boy, I threw it all away. How could I think of tables and chairs, when I was giving my life to my work? Besides, I always felt that the more I was plagued and punished, the more certain I was to get out the best in me: solitude and want are the twin nurses of the soul."

"But didn't you wish to get any recognition, any praise?" I broke in.

"I knew by this time," he answered, "that, in proportion as my work was excellent, I should find fewer to understand it. How many had I seen come to praise and honor while Rossetti fell to nerve disease and madness; and yet his work endures and will endure, while theirs is already forgotten. The tree that grows to a great height wins to solitude even in a forest: its highest outshoots find no companions save the winds and stars. I tried to console myself with such similes as this," he went on, with a deprecatory smile, "for the years passed and I seemed to come no nearer to success. At last, the way opened for me a little, and, after eight or ten years of incessant experiment, I found that partial success was all I should ever accomplish. Listen! There is not one pair of eyes in a million that could ever see what I had taught myself to see, for the passion of the soul brings with it its own reward. After caring for nothing but truth for twenty years, thinking of nothing but truth, and wearying after it, I could see it more clearly than other men: get closer to it than they could. So the best part of my labor—I mean the highest result of it—became personal, entirely personal, and this disappointed me. If I could do no good to others by it, what was my labor but a selfish gratification? And what was that to me—at my age! I seemed to lose heart, to lose zest. . . . Perhaps it was that old age had come upon me, that the original sum of energy in me had been spent, that my bolt was shot. It may be so.

"The fact remains that I lost the desire to go on, and, when I had lost that, I woke up, of course, to the ordinary facts of life once again. I had no money; I was weak from semistarvation and long vigils, prematurely old and decrepit. Once more, Gabrielle came to my assistance. She fitted up this room, and then I went out to sell my glasses, as a peddler. I bought the tray and made specimens of all the spectacles I had made, and hawked them about the streets. Why shouldn't I? No work is degrading to the spirit, none, and I could not be a burden to the one I loved, now I knew that my best efforts would not benefit others. I did not get along well: the world seemed strange to me, and men a little rough and hard. Besides, the police seemed to hate me; I don't know why. Perhaps, because I was poor, and yet unlike the poor they knew. They persecuted me, and the magistrates before whom they brought me always believed them and never believed me. I have been punished times without number for obstruction, though I never annoyed anyone. The police never pretended that I had cheated or stolen from anyone before; but, after all, this latest charge of theirs brought me to know you and gave me your friendship; and so I feel that all the shame has been more than made up to me."

My heart burned within me as he spoke so gently of his unmerited sufferings. I told him I was proud of being able to help him. He put his hand on mine with a little smile of comprehension.

A day or two later curiosity awoke in me again, and I asked him to let me see a pair of the new glasses, those that show the ultimate truth of things.

"Perhaps, some day," he answered quietly. I suppose my face fell, for, after a while, he went on meditatively: "There are faults in them, you see, shortcomings and faults in you, too, my friend. Believe me, if I were sure that they would cheer or help you in life, I would let you use them quickly enough; but I am beginning to doubt their efficacy. Perhaps the truth of things is not for man."

When we entered the court on the day of Penry's trial, Morris and myself were of opinion that the case would not last long and that it would certainly be decided in our favor. The only person who seemed at all doubtful of the issue was Penry himself. He smiled at me, half pityingly, when I told him that in an hour we should be on our way home. The waiting seemed interminable, but at length the case was called. The counsel for the prosecution got up and talked perfunctorily for five minutes, with a sort of careless unconcern that seemed to me callous and unfeeling. Then he began to call his witnesses. The workman, I noticed, was not in the court. His evidence had been rather in favor of the accused, and the prosecution, on that account, left it out. But Mr. 'Allett, as he called himself, of 'Igh 'Olborn, was even more voluble and vindictive than he had been at the police court. He had had time to strengthen his evidence, too, to make it more bitter and more telling, and he had used his leisure malignantly. It seemed to me that everyone should have seen his spite and understood the vileness of his motives. But no; again and again, the judge emphasized those parts of his story which seemed to tell most against the accused. The judge was evidently determined that the jury should not miss any detail of the accusation, and his bias appeared to me iniquitous. But there was a worse surprise in store for us. After Hallett, the prosecution called a canon of Westminster, a stout man, with heavy jowl and loose, suasive lips, Canon Bayton. He told us how he had grown interested in Penry and in his work, and how he had bought all his earlier glasses, the Rossetti-glasses, as he called them. The canon declared that these artistic glasses threw a very valuable light on things, redeemed the coarseness and commonness of life and made reality beautiful and charming. He was not afraid to say that he regarded them as instruments for good; but the truth-revealing glasses seemed to excite his utmost hatred and indignation. He could not find a good word to say for them: they only showed, he said, what was terrible and brutal in life. When looking through them, all beauty vanished, the charming flesh-covering fell away and you saw the death's-head grinning at you. Instead of parental affection, you found personal vanity; instead of the tenderness of the husband for the wife, gross and common sensuality. All high motives withered, and, instead of the flowers of life, you were compelled to look at the wormlike roots and the clinging dirt. He concluded his evidence by assuring the jury that they would be doing a good thing if they put an end to the sale of such glasses. The commerce was worse than fraudulent, he declared; it was a blasphemy against God and an outrage on human nature. The unctuous canon seemed to me worse than all the rest; but the effect he had on the jury was unmistakable, and our barrister, Symonds, refused to cross-examine him. To do so, he said, would only strengthen the case for the prosecution, and I have no doubt that he was right, for Morris agreed with him.

But even the prosecuting witnesses did not hurt us more than the witnesses for the defense. Mr. Penry had been advised by Mr. Morris to call witnesses to his character, and he had called half-a-dozen of the most respectable tradesmen of his acquaintance. One and all did him harm rather than good; they all spoke of having known him twenty years before, when he was well-to-do and respectable. They laid stress upon what they called his "fall in life." They all seemed to think that he had neglected his business and come to ruin by his own fault. No one of them had the faintest understanding of the man, or of his work. It was manifest from the beginning that these witnesses damaged our case, and this was apparently the view of the prosecuting barrister, for he scarcely took the trouble to cross-examine them.

It was with a sigh of relief that I saw Mr. Penry go into the box to give evidence on his own behalf. Now, I thought, the truth will come to light. He stated everything with the utmost clearness and precision; but no one seemed to believe him. The wish to understand him was manifestly wanting in the jury, and from the beginning the judge took sides against him. From time to time, he interrupted him just to bring out what he regarded as the manifest falseness of his testimony.

"You say that these glasses show truth," he said. "Who wants to see truth?"

"Very few," was Penry's reply.

"Why, then, did you make the glasses," went on the judge, "if you knew that they would disappoint people?"

"I thought it my duty to," replied Penry.

"Your duty to disappoint and anger people?" retorted the judge; "a strange view to take of duty. And you got money for this unpleasant duty, didn't you?"

"A little," was Penry's reply.

"Yes; but still you got money," persisted the judge. "You persuaded people to buy your glasses, knowing that they would be disappointed in them, and you induced them to give you money for the disappointment. Have you anything else to urge in your defense?"

I was at my wit's end; I scarcely knew how to keep quiet in my seat. It seemed to me so easy to see the truth. But even Penry appeared indifferent to the result, indifferent to a degree that I could scarcely explain or excuse. This last question, however, of the judge aroused him. As the harsh, contemptuous words fell upon the ear, he leaned forward, and, selecting a pair of spectacles, put them on and peered around the court. I noticed that he was slightly flushed. In a moment or two, he took the glasses off and turned to the judge:

"My lord," he said, "you seem determined to condemn me, but, if you do condemn me, I want you to do it with some understanding of the facts. I have told you that there are very few persons in this country who have any faculty for truth, and that the few who have, usually have ruined their power before they reach manhood. You scoff and sneer at what I say, but still it remains the simple truth. I looked round the court just now to see if there was anyone here young enough, ingenuous enough, honest enough, to give evidence on my behalf. I find that there is no one in the court to whom I can appeal with any hope of success, but, my lord, in the room behind this court there is a child sitting, a girl with fair hair, probably your lordship's daughter. Allow me to call her as a witness, allow her to test the glasses and say what she sees through them, and then you will find that these glasses do alter and change things in a surprising way to those who can use them."

"I don't know how you knew it," broke in the judge, "but my daughter is in my room waiting for me, and what you say seems to have some sense in it. But it is quite unusual to call a child, and I don't know that I have any right to allow it. Still, I don't want you to feel that you have not had every opportunity of clearing yourself; therefore, if the jury consent, I am quite willing that they should hear what this new witness may have to say."

"We are willing to hear the witness," said the foreman, "but really, your lordship, our minds are made up about the case."

The next moment, the child came into the court—a girl of thirteen or fourteen, with a bright, intelligent face, a sort of shy fear troubling the directness of her approach.

"I want you to look through a pair of spectacles, my child," said Penry to her, "and tell us just what you see through them," and, as he spoke, he peered at her in his strange way, as if judging her eyes.

He then selected a pair of glasses and handed them to her. The child put them on and looked round the court, and then cried out suddenly:

"Oh, what strange people; and how ugly they all are. All ugly, except you who gave me the glasses; you are beautiful." Turning hastily around, she looked at her father and added, "Oh, papa, you are—Oh!" and she took off the glasses quickly, while a burning flush spread over her face.

"I don't like those glasses, she said indignantly, laying them down. "They are horrid! My father doesn't look like that."

"My child," said Penry, very gently, "will you look through another pair of glasses? You see so much that perhaps you can see what is to be, as well as what is. Perhaps you can catch some glimpse even of the future."

He selected another pair and handed them to the child. There was a hush of expectancy in the court; people who had scoffed at Penry before and smiled contempt, now leaned forward to hear, as if something extraordinary were about to happen. All eyes were riveted on the little girl's face; all ears strained to hear what she would say. Round and round the court she looked through the strange glasses and then began to speak in a sort of frightened monotone:

"I see nothing," she said. "I mean there is no court and no people, only great white blocks, a sort of bluey-white powdered as with sugar. Is it ice? There are no trees, no animals; all is cold and white. It is ice. There is no living creature, no grass, no flowers, nothing moves. It is all cold, all dead." In a frightened voice she added: "Is that the future of the world?"

Penry leaned toward her eagerly:

"Look at the light, child," he said; "follow the light up and tell us what you see."

Again a strange hush; I heard my heart thumping while the child looked about her. Then, pulling off the glasses, she said peevishly:

"I can't see anything more: the light hurts my eyes."

DEATH IN PRISON

Matthew Penry whose trial for fraud and condemnation will probably still be remembered by our readers because of the very impressive evidence for the prosecution given by Canon Bayton, of Westminster, died, we understand, in Wandsworth Prison yesterday morning from syncope. —Extract from the *Times*, January 3rd, 1900.

THE
HOLY MAN

(After Tolstoi)

PAUL, THE ELDEST SON of Count Stroganoff, was only thirty-two when he was made a Bishop: he was the youngest dignitary in the Greek Church, yet his diocese was among the largest: it extended for hundreds of miles along the shore of the Caspian. Even as a youth Paul had astonished people by his sincerity and gentleness, and the honors paid to him seemed to increase his lovable qualities.

Shortly after his induction he set out to visit his whole diocese in order to learn the needs of the people. On this pastoral tour he took with him two older priests in the hope that he might profit by their experience. After many disappointments he was forced to admit that they could only be used as aids to memory, or as secretaries; for they could not even understand his passionate enthusiasm. The life of Christ was the model the young Bishop set before himself, and he took joy in whatever pain or fatigue his ideal involved. His two priests thought it unbecoming in a Bishop to work so hard and to be so careless of "dignity and state," by which they meant ease and good living. At first they grumbled a good deal at the work, and with apparent reason, for, indeed, the Bishop forgot himself in his mission, and as the tour went on his body seemed to waste away in the fire of his zeal.

After he had come to the extreme southern point of his

diocese he took ship and began to work his way north along the coast, in order to visit all the fishing villages.

One afternoon, after a hard morning's work, he was seated on deck resting. The little ship lay becalmed a long way from the shore, for the water was shallow and the breeze had died down in the heat of the day.

There had been rain clouds over the land, but suddenly the sun came out hotly and the Bishop caught sight of some roofs glistening rosy-pink in the sunshine a long way off.

"What place is that?" he asked the Captain.

"Krasnavodsk, I think it is called," replied the Captain after some hesitation, "a little nest between the mountains and the sea; a hundred souls perhaps in all."

(Men are commonly called "souls" in Russia as they are called "hands" in England.)

"One hundred souls," repeated the Bishop, "shut away from the world; I must visit Krasnavodsk."

The priests shrugged their shoulders but said nothing; they knew it was no use objecting or complaining. But this time the Captain came to their aid.

"It's twenty-five versts away," he said, "and the sailors are done up. You'll be able to get in easily enough but coming out again against the sea breeze will take hard rowing."

"Tomorrow is Sunday," rejoined the Bishop, "and the sailors will be able to rest all day. Please, Captain, tell them to get out the boat. I wouldn't ask for myself," he added in a low voice.

The Captain understood; the boat was got out, and under her little lugsail reached the shore in a couple of hours.

Lermontoff, the big helmsman, stepped at once into the shallow water, and carried the Bishop on his back up the beach, so that he shouldn't get wet. The two priests got to land as best they could.

At the first cottage the Bishop asked an old man, who was cutting sticks, where the church was.

"Church," repeated the peasant, "there isn't one."

"Haven't you any pope, any priest here?" inquired the Bishop.

"What's that?"

"Surely," replied the Bishop, "you have some one here who visits the dying and prays with them, some one who attends to the sick—women and children?"

"Oh, yes," cried the old man, straightening himself; "we have a holy man."

"Holy man?" repeated the Bishop, "who is he?"

"Oh, a good man, a saint," replied the old peasant, "he does everything for anyone in need."

"Is he a Christian?"

"I don't think so," the old man rejoined, shaking his head, "I've never heard that name."

"Do you pay him for his services?" asked the Bishop.

"No, no," was the reply, "he would not take anything."

"How does he live?" the Bishop probed further.

"Like the rest of us, he works in his little garden."

"Show me where he lives: will you?" said the Bishop gently, and at once the old man put down his axe and led the way among the scattered huts.

In a few moments they came to the cottage standing in a square of cabbages. It was just like the other cottages in the villages, poverty-stricken and weather-worn, wearing its patches without thought of concealment.

The old man opened the door:

"Some visitors for you, Ivanushka," he said, standing aside to let the Bishop and his priests pass in.

The Bishop saw before him a broad, thin man of about sixty, dressed half like a peasant, half like a fisherman; he wore the usual sheepskin and high fisherman's boots. The only noticeable thing in his appearance was the way his silver hair and beard contrasted with the dark tan of his skin; his eyes were clear, blue and steady.

"Come in, Excellency," he said, "come in," and he hastily dusted a stool with his sleeve for the Bishop and placed it for him with a low bow.

"Thank you," said the Bishop, taking the seat, "I am somewhat tired, and the rest will be grateful. But be seated, too," he added, for the "holy man" was standing before him bowed in an attitude of respectful attention. Without a word Ivan drew up a stool and sat down.

"I was surprised to find you have no church here, and no priest; the peasant who showed us the way did not even know what 'Christian' meant."

The holy man looked at him with his patient eyes, but said nothing, so the Bishop went on:

"You're a Christian: are you not?"

"I have not heard that name before," said the holy man.

The Bishop lifted his eyebrows in surprise.

"Why then do you attend to the poor and ailing in their need?" he argued; "why do you help them?"

The holy man looked at him for a moment, and then replied quietly:

"I was helped when I was young and needed it."

"But what religion have you?" asked the Bishop.

"Religion," the old man repeated wonderingly, "what is religion?"

"We call ourselves Christians," the Bishop began, "because Jesus, the founder of our faith, was called Christ, Jesus was the Son of God, and came down from heaven with the Gospel of Good Tidings; He taught men that they were the children of God, and that God is love."

The face of the old man lighted up and he leaned forward eagerly:

"Tell me about Him, please."

The Bishop told him the story of Jesus, and when he came to the end the old man cried:

"What a beautiful story! I've never heard or imagined such a story."

"I intend," said the Bishop, "as soon as I get home

again, to send you a priest, and he will establish a church here where you can worship God, and he will teach you the whole story of the suffering and death of the divine Master."

"That will be good of you," cried the old man, warmly, "we shall be very glad to welcome him."

The Bishop was touched by the evident sincerity of his listener.

"Before I go," he said, "and I shall have to go soon, because it will take us some hours to get out to the ship again, I should like to tell you the prayer that Jesus taught His disciples."

"I should like very much to hear it," the old man said quietly.

"Let us kneel down then," said the Bishop, "as a sign of reverence, and repeat it after me, for we are all brethren together in the love of the Master"; and saying this he knelt down, and the old man immediately knelt down beside him and clasped his hands as the Bishop clasped his and repeated the sentences as they dropped from the Bishop's lips.

"Our Father, which art in heaven, hallowed be thy name."

When the old man had repeated the words, the Bishop went on:

"Thy kingdom come. Thy will be done in earth as it is in heaven."

The fervor with which the old man recited the words "Thy will be done in earth, as it is in heaven" was really touching.

"Give us this day our daily bread. And forgive us our debts,* as we forgive our debtors."

"Give . . . give—," repeated the old man, having apparently forgotten the words.

* This form of the Lord's Prayer is evidently taken from Matthew.

"Give us this day our daily bread," repeated the Bishop, "and forgive us our debts as we forgive our debtors."

"Give and forgive," said the old man at length. . . . "Give and forgive," and the Bishop seeing that his memory was weak took up the prayer again:

"And lead us not into temptation, but deliver us from evil."

Again the old man repeated the words with an astonishing fervor, "And lead us not into temptation, but deliver us from evil."

And the Bishop concluded:

"For thine is the kingdom, and the power, and the glory, for ever. Amen."

The old man's voice had an accent of loving and passionate sincerity as he said, "For thine is the kingdom, and the power, and the beauty, for ever and ever. Amen."

The Bishop rose to his feet and his host followed his example, and when he held out his hand the old man clasped it in both his, saying:

"How can I ever thank you for telling me that beautiful story of Christ; how can I ever thank you enough for teaching me His prayer?"

As one in an ecstasy he repeated the words: "Thy kingdom come. Thy will be done in earth as it is in heaven. . . ."

Touched by his reverent, heartfelt sincerity, the Bishop treated him with great kindness; he put his hand on his shoulder and said:

"As soon as I get back I will send you a priest, who will teach you more, much more than I have had time to teach you; he will indeed tell you all you want to know of our religion—the love by which we live, the hope in which we die." Before he could stop him the old man had bent his head and kissed the Bishop's hand; and tears stood in his eyes as he did him reverence.

He accompanied the Bishop to the water's edge, and,

seeing the Bishop hesitate on the brink waiting for the steersman to carry him to the boat, the "holy man" stooped and took the Bishop in his arms and strode with him through the water and put him gently on the cushioned seat in the stern sheets as if he had been a little child, much to the surprise of the Bishop and of Lermontoff, who said as if to himself:

"That fellow's as strong as a young man."

For a long time after the boat had left the shore the old man stood on the beach waving his hands to the Bishop and his companions; but when they were well out to sea, on the second tack, he turned and went up to his cottage and disappeared from their sight.

A little later the Bishop, turning to his priests, said:

"What an interesting experience! What a wonderful old man! Didn't you notice how fervently he said the Lord's Prayer?"

"Yes," replied the younger priest indifferently, "he was trying to show off, I thought."

"No, no," cried the Bishop. "His sincerity was manifest and his goodness too. Did you notice that he said 'give and forgive' instead of just repeating the words? And if you think of it, 'give us this day our daily bread and forgive us our debts as we forgive our debtors' seems a little like a bargain. I'm not sure that the simple word 'give and forgive' is not better, more in the spirit of Jesus?"

The younger priest shrugged his shoulders as if the question had no interest for him.

"Perhaps that's what the old man meant?" questioned the Bishop after a pause.

But as neither of the priests answered him, he went on, as if thinking aloud:

"At the end again he used the word 'beauty' for 'glory.' I wonder was that unconscious? In any case an extraordinary man and good, I am sure, out of sheer kindness and sweetness of nature, as many men are good in Russia. No wonder our *moujiks* call it 'Holy Russia'; no wonder, when you can find men like that."

"They are as ignorant as pigs," cried the other priest, "not a soul in the village can either read or write: they are heathens, barbarians. They've never even heard of Christ and don't know what religion means."

The Bishop looked at him and said nothing; seemingly he preferred his own thoughts.

It was black night when they came to the ship, and at once they all went to their cabins to sleep; for the day had been very tiring.

The Bishop had been asleep perhaps a couple of hours when he was awakened by the younger priest shaking him and saying:

"Come on deck quickly, quickly, Excellency, something extraordinary's happening, a light on the sea and no one can make out what it is!"

"A light," exclaimed the Bishop, getting out of bed and beginning to draw on his clothes.

"Yes, a light on the water," repeated the priest; "but come quickly, please; the Captain sent me for you."

When the Bishop reached the deck, the Captain was standing with his night-glass to his eyes, looking over the waste of water to leeward, where, indeed, a light could be seen flickering close to the surface of the sea; it appeared to be a hundred yards or so away.

"What is it?" cried the Bishop, astonished by the fact that all the sailors had crowded round and were staring at the light.

"What is it?" repeated the Captain gruffly, for he was greatly moved; "it's a man with a grey beard; he has a lantern in his right hand, and he's walking on the water."

"But no one can walk on the water," said the Bishop gently. "It would be a miracle," he added, in a tone of remonstrance.

"Miracle or not," retorted the Captain, taking the glass

from his eyes, "that's what I see, and the man'll be here soon, for he's coming toward us. Look, you," and he handed the glass to one of the sailors as he spoke.

The light still went on swaying about as if indeed it were being carried in the hand of a man. The sailor had hardly put the night-glass to his eyes, when he cried out:

"That's what it is!—a man walking on the water . . . it's the 'holy man' who carried your Excellency on board the boat this afternoon."

"God help us!" cried the priests, crossing themselves.

"He'll be here in a moment or two," added the sailor, "he's coming quickly," and, indeed, almost at once the old man came to them from the water and stepped over the low bulward on to the deck.

At this the priests went down on their knees, thinking it was some miracle, and the sailors, including the Captain, followed their example, leaving the Bishop standing awe-stricken and uncertain in their midst.

The "holy man" came forward, and, stretching out his hands, said:

"I'm afraid I've disturbed you, Excellency: but soon after you left me, I found I had forgotten part of that beautiful prayer, and I could not bear you to go away and think me careless of all you had taught me, and so I came to ask you to help my memory just once more. . . .

"I remember the first part of the prayer and the last words as if I had been hearing it all my life and knew it in my soul, but the middle has escaped me. . . .

"I remember 'Our Father, which art in heaven, hallowed be thy name. Thy kingdom come. Thy will be done in earth as it is in heaven,' and then all I can remember is, 'Give and forgive,' and the end, 'And lead us not into temptation, but deliver us from evil. For thine is the kingdom, and the power and the beauty for ever and ever. Amen.'

"But I've forgotten some words in the middle: won't you tell me the middle again?"

"How did you come to us?" asked the Bishop in awed wonderment. "How did you walk on the water?"

"Oh, that's easy," replied the old man, "anyone can do that; whatever you love and trust in this world loves you in return. We love the water that makes everything pure and sweet for us, and is never tired of cleansing, and the water loves us in return; anyone can walk on it; but won't you teach me that beautiful prayer, the prayer Jesus taught His disciples?"

The Bishop shook his head, and in a low voice, as if to himself, said:

"I don't think I can teach you anything about Jesus the Christ. You know a great deal already. I only wish—"

THE KING
OF THE JEWS

THE PERSONS

HUSHIM. *A woman of the tribe of Benjamin; wife of Simon and mother of his two sons, Alexander and Rufus.*
SIMON. *Of Cyrene, who owns a field in the country outside Jerusalem, on the way to Bethel.*

THE SCENE: JERUSALEM

Time: The First Hour of the day of Preparation

HUSHIM. Now you know what to do, don't you? You must go to the Temple by the second hour and wait for Joad. When he comes he'll take you to the High Priest. You'll know Joad, he'll be dressed as a priest. Tell Joad he's the handsomest man you've ever seen; he's small, you know, and likes to think he's captivating. Compliment the High Priest on his sense of justice; say it is the finest in the world; say anything. . . . Don't be afraid of overdoing it; men love flattery.
SIMON (*nods his head*). I'll do my best.
HUSHIM. If I've not heard from you by the fourth hour I'll send Alexander to you to know the result, for I shall be very anxious. And the boy'll find out, he's so sharp. Don't

spare compliments. You must be doorkeeper in the Temple, and flattery is like honey, the less you deserve it, the more you like it.

SIMON (*going*).   I'll try to do what you say, Hushim.

The Eleventh Hour on the day of Preparation

HUSHIM.   Well? Have you got the post? You have been a time. Are you the doorkeeper of the Temple; have we the house in the Inner Court?

SIMON (*passing his hand over his forehead*).   I don't know.

HUSHIM.   Don't know; you must know. Was Joad there? He promised to speak for you. Did you see him?

SIMON.   I didn't see him. (*Sits down wearily.*)

HUSHIM.   Didn't see him! Wasn't he there? My uncle's brother, too, and he promised me: the liar. What did you do?

SIMON.   I did nothing. I'm tired, Hushim.

HUSHIM.   Tired! What's happened? Why don't you speak? What's the matter with you? Are you dumb or ill?

SIMON.   I'm not ill, I'm only tired.

HUSHIM.   Tired, you great hulk. Where have you been? What have you been doing? What's the matter with you? Can't you speak?

SIMON.   If you knew—

HUSHIM.   If I knew what? Oh, you make me mad. What is it? (*She takes him by the shoulder and shakes him.*) What's happened? Oh, you brute! Can't you speak?

SIMON.   You've no cause for anger, wife.

HUSHIM.   No cause! Have you got the place? What did the High Priest say? You must know that.

SIMON.   I don't know.

HUSHIM.   You don't know. You must be mad. This comes of marrying a foreigner, a fool, a great brute. They all said I'd repent it. Oh! Oh! Oh!

SIMON.   Don't cry, Hushim. I'll tell you everything.

HUSHIM (*drying her eyes*).   Tell me, did they make you

doorkeeper? That's what I want to know. Tell me that. You promised you'd be in the Temple at the second hour and here it is the eleventh. Where have you been all day? Where?

SIMON.   I'm sorry, wife; I forgot.

HUSHIM.   Forgot, sorry! What do you mean? Joad promised me to get you the place if the High Priest liked you. Did you get it? What did they say? Talk, man.

SIMON.   I'm so sorry. I forgot all about it. I have not been to the Temple.

HUSHIM.   You've not been to the Temple. And why not? Where were you? Don't say that Eli got the post. Don't say it or I'll strike you.

SIMON.   I'm very sorry. I forgot. I don't know who got it. I wasn't there.

HUSHIM (*sitting down*).   Oh! Oh! Oh! He wasn't there! Oh! Oh! Oh! Where have you been all these hours? What have you been doing? Where did you go? Where did you eat?

SIMON.   I've not eaten. I've—

HUSHIM.   Not eaten! Why not? What happened? Oh, why won't you speak! Talk, tell me!

SIMON.   I'll tell you everything; but I'm very tired.

HUSHIM.   Tell me first, who got the post? You must have heard.

SIMON.   I don't know. I've not heard.

HUSHIM.   At the fourth hour I sent Alexander to the Temple to find out whether you were chosen or not; when it got so dark I sent Rufus to my sister-in-law, Hoshed. I could not bear the suspense. They both come back without news. You must know who got the post.

SIMON.   No, I don't know. I didn't ask, but—

HUSHIM (*giving him wine*).   There! Now tell me everything. You went out to the field?

SIMON (*nods while drinking the wine*).   I was at the field till nearly the second hour working, then I came into the city.

When I reached the street which leads from the Temple to the Golgotha I could not get across it, there was such a crowd. They had all come to see some prisoners who were going to be crucified.

HUSHIM.   But didn't you push through?

SIMON.   I got through the first file, but there soldiers kept the passage. I had to wait. No one was allowed to cross. . . . They told me there were three criminals. The people were talking about them. Two were thieves and one a rebel from the north, who had tried to make himself king. It was to see him the people had run together. Some said he was a prophet of God. . . .

After a little while the prisoners came by. The two thieves first, and then slowly the man, whom they called a prophet. He looked very ill. . . . (*After a long pause.*) They had platted a crown of thorns and pushed it down on his head, and the thorns had torn the flesh and the blood ran down his face. When he came opposite to me he fell and lay like a dead man; the Cross was heavy. . . . The Centurion ordered some of the Roman soldiers to lift the Cross from him and he got up. He seemed very weak and faint: he could hardly stand. . . . The Centurion came across to me and pulled me out, and pointed to the Cross and told me to shoulder it and get on. . . .

HUSHIM.   But why *you?*

SIMON.   I suppose because I looked big and strong.

HUSHIM.   Didn't you tell him you had to be at the Temple?

SIMON.   Of course I told him, but he thrust me forward and warned me if I didn't do as I was told, I'd have to go to the Temple without feet.

HUSHIM.   Oh, what bad luck! No one ever had such bad luck as you. No one. Why didn't you run away?

SIMON.   I didn't think—

HUSHIM.   Well, you carried the Cross? And then—

SIMON.   I went to lift the Cross; it seemed as if I were

helping to punish the man. While I stood hesitating, he looked at me, Hushim. I never saw such eyes or such a look. Somehow or other I knew he wished me to do it. I lifted the Cross up and got my shoulder under it and walked on. I did not seem to notice the weight of it, I was thinking of his look, and so we went through the crowd past Golgotha to the Hill of Calvary. On the top I put down the Cross.

HUSHIM. When was that? It must have been about the third hour. Why didn't you go to the Temple then? You see, it was all your fault. I knew it was! But go on, go on.

SIMON. I forgot all about the Temple, I could think of nothing but the man. He stood there so quiet while the priests and people jeered at him. . . . When the others were hung up, they shrieked and screamed and cursed. It was dreadful. . . .

When they were getting ready to nail him to the Cross I went over to him and said, "O Master," and he turned to me, "forgive me, Master, for doing what your enemies wished." And he looked at me again, and my heart turned to water, and the tears streamed from my eyes, I don't know why. . . .

He put his hands on my shoulders and said, "Friend, friend, there is nothing to forgive. . . ." (*Lays his head on his arms and sobs—*)

HUSHIM. Don't cry, Simon, don't cry. He must have been a prophet!

SIMON. If you had seen him. If you had seen his eyes. . . .

HUSHIM (*beginning to cry*). I know, I know. What else did he say?

SIMON. He thanked me, and though I was a foreigner and a stranger to him, and quite rough and common, he took me in his arms and kissed me. . . . I was all broken before him. . . .

He was wonderful. When they nailed him to the Cross

he did not even groan—not a sound. And when they lifted the Cross up—the worst torture of all—he just grew white, white. . . . All the priests about and the people mocked him and asked him if he could save others why couldn't he save himself? But he answered not a word. . . . I could have killed them, the brutes! He prayed to God to forgive them, and he comforted one of the thieves who was sobbing in pain. . . .

Oh, he was wonderful. Even in his anguish he could think of others, and yet he was the weakest of all. . . .

And then the storm burst, and I stood there for hours and hours in the darkness. I could not leave him, I waited. . . . Later some of his own people came about the Cross, weeping, his mother and his followers, and took him down, and they called him Master and Lord, as I had called him. They all loved him. No one could help loving him, no one. . . .

Above his head on the Cross, they had written, "King of the Jews." You Jews have no king, I know; they did it to mock him. But he was a king, king of the hearts of men.

HUSHIM. And with all that we've lost the place! What was his name?

SIMON. Jesus of Nazareth.

HUSHIM. What was it he said to you? I want to remember it to tell Hoshed.

SIMON. He called me "Blessed, for that I a stranger, who did not even know him, was the only man in the world who had ever helped to bear his burden."

A DAUGHTER
OF EVE

An old-fashioned square house on Long Island, set in a clearing of pine trees; a break in the cliff shows a little triangle of sandy beach and the waters of the sound dancing in the moonlight. Half a dozen men are sitting about on the stoop looking over the silvery waters.

The evening papers had published an account of Mrs. Amory's will which showed that she had left half a million dollars to a nursing home for mill-children in Philadelphia. The news set us all talking of the wonderful work she had done and her self-sacrifice. Most of us assumed that it was a religious motive that had induced this rich and, it was said, handsome woman to give years of her life to improving the lot of the city's waifs and strays.

The ladies had left us and gone up to bed; but we still discussed the matter. Suddenly Charlie Railton turned to Judge Barnett of the Supreme Court of the State of New York, who sat with his chair tilted back against the wall ruminating.

"Say, Judge, what do you think of it, anyway? I'd like to hear your opinion."

"I have no opinion of the matter," replied the Judge, taking the cigar out of his mouth and speaking very slowly, "I don't know women well enough to be sure about anything where they're concerned."

"Plead guilty, Judge," cried Railton, who was about thirty years of age. "Plead guilty and throw yourself on the mercy of the court; I guess you know women better than most of us, and they're pretty easy to know, it seems to me."

"I used to think so, too," said the Judge, "but I got kind o' puzzled once and I've never been sure since."

"How was that, Judge?" cried our host, one of the boldest speculators on the New York Stock Exchange, scenting a mystery.

"It's a long story," said Barnett deliberately, "and it's pretty late already."

We all protested and called for the story and the Judge began:

"It takes one a long way back, I'm afraid; back to the late sixties, and it's autobiographical, too; I guess it has every fault."

"Go on," we cried in chorus.

After being admitted to the Bar—he resumed—I went up to my mother's place in Maine to rest. Along in the winter I got pneumonia on a shooting trip and could not shake it off. I crawled through the summer and then made up my mind to go to California or somewhere warm for the winter; I had had enough of snow and blizzards. I spent the winter in Santa Barbara and got as fit as a young terrier.

In the spring I went to 'Frisco and there in a gymnasium and boxing saloon got to know a man who was about the best athlete I ever struck. Winterstein might have been heavyweight champion if he had trained, and he was handsome enough for a stage lover. He was just under six feet in height, with bold expression and good features; dark hair, in little curls all over his head and agate-dark eyes which grew black when he was excited or angry.

I found he was a better man physically than I was, and that was the beginning of our friendship; we soon became intimate and he told me all about his early life. He was born in the North of England, and became a sailor in the English navy, but he could not stand the rigid discipline, poor food, and harsh treatment. He deserted in Quebec while still a lad, and made his way to New York. He had not had much education, but he had improved what he had by reading. Like most men of intelligence who have not had a college training, he set great store by books and book learning, and got me to help him with mathematics. He had a captain's certificate, it appeared, but he wanted to know navigation thoroughly; he surprised me one day by telling me he owned a little vessel which was nearly ready for sea.

"I have just had her overhauled," he said; "would you like to come and see her? She's lying off Meiggs's."

"What do you do with her?" I questioned, full of curiosity.

"I go pearling," he said; "pearls are found nearly all 'round the Gulf of California. The fisherfolk rake in the oysters and lay them on the beach till they get bad and open of themselves. The children collect the pearls and keep them until I come 'round. I paid for the craft and have a couple of thousand dollars put by from last year's work."

"But where did you learn about pearls?" I asked.

"I worked for a man once and picked it up. Sometimes I make a little mistake, but not often. You see we go to out-of-the-way places where we reckon to give about a quarter what the pearls are worth. That leaves a wide margin for mistakes."

"But I had no idea that there were pearls in the Gulf," I said.

"Why not come along and see for yourself," he said. "I'll be starting in a week. The schooner had to have her bottom cleaned and the copper repaired, that's what's hung me up for this last month or so. Now I'm about right for another year. If you'd like to come, I'd be glad to have you."

"And make me mate?" I asked laughing.

"Commander," he replied seriously, "and you shall have ten percent of the profits."

"I'll think it over and let you know," was my answer.

The adventure tempted me, the strange life and work, the novelty of the thing: I resolved to go pearling.

I went with Winterstein to the wharf and he showed his craft to me. She looked like a toy vessel, a little schooner, a fifty-footer of about forty tons. She sat on the water like a duck, a little New England model with beautiful lines. Winterstein introduced me to his first mate, Donkin, and his second mate, Crawford. Donkin was a big lump of a fellow, six feet two in height, broad in proportion and brawny, a good seaman. Crawford I soon found out was an even better sailor and more intelligent, though of only average strength.

"What about the crew?" I asked Winterstein when we were alone in the little cabin.

"I want one more man and a boy," he replied laughing at my surprised face.

"But," I retorted, "you can't have three officers and one man."

"It's like this," he said: "Donkin has only been a second mate, but he gets a first mate's certificate provided he stays with me a year, and the same thing with Crawford. The work is not hard," he added apologetically, "they get good wages and a lift in rank and it suits them, and so I get first-rate work cheap. Four or five men can manage this craft easy so long as we don't strike a cyclone and there ain't much dirty weather in the Gulf."

A couple of days later Winterstein told me shyly that he had been married recently, and after I had congratulated him, he insisted that I must come and be introduced to the prettiest girl in California. All the way uptown he praised his young wife, and the praise I found was not extravagant. Mrs. Winterstein was charming: tall and fair with Irish grey eyes; her shyness and love of Winterstein put a sort of aureole about her. She was of Irish parentage: before her marriage her name had been Rose O'Connor. Nothing would do but I must call her Rose at once. The pair lived in a little frame house on the side of the bluff, where now there is a famous park. An old Irishwoman did the chores for Rose and mothered and scolded her just as she had done before her marriage. Rose, I learned, had been a teacher in the high school. In the next few days I saw a good deal of her. She was doing up her quarters and buying knickknacks for the cabin and tiny stateroom, and I naturally ran her errands and tried to save her trouble.

Whenever I ventured a shy compliment she always told me I must see her sister Daisy, who was at Sacramento in a finishing school. Daisy was lovely and Daisy was clever; there was no one like Daisy in her sister's eyes.

It was a perfect June morning with just air enough to make the sun dance on the ripples, when at length we were all ready on board and starting out of the bay.

Our crew had been completed by a young darky called Abraham Lincoln, who at once took over the cooking, and a sailor called Dyer, who was a little lame, but handy enough at his work.

The first part of the cruise was uneventful: it might have been a yachting trip. Day after day we sailed along in delightful sunshine, with a six or eight-knot breeze. The perfect conditions would have been monotonous had we not amused ourselves with fishing. One day I remember we got rather rough weather and when Winterstein, Donkin and myself took our bearing next day we found that we had been swept some distance to the westward.

It was Crawford who solved the enigma for us. He told us there was a current called the West Wind Drift, which set across the Pacific from east to west as if making for 'Frisco and then flows down the coast from north to south till it meets the north equatorial current which comes from the south and sweeps out to the west, carrying the tail end, so to speak, of the drift with it. Where the two opposing currents meet off the South California coast, one often finds a heavy sea and variable crosswinds. But as soon as we turned into the Gulf the fine weather began again.

The trading which I had hoped would be full of adventure turned out to be quite simple and tame. We ran along the shore, stopping wherever there was a village. Usually we dropped anchor pretty close in and rowed ashore. At nine places out of ten Winterstein was known. The fishermen brought out their little cotton bags of pearls and we bought them. Curiously enough, the black pearl, so esteemed today, had then no value at all. Whenever we bought a packet of white pearls, the black ones were thrown in as not worth estimating. The pink pearls, too, had no price, unless they were exceptionally large or beautifully shaped, and even then they were very cheap. I began to collect the black pearls to make a necklace for Mrs. Winterstein. I was half in love with her I think from the beginning. She was not only very pretty but laughter-loving, and girlish, and her little matronly airs sat drolly upon her. Everyone on board liked her, I don't know why. I suppose she wanted to please us all, for she was full of consideration for everyone. I have never seen any woman who appealed so unconsciously and so directly to the heart, and her happiness was something that had to be seen to be believed. She simply adored her husband, waited on him hand and foot, and pampered all his little selfishnesses. She was only unhappy when away from him, or when it was rough weather and she was seasick. Curiously enough, in spite of the long cruise, she never became a good sailor. In fine weather she was all right, but the moment *The Rose* commenced to bob about, Mrs. Winterstein used to retire to her cabin.

I told no one about the necklace. I simply annexed all the black pearls and determined to get them strung together as soon as we got back to 'Frisco. I never landed without asking after them, and even went so far as to buy some which were being used by the native children as trinkets. I remember once coming across an extraordinary specimen as big as a marble, perfectly round, and with a perfect skin. We were passing a cabin where a couple of mestizo girls of fourteen and sixteen were seated on the sand playing a game of bones, which I think must be as old as the world, for the Greeks knew it as astragalos. You throw the round bones up into the air and turn your hand round quickly and catch them on the back. Among the five bones was a black pearl, which I admired at once and bought for a quarter, I think. I can still see the half-naked girl-child as she handed it to me. She stood on one leg like a stork, and with her right foot rubbed her left ankle, while glancing at me half-shyly out of great liquid dark eyes. She had only a red calico wrap about her body, out of the folds of which one small round amber breast showed: but she was evidently unconscious of her nudity—a child in mind, a woman in body.

I have absolutely nothing interesting to tell of this first cruise. We stopped once where the sea must have receded from the land, for the town was some four miles inland. I have forgotten the name of the place, but it was quite a town—some two or three thousand inhabitants. The smell of the oysters on the sea beach, I remember, was overpowering. Thousands and thousands of bushels had been left to rot. Our harvest of pearls here was so large that Winterstein resolved to go back to 'Frisco at once and market his goods. We were all tired of fish and biscuits varied with sowbelly fiery with salt and black with age.

The return trip was just as uneventful as the voyage

out. Winterstein's profits were beyond all his former experiences. After paying all expenses, giving me my tenth, and dividing another tenth between the two mates, he cleared up something like six thousand dollars for two months' work.

He was naturally eager to get to sea again, but there was a difficulty. Rose found that her sister had left Sacramento, and had come to live in 'Frisco. She had got work, too, I gathered, in a shop and refused absolutely to be a schoolgirl any longer or to accept her sister's advice. Rose was anxious about her and resolved to take her on board with us the next cruise. But for a long time Miss Daisy refused to come: she preferred, it appeared, to be entirely on her own and it was only when Winterstein joined Rose in solicitation that she finally consented. I was rather eager to see this very self-willed and independent young lady.

I was quite ready for another trip. It would please my mother, I thought, if I went back with a couple of thousand dollars in my pocket, and I had got my black pearls strung as a necklace for Rose.

Winterstein warned me that the next trip would perhaps not be so profitable, as he would leave out the chief places, which he had already touched at, and go to the more remote stations.

"Pearling," he said, "is like everything else in life—the easiest work is the best paid." His philosophy was not very deep, though his observation was exact enough.

We arranged to start one afternoon. I had been in town making purchases. It was wretched weather. A nor'easter had sprung up and blew sand through the streets in clouds. I only hoped that the departure would be postponed. I found Winterstein waiting impatiently for me, and his wife's sister, too, was on deck in spite of the rough weather. Winterstein introduced me to her. Daisy O'Connor did not make much impression on me at first; she was girlish-young and did not seem to be anything like so good looking as her sister. True, she had large dark brown eyes and good features, but she was smaller than Rose, and without Rose's brilliant coloring or charm of appeal. She treated me rather coolly, I thought. Winterstein seemed to be in a great hurry to get off.

"Why not put off going until tomorrow?" I asked. "As soon as we get outside she'll duck into it halfway up her jib."

"Tomorrow's Friday," remarked Miss Daisy.

"Surely you're not superstitious?" I laughed.

"Yes, I am," replied the girl, and a peculiar character of decision came into her face and voice.

"You know the old rhyme?"

She questioned me with a look, and I repeated the old chanty:

> Monday for health
> And Tuesday for wealth
> And Wednesday the best day of all,
> Thursday for losses
> And Friday for crosses
> And Saturday no day at all. . . .

"Thursday will be a bad start," I added.

"I like a bad start," she retorted; "a good start often means a bad ending." She spoke bitterly, I thought.

"A resolute little thing," I said to myself carelessly, while getting into my sea-togs.

In five minutes the anchor was up and the sails set and we were beating out to sea in the teeth of the gale. In the bay the wind came in gusts, but as we held toward Lime Point it settled down to a steady drive which heeled us over till the lee scuppers were under water. Every moment it blew harder. When we went about and opened out the Golden Gate, *The Rose* went over, over till it looked as if she would turn turtle. I laid hold of the main rigging to keep my feet and get the spindrift out of my eyes. Ten feet from me was the girl with one hand on a stay, her slight figure braced against the gale, evidently enjoying the experience. A different voyage from the first, I thought to myself, and under different auspices. But the work and danger stopped thought. As soon as we were out of the Golden Gate and clear of Point Bonita the sea began to pile up and break in masses on the bar. We were in for a dirty night. In five minutes we were all wet to the skin. The girl had gone below. The companion, skylights and hatches were all battened down and made snug and not a moment too soon. The sea on the bar was terrific: again and again the green water buried the decks, but as soon as we had got outside and turned her bows southward, the gale came fair on the quarter and the little "saucer" as I called *The Rose* made good weather of it, lifting easily to the great combers and swooping along their shoulders into the night for all the world like some white sea-bird.

The coming on board of Daisy O'Connor altered everything. I was too young at the time to explain, or even understand what was taking place. The interest which used to center in Rose and Winterstein and abaft the companion, now followed Daisy all over the ship. For the girl was never long in one place and divided her favors impartially among all the men on board. Now she walked his watch talking to Crawford, or sat discussing a book with me. She was less with Winterstein than with any of us, which was not remarked, because the weather still continued boisterous and gave him a good deal to do between the stateroom in which his wife spent most of her time and the wave-swept deck.

In every way this cruise was different from the first, less pleasant, if more exciting. The first thing I noticed was that Donkin, who appeared to like Winterstein on the first voyage, now disliked him. Winterstein spoke sharply to him one day about the way the jib was sitting:

"That jib's shivering," he said, "it's not set flat, take a pull at it."

Donkin looked at him and said sulkily:

"That's because she's steered too free."

"That's all you know about it," replied Winterstein cheerfully, "at any rate take a pull at the sheet."

The look of contempt and anger which Donkin threw at the skipper surprised and shocked me. I did not even then notice that Daisy was standing to windward almost between them. It only occurred to me long afterwards. *The Rose*, which had been the most comfortable craft in the world, had become an ordinary sort of vessel.

The weather was very unsettled; usually we had more than enough wind and a heavy lop of sea, and the little saucer, tossed about like a cork.

Three days out of four Rose O'Connor kept to her berth, and never showed at all even at mealtimes, and Daisy O'Connor took her place on the deck and in the cabin as well. Day after day Winterstein and I lunched with her alone. The door leading into Rose's stateroom was generally closed. It was impossible not to be interested in Daisy. She was very intelligent and self-centered, and as reserved as Rose was ingenuous and open. She struck me as being much older than Rose. She was a sort of enigma, and I could not help wanting to find the key to it. She never praised or complimented one as Rose did; her praise was a word or two, which seemed wrung from her, a tantalizing, proud creature.

One day we were running along under some bluffs; the wind was light and fitful; we had all the plain sails set. Rose was on deck, seated in a cane armchair to windward of the companion. Winterstein was a consummate seaman, and that day seemed a little anxious; he kept running down to look at the barometer, and had a word or two with Crawford, I remembered afterwards. Neither of them seemed to like the look of the weather. I paid small attention to externals, for Daisy was walking the deck with me, and I was telling her how I intended to put up my shingle in New York that winter and start my law office. She was looking her very best and I had begun to wonder whether she was not even more attractive than her sister. When she got excited, or when the wind blew a little sharply, her white skin would take on the faint pink tinge of a sea shell, and when interested her eyes would grow large and deepen in color. Altogether I was beginning to think her fascinating. Unconsciously I was transferring to her my old allegiance to Rose. Rose was not at her best this cruise; she looked washed out and pale; she did what she could, but the bad weather was against her. Clearly the spiritual center of gravity, so to speak, of the vessel, had changed, and I certainly was not blind to the fact that Daisy gave me more of her time than she gave to anyone else, though she would often have long talks with Donkin. The person she spent least time with was distinctly Winterstein.

While we were walking up and down talking, the wind suddenly ceased, and the little craft shot up at once on an even keel and set Rose's chair sliding. It was stopped by Winterstein, who took his wife below, and as we resumed our walk again I noticed that the look Daisy threw at her sister was more than indifferent; there was contempt in it. In a minute or two Winterstein came up again and stood near the mainsheet and every now and then we passed him. The wind was blowing again steadily and the schooner heeled over under it and all went on as before. Suddenly, without any warning, the wind veered round and blew from almost the opposite point of the compass. With a slash and crash the sails came flapping over our heads and the boom smashed inboard, as if we were going to jibe. I caught the companion to hold myself. Daisy was thrown past me and would have had a nasty fall had not Winterstein caught her in his arms. She tore herself loose angrily, and he sprang to the mainsheet and drew it taut and stopped the boom from going over. The helmsman, Crawford, had been almost as quick. No sooner had the squall struck us than he put the helm up and the next moment *The Rose*'s bow fell off and her sails filled again and she went on as before. In the nick of time Winterstein eased away the mainsail.

The fine thing in the occurrence was Winterstein's extraordinary speed and strength. There he stood holding the mainsheet, his magnificent athlete's figure etched against the sky. Before I had taken in his splendid unconscious pose, Daisy made an inarticulate exclamation as if she had caught her breath; but when I looked at her, her face was as composed as usual and without expression.

I thought at the time that the weather was chiefly responsible for the change in the moral atmosphere. It is impossible to be good-tempered if you are wet through by day and up half the night shortening sail or ready to shorten it. For the schooner after all was only a small craft, and heavily sparred even for summer weather. The sails, it was evident, were too big for her, though Winterstein declared he had never seen such weather in September. I had never had harder work. Three days out of the four we worked all day long and half through the night. The little craft was undermanned. And though we were all strong, five or six pairs of hands cannot do the work of ten or twelve, and no man can be in two places at once. Our tempers began to get ragged.

On the first trip Crawford had been a great friend of mine; he was really a fine sailor and intelligent besides, and whenever I wanted to know anything, I used to go and talk with him, and even in 'Frisco I took him out with me to the theatre once or twice, and was very much amused by his shrewd comments. But one day he called me to help him hauling in the jib.

"Bear a hand, damn you," he cried. I was amazed.

"What's the matter, Crawford?" I said afterward, but he turned on his heel and muttered something about "lazy" in such a tone that I replied:

"Lazy or not, you had better curse someone else."

But afterwards, in cool blood, I could not help asking myself what it all meant. I could find no reason for Crawford's change of manner. "Lazy" stuck in my mind. The day before had been fine and I had sat in a chair near Daisy, and read Whittier to her, but that could have nothing to do with Crawford I decided, who seemed to me quite old: he must have been nearly forty.

The weather made little difference to Daisy. She was up on deck in all weathers, and seemed fairly to revel in a hard gale. When it was dry she used to wear a tight-knitted thing, like a long blue jersey, which outlined her slight figure, and when it was wet she would put on a waterproof, and tuck her hair inside a close hood, which seemed to frame her face lovingly; I liked her best when it simply blew hard, and we could walk about and talk.

About this time I began to notice that Donkin was trying in his uncouth way to make up to her. He seized every opportunity of talking to her and advising her. It was a remark of Crawford's that opened my eyes. They were standing together chatting one day when Crawford looked at me over his shoulder and said:

"She does not care for him any more than she cares for the mainmast, but the big fool thinks she does."

A pang of surprise and anger told me that I cared more than I admitted to myself. The idea of Donkin, great, ugly, sullen Donkin, side by side with that beauty and fine intelligence.

"Beauty and the beast," I said. Crawford looked at me and turned aside: I realized that I had spoken bitterly.

All this time there seemed to be less change in Winterstein than in any of the rest of us. Day after day and night after night he did two or three men's work, and did not seem to feel fatigue or need sleep. He was helped, of course, by his magnificent health and strength. He appeared to take it as a matter of course that I should monopolize Daisy, and we talked together at mealtimes almost as if he were not in the cabin. Our talk was mostly of books and works of art in which it was impossible for him to join. He listened, indeed, but could hardly expect to interest her in books as I could. Sometimes I read scraps of Shelley or Swinburne to her, and it was a treat to see her face flush and change with the varying emotions. Her eyes were extraordinary; they drew the very soul out of one and tempted one perpetually to more passionate expression. Talks begun in the cabin continued with us on deck. No one made me talk as she did. She was something more than a sympathetic listener. She made one want to draw forth her interest or rare word of praise. But if she showed intense emotion about a piece of verse or some wonderful cloud-effect, her interest was always impersonal. As soon as the talk became at all sentimental she would break it off and her eyes would grow inexpressive as brown stones.

After we had rounded the peninsula and turned into the Gulf, the weather suddenly improved. Day after day we floated along with a light breeze under a pale-blue sky, tremulous with excess of light. Day after day now Rose came up and we had tea and even dinner on deck. But somehow or other Rose never regained her position: we like her and turned to her, attracted by her smiling good humor, but the spiritual interest of the ship was centered in her sister. Everything in Rose was open, comprehensible, from her flowerlike beauty to her manifest devotion to Winterstein, but Daisy was a closed book, a tantalizing puzzle; for all of us she had the charm of the unknown and unexplored. She entered into no direct competition with her sister; she simply kept apart as a rival queen and there could be no doubt that her court was better attended. You flattered Rose and paid compliments to her, the other you studied and sought to interest. Rose was always more than fair to her sister. In fact she praised her and made up to her timidly, like the rest of us. One day Winterstein had gone down for a pair of loose boots for his wife, as she wanted to walk. While he put the boots on we naturally talked of feet. I praised Rose's feet, but she would not have it:

"My feet are huge," she said, "in comparison to Daisy's. I take fours and she takes ones, don't you, Daisy? Show them."

Daisy looked at her with a little smile, but did not follow her advice.

"Come, Daisy, show us," I said.

She turned smiling inscrutable eyes on me and that was all. Suddenly Winterstein laughed.

"Daisy wants to spare us," he said. Her face hardened.

"Daisy does not think it a matter of any moment," she said, "but if you are all agreed, there you are," and she pulled her feet together and drew up her skirts deliberately, showing tiny feet and two nervous, slight ankles. But almost at the same moment she sprang to her feet:

"Are you coming?" she threw to me, and walked down the deck.

"What wonderful feet you have," I said, "almost too small for your figure."

"Why should very small feet and hands be admired?" she said, turning to me.

I could not give her the answer that came into my mind, and hesitated, seeking some other explanation.

"It's traditional. . . . I hardly know," I hesitated and sprang to knowledge for evasion. "All Greek statues of women have large feet," I remarked.

"But there must be a reason," she said, and her eyes probed mine.

"Yes," I replied, feeling annoyed with myself for getting red. She took it all in coolly and then changed the conversation, perhaps she understood more than she admitted.

In the Gulf we called at various small stations and did fairly well with the pearls. Rose had given Daisy my black pearl necklace, I noticed: it seemed strange to me that all the affection should be on Rose's side.

The weather got finer and finer: it became so hot indeed that Winterstein fixed up an awning from the companion to the poop. We used to keep the awning cool by throwing a couple of buckets of water on it before Rose came on deck, for she felt the heat intensely.

About this time I began to guess that her paleness and languor had a cause, and we all felt more kindly toward her if that were possible. But the fact itself seemed to set her more and more apart, putting her outside our circle. The heat seemed to affect Daisy no more than it affected the rest of us. I used to get up nearly every morning and bathe, and when there was a wind Donkin or Crawford used to throw a bucket of water over me and I hopped about on the for'castle to dry myself. If there was no wind I went overboard, keeping near the vessel because of the sharks. One day I had just run up after my bath, I was still drying my head, when Daisy came on deck.

"Oh, how I should like a swim," she said. "I've been so hot in that stewy cabin."

She did not look hot, she was always the picture of neatness. But Donkin put his oar in at once.

"Nothing easier, Miss Daisy."

When had he commenced calling her by her Christian name, I wondered angrily.

"Oh, but the sharks," she said. "If one were to bite a foot off, or a hand, I should kill myself. I do not mind death, but I would not be deformed for anything."

"We could rig a sail out on the yard, so that you could have four feet of water, and yet be perfectly safe," he replied.

"Oh, how splendid," she said, "I wish you would."

"In ten minutes, Miss Daisy," he said, and turned away to the work, Crawford following at his heels.

"I must go down and get ready," she said, "but won't you come in with me, you won't mind bathing again, it will give me courage?"

"I have no bathing things," I said, "but I can probably get a suit ready for tomorrow."

"What a pity," she pouted, "bathing alone is no fun. Can't you make something do?"

"I daresay I can," I replied.

"Please," and she disappeared down the companion.

I went below and got myself ready with a loose flannel shirt, and a pair of duck trousers cut off at the knee, promising myself to hem them round next day. The rummaging about took me some time, and when I came on deck Daisy was already waiting and all the preparations had been made. A yard had been sheered out from the ship and stayed against the bulwark and companion. From the end of it a square sail had been let down by a cross yard at the end of the spar. The sail dipped into the water and formed a bath of perhaps twenty feet long, fifteen feet broad and four or five in depth. The gangway opened into the middle of it, and the little ladder led down to the water's edge. When I came up, Daisy was thanking them.

"Did you ever see such a perfect bath?" she said, turning to me. "Isn't it clever of them. I think you sailors," and she looked into Donkin's eyes, "can just do anything." (The fellow's weather-beaten hide flushed to brick red.) "It was Mr. Crawford," she added, "who thought of putting the sail by the gangway. He thinks of everything."

She was diabolically clever; for the praise was deserved. Crawford's white face paled and he fidgeted under her eyes.

Daisy had on a little green cap, into which she had tucked her hair, and a great white bath sheet. Winterstein came up from below and stood close by.

"Will you go first?" I said.

She turned and undid the tapes at her neck, and let the bath towel slip onto the white deck. She was in pale green with knickerbockers; a little tunic cut low at the neck fell over her hips. Her arms were bare, and her legs from the knees down. Everything suited her. She was adorable—girl and woman in one. The next moment she had slid down the ladder into the sea and was swimming about. In a moment I joined her, and then she explained to me that she could never float.

"My feet always go down," she said, "and before I know it I am standing on my feet upright in the water." Again and again she tried to float, but always with the same result. I wondered if she knew how provocative she was, as she lay there with the men leaning down from the bulwarks, all staring at her with hot eyes. When she came on deck she did not disappear at once into the bath cloak, which Donkin held ready for her. She stood there among the men on deck in her semi-nudity, and cried:

"Oh, I have enjoyed myself; it has been perfect. I am so much obliged to you," she said, turning to Donkin, "and to you, too, Mr. Crawford."

I noticed that Dyer at the helm devoured her with his eyes while Abraham's black face grinned from the for'castle hatch.

"It was kind of all of you," she went on, "the water was not a bit cold. You will put the sail down tomorrow, won't you?" she said to Donkin, as she stretched her arm backwards over her head to get the cloak. The movement threw her little breasts upward into sharp relief; the next moment she had drawn the cloak about her with a little gay laugh and disappeared down the companionway. It was as if the sun had gone out. For a moment we men stared at each other, and then I went forward to change my things while Donkin and Crawford busied themselves getting in the sail. Suddenly I heard Winterstein's voice:

"Here, you Abraham, bear a hand with the swab here and dry up this water. As you've come on deck you may as well do something." I turned in surprise, the tone was strangely hard and menacing, utterly unlike Winterstein, but I did not catch a glimpse of his face, for as soon as he had given the order he turned away to stare at the land over the poop.

What was the meaning of it all, I asked myself, but I soon put the query out of my head, because I did not want to dull the vivid image of the girl's beautiful figure which had been revealed to me. Was anyone else as lovely? I asked myself. Her feet were like baby feet. The marks of sex in her figure were so slight that they merely accentuated the beauty of the slim round outlines. What provocation in the crooked girlish arms, what a challenge in the inscrutable mutinous eyes. She had been delightful to me in the sea: she turned to me familiarly for help; I had touched her firm flesh again and again, and I was intoxicated with her as with wine.

I did not see Daisy again that morning until lunchtime, or dinner as we called it. I had fished, persistently, and called out loudly whenever I had the opportunity, hoping that it would bring her on deck, for she reveled in fishing, and was easily the champion because all the men vied with each other in picking the most attractive baits for her. In this game Crawford was easily first. He brought up a piece of red flannel one day, cut into the shape of a narrow tongue; on the other side of it he had sewn a glittering piece of white satin. Equipped with this bait no one had a chance with Daisy. She had caught three fish to my one, and as Donkin or Crawford was always at hand to pull up the wet line for her and take the hook from the fish and put the bait straight again she had little to do except amuse herself.

At lunch she took all my compliments in complete silence.

"You would be able to float," I insisted, "if you would arch your back and keep your head right back."

But she would not have it.

"I do arch my back and put my head right back, but my feet pull me upright."

"Such tiny feet," I replied, "have not the power to pull anyone down."

"You shall try, tomorrow," she said. "I will keep as rigid as you please, and you shall put your hand under my back to see whether I am stiff."

Winterstein suddenly spoke:

"Why don't you put that French thing on, that knitted thing instead of the tunic?"

"Do you mean the maillot?" she said slowly, looking him straight in the eyes.

He nodded. His expression I remembered afterward was a little strained.

"I have not worn it," she said with her eyes on the cloth, "since I bathed at the Cliff House, but as you wish it," she added slowly, "I will put it on," and she turned away indifferently. There was a tension in the air, but not on her side I thought as much as on his, but why?

"What is the maillot like?" I said, showing her that I knew the French word.

"It's a knitted thing," she said; "all the girls used to wear them and little French slippers. You know we have parties in the baths. I have got all the things still. I'll put them on tomorrow. I think they suit me. Some people used to say so," she added slowly.

Winterstein got up, and went into his wife's bedroom for something or other. When he returned I was leaving the cabin. Daisy called to me on the way up that she would bring Browning with her. She was sensitive to beauty of words or music and extraordinarily intelligent; I delighted to read her my favorite poems.

If I were a storyteller I'd try to make all you people feel

what we felt next morning. The weather was perfect, the sea like glass: the little schooner seemed to breathe gently as if sleeping on the oily swell. Rose came on deck early and established herself under the awning. I thought that her presence would make a difference, would act as a restraint on her sister and I wished her away. I had got my bathing things in some sort of order the evening before. I rather fancied myself in them. I had not been on deck more than five minutes when I noticed a sort of subdued excitement in everyone. All the men were on deck and they had all rigged themselves out more or less. Donkin was shaved and so was Crawford, Dyer limped about in clean ducks, and Abraham Lincoln had mounted a large white collar with a scarlet and blue tie. Winterstein alone had made no change. He talked to his wife while moving about whistling for wind as if indifferent. . . .

For the first time I noticed clearly that Rose was soon to become a mother. Her face was a little white and drawn, and when she tried once or twice to take a few turns with Winterstein you could see that her figure had altered in spite of the loose dress she wore. I was looking over the little lifeboat which we carried on the davit amidship when I heard Daisy's voice.

"What a perfect day," she said, "and how delightful everything looks. I know I shall enjoy the bath."

Naturally I went toward her. She was standing close to the companion. Rose was sitting a yard or so behind it with her chair against the mahogany top. Everyone was on the tiptoe of excitement. Donkin, Crawford, Abraham Lincoln, all moved like steel nibs toward the magnet, except Winterstein. The girl had her back to the men. Suddenly she opened her wrap a little to show herself in her maillot to her sister. Winterstein and I could not help seeing her as well. It caught my breath. For one moment I thought she was naked. The maillot was white; the meshes of it showed the rose-colored skin beneath. She looked like an ivory statue by some modern French artist: she was rounder, more womanlike than I had pictured her immaturity.

"Oh, Daisy," cried Rose.

"He told me to put it on," said Daisy defiantly looking at Winterstein while drawing the cloak about her again. "You used to say it fitted me perfectly," she added, "and liked me in it."

"Yes," said Rose, amiably, leaning back and closing her eyes, as if in pain or weariness, "it does suit you, but somehow or other it was different when half a dozen of you children were all wearing them in the bath; besides you've grown, I suppose, and it's in the open and men about . . ."

"I'll take it off," said Daisy in the hard clear voice which I had come to recognize as a sign of annoyance.

"Oh, no," said Rose, "I'd bathe in it now I had it on. Go on," she said smiling, "the dip will do you good."

The girl turned and without a word went down into the cabin. In a minute or two she appeared.

"Will you go down first," she said to me, "and I will dive in."

She stood in the gangway with the shapeless wrap about her. I nodded, for my mouth was dry, and without more ado, threw myself into the sea, and in a moment was standing on the sail dashing the water from my eyes. Daisy opened the wrap slowly and took her arms out of the sleeves with a sort of serpentine movement, infinitely graceful and provocative. She had put on her little tunic over the maillot. I was glad the outline was draped; but having seen her in the maillot the vision of her form was still with me in its half-ripe seduction. But being hidden from the other men it seemed mine and private. Yet I noticed that Donkin received her bathing cloak mechanically without taking his eyes off her. As she stood above me she swayed backward—down, down, the lines of her flexible young body changing every moment and let herself glide into the sea. All the time she stood poised on the deck there was a steel band of hate around my chest. I do not think the girl knew what she was doing. I do not believe she could have imagined the rage of desire her beauty called to life in these men who had been a month at sea, eating heartily while breathing in the tonic sea air. As soon as she was in the water beside me all anger vanished; she seemed to belong to me then, and I wondered whether she liked me to touch her; at any rate she was not adverse to learning anything I suggested and naturally I was fertile in suggestions.

Suddenly she said she would float; she would arch her back and put her head back as far as she could, and I must put my hand under her waist and support her, then I would see how impossible it was for her to float. I did what I was told without thinking, and at first she floated and I looked into her face and cried:

"You see, you see." But she was not looking at me, her face was set hard, there was a sort of defiance in it. I followed her glance up and saw Winterstein leaning over the bulwarks gazing down on her. I seemed to catch for the moment a sort of tension between them and then slowly the vaselike outlines of her hips sank lower into the water, and she came up smiling:

"See how my feet drag me down," she said, pushing her right foot up through the water in comic dismay, as if to show me how heavy it was.

Winterstein had left the bulwarks, but Donkin was looking down at her and Crawford and the others all drinking her in with greedy eyes. She swam about a little and then climbed up the ladder and stood at the top of it, half in the hot sunshine, and half in the shade of the awning—to get warm, she said. My foot was on the lower rung of the ladder, I was so close to her that I could see every line of her body, the adorable roundness, and the

fine nervous grace of it. I could scarcely refrain from putting my hands on her as she stood there swaying just in
front of me, with the wet tunic clinging to her like skin
and showing all her adorable nudities.

"It is too delicious," she said with a little shudder, "the
water is warmer than the air. The air makes me shiver,
but the water is warm like new milk. You should come
and bathe, too, Rose."

"Put on your wrap and change quickly, or you'll catch
cold," said Rose, who had picked up her things and was
going down to the cabin. She spoke a little tartly, I
thought.

The girl turned and let Donkin wrap the bathing cloak
about her without a word. I caught sight of her as she
turned, and the vision of her is with me still. I've wondered since if there ever was a more perfect figure, or if
anyone else could be so slim, with such tiny round breasts
no larger than apples. I can still see the dimples in her
arms at the elbow and the drips of water diamonding the
rosy skin as she lifted up her arms to take the cloak which
Donkin was holding.

The next moment she had vanished down the companion. I stepped forward. Donkin and Crawford were
standing close together still staring after the girl. As she
disappeared they turned and perhaps by accident jostled
each other: in a flash their jealous hate flamed. Before one
could think Donkin was holding Crawford by the throat
while Crawford was striking him in the face savagely. The
next moment Winterstein had thrust them apart.

"Are you mad?" he said to Donkin in repressed low
voice. "I'm ashamed of you," he added, turning to Crawford and speaking more naturally. Donkin glowered sullenly while Crawford muttered something and went forward. As I followed him Lincoln's black face went down
the fore-hatchway and Dyer turned to take up his watch
again; but not before I had noticed a certain antagonism on

every face; they all reminded me of a set of dogs on the point of fighting—all rigid, with bared fangs and hating eyes.

The rest of the day passed in a sort of stupor, Rose was on deck nearly the whole time, Winterstein always in attendance. Daisy and I walked the deck a good while together; I got her to say she liked me, but when I pressed her to say how much, she only laughed and changed the subject. She had a long talk with Donkin and another talk with Crawford; she even managed to smile at Dyer and transport him into the seventh heaven of delight. For the time I began to realize her insatiate vanity; she wanted all the men to admire her. I raged against her in my heart, raged the more because I was in the toils. I would have given ten years of my life to have been able to have taken that slight figure in my arms, to have crushed those little breasts against mine and kissed the flower of her mouth.

But of all this she seemed unconscious, she was simply herself, quiet, aloof, and inscrutable till late in the afternoon, when a little breeze sprang up, a land breeze which gave the light schooner three or four knots an hour—good steering way. Then she had the lines up and fished from the poop. Donkin and myself waited on her, while Winterstein walked up and down beside his wife from the poop to the companion and from the companion to the poop in silence. Dyer steered and Abraham Lincoln came grinning to us every now and then to bring fresh bait for Miss Daisy. . . .

The catastrophe came with startling suddenness. I see now that it must have come, that it was all prepared, inevitable. Yet the unexpectedness, the tragic completeness of it were overwhelming. It seems to have blotted out all that went before so that I do not know whether it was two or three days or half a dozen days later than the bathing or not. Anyhow we had lively breezes; the spar had to be taken in and the extemporized bath dismantled. We had called, I remember, at Mulege near Los Coyotes, and had had a good haul of pearls and a lot of hard work.

One afternoon we had been working hard and had had to row the boat for four or five miles over shallow water to a village where the inhabitants, we found, had collected pearls for years and years and had never before been visited. The bargaining was interminable. The fisherfolk had no standard of value. One man wanted a dollar for three or four fine pearls, another wanted fifty dollars for an insignificant bad specimen, and we were on the strain of all day bargaining and cajoling. I was tuckered out when I got into the boat and took the bow oar to Donkin's stroke while Winterstein sat in the stern sheets. I think Winterstein, too, must have been tired and exasperated, for he scarcely spoke all the way to the schooner.

When we got on board a six-knot breeze was blowing. After telling us to keep our course, Winterstein went below. I went down, too, and had a sleep: when I came up again I felt refreshed and vigorous.

The night was wonderfully beautiful. The moon rose like a crimson wafer through a thin heat mist, but soon shook herself clear of her trailing garments and walked the purple like a queen. I noticed for the first time that the moon's radiance lent the edges of the nearer clouds a brownish smoky rose tinge. As the night wore on the fleecy round clouds gathered closer together like silver shields hanging heavily against the blue vault; the moonlight grew fitful.

When I went down Daisy and Winterstein were both on deck. They were standing near each other just by the poop. When I came up after having had a cup of coffee and a biscuit they were still talking at intervals. She was sitting on the companion while he stood in front of her or moved away and then came back. I went forward to do something and when I returned they were still talking, which seemed strange to me, for they seldom exchanged more than a word or two. Every now and then she laughed, and the laugh was hard and clear: she was scornful I thought. They seemed so preoccupied that I was annoyed and would not join them. Abraham Lincoln at the tiller was almost out of earshot. I suppose I was jealous. I noticed that when the moon came out from the darkening clouds they were some distance apart, but as soon as the light was veiled they seemed close together again. I was furious, my pride prevented me going near them, yet I could not but stare toward them at intervals, jealously watchful. Suddenly while I was a little to windward, just in line with the helmsman, the moon came out, and I saw Winterstein take Daisy's head quickly in his hands and kiss her on the lips; my heart had stopped. The moon showed everything as if it were daylight. I took a quick step forward when just as suddenly I became aware that Rose had come out of the companion and had seen her husband kissing her sister.

For a moment she stood petrified. I heard a faint exclamation, or was it merely her breath caught in a gasp and strangled? She turned and moved across the deck with her hand across her face. She struck the low bulwark and there was a splash in the water. The next moment Winterstein had sprung to the side and plunged in after her. The second splash seemed only a couple of seconds after the first. I jumped to the helm only just in time; for the darky had let it slip from his hands and was staring round where Winterstein disappeared. I crammed the tiller hard down, shouting:

"Man overboard, man overboard."

The next moment Crawford sprang on deck. The little schooner was fluttering in the wind: she came about with a jerk just as Crawford and the darky dropped over the side into the dingy and began rowing back.

"What is it?" cried Donkin, running aft.

"Mrs. Winterstein fell overboard and Winterstein went

after her. How long shall we take to get back, do you think?"

"It is a quarter of a mile," he replied, while loosening a life buoy.

"Then we must pick them up?" I said.

"Of course," he answered. "I guess Winterstein's a good swimmer."

"First rate," I replied, but my heart was hurting with fear.

At this moment Daisy passed across my line of vision going to the bulwarks to look ahead. The moon was full out and the light quite strong again. I looked at her face and it seemed as if she were excited, expectant, resolute; no trace of horror, or fear. I gasped and suspicion came to me. Could it be that she had wished for it? Her sister—it was impossible.

Two minutes more and we were alongside the boat again. Crawford had everything ready as usual and had gone to the very spot, and as we came up the wind beside the boat I left the helm to the Negro and leaned over the bulwarks. I was just in time to see Winterstein come to the surface and haul himself up by the stern of the boat.

He stood there poised for a moment, and then hurled himself into the sea again as if he would go to the very bottom. My heart sank: he had not found her yet.

I called to Crawford to know if he had seen any trace of Rose.

"No sign," he replied, "and this is the skipper's fourth or fifth dive. I guess it's no good."

"I think you ought to come into the boat," he said a moment later, "and get Winterstein to come on board. He'll kill himself with his diving. I've never known a man keep down so long; he can't do it again."

I jumped into the boat, and a couple strokes took us to the spot where Winterstein had disappeared. We stared down on the dark surface, but there was not a sign or a sound. It seemed incredible that any man should be able to stay under so long.

Suddenly Crawford cried, "There he is," and gave a couple of strokes with his oar: slowly the body came to the surface. As we caught hold of him we saw that the blood was streaming from his nose and mouth and ears.

"He's killed himself," said Crawford, "I thought he would."

We got back to the schooner in a moment and lifted Winterstein on board.

As I was helping to carry him toward the companion with his head in my hands, Daisy caught hold of me:

"Dead?" she cried, her eyes wild in the frozen face.

"I don't think so," I replied, "he stayed under too long. We must get him downstairs and bring him to."

"Ah," she gasped, and let my arm go.

We carried Winterstein down to the cabin, turned him over and poured the water out of him. Afterwards I blew whisky up his nose and poured some down his throat, and in a few minutes he revived.

"Where is she?" he said, struggling to rise. "Have you got her?"

"It's no good, Skipper," cried Crawford, holding him down. "We did our best. You did all one man could. She must have gone straight down. There's not a sign of her."

"I must find her," he said, struggling up. But he was too weak, he fell back fainting.

I do not know how the hours passed. I felt dazed; but with an ache at my heart and a sort of vague dread; it was all incredible to me. I could not believe that Rose was dead, drowned, that I should never see her again, that charming woman with her appealing, passionate soul. It was too awful to realize. I thought I'd wake up and find it all a bad dream. Suddenly I noticed that my legs were cold. I put my hand down, my trousers were dripping wet from carrying Winterstein. The next moment I became conscious that I was dead tired, drunk tired, my eyes were closing of themselves. Instinctively I turned into the for'castle, stretching myself on the lockers and slept. . . .

When I awoke I did not know where I was: everything was strange to me. Then I remembered, and with the remembrance came the iron band about my chest constricting my heart. I got up and went on deck. No change there. The schooner was just drawing through the water, the sun shining; the light dancing on the wavelets; and air like wine. Dyer was at the helm. If only last night could have been blotted out. I could scarcely believe it was real. As I went aft, Crawford met me:

"How's Winterstein?" I asked.

"Sleeping now," he replied, "but he's been mighty bad. I never saw a man so done up—never. How did it happen? How did his wife go overboard? You saw it," and his eyes probed mine.

"She came out of the companion," I said, "the deck was on a bit of a slant . . . it all happened so quickly." I felt myself flushing. I was angry with my hesitation.

"But why did she? How did she sink like that?—it's mighty curious," he added suspiciously.

"Have you seen Miss Daisy?" I asked to change the current of his thought.

"Miss Daisy," he repeated, emphasizing the Miss, so that I noticed how strange it was for me to use the formal courtesy, "Miss Daisy ain't been up yet. The nigger thinks 'twas jealousy between the two sisters; but he saw nothing. You must have seen."

I had time to recover myself, and chose a better way of putting him off the scent:

"It's awful, awful"; I said, as if to myself. "I can't understand it." Crawford grunted, still suspicious.

But in spite of the tragedy, the suspicions, and the dark cloud of fear that hung over me as to what might happen next, the ordinary routine of life went on—luckily for all of us. A little after Abe called to me from the for'castle to come and have a cup of coffee. I found I was very hungry and after breakfast felt much better, more hopeful I mean, and fitter to meet whatever might occur.

Half an hour later, Crawford was at the helm steering. I was standing near the foremast when suddenly Daisy came out of the companion and spoke to Crawford in passing. He replied in a monosyllable, without the usual greeting, and then stared up at the mainsail as if there was nothing more to be said. The instinctive puritanism of the race spoke in his awkward rude rebuff. I saw the color flood her cheeks and then ebb away. I loathed the man; I could have beaten him for his insolence; yet I was glad he had insulted her: why? She deserved it all and more, I thought hotly—and yet—she walked up the slanting deck, her little figure thrown back proudly. I crossed the windward between the masts to cut her off: why? I don't know. I only know that passion was in me; she seemed so far away from us all with that level, unseeing, unwavering glance; the proud aloofness attracted me. I had never before understood the fascination of her personality, of her courage. When we met she stopped and her eyes held me.

"I know you never meant it, Daisy," I said tamely and held out both my hands to her.

"Are you sure?" she replied, her eyes searching hard. The words shocked me. I did not realize that having just been insulted, she was all mistrust and temper; if only I had said the right word; but her pride angered me and for the moment I took her question that may have only been doubt of me for an admission of guilt. Fool that I was.

"God," I exclaimed violently and stepped back. Her face hardened and she swept past me without another word or look, leaving me there confused, angry, wild, and back of all full of forgiveness—of admiration.

I could not but dread the first meeting with Winterstein. What would he say, how would he take it all? I had

not much time to let imagination wander. As I turned in
my walk, he was there. His appearance was shocking; it
wasn't only that he was white and seemed ill; his clothes
hung on him; he was shrunken and his eyes were bad to
look upon—despairing—sad at one moment, the next hot
in self-anger and exasperation.

I went to him at once, my heart full of pity. I saw he
was all broken.

"I'm glad you're up," I cried cordially; "the air'll do you
good."

He looked at me with such dumb misery in the glance
that my eyes pricked: he nodded his head once or twice
and then went over to the low poop and sat down.

A little later Dyer went to him and said breakfast was
ready. He shook his head merely and sat on gazing mood-
ily at the water.

The same thing happened at dinner time, but when
pressed to eat by Crawford he replied, " 'Twould choke
me. I'm all right."

The sweet old routine of life had done me good so I
thought it would do good to everyone and should be kept
up; accordingly I went to dinner in the cabin as usual. As
Daisy did not appear I knocked at the stateroom and asked
her to come. A minute or so later, she entered quietly, but
she hardly ate anything and spoke not at all. At supper it
was the same thing.

Winterstein sat on the poop till far into the night. When
Crawford came on watch, I took Winterstein below: he
said merely, "I shan't sleep," but threw himself on the
cabin sofa without undressing.

The next day passed in the same way, but before dinner
Crawford told me that he could not get Winterstein to take
anything.

"If he doesn't eat, he'll go crazy," he said. "He's just
eatin' himself."

I told this to Daisy. She looked at me with set face.

"I have no influence," she said slowly, as if speaking to herself, "no influence, but I'll try." Her face went rigid as she spoke. I nodded and went with her up the companion ladder. But Winterstein didn't yield at first to her asking; he shook his head, merely saying, "I can't."

"The soup will help you," she said, and then slowly, "Rose would wish you to take it!"

"O, God!" he cried starting up and stretching out his arms, as if he couldn't bear to hear the name—and then sank down again. She put the cup in his hands and he took it and drank, and then relapsed again into his moody brooding silence.

When she returned she went straight to her cabin and so another day went by.

The next day Winterstein took some soup I brought him. In the evening Crawford proposed to return at once to 'Frisco.

"I don't like his looks," he said; "he's worrying himself crazy and I guess the sooner we all get away from each other the better; perhaps we'll be able to forget the whole darned thing then and live again."

Donkin agreed with him, and so did I and the ship's course was altered.

Daisy got into the way of walking the deck with Donkin. He adored the very planks she trod on and perhaps that touched her. Anyway, she was with him now more than with any of us. It made me angry and scornful, kept my jealousy alive, prevented me from understanding her or forgiving—I always saw the two heads together and the fatal kiss.

In this puzzling world mistakes or blunders often have worse results than crimes. The momentary yielding to passion brought the tragedy and the first tragedy inevitably drew on another.

We had got into the Equatorial Current and were making fine time up the coast toward 'Frisco. The weather was just what sailors like: a fair wind perfectly steady day after day; bright skies, and blue seas with scarcely a white horse to be seen. We did not alter the set of the canvas for days together; there was nothing for us to do. Unfortunately nothing to take our minds off the tragedy, nothing to change the feeling of misery and apprehension. I never passed such miserable days: they seem like a nightmare to me still.

One morning I heard a row on deck and then what sounded like a shot. I threw a coat on and ran quickly up the companion. To my astonishment there was no one steering, the helm was lashed amidship. I heard a shout from overhead and saw Donkin and Crawford in the main rigging near the heel of the topmast. The next moment I noticed Winterstein seated on deck between the two masts. He was playing with a dead snapper making believe it was about to bite him, drawing his hand away quickly from the dead mouth with a cackle of amusement.

"Good God!" I wondered, "what's the matter?" As I went toward him it suddenly came to me: "He's mad," I said to myself. I was all broken up with pity.

The men in the rigging shouted, "Look out," just in time to put me on my guard: for Winterstein had a revolver beside him, and as soon as I came within his line of vision he took up the gun and leveled it at me crying:

"There's another of 'em," and fired without more ado.

I called out to him and backed away, but as he was preparing to fire again, I slid across the deck to the lee rigging and went up as fast as I could. Neither Donkin nor Crawford had anything new to tell me, except that Crawford had been slightly wounded by the first shot Winterstein had fired at him. It had just touched the right shoulder.

"It burns a bit," he said, "though it's not much more than skin deep."

The Negro and Dyer, it appeared, had both fled to the for'castle. We quickly resolved that the moment Winterstein went down below, one of us should seize him and the others tie him up.

"If I could only get him away from his gun," said Donkin, "I'd find out in five minutes whether he's as strong as he thinks himself."

"You'll find out how strong he is soon enough," I replied. "He's about the best man with his hands I ever saw. It will be all the three of us can do to get the better of him."

"I've never seen the man yet," said Donkin sturdily, "I was afraid of."

The trial came very soon. Of a sudden Winterstein stood up, threw the dogfish overboard and leaving his revolver on deck walked quickly aft, and disappeared down the companion. The next moment we slid down to the deck, Crawford arming himself with an iron belaying pin, a fearsome club at close quarters. I crept stealthily along the weather bulwarks to the companion and Donkin strode boldly down the deck. I think it must have been Donkin's heavy step that Winterstein heard; for just before I got to the companion he passed up it like a flash and stood facing him.

"Ho! Ho!" he cried, laughing, "Mr. Donkin wants some gruel, does he? Take it, take it then," and jumping in as lightly as a ballet dancer, he struck out right and left. His left caught Donkin in the face and the blood spurted as if the man had been hit with a hammer, the second blow caught him on the neck and hurled him down.

"Ho! Ho!" cried the madman again, dancing about so as to face Crawford.

"Crawford wants some, too."

Fortunately for Crawford, Donkin was a very strong man, and scarcely had he been knocked down when he picked himself up again. He was angry, too, and his anger did him no good. With his head down like a bull he rushed at the skipper. Winterstein sidestepped him to windward and as he passed caught him a left-handed shot under the ear with such force that Donkin seemed to touch nothing till he crashed into the lee bulwarks and lay there quiet enough. My chance had come: Winterstein was a yard from me. As he struck Donkin I threw my arms about his waist from behind, pinning his right arm to his side. At the same time with the instinct of the wrestler I lifted him from the deck so as to make him as helpless as possible. For a moment he struggled wildly, roaring like a bull; then in a second broke my grip and got his right hand free. But I still held him and as I was well behind him he could not get at me easily. But he was too strong. The next moment his right hand had caught my collar and shifted to my neck and ear, and I felt myself being dragged round. I knew that the struggle could only last a second or two, and just as I was expecting his blow I heard a thud; the writhing form in my arms grew still and heavy and slid down on the deck. Crawford had run across and struck Winterstein on the temple with the iron belaying pin. Almost at the same moment Dyer and Abraham Lincoln ran up on deck. We hauled Donkin up out of the lee scuppers and told Dyer to throw water over him. We then wiped Winterstein's bleeding head and carried him down below to his berth, where we tied his hands and feet. Just after we had laid him out, Daisy came out of her little stateroom. She looked at us and in a phrase or two Crawford flung the tragedy at her. She did not seem to notice the man. She came straight to Winterstein.

"Leave him to me"; she said imperiously, kneeling down beside him.

The second tragedy seemed to fall on numbed senses. I scarcely remember any sequence of time in what occurred afterwards. I knew it soon came on to blow, but whether it was that day or the next or later, I could not tell. I remembered that Winterstein appeared on deck again and sat in his old place on the poop gazing out over the sea. His madness seemed to have left him, but his brooding silence now was often broken by periods during which he moved about muttering to himself incessantly. Crawford said he was talking of his wife or to her. He was tragic, terrible—a figure of despair.

We had altered our course again and were steering nor'west. The nor'west wind had grown to a gale, while the current was running strong under our feet. Between the tide and the wind the sea grew into hillocks and hills and still it blew harder and harder. . . .

Long ago we had taken all the sails off her, leaving only a storm jib and a rag of tarpaulin in the mainmast rigging aft, and under these two handkerchiefs the schooner lay over so that her masts were near the water.

Late in the afternoon Crawford asked me to keep a sharp lookout.

" 'Frisco?" I asked, and he nodded.

I never was so glad of anything in my life, the band round my chest seemed to loosen.

The sun was going down in a sort of yellow glare. For over an hour or so Winterstein had been standing by the tarpaulin in the mainmast rigging staring over the waste of water. I clawed my way aft to him. The tarpaulin sheltered us from the fury of the wind and made an oasis of quiet in the uproar.

"We'll soon be in 'Frisco!" I cried.

He looked at me with unseeing hopeless eyes: my heart turned to water. Suddenly he caught me by the shoulder.

"I can't stand it," he said, as if confiding to me; but in a tone so low I could hardly hear him. "I can't stand it."

"Time will soften the pain," I said. The words rang false even to me.

"No, no," he shook his head. "It gets worse. If it had been an accident, I might have stood it: if some one else had done it, perhaps; but I did it, I: that's the thorn that festers and stings and burns, and gets worse not better, worse all the time. . . . I was glad to go mad: I wish I could go mad again and not think of it all the time." And he passed his hand over his forehead in weary wretchedness. . . .

"If I hadn't loved her so, I might sleep now and then and forget. I never cared for any other woman: she was perfect to me from the beginning. Hell," he broke off raging, "what sort of a fool was I—er? was there ever such a fool—a damned fool—damned. . . .

"I don't know why I did it: it just took me at the moment. Hell," and his eyes were wild. "I'm not fit to live: this world's no place for fools," and he laughed mirthlessly. . . .

"I can't stand it, I just can't stand it! Oh, my sweet: fancy hurting you! . . .

"Is there any other life, eh?" I could not answer—my heart ached for him. "I never took much stock in it; but I'll soon know. So long," and he turned into the force of the wind and strode aft. Even then I noticed that he could walk the deck in the gale that seemed to blow my breath down my throat and choke me.

I clawed my way forward again. Winterstein was beyond my help. I was glad of the gale and the wild seas and the danger, I didn't want to think. I was filled with fear and pain. . . .

The wind came harder and harder. The tremendous weight of it seemed to flatten the sea, and you could only put your head above the bulwarks if you held on with both hands.

All that night Crawford stuck to the helm and it needed all his seamanship to bring us through the storm.

At twelve o'clock we lifted the light and a little later we got a little under the shelter of the land and the sea was not so bad. But the bar gave us an awful half hour. The little schooner came out of the broken water with deck swept clean: the boat had gone and all the bulwarks, and *The Rose* was leaking in a dozen places: she would never go to sea again.

When we came to anchor off Meiggs's wharf about three o'clock, we had all had enough of it. In spite of the fear that the little schooner might founder under us and though I was freezing cold and wet, I went below and slept without turning in. I had not had a wink for two nights and had eaten nothing but a biscuit for thirty-six hours.

Crawford woke me, bright sunshine fell down the hatchway: as soon as I opened my eyes, I knew something was wrong.

"What is it?" I cried.

"Winterstein went overboard in the night," he said, "I don't know when, and the girl's been in faint after faint. Donkin's going to take her up to the house. I guess you had better get up, she may want to see you. But don't say anything harsh to her: she's had it bad enough."

I was on deck in five minutes in time to see Donkin bring Daisy out of the companion and take her across the ladder. He fairly lifted her into the boat, and as he turned to row her ashore I caught a glimpse of her face. It made me gasp: I never saw such a change, never. Her face had gone quite small like a little child's, and as white as if it had been made out of snow. . . .

I could not stop on board the schooner; I guess everybody left it as soon as he could. I came East the same week and never saw any of 'em again.

A pretty bad story, ain't it? A brute of a story. Just like life. No meaning in it: the punishment out of all proportion to the sin. Sometimes it's like that. Sometimes things a thousand times worse go unpunished and then for a little

mistake or slip, tragedy piles itself on tragedy. There ain't
no meaning in it, no sense. I don't believe there's any purpose either, anywhere it's just chance.

The Judge broke off.

The dreadful story had held us; now some of the men
stretched themselves, lit cigars, or took drinks, but no one
spoke for quite a while.

Suddenly Charlie Railton said:

"That Daisy was a wild piece; but I thought you were
going to tell us something about Mrs. Amory, Judge. I
thought perhaps you knew her."

"I knew a good deal about her," replied Barnett quietly,
"though I never met her. I was mixed up in her affairs
after her husband died. I was agent for the land she
bought for almshouses. I let her have it cheaper because of
the object."

"I ought to have met her a dozen times, but I never did,
strange to say. Of course I knew all about her for the last
two or three years. I knew she was a mighty good woman.
Her lawyer, Hutchins, whom I knew well, always said so,
said she was the best woman he ever saw, and one of the
kindest. Amory just worshiped her, I believe, and she
brought up his daughters by his first wife splendidly. She
had only one child of her own and it died. It nearly killed
her, Hutchins said. A mighty good woman, and I ought to
have met her a dozen times, but it never happened
so. . . .

"When she died Hutchins insisted that I should go to
the funeral. You know the house. I guess it's one of the
finest in the States. They laid her out in the music room.
It looks like a church with its high painted windows and
old tapestries and open timber roof: the paintings are all
masterpieces: three or four Rembrandts, I believe. Well,
they did the room up as a *chapelle ardente*—and laid her out
there in state, and all Philadelphia went to visit and a good
many of her girls cried over her. I went with Hutchins

and nothing would do but he would have me go right up to the coffin. The moment I looked at her, the moment I saw her face, the little face no bigger than your hand, all frozen white; I knew her. That was the face I had seen in the boat when Donkin rowed her ashore thirty years before, 'Jezebel's daughter,' I used to call her to myself. . . .

"I was just struck dumb, but I knew that was why I had never met her. She had not wanted to meet me. I was a bit surprised when two or three days later I had a letter from her. Hutchins had to read the will and in it he found a letter addressed to me. I have not got it by me, but I can tell you some of what was in it; she had no reason to be ashamed of it. I was wrong to judge her as I did at the time. Young people are mighty severe in their judgings. As you get older you get more tolerant. . . .

"With the letter there was a little box, and in the box a string of black pearls, the same I had given her sister. Mrs. Amory began by telling me that she had wanted to give them back to me, as soon as Donkin had told her they were mine, but all trace of me had been lost, and she had never heard of me again till long after her husband's death, when the end was near. She asked me to give the black pearls to my eldest daughter Kate, and she left me a string of white ones to give to my youngest daughter. She seemed to know all about us. . . . She told me I had always misjudged her and I guess I had. . . .

"Winterstein, it appeared, knew her first; used to meet her at the baths and swim with her and make up to her. She thought he was in love with her, and girl-like gave him her soul; made him her god. Just before she went back to school she brought him home and introduced him to her sister, thinking that through her sister she would keep in touch with him. She heard no more till her sister told her they were married. She said it drove her nearly crazy. . . .

"I guess Rose never knew that Daisy loved him, but it was a bad tangle. Daisy did not say that Rose knew, but she said Rose ought to have known—anybody would have known. I think she was wrong. She was judging Rose by herself; she was mighty quick and observant while Rose just lived like a flower. Besides, Rose would never have wanted her on board the schooner if she had even suspected the truth. No; Rose acted in all innocence. But Daisy couldn't see that; she was hurt too badly to judge fairly.

"She did not excuse herself in the letter. She confessed it was her wounded vanity led her to provoke Winterstein. But she had no notion of anything worse. 'I saw he admired me,' she said, 'and that pleased me. I was hard and reckless; I felt hurt and cheated: he was mine and I could have made a great man of him, I thought. Oh, I was horribly to blame; but he caught my head that night and kissed me against my will. I could not get away. If I had been standing up, his lips should never have touched me. You will believe me; won't you? and forgive me; now that I am dead?'

"I forgave her all right," the Judge said, "or rather I understood her and there was nothing to forgive. There's Angel and Devil in all of us, Charlie, and the Heaven and Hell, too, is of our own making, it seems to me. . . ."

AKBAR: "THE MIGHTIEST"

Iℕ ᴛʜᴇ ʜᴇᴀʀᴛ ᴏꜰ ᴀsɪᴀ, in the great Temple of Samarkand, are three tombs: one to Timour, the first of the Mughal Conquerors who overran Asia; one to Akbar, his descendant, who as a youth won India and established an empire; and one to Akbar's master and counsellor, Abulfazl. Akbar's tomb, erected by himself, is quite a small and insignificant one, and there the Conqueror rests quietly enough these three hundred years and more now at the feet of his teacher. The simple grandeur of the great sarcophagi, the humility of the invincible emperor quickened my curiosity, first awakened by the name given to him of "Akbar," which means the "Mightiest" or "Highest," and is generally used as an attribute of God. Was he really a great man? Who gave him the astounding title? How came it to stick to him? Why was he the only conqueror in recorded time whose empire endured for centuries after his death?

Samarkand, too, interested me. It is one of the oldest cities in the world: even the stones of the strong houses are eaten into by the centuries and colored with the patine of time, and its chief citizens are tanners now and goldsmiths as they were two thousand years before Christ, when it was called Marcanda. But again and again I left the bazaars and dark shops, with their silk praying-rugs that take a generation to weave, and barbaric jewels—sky-blue turquoises as large as filberts, carved amethysts as big as hens' eggs, and sapphires sold by the ounce—to return to the Temple.

One day, in an Armenian's den in the bazaar, I found a Crusader's sword, and a suit of chain armor that must have belonged to one of the knights who followed St. Louis to the Holy Land. The owner of the shop talked the Levantine jargon, which is based on modern Greek, and so I could make myself fairly understood. In his cautious way he took a polite interest in me, as a customer, and when I explained to him that I was interested in the cathedral, and especially in Akbar and his life, he told me he would send a compatriot of his to the caravanserai, a learned Sunni, who would give me all the information on the subject I could desire.

The next day I found a Sufi waiting for me, who looked the priestly part, whatever his practice may have been. He was of middle height, yet impressive by reason of impassivity. The slow quiet ways of the immemorial East seemed to have moulded his gentle, deferential manners. I have never seen so expressive a face that changed so little. It was of the purest Persian type: a narrow oval, the features almost perfectly regular, though the nose was slightly long and beaked, the eyes long, too, and dark brown, almost the black-brown of strong coffee; he might have been anywhere between thirty and forty-five. He introduced himself as having been sent to me by the merchant, and placed himself at my disposal. I told him that what I wanted to know was the story of Akbar—how he came to power, why he built himself a small tomb at the feet of his teacher. Was there any reason for his humility, any spiritual significance in it? Had he no woman in his life, but only a man-friend?—a host of questions.

The Sufi bowed and told me he would do his best to answer me: would I care to hear the popular story? I responded eagerly that was just what I most wanted. Then he was afraid his knowledge of Greek might be insufficient: would I mind if now and then he availed himself of a dictionary? And he pulled a little shabby, dog-eared booklet out of his pocket, which was issued in Leipzig, and contained words in Persian, Hindu and modern Greek.

I assured him I was chiefly curious about Akbar himself. Did the great fighter really become a sort of religious teacher and put forth a new religion? He assured me he would tell me everything as it had been told to him when a boy. I thanked him; that was what I desired.

"Everyone knows," he began, "that Akbar's real name was Jelàl-ed-Din Muhammad. He was born at Amarkot in 1542, when his father was fleeing to Persia from Delhi. In 1555, when the boy was thirteen years of age, his father died. Jelàl gave the control of his kingdom to Bairam Khan as regent, and occupied himself with games and physical exercises. Bairam Khan set to work to subdue the provinces that had revolted from Jelàl's father. He carried out his work with such relentless cruelty that his name became a byword from the banks of the Ganges to the Caspian. He brought peace, it was said, the white peace of death!

"Till he was about eighteen Jelàl gave himself to sports and poetry like other youths, and thought little about governing. He was the most enthusiastic polo player of his day, and one story told about him depicts his strength of body and impetuous intensity of character better than pages of description. He was surprised once by nightfall in the middle of a close game; he resolved to go on till he had gained the victory. Accordingly he had balls made of palás wood that burns a long time, and with these fiery balls he continued the game till his side had won.

"I always see Akbar, in my mind, galloping furiously in the dark after a ball of fire; that seems to me symbolic of the intense spirit of the young conqueror. When he was

sixteen or seventeen he began to listen to criticisms of
Bairam Khan. He even made some pertinent suggestions;
and the Minister-General, jealous of his power, looked out
a lovely girl for him and persuaded him to take her to
wife. With the cunning of the East Bairam Khan knew
that the best way to lead princes was with such silken
strings.

"A year or two later the king had his first real shock:
one evening he was poisoned and came near death—only
recovered, indeed, because he took violent emetics on his
own initiative before the doctor had time to come to his assistance. Who were the culprits? The king knew intui-
tively. There must be a conspiracy between two, he said:
between the chief cook, who alone prepared his food, and
his wife, who had cajoled him into eating it without waiting to have it tasted. He had the chief cook before him,
and in five minutes wrung the truth out of him and found
that his suspicions were correct. His dismissal of the
wretch was equivalent to a sentence of death. The culprit
was strangled before he left the antechamber. While that
was going on Jelàl strove to compose his spirit by writing a
sonnet, but he could hardly please himself even with the
first verse.

"He could not shirk the question: What was to be done
with the girl? At length Jelàl called her before him and
asked her simply why she had conspired with the cook.
What had he done to make her hate him?

"The girl shrugged her shoulders disdainfully and kept
silent.

" 'Do you love cooks better than kings?' asked the monarch at last; and the girl burst forth:

" 'We women love those who love us and care for us.
When did you ever care for anyone but yourself? You
think more of winning a chaugan game than of winning
love. A woman to you is a plaything. How can you expect
love when you never give it?'

"The king was shaken with surprise and doubt. After all, the girl was right enough and what she said was true. He had always treated her as an instrument of pleasure. Why should he expect gratitude and affection from her?

"What was he to do with her? . . . this woman he had loved and trusted?

"He was utterly at a loss till a thought struck him. In spite of his diabolic cruelty, or because of it, Bairam Khan had been successful in life. He had conquered provinces and subdued cities; he should know how to deal with a faithless woman. So Bairam Khan was summoned to the presence and asked by the king for his advice. The old warrior pronounced himself decisively.

" 'A great ruler should be beloved by his friends,' he said, 'and feared by all the rest of the world. The Emperor Jelàl is already beloved by all who know him. He must make himself feared so that whoever in the future dares to think of revolt shall have the cold of death in his nostrils. The girl should be hung up in public and sliced to death with a sharp tulwar. That is the most lingering and most painful death that can be inflicted on a woman. It might be so managed,' he concluded, 'by beginning with the hands and going on to the feet, that the agony would be prolonged for more than an hour. The emperor himself should preside at the ceremony.'

"The young monarch heard him attentively to the end and then:

" 'What would the pain of the woman profit me?' he asked sharply.

"Bairam Khan answered: 'The punishment of the wrongdoer is the protection of the powerful.'

"The young king stared at him. 'The powerful need no protection,' he said; and, after a pause, added in a loud, severe voice:

" 'You have taught me, Bairam Khan, that what men say about you and your cruelty is true. Hitherto I have lived for my pleasures and left the care of my kingdom to you. Now I'll take the rule into my own hands and allow you to make the Holy Pilgrimage.' (This was practically an order to Bairam Khan to make that pilgrimage to Mecca which ensures salvation.) And the young king, with that generosity which was always a marked trait in his character, added:

" 'A suitable jaghir out of the parganas of Hindustan shall be assigned for your maintenance and transmitted to you regularly.'

"Thus dismissed, Bairam Khan stood stock-still for a moment and then salaamed till his forehead rested on the floor before he rose and backed out of the hall.

"Jelàl then called the defiant girl before him again. 'You can keep the jewels,' he said, 'and all the other gifts my love bestowed upon you.' The girl glanced aside indifferently, as if she had not heard. 'I cannot punish where I have loved,' the king went on slowly, 'nor give you pain who have given me pleasure.'

"The girl looked at him still in suspicion, unconvinced.

" 'What are your gifts to me?' she snapped. 'I shall be killed before I leave the palace.'

"And the king answered: 'You shall go in peace, still keeping the name and honor of the king's chosen.'

"On hearing this the girl cried aloud: 'The king is indeed the king.' And, falling on her knees, bowed herself before him.

"And the king continued: 'One of these days I shall come to Agra and there build you a house, and you shall live in it and speak to me freely.'

"And the woman looked long at him, as if seeking to divine his meaning, and then turned and left the Court without a word and went to live in Agra. From her the king had learned many things only known to women. . . .

"When the rule was taken away from Bairam Khan he

rebelled, but was quickly broken in battle by the king, and then as quickly forgiven and sent on his way to Mecca. On the point of embarking he was stabbed in the back by one he had wronged, and died with all his sins unpardoned. Jelàl continued the promised jaghir to his children. . . .

"Ten years later the young king had overrun all India north of the Deccan and subdued it, spreading his fame the while from Delhi to the Dardanelles—indeed from end to end of the civilized world as the civilized world then was. Men began to wonder at him, and his constant successes awed them; some even passed from praise to adoration, calling him 'Akbar.' But he would not use the name: didn't deserve it, he said; his victories had all been easy. . . .

"It was after he had subdued Kashmir that the first severe trial of his life took place. The king of distant Khandesh had sent an embassy to him, congratulating him on his conquests, and, according to custom, the emperor sent him back a firman, thanking him and saying that he would take one of his daughters to wife as a pledge of enduring amity.

"The king replied that he felt himself greatly honored by the proposal, and with the letter dispatched his youngest daughter with a great retinue and many gifts. She turned out to be a beautiful girl, as those Northern women sometimes are, but very proud. The emperor, being only thirty-two at the time, fell to desire of her at the first meeting. Strange to say, she held aloof from him; would not go into the harem even as a queen, and was not to be won by prayers or promises.

"When the king in a moment of passion threatened to take her by force she plainly told him he could take her body perhaps, but her spirit and her heart were her own, and he would never gain them by violence.

"The king then tried to win her by gifts and kindness, by rich jewels and great shows staged in her honor—

shows in which hundreds of wild beasts fought for days, such shows as had never been seen before in the world. The girl was flattered and pleased in spite of herself. One combat in especial interested her. When she saw a pair of wild stallions fighting with superb pride and fierceness she cried out with delight and admiration, for the wild desert horses fought standing up on their hind legs, striking with their front feet and ever seeking with open mouth to seize the adversary by the crest and hurl him to the earth. This conflict pleased the girl much more than the deadlier, bloodier strugglings of tigers and bulls which the emperor staged for her amusement.

"But when it came to lovemaking she withdrew into herself and again and again denied the monarch, now passionately, now sullenly.

"One day the king threatened to send her back home, and she retorted that nothing would please her better; and when he questioned her further she confessed boldly that one of the young nobles about her father's Court had attracted her. It appeared that the courtship had not gone beyond glances, the girl admitting ruefully that her father would never allow her to marry a mere subject, as he believed himself to be directly descended from God. This new and unexpected difficulty enraged the emperor. He was at a loss, too, irritated by his own indecision and fear of taking a wrong step.

"Fortunately good counsel was at hand. An Arab, named Mubárak, whose ancestors had settled in Rajputana, was renowned for wisdom, and as his two sons grew to manhood they became famous as having inherited their father's genius. Shaik Faizi, the elder, was known everywhere as a doctor and poet. He had composed many books and won popularity by always attending the poor for nothing. His younger brother, Abulfazl, was an even greater man. When only fifteen years old his learning was the wonder of the district, and by twenty he had begun to teach in the mosques. The Persian proverb says that no tree grows very high which comes to maturity quickly. But Abulfazl was an exception to this rule. Jelàl induced him to abandon his intention of giving himself up wholly to a life of meditation at twenty-three, and took him into his own suite. Though eleven years older than Abulfazl, the king grew to respect him more and more, and their intimacy developed into a mutual understanding and affection. At his wits' end to know how to win his proud wife Jelàl turned to Abulfazl.

" 'In love and war,' he said, 'no one should ask for counsel. But in this absurd difficulty I'd like to know whether anyone can find a way where I see no sure outlet.'

"After some time for thought Abulfazl told him there were many ways and they all reached the goal—with time.

" 'I'm faint with desire,' cried the king; 'wild with impatience.'

" 'Is she wonderful in beauty, or in mind, or in character?' asked Abulfazl.

" 'In all!' exclaimed the king. 'She's without a peer in the world.'

"Abulfazl smiled. 'The madness of love speaks through you. Such desire is mere ignorance. Enjoy her once and the glamour will be gone.'

" 'But the joy will be mine,' cried the king, 'and the memory. The illusion of love and desire are the chiefest pleasures in life. Bare us of them and what would life be worth?'

" 'More than you would believe now,' said Abulfazl. 'But what is her real power over you?'

"The king thought in silence. 'Her courage,' he replied, 'and, to tell you the truth, her disdain of me and, of course, her loveliness.'

" 'It is a great opportunity,' said Abulfazl, 'to win the

great fight with one blow. The only course worthy of my lord is that he should conquer himself and subdue his passion.'

" 'Impossible!' cried the king. 'She is in my blood, in my brain, in my heart. If I don't win her I shall have lost the world.'

" 'So it seems to you now,' rejoined Abulfazl, smiling, 'and were you anyone else I would advise you to go into Persia, far away from her, and there give yourself up to other beauties and lose all memory even of this one woman; but my lord should take the high way. If you can conquer such a passion you can do anything. It is not the food that gives the pleasure, but the appetite. Restraint will increase your desire and any new girl will seem wonderful to you.'

" 'Do you know what you are advising?' asked the king, turning on him with hard eyes.

"Abulfazl nodded his head.

"With one movement Jelàl was on his feet.

" 'So be it,' he said quietly, after a pause. 'If you have made a mistake you shall be impaled. If by following your advice I lose my joy of life and my delight in living I shall see you die with pleasure; but if you are right, and by conquering myself I win content, you shall be master in my kingdom and I shall be second to you.'

" 'You would not be my master,' replied Abulfazl quietly, 'if you could thus punish your best friend.'

" 'I am my own best friend,' retorted the king gloomily; 'but love is surely a madness and there may be some wisdom in your counsel.'

"For a month the king went in and out and paid no attention to the girl or to Abulfazl. He then started off suddenly to Agra, and when he returned he sent for Abulfazl again:

" 'You were right in one thing,' he said, 'and wrong in another; fasting does sharpen appetite amazingly, but you were wrong when you said any dish would give pleasure. I want nothing but this one girl: no other can tempt me, and I am mad with longing for her.'

" 'I have thought, too, while my lord was absent,' said Abulfazl, 'it may be that the princess is indeed the king's complement and meant for him. In that case seek her out, get to know her soul and body, and give her time and occasion to know you. As you are greater than she is she will be drawn to you—that's the law; the greater draws the less; besides, she is already curious about you. She will love you. In this way you may both win love and make love your servant.'

"The king broke in:

" 'The woman at Agra told me to hide my desire and make the girl fear she had lost me. Women, she said, all want what they can't have or what is above them.'

" 'All men too,' said Abulfazl, meeting the king's eyes and smiling as he spoke, for he saw that the master was again at one with him; 'the woman's counsel is wise.'

"Jelàl then began what he always afterwards called his 'discipline.' It was a long struggle and only one or two incidents in it were decisive. Each day the princess was told to attend the king while he listened to complaints in the morning and gave judgments in the Great Hall. Now and again in difficult cases he would ask her advice, but he seldom took it, and soon the girl had to admit to herself that the monarch knew life and men better than she did. But just when she was getting impatient under cumulative evidence of her inferiority, the king with fine wit took care to praise her for some mental quality or grace of spirit she did not possess, and this appreciation pleased her greatly.

"In spite of his passion Jelàl pretended to take only a mild interest in her and showed himself always engrossed in affairs of State. Still the girl would sometimes smile to herself, as if she saw through his acting. But when she let her eyes rest on him or encouraged him by smile or word, and he would turn away to talk to some Minister, she would grow thoughtful, and the women of the harem said her temper was not so even as it used to be.

"As soon as the woman at Agra learned that the king had aroused the girl's interest and made her doubt her empire over him, she advised him to send for her lover and offer to marry them, and the king consented, for the counsel pleased him. He himself had noticed from time to time an uncertain humility in the girl's manner and in her eyes a sort of appeal. Others noticed that she had begun to drape her tall figure after the fashion of the women in the harem, and now swathed herself so closely that her shape could be seen through the soft stuffs just as if she had been coming from the bath.

"It was in this mood that the lover of her girlhood appeared to her. Half unconsciously she had idealized him and exaggerated his charm to herself, and now she saw that the attraction he had had for her had completely disappeared, and to her consternation she realized that he was much more concerned to win the emperor's favor than her love. He seemed to her paltry and immature; yet she could not bear to admit her mistake to the great king. What was to be done? She resolved to carry it through.

"In full Court the king came to her, leading the Khandesh noble: 'Here, lady,' he said, 'is one who loves you, and your father consents to your marriage.'

" 'Only if Akbar wishes it,' added the unfortunate youth, bowing low.

"As the girl flushed with anger at her suitor's obsequiousness, the king turned away and shortly afterwards left the palace.

"Next day the girl heard that he had gone again to Agra and the women of the harem assured her that he had gone back to his first wife, for men visited a woman for only one thing. It was noticed that the girl seldom spoke of her betrothed, and when the king returned she prayed him to see her.

"Schooled by Abulfazl the king replied that he would surely see her as soon as he had concluded some urgent business, and he kept her waiting nearly a week. By this time the girl had grown sick with fear lest she had lost the monarch's love. When she was admitted to his presence she could only cry:

" 'My lord, my lord.'

" 'What can I do to pleasure you?' asked the king. 'Will you be married to your compatriot at once?'

"The girl saw that his eyes were laughing and took it that he despised her.

" 'As the king does not want me,' she retorted proudly, 'I wish to be sent back to my father.'

" 'But you said you didn't want the king,' persisted the monarch, 'and you loved this young man. Why have you changed?'

" 'I was young,' she said, gulping down the lump in her throat, 'and knew no better.'

" 'And now?' asked the king.

" 'There is only one man in the world for me,' she said, 'and that is the king,' and she lifted her eyes to his and gave herself in the look.

"Though his heart thrilled with joy, the king kept his control: 'Go to the harem,' he said, 'and wait for me.' And she turned, glowing, and went like a child.

"In the harem the king found her another woman. After he had convinced her of his love she broke into praises of his looks and strength, and when he said that there were many handsomer and stronger men she wouldn't listen, but covered his mouth with her hand and declared that there was no one in the world like him, and that he was the most splendid man in the Court, though he was only a little taller than the average.

"Because she was very fair, with skin like ivory and eyes as blue as sapphires, she praised his black eyes and hair and his loud, deep voice, and even the small wart on the left side of his nose; he was her god, the 'Most High—Akbar,' she exclaimed, and she would never call him by any other name.

"But when he told her he would have to earn it first, and thus recalled to his ambitions made ready to leave her, he found another woman still.

" 'You shall not go!' she cried boldly; 'the cook's mistress at Agra calls, you shall not go!'

"And when he said that he went to Agra for counsel and not for love, for the woman was cunning and had taught him much, she wouldn't have it.

" 'You shall not see her,' she panted, 'not yet—not till you know me better—promise, not till I give you leave!'

"She was so passionate in her pleading that the king promised and caressed her, and then she burst into tears and said he might go if he liked, but it would break her heart and she was very unhappy and— Her tears set off her beauty better than her pleading or her pride, and her quick changes of mood charmed the king, who could not help showing his astonishment. He had thought her proud and reserved at first, he said, and at that she smiled deeply, saying love was a magician and fashioned a woman to her lord's desire.

" 'But you did not love me at first,' he said; 'it was only by feigning indifference and holding off that I won you.'

"At that she looked up at him from the divan, smiling. 'It was the wise Abulfazl, was it not, who gave Akbar that counsel?' And she said this though she knew in her heart the counsel came from the woman at Agra, but she would not keep her memory alive by making mention of her.

"The king was astonished by her intuition.

" 'How did you guess,' he asked, 'that I went to him for counsel?'

"She pouted and said carelessly: 'If I had not loved Akbar from the beginning, no holding off would have won me.'

" 'But if you loved me why did you plague me so at first by pretending coldness and aversion?'

" 'Because I loved,' she said. 'I saw that all things came to Akbar too easily and so I held away, though when he took me in his strong arms and kissed me in spite of my resistance I almost yielded.'

" 'Akbar blamed himself afterwards for forcing you,' said the monarch.

"Again, unexpectedly, she laughed aloud:

" 'You child!' she cried, 'you child! You would never have tasted my lips had I not let you; the resistance, like the coldness, was all feigned. There! I've given my secret away. We women are all traitors to ourselves.'

"In wonder the king exclaimed:

" 'I believe you know more about women than even the woman I have called "wise" at Agra!'

"The smile left her face and a change came over her: 'All women know women,' she said, 'but she is a vile creature, fit only for the bazaar.'

" 'Why do you say that?' asked the king, and the girl responded: 'If anyone killed my lover I would never forgive him, never. When he put his hands on me I should feel the blood sticking on them; hate would be in my heart for him, and I'd curse him by day and by night.'

" 'He was only a cook,' said Akbar.

"But the girl wouldn't have it.

" 'If I had stooped to my lover, still more would I have felt his loss: it is our sacrifices for you that endear you to us!'

"Suddenly the king turned on her, for he was curious:

" 'Why did you resolve all at once to yield to me?'

"She answered quietly:

" 'When Akbar brought that man here and offered me to him before the Court, my heart was as water lest I had lost my lord's love: I had enough of the struggle or'—and she took his head in her hands and kissed his mouth— 'I wanted you—' And she sighed in content.

"That first communion with his love showed the king that the instinct of his desire had been right and that he had an extraordinary mistress—as changeful as the sky in the monsoon and charming with all the gaiety and liveliness of girlhood; but he was soon to find that she was more.

"Almost from the first day she made up to Abulfazl, and not only won his admiration and affection but found out from him quickly sides of the king's character which she might otherwise have been years in discovering. From this counselor she learned that the deepest motive in the king was his ambition, and not ambition merely to conquer, or even to consolidate his empire, but to grow himself, to become wiser and better than any man on earth. Her lover was indeed a king of kings.

"She even found out from Abulfazl without his knowing it the true explanation of the kindness shown to the woman at Agra.

" 'The king doesn't keep her now for counsel,' he said, 'but to remind him of what he first learned by forgiving. He wishes now that he had forgiven the cook. I believe,' he added, 'that if the cook had lived the king would long ago have sent him to his love at Agra.'

"At that the girl gasped; for such magnanimity was beyond her. But she had learned the chief lesson, that Akbar, like all great and generous natures, was to be moved by an appeal to the highest much more easily than by tempting the animal in him or by urging his own self-interest. And with this key in her hands and her woman's intuition that everything is to be done with a man by praise, she became a real companion to her lord and an inspiring helpmate. She pleaded for the gentler virtues, and Akbar, having already begun to realize that a great man should have a good deal of the woman in him, was ready to listen to whatever was wise in what she said and to profit by the new insight."

And here the Sufi stopped, as if he had come to the end of the story; but I was too interested in Akbar to let him off so easily.

"You have told me half the tale," I began, "and have told it fairly well for a learned man; but you have left the more important part unexplained. I understand now why 'Akbar' honored Abulfazl and why men honored Akbar; but I don't see yet why Abulfazl wrote Akbar's deeds and words and showed such unfeigned admiration of his master."

"Jelàl was not called 'Akbar' for nothing," replied the Sufi: "he was the first Conqueror whose empire survived him, and it survived because it was built on sympathy and not on suspicion, on love and freedom and not on fear and hate."

"What do you mean exactly?" I asked.

"Previous conquerors," said the Sufi, "held down each province they subdued by a standing army. Akbar not only allowed each province to govern itself, but gave the peoples greater freedom than they had had before, while insisting on complete religious toleration. Personal ambition even found scope and security under his rule. That was why his empire lasted till the white traders conquered Hindustan two hundred years later."

And again the Sufi paused.

"You have yet to tell me," I persisted, "when and why he took the name of 'Akbar': was it pride or—?"

"The best Mussulmen," said the Sufi, "blame him for taking the divine attribute—'The Highest,' but if ever a man deserved it, he did. His mind was never at rest. When there were no more foes to conquer he invited to his Court Lamas from Tibet and Padres from Goa, and was the first to declare that Jesus was not only a great prophet, as Mohammed had said, but greater than Mohammed himself, the greatest of all. Jesus and Mohammed, he used often to say, were like stars in the heaven, and greater and brighter luminaries would yet come to throw radiance on the ways of men. He even went so far," and the Sufi whispered the words as if in dread of some eavesdropper, "as to assert that every man might be Mohammed and Jesus besides being himself, for he too had come from God as they had come."

"Interesting," I said; "and so Akbar lived as a god, 'happy ever after.' "

"No, no," cried the Sufi with Eastern wisdom; "happiness is not for wise or great men: Akbar was tried beyond the ordinary. His two favorite sons drank themselves to death, and the son who ultimately succeeded him in the empire revolted against him and got his friend Abulfazl murdered. That grief and disappointment changed all life for Akbar. What good was vengeance and what profit was there in anger when he knew by a sort of instinct that wild envy and jealousy had induced his son to kill a better man than himself.

"Akbar saw he might as well forgive his son, for nothing he could do would bring Abulfazl back to life or put light again in those kindly hazel eyes which were always warm with love for him.

"The murder of Abulfazl, who was too gentle to have any enemies, brought the nothingness of life very close to Akbar. From the afternoon when the sad news reached him he resolved to live as if every day were to be his last; that marked his conversion to the ideal life. . . .

"In maturity he had been gross of body, as strong men often are who carry the appetites of youth into middle age;

but after this Akbar became an ascetic and lived altogether on rice and fruit."

"Did he ever take the title of Akbar himself?" I interjected.

"It was given to him very early," explained the Sufi, "by many when he was only thirty; but he never took it himself till after Abulfazl's death. We can see how he came to it," the Sufi added, as if in apology, "for he was always frank and sincere as a child. His studies of various prophets had taught him that they were all alike in some qualities, and recognizing in himself in later life the same characteristics of gentleness and loving-kindness, he came to believe that he, too, was divine and sent by God as His vicegerent on earth, or khalifa."

"Very interesting," I could not help interjecting. "Did he then speak of himself as the khalifa?"

"He did," replied the Sufi solemnly, "and in this conviction he put forth a new creed, Din-i-Ilahi—'The Divine Faith'—which contained the best in a dozen religions, and so long as he lived it was adopted and practiced throughout the empire."

"You amaze me," I cried; "what was this new religion?"

"Akbar," replied the Sufi slowly, "took the ceremonies of it from the Parsees and the spirit from Jesus, and he built the Ibadat-Khana or palace-temple at Fatepur-Sikri for men of learning and genius; and there he gathered about him prophets from Persia and painters from Francia, and allotted pensions to writers and saints and men of talent of all kinds, and his fame spread abroad throughout the world. All over his empire he built roads and founded schools, for there was peace in his time, though men said he had 'forgotten how to punish.'. . ."

"But was his religion followed?" I asked. "Had he any real converts?"

"Myriads of disciples and hakim," replied the Sufi, "for in love of his wife he took Mohammed's heaven into his gospel and said that perfect happiness was only to be found in the love of women. . . ."

"What was his end?" I asked.

"Alas! alas!" exclaimed the Sufi, "it came all too soon. He worked too vehemently, always galloping in the dark after that flaming ball, so that he died worn out when he was only a little over sixty; but he had the consciousness of having lived a great life and left a noble example. Some of us still believe," added the Sufi, as if speaking to himself, "that he was indeed a son of God, the true Khalifa, and the faith he set forth was worthy of the name he gave it—'The Divine.'

"Toward the end of his life, though he always passed much of his time in the harem, it was for counsel chiefly, and there it was said that he was happy, for he would have no other companion but his wife, the king's daughter, though she was childless, and she was at his side when the darkness took him."

ST. PETER'S DIFFICULTY

ONE DAY PETER was greatly disturbed. He wanted to leave the Gate of Heaven and his duties there for a few minutes, so he called his brother Andrew to take his place.

Andrew was very willing to play guardian, but Peter was afraid to leave him in charge.

"Mind now," he cautioned him, "don't let anyone in who is not entitled to enter. Don't act on your own judgment. Ask the Recording Angel and go by his assurance only, and remember that those who have a right to get in will always get in, and a little delay will not harm them, for son of man or daughter of Eve was never too humble. Take care now and make no mistake."

Andrew assured Peter again and again that he would follow his directions to the letter, and at length Peter hastened away toward the Throne, his business brooking no delay.

On the way he met Jesus, and after some hesitation could not help unburdening his heart to Him:

"A dreadful thing has happened, Master," he began, "and I want you to believe that I am not to blame. I have been given charge of the gate and have never left it for a moment till now, and I pledge you my word I have never let a single person inside who has not a perfectly clean sheet. No one can be more grateful for all the privileges of Heaven than I am. You believe me, don't you?"

Jesus bowed His head with smiling eyes.

"I am sure, Peter, you have been an admirable guardian," He said, "but what is troubling you now?"

"The other day," began Peter, looking up at Him with sidelong intent eyes, "the other day I met a little blind girl whom I certainly never let into Heaven. Oh, Master, Master, someone is admitting them; I can do nothing and I shall be blamed for someone else's fault."

Jesus put His hand on Peter's shoulder: "We do not blame easily, do we, Peter? But who do you think is letting them in?"

"I cannot sleep or eat for thinking of it," replied Peter evasively; "please help me."

"How shall I help you?" asked Jesus.

"Come tonight at eleven o'clock when all is quiet and I will show you everything."

Jesus looked at him in some surprise, but answered simply: "I will be with you, Peter."

That night Peter took Jesus and guided Him by the hand all along the rampart to the first great bastion; then he whispered to him to wait in the shadow and he would see. And lo! a few minutes later they were aware of a woman's figure close to the battlements. They both saw her unwind her girdle and let it down over the wall; in a few moments a little hunchbacked creature climbed up, took one or two halting steps and then cast himself down on his face before the woman and began kissing the hem of her garment.

At once Jesus drew Peter away, and as they went toward the gate, out of earshot, He said: "My mother!"

"Yes, it is Mary," Peter began, "and what can I do? Those she lets in are all deformed like that wretched hunchback; she helps only the maimed and the halt and the blind, and some afflicted with bleeding, putrid sores—

dreadful creatures; they would shame even an earthly city. But what am I to do, Master?"

"Peter, Peter!" said Jesus, and the luminous great eyes dwelt on him, "you and I had not even deformity to plead for us—"

THE
EXTRA
EIGHT DAYS

Léon fornageot had lost his place as a notary's clerk; he had been proud of his position, and really dressed the part. He always wore a frock coat and a white tie; his short whiskers, too, cut English fashion, gave him, he thought, an air of dignity. But once out of work he fell to pieces very soon.

Madame Fornageot now dressed him and fed him, and did not forget to tell him so even when pouring out the glass of water for him, with which he had now to content himself. She was always reproaching him; in a crowd she did not hesitate to push him. He would turn on her: "Amelie! do not be brutal; I cannot be quicker than I am going; there is someone in front of me." "Yes," she would reply angrily, "there's always someone in front of you."

The rage of Madame Fornageot, with her spirit of economy, can be imagined when Grabiche, a cousin of her husband, presented himself one evening at seven o'clock and invited himself, if you please, to dinner. They had not met for twenty-five years. Young Grabiche then was fat and joyous, and used to sing songs in a café concert—naughty songs, disgusting songs, according to Madame Fornageot, "A pretty family yours!" she sighed afterwards to her husband.

But now here was a new Grabiche, a Grabiche of fifty-five years of age—fatter than ever, redder than ever, and under his right arm an immense paté and under his left a bottle. "We will have a jolly dinner," he cried. "Uncle Cyprien gave me your address."

Madame Fornageot smiled, because she had noticed that although the tweed suit of Grabiche showed marks of wear, still across his immense stomach there was a beautiful gold chain, and on one rather dirty finger a large diamond.

"Do you still sing at la Chaussée Clignancourt?" she asked.

"No!" cried Grabiche. "Oh no! It is the others now who sing for me."

He explained that he had seen how the directors employed singers and got the chief profits for themselves, so after ten years of economy he bought an establishment of his own, "Le Cri Cri," and baptized it "The Music-Hall des Rigolos" (those who mean to enjoy themselves). "Now, my children," he added joyously, "I gather in my thirty thousand francs a year without any trouble.

"The essential is never to have any trouble. My father and mother gave me a salt mouth: I do not drink because I like it, but I drink because I am always thirsty. I live well and save nothing. I am not married and have no children—indeed, Fornageot, you are my only heir, and if I kick the bucket before you I will always leave you enough to drink to my health. . . . Do not shake that bottle, man, that's good wine!"

After the dinner he took them to his music hall: a dreadful clientèle—men without collars and women without any hats. The director put his relatives into a box, and the young fellows in the audience in front of them kept making fun of them, especially of Madame Fornageot, who had put on some little curls.

"They like to amuse themselves," explained Grabiche. "They will not throw anything at you. I know them nearly all"; and suddenly noticing one of the guttersnipes who was making fun of Madame Fornageot's headdress, he cried:

"Look here, Calves-liver, you shut up or I will come and talk to you!"

In the entr'acte he took Léon Fornageot behind the scenes. They came immediately upon half-a-dozen women in every state of undress, three or four playing cards in a corner waiting for their turn.

Grabiche introduced them: "My English dancers: Rosa, Carmen, Bijou and Mélindie. Do not get up, my dears!— only a relation." Fornageot bowed gravely to Monsieur Ernest, a comic, and Mademoiselle Laura Ponestier, who seemed to be able to walk about on her hands as easily as on her feet. He bowed also to Chung-Li, a Chinese juggler, who had the accent of Montmartre, and to the Kreitzer family, newly imported from Vienna.

Grabiche ordered drinks, and as soon as they came, "This is the life that pleases me," he cried to Fornageot. "I change the entertainment every eight days, but whenever I find a little girl that I like, instead of sending her away I keep her a week longer—that is a little present I make to myself. She is like the manageress for a whole week, never more. Both my public and myself like change. At the end of a fortnight she must go: they can cry or groan, I pay no attention.

"That is why whenever I change the bill here they ask, 'Who is going to get a week longer?' "

"Grabiche!" Fornageot cried reproachfully. "Grabiche!" But Grabiche did not even notice the moral reproach.

When they came back they found Madame Fornageot very vexed, troubled too, a little. She kept looking at her husband to see the effect that had been produced upon him. But Léon had his old air of a head clerk who was impenetrable. All he said was: "I was never behind the scenes before; it is all excellently arranged. The lady artistes were playing cards." . . .

From this moment on, every Sunday Grabiche paid a visit to Fornageot. He always came provided with food and rich wine. Madame Fornageot was once able to recommend a sentimental song to him, and he always said afterwards she was born for the theatre because the sentimental song had a success.

One Sunday when Grabiche came Fornageot noticed that he was redder even than ordinary, and could not walk straight. Instead of wine, too, he had brought a bottle of old Cognac.

"I am not well," he said. "I need to be screwed up a peg or two. I am going to watch you folk dine, and I shall just be content with a glass or two of old Cognac in which I dip a crust; that is my remedy for all ailments."

"It would perhaps be better—" insinuated Léon Fornageot.

But Madame Fornageot cried: "Leave your cousin alone; he knows best what is good for him."

"You are right," cried Grabiche. "I am too well, my blood is too strong, that is the terrible part of it; but I'll pour out a little of this Cognac. I have a sort of vertigo—a noise, too, a rumbling in my ears. I'll have a glass of this Cognac and I shall be all right."

The Fornageots noticed that the first three glasses turned him to violet instead of red, but Madame Fornageot helped the soup and they began to eat. Suddenly Grabiche put out his right hand and closed it in the air.

"The bottle is by your side," cried Madame Fornageot. He tried to reply, but it ended in a sort of groan. His face became blue instead of violet, and he fell forward on the tablecloth.

"He is drunk!" cried Madame Fornageot.

He was dead. . . .

There were long formalities, but at the end of three or four months, thanks to M. Fornageot's training as a notary's clerk, the couple came into possession of the Music-Hall des Rigolos and of about five thousand four hundred francs in cash. The music hall was not easy to sell, but it was evident that with a little care it would bring in twenty or thirty thousand francs a year. It was a fortune for the Fornageots, and they did not hesitate to grasp it.

Madame Fornageot put herself before the cash-desk and engaged a strong man to turn out any riotous spectators, and Fornageot carried on the music hall.

Monsieur Fornageot's whiskers became more important than ever. He was always now in a frock coat and perfectly new white tie. And before long his temptation came. There was a little Italian dancer whom he pinched as she passed him and who smiled so sweetly at him that he made up his mind he would follow the example of Grabiche and give her—an extra week.

But he found it difficult to tell Madame Fornageot, for Madame Fornageot now had put on great airs. She constantly wore her jewelry. He noticed, too, that she rouged her cheeks a little, and that she always put on artificial curls. But the charm of the Italian dancer was invincible. M. Fornageot determined to speak plainly. So the same evening he went to the cash-desk where Madame Fornageot was arranging all the moneys:

"That little lace necklet suits you, my dear," he said; "I want to propose something—"

But Madame Fornageot interrupted him: "You know the tightrope dancer, he is very successful; he has made a hit, and as it is the custom here, when the proprietor is content with the performance, I am determined to give him an extra eight days."

M. Fornageot found nothing to say!

A MAD LOVE
The Strange Story
of a Musician

A little more and how much it is;
A little less and what worlds away.
                                    —BROWNING

THE SCENE, VIENNA; the time, October in the early eighteen nineties.

I had been studying at the University a couple of semes-
ters and had fallen in love with the gay good-humored
capital. In the Laudonstrasse I had two rooms and a
bathroom. I put an Oriental rug or two in my sitting room
and I had to laugh when the maidservant, the first time
she came into the room, took off her boots for fear of hurting the carpet. It was a symbol to me of the contrasts so
characteristic of Vienna between the primitive simplicity
of a peasant folk and the stately ceremonial of the Court
and extravagant luxuries of the nobility. The many-
colored cosmopolitan life drew me from my books; and
I'm afraid I was a poor student.

One day, seduced by the beauty of the afternoon, I
made up my mind to take a long walk. I went down the
Prater to the river. The great drive spread before me,
tempting me on, but I had started too late; the carriages
were all returning to the city at high speed; night was
drawing down and there was a premonition of rain in the
air.

I had walked perhaps a quarter of a mile beside the river
when my attention was drawn to a Schutzmann who had
gone over to wake a man on one of the benches. He stood

before the huddled-figure, speaking to it but getting no answer. I paused to see what he would do. He said something more, still no reply. Shrugging his shoulders he went off unconcernedly with the easygoing good nature of the Viennese. A glance showed me a man with a greyish beard sleeping heavily. Exchanging a smile of comprehension with the Schutzmann, I went on my way briskly, hoping still to get a walk before it rained.

An hour later a slight wind had arisen, and the leaves began to whirl down from the trees and a slow drizzle began. The gay scene of the afternoon, with the sparkling river and the stream of carriages and well-dressed people, had all vanished, and as I walked back the desolation of the autumn evening grew on me.

As I neared the town I thought of the wastrel on the bench, and when I got opposite him I was struck by the fact that he did not seem to have moved in the meantime; he was still huddled up in the corner, with his head on his left arm; I could just distinguish the tuft of his beard.

"He'll get wet," I thought to myself. "I had better wake him."

I went over and spoke to him, grasping his shoulder. No response; the sleep was too profound. A vague disquieture came over me. I touched his right hand, which was lying on his knee, and started back; it was cold. Could the man be dead? I pushed his leg and it moved with my hand; he was not dead, but sleeping the sleep of profound exhaustion.

I shook him vigorously, and after a moment or two he turned his head and looked at me.

"Wake up," I said, "you'll catch your death of cold here."

At first he did not answer. His face struck me. The eyes looking at me were not large, but young and unfriendly-keen, a light blue that went with his rufus hair and bronzed complexion. The beard was reddish-grey and unkempt, but at the first glance I noticed his beaked nose and strong, bony jaws: the face of a man of character, strong and well-balanced. A small moustache shadowed the mouth; the lips were well-cut, sensitive but not sensual. If this man had come to grief, I said to myself, it was not through fleshly lusts. What could be the cause?

He was not badly dressed. His hands were clean and cared for. Why did he not speak?

"It is too cold and wet to sleep here," I attacked again. "Wake up; you must feel cold already."

"What is that to you?" he said slowly. "Leave me alone!"

"I was afraid you'd catch cold," I stammered in surprise.

"And if I want to catch an everlasting cold, what's that to you?"

I was nonplussed—the man's language, the extraordinary resolution in the toneless voice—all staggered me.

"I happened to touch your hand," I said, "and found it cold, so I was afraid you'd get really ill sleeping here in the wet."

"Oh, be damned!" he barked. "I was happily unconscious till you called me back to life. What possessed you? Couldn't you leave me alone? I had left all the misery of living behind; now it's all to do over again. Go away."

"Will you, an educated man," I said, "allow yourself to die here of cold like a starved dog? Come, man, have another wrestle with fate."

He did not move, but simply looked at me. "I don't want another wrestle," he said, in the same slow, toneless voice. "I am more than halfway through. Leave me alone!"

"You are not halfway through," I exclaimed, feigning a laugh, "you'll probably get pneumonia and have a dreadful month in the hospital."

"I am cold all through already," he said. "I have not eaten for a week. Death is at my heart."

I was young and have more than a grain of obstinacy in me; I could not leave him to die.

"If I wanted to die," I exclaimed, "I would take the pleasantest way out."

He didn't even answer; his eyes closed as if weary!

I persisted. "I'd go out like an artist, warm and happy. I'd meet Death rose-crowned like a conqueror."

His eyes lightened, then his eyebrows went up and he made a motion with his hand as if to say: "Have it as you will."

A passing fiacre stopped at my lifted hand.

"Come," I said, "I have a few gulden to spare."

"You will have to carry me," he replied. "I'm stiff."

His immobility struck me. He had not moved all the time we had been talking. I put an arm round his waist and tried to lift him. The driver with the ready serviceability of the Viennese had hopped down from his box and now came across and helped me; with his aid we got the man in the fiacre and I gave the driver my address.

On the way, my strange companion said nothing; with shut eyes he leaned back in the cab. When we got to my lodgings, the Kutscher sprang off the box and came to the door.

"Can I help the gentleman?"

"I wish you would," I replied. "It is only two flights up."

In a few minutes we had got the man into my bedroom and put him in an easy chair.

"Go to the restaurant at the corner," I said to the driver, "and get me a bowl of hot soup, will you, and some hot water? I have brandy here and wine."

"Certainly, sir," he said, and hurried off immediately.

I got out some warm winter underthings and tried to get my friend's coat off, but found it very difficult. I went and got him a glass of brandy, but the moment he tried to swallow it he spluttered it all out.

"I'm sorry," he apologized. "It's like liquid fire."

I made it weaker with some water and gave it to him again and he got it down, but the real help came when the coachman returned with some hot soup and bread. I arranged it on a little table and the first spoonful brought life back to the half-starved man. Meanwhile the coachman busied himself taking off the man's boots and putting on a pair of thick socks I handed him, and after the soup had taken effect we managed to undress him and pack him away in the bed.

"You are all right now," said the coachman, rubbing his hands. "You'll be asleep in five minutes. I wish I had such 'tendance."

The hint was not lost on me. When paying him I gave him a glass of brandy, for which he thanked me by calling me "Herr Baron!" with the instinctive desire of the Viennese to please.

When he had gone I turned to the bed.

"I am not inclined to sleep," said my friend. "And you don't even know my name."

"There is time for all that," I replied.

"It wouldn't convey anything to you," he said, "for nobody knows me here; but my name is Hagedorn— Emanuel Hagedorn."

"A long sleep will do you good," I said. "If you let yourself go, you will soon be asleep. Tomorrow is another day."

I took his clothes and boots into my little sitting room and closed the door. The boots I found were well made; the clothes travel-stained, but good—they only needed brushing and pressing. Meanwhile I would have to arrange a bed for myself in the sitting room. I went down to see the landlady and soon got everything in order.

Suddenly I remembered that I had not eaten, so I went out and had a meal at the Ried Hof nearby, where I sometimes went when the weather was bad. When I came back my bed was made up on the sofa and a little wood fire was burning on the hearth.

I listened at the door but heard nothing in the bedroom save regular quiet breathing. Reassured, I went to sleep. In the morning I was up early, but I had scarcely moved across the floor when I heard sounds in the other room. At almost the same moment the maid knocked, bringing coffee and bread and Hagedorn's clothes. I called through the door, "Good morning!" and went on dressing.

Half an hour later there was a tap at my door and Hagedorn came in quietly—self-possessed. As I stood up he nodded to me and we were for a moment opposite each other. I caught my breath; he was so calm and completely master of himself, without a trace of humility; there was an air of assured strength about him that was imposing.

I pointed to the armchair near me and said: "Won't you sit down? Please throw off ceremony."

He took the chair at once.

"How do you feel now?" I asked.

"Perfectly well," he said, "without a trace of cold or even cough; I never felt better. Fasting must be good for one. My head is perfectly clear and I am fairly strong."

"You will be better after a good meal," I responded. "Where would you like to dine?"

"It is a matter of indifference to me," he said. "I am in your hands in more senses than one, though I must warn you again, sooner or later you will recognize that your help and kindness have been wasted. You see," he went on, "it was not a sudden resolve on my part, but a slowly ripening resolution that still holds, though I recognize the sense of what you said, that if one must kill oneself, one should choose the pleasantest way. Very practical, you English."

"I am not English," I broke in, "but Celt, and not very practical, I fear, but I feel that whoever wishes to swim can swim."

He laughed grimly. "Women float almost in spite of themselves," he said, "fat hips and small head; they are only pulled down by their clothes—vanity. The athlete or thinker, head and muscles, goes under unless he swims—fat floats."

"What age are you?" I broke in. The night before I thought he was fifty; now he looked much younger.

"Not thirty-four," he replied. "You are astonished. My beard turned grey in the last three or four months." He had shaved it off, I noticed. "It is hard to make up your mind to leave life—it costs blood!"

"I don't want even to hear the story yet," I said. "I want you to have a couple of days' rest and get quite well and strong."

"As you will," he replied, "but you are warned."

Two or three days passed, and as if by mutual consent we kept off the topic that was in both our minds. I did not go to the University, but instead took long walks with Hagedorn. It happened to be beautiful weather, almost like an American fall with its bright sunshine but softer, gentler skies, and the Viennese were gay and laughter-loving as only Viennese can be. Hagedorn did not talk much, and yet he impressed me as a man of real power. We went to the theatre almost every night. When I proposed the Opera he shook his head. "I call it the house of prostitution," he said; "hateful, for it should be a Temple."

"Is it the operatic form you dislike?" I questioned, "or music?"

"Music is only in its infancy," he remarked contemptuously, "and opera is a bastard form."

"What do you mean by infancy?" I asked.

He shrugged his shoulders and didn't answer for a moment, and then began.

"Did it never strike you that other arts, arts of seeing, like drawing and painting, are universal; whereas music, the art of hearing, is merely national, or, if you will, European? As soon as our artists saw Chinese paintings and Chinese sculpture they recognized their greatness; Chinese pottery, too, ranks above our own. Even Japanese color-prints revealed to us new decorative possibilities; painting is an art with a universal appeal. But music! Let a Chinaman listen to a Wagner opera or a Beethoven symphony and he just shrugs his shoulders; it's all to him a medley of unpleasant, or at best, meaningless noises. Go yourself to hear Japanese music and you will find nothing in it that appeals to you. Music as yet is in its infancy and I don't care to listen to the babbling."

This was not the first time the man had surprised me with new thoughts. As he sat there, turned sideways in indifference, his face, I thought, had the carved outlines and color of a Venetian bronze. Every hour he interested me more; he had taste in food and wine, I noticed, and the manners of a great gentleman; he was surely "someone," as the French say.

A few days later we went to an open-air restaurant outside the town, and after a good meal sat talking; or, rather, I talked about writing and writers, in doubt whether I should ever do anything worthwhile.

Suddenly Hagedorn broke out:

"Why put off the day of reckoning? I would not be better than I am, and you ought to know how hopeless this rescue work of yours is? I may even be able to do you some good, show you how foolish the whole struggle of life is, especially for the artist."

Full of curiosity, I acquiesced. "Let us walk back and talk it over," I said. And back we went to my rooms.

He took a cigar and I lit a cigarette, and we sat opposite each other for what I felt was going to be an interesting talk, for in this week or so of intimacy Hagedorn had made a profound impression on me; his casual remarks were often original, indeed curiously provocative and stimulating. He was a few years older than I, but he had the air of being much older, much more experienced. He had evidently drunk deep of life. I had barely sipped the cup; yet I resented a little the sort of authority that sat naturally upon him.

"I want to tell you the whole story," he began, "because you'll understand it. I am an artist and you are training yourself to be an artist in words. It is we artists who come to the worst grief, not because we are weak, as the Philistines imagine, but because our burden is intolerably heavy—heavy, I often think, in proportion to our gifts."

"What do you mean?" I exclaimed. "The burden should surely be light, if the gifts are great."

He shrugged his eyebrows in a way he had of indicating polite tolerance of my ignorance. "You will hear," he said. "There are to my mind two sorts of artists. The best artists are great men first and artists afterward. You may have noticed that I did not agree when you spoke of Beethoven and Wagner in the conventional way. These men are both great because they were great men, not because they're great musicians. Wagner would have been, in my opinion, an even greater writer than musician, if he had given himself to literature. His early libretti are finer than his music.

"Then you have an artist like Franz Hals, who is a born painter, or Watteau; his very colors please you like a child's smile; there is joy and beauty in the mere tints. Everyone can see that Watteau is infinitely more gifted as a painter than Rembrandt; Rembrandt carries it because he was the greater man."

"How are you so sure he was the greater man?" I asked. "Where do you find the shortcoming in Watteau?"

Hagedorn paused for a moment, then began. "Do you know his 'Embarquement pour Cythere' in the Louvre?"

I nodded, and he went on: "You have the advantage of me. I have only seen a print; but the motive is that couples in love are going to sail to the Isle of Venus. The first couples are away up on a hill in the right-hand corner of the canvas; then to the left of them other pairs, and finally down by the water's edge on the lower left side, the boat. But the procession should have started from the left-hand top corner and gone down to the right; our eyes, probably through reading, move more easily from left to right. Had Watteau thought over the matter he could not have made such a blunder in construction. The brain work in Rembrandt is far higher."

"Of course, of course!" I cried. "A fair illustration."

Hagedorn went on. "I often think a great painter should be able to paint a wonderful picture by merely putting different colors on a canvas without any representment of reality or likeness to the actual."

"Then you're a painter," I cried.

"No, no!" he said. "I am nothing. I was a musician with an extraordinary gift. Whether I had any greatness in me, you will be able to judge better than most; but I came to believe that I had.

"My father was a Kapellmeister in Salzburg; pure German, I believe. My mother was a singer who lost her voice with me, her first child. She must have been a Jewess, I think, but I never saw a pair that loved and lived in such unison as my father and mother. No one could have had a happier childhood than I. When I was six or seven they found out I had a wonderful ear, and they tried to keep me away from music. My father had a dread of precocity and infant prodigies. He always said that Mozart would have lived much longer and done much better work if he had not begun so early. He used to condemn our practice of starting racehorses at two years of age; he thought if we started them at five or six we should have better horses. And I dare say he was right. He had brains, my father, and my mother agreed with him in everything and always did what he wished.

"They sent me to school, and school was easy for me. I

had a quick, retentive memory and learned without trouble. I tell you all this not to praise myself, but to make you understand the tragedy. Then I got to know a shoemaker who lived near us who had a violin, and I used to go round and play with him. I don't know how I learned, but I did. One day my father, who had been first violin in the orchestra at the Opera, took out his violin and played for us—I forget what. I was about ten. I took the violin from him and began to play. You should have seen his surprise and my mother's pride, and my own gratified conceit. I shall never forget that day! But Fate hates the favorites of Fortune!

"After that they set me free. My father was delighted to teach me instrument after instrument, and I learned three or four, including the cello and the piano."

"Do you know four instruments?" I broke in.

"I can play any instrument," he said carelessly.

"Good God!" I exclaimed, "and you found it difficult to make a living?"

"No, no!" he cried. "I never said that. I've found it difficult to live, but I never had any difficulty in making a living. It's our dreams kill us. It is the heaven we see before us and cannot realize, or the Paradise we've been driven out of that makes life disgusting to us and kills us. We artists die of our dreams as of the plague."

"I do not understand," I said. "Go on, please."

"Let me come to the point at once," he said. "I am one of the few persons born with an ear for music; there are not three in a generation; I've never met another. You don't know why or how Bach arranged his *Wohltemperirte Klavier*, do you?"

I shook my head.

"It would take too long to explain; but the piano is still imperfect. Take C sharp and D flat. They both sound the same to you; but C sharp is twelve vibrations faster than D flat. I can hear them; anyone can hear the difference on the violin. The violin can give you the true note; the piano doesn't; that's why a great violinist is often out of pitch with an orchestra, and why the only good music is that of a string quartet."

"But you," I cried, "can you hear all that?"

"I have absolute pitch," he replied. "You do not know what that means. It means that between two notes that succeed each other you hear only an interval. I know myriads of tones between them. Our musical notation is all imperfect.

"Now, what does this imply? The painter is able to give you an idea of any living thing at once in three or four strokes. He can show you the difference between a woman's figure and a man's; between a cow and a buffalo; between a lion and a tiger. He can represent anything he sees: why can't the musician represent anything he hears? Why isn't he able to give you the songs of birds, the sound of the wind in the trees, the long withdrawn rustle of the tide ebbing on a beach? Because music is a half-art, and the sounds in Nature are infinitely too complex for our silly scales."

"But did not Wagner give us a storm at sea in *Der fliegende Holländer?* And what of the Waldvogel in *Siegfried?*" I asked.

Hagedorn laughed scornfully: "Talk to me of that storm; it's childish, and the Waldvogel! Why not ask a painter to paint the woodbeast? He'd ask you, 'Which one, squirrel or bear?' The woodbird is just as ridiculous. Wagner had to use a flute for his bird's note, simply because there is a sort of surface likeness between a blackbird's song and a flute, but the violin can give the tone much better if he had only known it. Don't let us talk of Wagner as a musician!

"Mascagni tried to give the nightingale in *Parisina;* the song went on for forty-five minutes and was intolerably bad; they had to cut out the bird. I gave that opera the name it's known by now in Italy, 'Opera a forbici—the opera with the scissors.' Do you remember *The Creation*, by Haydn, and the beasts in it? Isn't that imitation ridiculous?"

I nodded.

"But can you render the nightingale's songs?" I probed.

He bowed his head: "So that any nightingale near will answer me at once, even in broad daylight."

"Good God!" I cried in astonishment.

"I can give you the music of the wind in the trees, too," he went on, "or of the sea in storm or calm; I can imitate whatever I hear, exactly as a draughtsman-artist can reproduce any form or any scene at will."

"What a gift!" I cried again.

Hagedorn shrugged his shoulders. "That's the alphabet of my art; but the gift made me infinitely conceited, and was one cause of my undoing.

"My parents got so proud of me that they humored me in everything. I began to appear at concerts and to show off. My father did all he could to hold me back; he kept me on at school till I was about fourteen, but I would not hear of the University. I did not go through even the top classes in the gymnasium. Life tempted me terribly and lessons were intolerable to one who had tasted the heady wine of applause from great audiences. Girls sought me out like moths seek a light, and I was eager to meet them. I got into life too deeply, and drank too deep with that desperate, unquenchable thirst of youth. I took double mouthfuls, as the French say. . . .

"The only thing except making love and kissing I would practice was my violin, unless, of course, I was learning some new instrument; but that was part of my showing-off. I really had only to conquer the little technical difficulties peculiar to each instrument, and almost at once I was master of it. I knew its weaknesses and its powers by instinct, and soon got to the end of them. But a violin—if you get a good one—has hardly any limitations; its virtues are yours and its shortcomings yours—"

"I would give anything to hear you play," I exclaimed. "We must get a violin. But, I cannot afford a Stradivarius," I added lugubriously, "I am quite poor."

"A Stradivarius is not needed," he replied. "I can find a violin as good as any Strad here in Vienna in a week; the best things have few lovers."

"What would such a violin cost?" I asked.

"Oh! anywhere from fifty to two hundred kronen; it's a matter of chance; I may not find one in a month."

"I will let you have the money," I said. "I want to hear you play so much. But weren't you in request everywhere; weren't you tempted at every moment by big offers?"

"I was in Paris playing on my own hook," he replied, "with an apartment on the Grand Boulevard before I was seventeen. That same summer I played at the Albert Hall in London. I do not need to tell you what my *nom de théâtre* was. It's better forgotten. Gifts don't matter; it is by the soul alone we count."

"But how did you come to grief?" I asked. "You had everything: health, fine presence, extraordinary talent; eminence in an art while still a youth. What brought you to despair?"

"Looking back," he said, "it seems to me that a good many causes combined over several years; but I would prefer, if you are content, to let you find out for yourself. The forces are all there still; they are operating now as before, but I think you ought to be convinced first that I am not bragging or extolling my powers unduly. If you'll buy me a violin, you'll always get your money back for it, and a few days practice will make it easy for me to show you what I can do."

I gave him the money the same day, and for nearly a week afterwards scarcely saw him, except at an occasional meal; then he appeared with a violin.

"Fortune favored me," he said. "I've got an Amatis—as good an instrument as one could wish to have; luck has always been with me. Now if you are going regularly to your lectures, I will practice here every morning, and you may make any arrangements you like for hearing me play, say, on Tuesday week, and I will try to show you that you did not help a wastrel."

Having started as a journalist in the States, I had formed connections with some newspapers in Vienna and got to know a good many critics. Since meeting Hagedorn I had talked to two or three of my journalist friends about him, and now I told them of his extraordinary powers and got them all intensely interested. I issued invitations for the next Tuesday afternoon, and besought all the journalists I knew to bring any real critics with them. They all told me they would turn up, and one in particular, the best writer on a musical weekly, declared he would have a great surprise for us; he would bring one of the greatest artists in the world to hear my friend. I could not help going in and reading his cordial, kindly letter to Hagedorn, hoping it would excite him and nerve him to do his very best. He listened to me reading the letter and then said:

"I am glad for you, my friend; your probation won't be long."

"But don't you see!" I exclaimed. "If this great musician takes you up, swears you are extraordinary, anything, everything may come to pass."

He shook his head. "It is not a cancer spot you can cut out," he said, "or a sore to cure. But I shall be ready. You'll see. Only do not let them see me or meet me. Keep them in the other room."

I was a little surprised, but I arranged chairs in my sitting room so as to seat about twenty-five or thirty people.

When the great afternoon came I was intensely excited. The room was crowded—forty people instead of twenty-five, and all on tiptoe of expectance. Suddenly the musical critic entered, bringing with him Joachim.

"I don't need to introduce Joachim to you," he said, "the greatest violin player in the world."

Of course, I insisted on his taking the seat of honor, and I could not help sneaking into the back room to tell Hagedorn that Joachim had come to hear him. He smiled, but his eyes were sad, and I returned a little chilled. He had given me the outline of the program, and it ran something like this:

1. A young nightingale learning to sing.
2. A nightingale after he has found his love.
3. How he should sing.
4. A Comment on Life.

I announced the first three, and we all sat down to listen in strained attention. After a little pause the nightingale's notes began to fall like golden beads. At the first break in the voice—extraordinarily lifelike—I saw Joachim start, and from that moment I knew Hagedorn had conquered. There was a hush when he stopped playing, and after a moment, quiet applause—I had almost said reverent applause—silenced almost immediately by new notes that rang out in a song of desire and joy.

Words cannot describe such sounds; at least I have no words to describe them. I can be excused for not attempting a task beyond Shelley's powers. But as the music ceased, Joachim jumped to his feet and silenced the clapping: "No applause," he said, "let us hear the next; it is most astonishing."

A moment or two later the next song began—what the nightingale should sing. It went from panting desire to throbs of joy, and from joy to triumph, and then came broken wailing notes caught up now and then with faint reminders of the love-ecstasy. Then—abruptly—silence. Joachim started to his feet again.

"He is not only a great master of the violin," he said, "but a great, great musician. Who is he? Please let me meet him."

I stood between him and the door and told him that my friend did not want to be known. The surprise, the admiration of all was manifest. Everyone declared that the performance was wonderful, epoch-making. One after the other found new words with which to praise the unknown master.

Suddenly Hagedorn began to play again. I announced "A Comment on Life!" In absolute silence everyone began to listen.

What was he playing? It was all light and gay and hopeful, like a spring morning, the joy mounting rapidly to passion and delight; higher still to rapture, and then—idiot laughter tore the air! A phantasmagoria began of all sorts of emotions mixed together—joy and pleasure broken by dreadful, meaningless chucklings; moanings and imprecations shrilled to shrieks and ravings, only to die away in ghastly mutterings. We looked at each other; plainly the musician was depicting a madhouse. Exquisite moments of joy and sighs of pleasure, ending in howls of rage and ear-piercing screams—appalling! Then a heavy silence!

No one applauded. I looked up. Joachim was shaking his head.

"Dreadful! Dreadfully painful," he said. "Art must not give itself to pain. What a pity! A most remarkable mastery. What a pity!" and he hurried from the room. No wish to meet Hagedorn now. The men vanished as quickly as they had come. One alone remained. A young fellow I had scarcely noticed, a critic on a daily paper, since famous, then just beginning to be known.

"Great work!" he cried to me. "Let them all go. I have listened to the greatest violinist I ever expect to hear; greater than Joachim, greater than anyone; a great original master; I must meet him!"

"Come and dine tonight and I will see if I can bring him," I said.

"Tell him from me," said the young man, "that I am on my knees before him. He is a great, great man—astounding!"

When he had gone I hurried into the next room to see Hagedorn. He had laid his violin on the bed and was seated in the armchair.

"You heard," I said.

"Everything. Your Joachim was characteristic; true to type, as I knew he would be. The imitations pleased him; my mastery of the instrument even. He has some greatness in him; but the moment I showed him a little more than he was prepared for—revolt, resentment—'Art was not made,' if you please, 'to give itself to pain.' Instead of a madhouse I ought to have given them a Jew Jeweller's Heaven with golden streets and pearly gates—a childish vision of a tawdry Paradise. But, I hope you are satisfied, my friend?"

"More than satisfied," I replied. "Satisfied that everything you have told me about yourself and your art is true; that you are the greatest musician I have ever heard or expect to hear. I believe you are a great man, too, and I am infinitely sorry for you. You heard what young Neumann said. Do you expect, out of forty fools, to get more than two to see you as you are? I think this is the only city in the world in which you could find two enthusiastic admirers!"

He put his hands on my shoulders.

"You are a great boy," he said, "and if anybody could help me, you would; but it's too late, if, indeed, it were ever possible."

That night young Neumann came to dinner and Hagedorn allowed me to introduce him as the violinist. Neumann said everything I have said here, and said it at far

greater length and better, or at least more enthusiastically.
He admitted with gay laughter that if he had only heard
the madhouse thing he would not have come back for
more, but he declared that it seasoned the nightingale's
songs and formed the most perfect contrast to them.

"I want you to play me the thing in all music I love
best," he said to Hagedorn. "It's the song of—"

"Stop!" cried Hagedorn. "Don't say another word; don't
tell me what it is." And he went into the inner room and
began to play.

"He has guessed right," said Neumann, as the strains
floated through the room. And for a wonderful quarter of
an hour we listened to the love duet in the second act of
Tristan, marvelously rendered, perfectly, so that expectation was surpassed, desire sated.

When he came into the room again Neumann took his
hands, with tears in his eyes and said simply: "I cannot
thank you. Words are nothing."

"Let us go and dine," I said, and we went out together.
But during dinner we were all very silent. There did not
seem much to say, and when we returned to the house and
Neumann left us at the door, I could only say to Hagedorn: "It has been a great day for me, a great day."

He nodded and went into his bedroom without a word,
but I noticed now that his face had something sphinxlike
in it; it was as if carved in stone to endurance.

The next morning Neumann called, just as the coffee
came.

"I have been up all night," he said, "utterly unable to
sleep. I could scarcely wait till it was eight o'clock so that I
might come round and say that I put myself at your service. Whatever I can do in Vienna I will do. You ought to
have been known ten years ago from one end of the world
to the other. Give me the chance of telling Vienna who
you are and of showing them what you can do."

Hagedorn smiled. "It is really kind of you," he said. "Talk it over with my friend here and decide whatever you please."

"We must give a series of concerts," cried Neumann in wild excitement; "subscription concerts, half a dozen or a dozen, in a large hall, but not too large. I know the very place. We will put the price high and every seat will be filled, and after the first concert every ticket will be worth fifty times its weight in gold. I know Vienna. It is not deaf to genius. I feel sure of a triumph."

"Not a dozen concerts," interrupted Hagedorn. "Say three, if you like."

"I want a crescendo effect," argued Neumann. "Please give me six concerts and write the programs. I am sure you can do anything you want to. Pick the musicians you care to honor and give their little-known pieces. Only play one or two of your own things in each concert. Match yourself with the greatest. I tell you, man, it will be a triumph!"

It was good to hear him. That was what I felt, too. Surely, surely it was possible to save such an extraordinary genius.

We soon found that our task was going to be an easy one. Neumann got the hall and Hagedorn gave me the programs for three concerts. He had headed them: "Old Masters; Modern Masters; The Future." Neumann begged for more, but he shook his head.

"I want to repay my friend here," he said. "That's all."

Neumann declared that with six concerts we would make fifty thousand kronen—a sum far beyond our hopes or wishes—but he begged so hard that at length Hagedorn consented. I did not interfere with a word. I had already grown doubtful of my right to interfere: *The heart knoweth its own bitterness.*

Finally they settled on four concerts. I could scarcely wait for the first one. At Neumann's request Hagedorn had made the programs very long. He began by playing some well-known things from Bach, and insisted on playing them on the instrument for which they were intended—the harpsichord. In his hands the little tinkling instrument became a wonder, and for the first time in my life a fugue of Bach showed itself as an exquisite thing, a jewel as beautiful as a sonnet of Wordsworth—divine music, impeccably perfect.

Then he played Beethoven's *Sonata* in B flat: we all had heard it again and again. I had never realized it was so wonderful. Then Mozart: grace and sweetness and joy incarnate.

And then Wagner; the famous passage in the *Meistersinger* that is, after all, the great egotist's own trial and supreme triumph.

They were all rendered as I have never heard them rendered before or since, and the audience was enthusiastic as only a Viennese audience can be. For ten minutes the whole program was interrupted while men stood on their chairs and women clustered together like a flock of doves in front of the platform applauding, laughing, chattering, crying. Really, they seemed to know how great a man he was.

When the women began to crowd into the aisle Hagedorn left the stage. He had insisted upon not even giving his name; the concert was given by "a musician." Only Neumann and I were on the stage, and I went out with Hagedorn.

When the tumult subsided he came in again and began to play on the violin. First a fugue almost like Bach's, but better. Then he gave us imitations of all the masters, more beautiful than the originals. Then a pause, and he began a lark's song. Just a lark's song some summer morning on a sun-bathed down or upland. What a song! The soul of joy was in it; it was simply irresistible. When he had finished and had bowed and walked off the stage, the audience went mad. In two minutes they had crowded on to the stage. They must see him and speak to him. But when I went out to get him I found he had left the theatre. I went back and told the people that it was impossible to find him. The afternoon papers told us that the price of the remaining seats for the next three concerts had trebled. Neumann was more than delighted.

"Let me see him," he cried.

"Go and find him," I said. "You may have more influence with him than I have. I want him encouraged."

"Encouraged!" exclaimed Neumann. "He must need a lot of encouragement if such appreciation is not enough for him," and away he went.

When I got home I found Hagedorn had not yet returned. He came in about half-past six quietly, and we went out to dinner. I had never known him more depressed.

"All this enthusiasm has made no difference to you?" I asked.

He shook his head, and his eyebrows went up.

"The price of the seats has trebled," I went on.

He shrugged his shoulders.

"But why, why are you so hopeless?" I cried. "Neumann says he has never seen such enthusiasm. The director of the Opera House has written to him, asking for your name and address. It seems his wife and daughter were in the audience and are wild with admiration."

Hagedorn shook his head. "I've had it all before," he said, "ten years and more ago. Praise does not satisfy the heart, my friend. Life to me is like an obscene monkey's cage: I could give you the gibberings and scratchings, the rages and sensualities; but what good would it all do? . . .

"When I was able to take life seriously, able to hope and enjoy, I failed; the audiences never wanted the best in me, never; but the imitations and childish things. I went on, in spite of the growing conviction that I was born out of due time. Five hundred years hence someone will come who will do my work, and find perhaps half a dozen who know him and want him; today it is too soon, and I have no wish to encourage or help men; I'm sick of them and their sordid squalor and soulless stupidity.

"Life tests all of us to breaking point," he went on, after a long silence. "I know now that the road I trod is the upward road and has been traveled by all who grow. The higher we climb in this world's esteem the heavier our fall. You remember the text in the Bible, *'Those whom He loveth He chasteneth.'* It is so true, that; divinely true. Those whom He loveth He chasteneth, continually, perpetually, without letup, to the very limit of their endurance. To those whom He hates He gives everything, lavishly and then the fall is—fatal. 'Twas here in Vienna I met my Fate: you may as well hear the whole story now though it's not worth the telling. . . .

I used to send my mother newspaper clippings of my triumphs, and for one reason or another, she was always calling me back to her, always wanting me near her. Her mother's heart was full of apprehension; perfect love is one with fear. Well, I came back to her more than once to rest and recruit. But I no longer shared their religious belief (my mother had long before accepted my father's Lutheranism, and that made a coolness). Besides, the hope of the ideal always tempted me away again, and a year or so later I would return again to see her and to brag.

When I was about twenty-two or three I stayed away some years—a foolish, light love affair in Paris that ripened me—but again I returned just before I was twenty-six with two hundred thousand gulden in the bank. I was rich: I loved horses and drove them in the Prater where you found me! drove them tandem, drove four-in-hand, and generally had a pretty girl beside me on the box seat.

When I went to the Opera I used to go behind the scenes and

brag to my heart's content. With that charming humor of the
Viennese they would push me on the stage to play something in
the middle of an Opera. No one could have been more favored
than I: and then without warning—my Fate.

One evening I was at a loose end. I did not know what to do
with myself or where to go. I had just got rid of a girl who was
plaguing me with her love which I had tired of; it was too
complete, had no limit, no sparkle; nothing bores like meek adoration.

I had been dining at a restaurant in the Ringstrasse when a
couple of men came up to me, one a journalist named Goldescu,
and the other a musical critic on some paper, I forget his name.
They were wild to take me to see a dancer—"as great a dancer,"
Goldescu said, "as you are a musician. She will be on tonight
for half an hour."

I had nothing to do and nothing better to propose, so I went
with them. It was a little restaurant in the Roumanian quarter—
a cellar in fact, long, low and no doubt dark in the daytime. We
went down a dozen steps to it. A crowd of common people sat
about drinking the sour Roumanian wine, Dragasan. The first
phrase I heard was "*Datche me vin*,"—almost pure Latin. Rou-
mania was a Roman colony under Trajan.

The proprietor played the Roumanian national instrument,
the Kobza, a sort of cross between the guitar and mandolin, and
as I got accustomed to the smoke I saw that there was a low
stage at the far end of the room. It might have been six or eight
feet deep and perhaps a foot high, with a green baize curtain in
front of it. No pretense of footlights except two gas jets in the
corners and one in the middle.

I could not drink the common wine but the proprietor began
to treat us with a good deal of politeness and soon brought me a
Tokai which was excellent—one of the great wines of the world.

My friends talked. Goldescu was a clever fellow and interested me perhaps because he was of a different race, and too
cynical even to believe in virtue, much less seek it.

After trying to eat one of their strange salads I asked when the
show was going to begin and the proprietor told me he would
bring Marie on as soon as he could, but she did not usually appear till eleven o'clock. There was a comic singer who bored me

to extinction and then the proprietor came out beaming: "She has come and will appear immediately."

I drew my chair clear of the table so as to have an uninterrupted view down the middle of the room. The curtains were drawn aside and we saw a girlish figure on the stage; Goldescu had said something about her being a Jewess; but she was not of the Jewish type, I thought. Her nose was small and straight; true, her eyes were large and dark and her hair black; but her lips, too, were refined and pretty; and with a certain sense of color contrast she had thrown yellow veils about her. She was just pretty, I concluded; very pretty even, but nothing more. I had seen more beautiful women but—there was something provocative-intense about her, besides a dainty aloofness and self-possession.

The music began—a sort of slow, vague theme, and Marie began to dance; at first very slowly, gracefully, and as she danced she discarded veil after veil. The music took on character. I began to see that it was a sort of representation of love, such a theme as you might witness any evening at the Opera, only there was no pirouetting here, or fast little runs and poisings on a toe; nothing acrobatic; simply at first lithe swayings, hesitations and refusals—reserve apparent always and a sort of fugitive grace; then the yielding little by little, the figure growing clearer as the veils went, till she stood outlined before us, and reached complete abandonment by sinking down and backward on the stage with outstretched arms while the curtains drew together shutting her off.

It was charming, graceful, clothed with beauty and the modesty of art. The applause was tremendous; they called for the dance again and again, but no one came. We called too, and applauded loudly, insistently; at length the proprietor went behind the scenes but came back disconsolate. Marie refused to do anything more or to come out. She would bow to the audience when she was dressed and that was all.

I don't know how it was, but the simplicity of her methods grew upon me. She was a real artist; her form more perfect even than her face. For some reason or other, in my Übermut (I was very arrogant) I thought I would bring her out, so I went over and took a violin from one of the musicians. The proprietor divining my intention, drew the curtains aside and I stepped on the stage and began to play. I first played some imitations of birds and then a love improvisation giving the spirit of her dancing. I had never played better. Still she did not appear. I put down the instrument and went off with my friends, content never to see the place again or the little Roumanian girl.

The days passed into weeks; it annoyed me to realize that I could not forget the dancer or blot her from memory. Often I asked myself: what was the secret of her influence; why did she live with me when more beautiful women were quickly forgotten? I could never find an answer. Time and again I was on the point of asking Goldescu to bring about a meeting and introduce me; but I disliked the cynical effrontery of the fellow and hated even to think of him in connection with Marie's reserved beauty and charm.

One day I met him walking with a girl. I saw the grace of her before I recognized who it was, and from some way off I noticed how people turned to look at her. When Goldescu introduced us she exclaimed:

"I hope you don't mind my disappearing the other evening. If you had stopped after your imitation of the lark I would have come out to meet you. I wanted to tell you how wonderful that bird's song was; but you rendered the very soul of my dancing with your music and that broke me all up. I could not come out in that *bouge* with red eyes."

"Very human, these artists," cried Goldescu in a comic voice, and we both had to smile.

"He's an artist," she said, "but I'm only a half-artist, an executant, my body's my instrument; it happens to be a good one, but if it were a poor one, I could do nothing; whereas he doesn't depend on the instrument at all; his art is in his soul."

"Charming of you," I protested, "but unjust to yourself. You rendered love delightfully. 'Twas like the Cherubino of Mozart; a quality of youth in it, of freshness and a hint of mature passion as well—an entrancing mixture."

She flushed slightly. "You don't know how good it is to be praised by you," she said simply, giving me her eyes. "If I could be deceived about myself your praise would do it, but—but—"

"What does the 'but' mean?" I asked. She pouted. "We

women always want perfection; don't praise me then. I am curious about you. You carry one's soul away by your playing, but who are you, *you?* You seem too young to have climbed the heights."

"Age is not a matter of years," I replied. "I'm as old as Time."

"A great phrase," she cried delightedly, "and true; oh, if only—"

"If you two want to make love," Goldescu interrupted, "why select the street?"

She shrank at that; so I raised my hat and said: "Please let me know where you dance next and I'll come."

I went; her eyes told me she understood that I could not bear our feeling to be cheapened by the Jew's appraisement.

"I've tried to give you a true impression of that first meeting," said Hagedorn, "but I've failed. It was all very simple and I've made it sound high-falutin'. I'm not an artist in words, you see. But to me she was a revelation, a miracle of frankness, sympathy—charm—

Ten minutes after I left her I could not help wondering why she went about with that Jew; what was the attraction, the connection? Fishy, it seemed to me; for I knew him, knew that no good thing could live in his atmosphere. I ought to tell you about him but I can't. I'm conscious I'm not fair to him; no human being could be as vile, sordid, soulless, unscrupulous, cruel and vain as I knew him to be. I've heard him boast of things an assassin would be ashamed of. Yet he was big and handsome in a common style, a good writer, a good actor, too, and always carried himself with an assured mastery in life. He always held the floor wherever he was. I remember his saying once he could always borrow money from the worldly-wise by saying: "Give me a hundred gulden; I don't promise ever to pay you back. You should be willing to pay for my society"; and from greenhorns by insisting it was a loan to be returned next day. The funny part of it was, he said, that a second loan was always easier to get than the first; humans hated to confess even to themselves that they had been fooled. And he believed as little in woman's virtue as in man's generosity.

"Their refusals," he used to say, "are all either coldness or calculation. Choose the right moment and—"

"And your mother?" someone retorted one evening.

"My race tells you," he responded.

A common nature and mind sharpened by life.

When we walked together a dozen girls gave him the glad eye for one who noticed me. Don't think I was envious of his gifts or looks; I never was envious in my life. But though he sought me out I had avoided him always till I found him with Marie.

Two or three days after that meeting on the street he sent me a wire to say he'd call for me at seven to take me to a new dance. I was ready and went with him.

"You lucky dog," he began. "She's always talking about you and your playing; it'll be your own fault if you don't win her, and she's a seductive little devil. I shouldn't be surprised if it was her first 'affair.' Fancy a professional dancer a virgin—everything's possible in this mad world! And she certainly has what the French call 'the devil in her body.' "

I could not discuss her with him. The thought of seeing her quickened my blood and with beating heart and glad eyes I went to my fate.

Yet all the preliminaries were hateful to me. When we reached the Concert Hall, the performance had begun, so Goldescu took me round to the stage door and went to her dressing room as if it had been his own.

"You know the way?" I asked in surprise.

"I should think so," he replied characteristically. "I've paid to learn it in every theatre in Vienna."

I could have struck the dog in the face.

At his knock she opened—"Come in"—and in we went though she was not half dressed.

"The days have seemed long," she said turning at once to me. "I have thought about you a great deal."

I, too, had thought about her; in fact I had hardly thought of anything else.

The stage bell sounded.

"I must get ready," she said, "forgive me! You'll come back?"

"I shall be delighted! After the show?" I asked.

"After my dance," she corrected, smiling. "I'll only need ten minutes to get rid of the greasepaint and change. I'll grudge the minutes."

She had voiced my very thought. "So shall I," I replied like an echo, and we went to our press seats in the front row.

Marie's dance was announced as "A Joy Dance," and she appeared all in rose; but the skirt was short and the stuff was so thin and soft that it clung and drew attention to the beauties of her figure in the most provocative way. My mouth parched while looking at her: I could scarcely draw breath and heavy pulses hammered in my temples. I was filled with a blind rage of jealousy; all these men seeing her nudity seemed an outrage.

"In the beginning dress was mere decoration," said Goldescu, "and not clothing, we are told. Marioutza is a true primitive, eh?"

I could not trust myself to speak. "How could she? Why?"

I was all interrogation and revolt; angry beyond control. Yet even in my rage I recognized that she was dancing marvelously; now like a lily swaying in water, now floating like thistle-down, seeming to rebound as lightly as she came to earth, and when the music quickened and she sprang from the stage, one really felt that she might go higher indefinitely—

> Like an unbodied joy
> Whose race has just begun.

It all showed such a union of rare natural gifts and long assiduous practice as only an artist could appreciate.

She ended her dance by springing into the wings and left us with the image of her willowy, slight figure outlined as distinctly as a figure on a Greek vase.

We walked about for a few minutes and on turning found her at the stage door.

"What did you think of it?" she asked with the anxiety of the true artist. For the life of me I could not answer as I wanted to.

"I liked it, of course," I said, "liked it immensely; but I preferred your love dance."

"Really?" she cried in such chagrined disappointment that I had to mitigate the rebuff. "I mean, love is a greater theme than joy," I began, "don't you think—"

Goldescu chose this moment to take his leave. "Don't let him cast you down!" he cried. "I've never seen you more entrancing: you're a marvel; but alas, I've something special on tonight," he added. We let him go almost without noticing him.

On our way to her rooms the girl enthralled me. She seemed to divine my secret thoughts and my jealousy vanished before her outspokenness. Our talk was confidential and intimate from the beginning.

"Your playing the other night," she began, "was magical, but I was overwrought by it and—and—I wanted to meet you under better conditions: you understand?"

Of course I understood. It was my own feeling.

"I want you to like my Joy Dance," she went on. "I wrote the music for it myself. Often as a girl the beauty of our river and woodland in summer and the song of the birds used to make me weep for joy. Bucharest is so lovely and I wanted to render that beauty that's one with joy and delight. I've a pretty figure and I'm glad of it. We all love beauty; don't we?"

I felt that I had been a brute.

"I know, I understand," I cried, "but I'm a man and had already put you apart and above everyone and when you showed your figure it made me jealous; it was petty of me."

"Let me explain it to you," she said with her childlike sincerity. "You know, we dancers look on our bodies as you do on your violin, as our instrument. You love a fine one and know all its good points and so do we. How often we used to laugh at some girl with big shoulders and bust trying to learn to dance: she couldn't; the instrument was not right."

"But do you like exposing yourself?" I asked; all my innate prejudices coming to rationalize my jealousy.

"I don't think of it in that way," she replied; "I want to express a certain emotion: I try to do it as perfectly as I can; I never even think whether I am showing a few inches more or less of figure. . . . Is that immodest of me? You know, I want you to know me as I am—my faults even. Others may take the greasepaint for my complexion; I want you to see me as I really am, heart and soul and all! . . . I think as a girl I was almost without modesty, in mind as in body. I used to picture and imagine all things to myself. I was dreadfully curious, longed to know this and that. The mind is immoral, isn't it? or rather it has nothing to do with morality?" And she looked up at me anxiously.

I nodded and she went on: "My mother used to be shocked at me. She was a Catholic and religious, and when she found me studying my figure in the glass (I often wanted to kiss it), she told me that I must be modest, and that the body was sinful.

"I couldn't believe it. I don't now. I love the curve of my neck, and my small breasts are lovely to me; and even my slender feet please me intimately."

I was shaken with delight: she was clear as crystal with a woman's depth and a woman's delight in her beauty. I smiled and she continued: "Am I immodest? I don't think so. If there were anything ugly about me, I'd conceal it and be ashamed of it. I hate my legs because the muscles show; but I can't help that; it's part of my art and I'm not modest or immodest about them: I just recognize the fact—"

"You dear!" I cried. "I've called modesty the fig leaf of ugliness."

"That's it, that's it," she crowed with delight; "that's the truth; the talk of the girls in the dance classes I call immodest; but—

"I like your strong, stern face," she broke off, "and the boy's eyes you have and your bronzed-air skin pleases me. Why shouldn't I say so? But most of all, your genius, your wonderful playing, the divine spirit in you—"

"You must hear me once at my best," I exclaimed. "I'll play for you better than I've ever played. Let me see. On Friday I play at Prince Lichtenstein's. Would you come?"

"Goldescu wants me to dance there," she cried. "Suppose we both perform in public, yet just for each other?"

She was ravishing and her eyes held mine; why were they so beautiful to me? Was it the long dark lashes or the brown brook depth? I can't say. For the first time in my life I knew love. I could not help touching her hips as we walked side by side; I was drunk with desire. I knew it was love I felt, love once for all, love that was deathless; this was my mate, the strength of my feeling frightened me. I longed to take her in my arms, but refrained—though the passion of admiration I felt for her and her sacred boldness was clear enough, I'm sure, for now and again her eyes gave themselves to mine.

At her door she held out her hand and though I wanted her lips I restrained myself. I had had so much; I did not want to go in. I wanted to drink the divine cup little by little and prolong the ecstasy. But I could not help putting my hands on her shoulders and looking deep into her eyes while I said: "Auf Wiedersehen! Mein Alles!"

"I'm conscious I've remembered badly," Hagedorn interposed. "I've given you no idea of her charm for me."

I went home as if on air, drunk with the hope that she loved me, crazy with desire sharpened by this and that picture of her slight fleeting girl's figure.

Next morning I awoke to find a letter from her begging me to send or bring her the music I had composed for her "Love Dance" so that, as she said, "even when dancing I may feel inspired by your spirit."

I sat down at once and wrote out the music and took it to her apartment that same afternoon. It was the first time I had seen her in her frame, so to speak. The drawing room was very simple; half a dozen photos of men and girl-friends; three or four prints of famous dancers, all sent her by Goldescu she told me, and nothing more except a piano and the usual furniture. At first she seemed shy; her eyes withdrawn; her hands, I remember, were very cold, but her face was lovelier than I had thought; she grew on one; surely her eyes were larger than the night before.

She made me talk about myself and my tours, of Paris, and London and Madrid; "People everywhere much the same," was her comment. I had to tell her of my mother and father and my beginnings and all I hoped to be and do.

Then a samovar was brought in and we had tea and afterward I went to the piano and played my "Love Dance" music for her and as I ended she put her hand on my shoulder and I could not help putting my arm around her waist seeking to draw her to me. At first she yielded and I thought she was going to kiss me;

but then she grew stiff and looked into my eyes and smiled, shaking her head:

> *"Touch hands and part with laughter,*
> *Touch lips and part with tears,"*

she chanted mischievously, the brown eyes alight. She pleased me so intimately that even her caprices were delightful. She wanted to try my music over before me; she played quite well I found, and then I had to play it again while she danced. "Oh, I shall have a new effect!" she triumphed. "You're a dear, dear magician" she cried, and for a moment put her glowing cheek against mine.

"I don't know why I record all this, but I want you to understand the full perfection of my love. Whatever she did or refused to do pleased me; her boldness of speech and virginal shrinking from even a kiss delighted me equally."

That evening at Prince Lichtenstein's was a triumph. She danced divinely and I really think my music helped her. I am sure as she sank backward on the floor while the music throbbed with passion and sang with delight, no human figure had ever shown a more complete abandonment.

The audience went crazy; you know our Viennese and how they love to show their feelings. Well, I never saw anything like the enthusiasm displayed that night. I suppose there were five hundred guests in the great ballroom; the best names in Austria, and they were all entranced. They cheered and kissed their hands to her in wild admiration.

She came to me before them all with glowing cheeks.

"O Master!" she cried, "what music. I felt as if I were in your arms. Do you really love me? Can you? Are you sure?"

For a moment I was tongue-tied and thought-bound, too.

"You know I love you," I heard myself say. And at once before them all she gave me her lips, as if we had been alone. I adored her for her noble courage.

Love to ordinary people is the event of their lives; but artists often have a tenfold keener delight. Suppose a sculptor suddenly finds in the woman he loves the most perfect model he has ever met. His passion is extraordinarily sharpened. Suppose a woman has tried for years and years to dance better than anyone else and suddenly finds her powers intensified by a musician who gives her surprising melodies, her esthetic ambitions are all realized beyond hope; if she's inclined to love the musician you can easily see how her passion will be heightened. That's how I explain the bursting forth of Marie's love. As for me, well, from the beginning she had been to me perfection perfected. At last I had found the ideal we all long for, and my very soul was ravished.

I looked up and the men and women were all smiling as I thought, maliciously or disdainfully (what were we to them after all but a musician and a dancing-girl). I had an inspiration. Taking her by the hand I led her over to Prince Lichtenstein and bowing said: "Prince, you have often been kind to me, but never so kind as tonight; for in your house I have found my bride."

Everyone applauded and shouted and Lichtenstein swore they must celebrate the betrothal of the two greatest artists in the world; and indeed we did celebrate it all night long for the early morning sunshine was gilding the house as the Prince took us to the door and sent us home in his State carriage with outriders, if you please, and all his guests cheering on the steps. And even then he would not let us go till I had promised to celebrate the marriage in his palace.

I took my love to her rooms and she would have me go in with her; so I sent the carriage home and stayed. And there with shining great eyes she told me she had loved me from the first and only wanted to make me happy and as I kissed her holding her in my arms I was more than happy, drunk with pride and joy, delirious with desire.

Next week my father and mother came to Vienna and I took a house and began to furnish it and Prince Lichtenstein sent me some pictures and others of the nobility followed suit. The Gross-Herzog Rudolph, who called himself my first admirer, gave me the whole drawing-room furniture—pictures and all— from one of his palaces.

Our marriage was an event but the part I liked best was that my mother had taken a great fancy to Marie and told me at the wedding she hoped to be a grandmother in a year.

They say happiness has no history and I found it true; I could tell you little or nothing of the next three years except that as I learned to know my wife's nature I loved her more and more. Positively she had no faults and a myriad of high qualities, all set off by gaiety and sweet temper.

After the first season in Vienna I took her for a tour through Italy and the second year through Spain. We learned everything together, languages and all. I found it easy with a few performances each year to increase our fortune; the only drawback to our joy was that we had no children, but neither of us missed anything; at least I certainly did not, and my wife assured me she was content. But she was always encouraging me to write an opera or an oratorio to show how great I was! The Passion of St. Matthew by Bach was her favorite; I ought to do a greater oratorio! I didn't want to face the work; I was continually plagued by the idea of making first a new and scientific musical notation. I wanted to go to China and Japan and learn their music and then build up a music which should include theirs and be as effective in Pekin or Kyoto as in Paris or Vienna. Meanwhile I worked constantly in my own lazy way and made up my mind to spend the next summer in Shanghai. Marie consented.

But that season in Vienna for some reason or other, perhaps to excite my ambition, she took up her dancing again, and got Goldescu to get her engagements and play publicity manager. I wrote several new themes for her and she certainly embroidered them superbly.

I don't think our passion had lost its keen edge; I found Marie a wonderful mistress with an extraordinary congeniality of taste and desires. It was she who first taught me to love pictures. If I proposed to go into the Carpathians in mid-winter to hunt bear and wolves, or in summer to go to the Lido at Venice for a week's bathing she clapped her hands and crowed joyful acceptance. Never was there such a joyous eager companion.

I often wondered what her own intimate wish was: had she desires apart from mine?

I had bought a little country place twenty or thirty miles from

Vienna and I went there frequently, sometimes without her, to put it in order.

Once or twice I had been annoyed by her liking for Goldescu; she always told me she had known him as boy and girl together, and had never even kissed him; his cynical effrontery, she insisted, disgusted her; but she had no good reason to give him up; he was so serviceable; she used him for this and for that and I believed her. I was too happy even to work at my art, too happy to measure how happy I was when the blow fell.

I had gone out to our country place one Saturday and found the water-tank that supplied the bathroom had burst and overflowed everywhere. I wired to Vienna for skilled help and stayed to set them to work. I wrote my wife I should not be in Vienna before Wednesday or Thursday and returned on Monday afternoon to get fifteen feet of piping that was urgently needed. I got the piping and saw that I had half an hour before I could catch my train. Naturally I drove to my home and went upstairs. The drawing-room door was ajar; hearing low voices I pushed it half open. On the sofa opposite was my wife nestling in the corner and leaning over her half behind her was Goldescu. As I was about to speak he leaned forward, lifted up her chin and kissed her on the mouth. I was petrified; literally unconscious that I drew the door to; suddenly I found myself at the stair-head, yards away, shivering with cold. Like a sleepwalker I passed down into the hall, picked up the coil of piping, went out the front door, found a droshky and drove to the station—mechanically!

I gave the coil of piping to the overseer, who told me I must have caught a chill and following his advice I went to bed. He gave me a hot rum. I fell asleep and four hours afterward awoke to a tempest of rage and hate that altered my whole nature.

The rest can be told briefly. In the morning I wired my lawyer who was also my father's; I told him the truth and begged him to tell it to my parents. I made over half of all I possessed to my wife, asked the lawyer to tell her the truth if she pressed for it and that evening took train for Venice. Since then I have been a wanderer over the face of the globe. I buried myself for two years in China and think I know their music now and their language and the spirit of that great people as well.

I went all through Japan time and again and understand, I think, their music.

But I've never done anything: the truth is I've never recovered from the shock of that afternoon. I used to hate her when I thought of it; often feared I should go mad with hate; but now I'm just cold to it all; it might have happened to someone else for all I care; but with my love I lost my love of life; all the uses of living became stale, flat and tedious to me.

"Three months ago I returned to Austria after six years of wandering, and went down to Salzburg. My father and mother have both died. I came to Vienna meaning to make an end; what was there for me to live for?

"You saved my life; for a brief space I've warmed myself with your inexhaustible strength and vigorous love of living, but it can't go on. . . .

" 'Everyone,' says the Russian, 'gets tired of holding up an empty sack.' You'd get tired in time, my friend, or if you did not, you must feel that I am tired already; I have traveled the path before, know all the toils and triumphs of it and therefore it all says nothing to me—nothing! I got the best of life too easily, too early; I can't struggle; I won't; it's fat that floats," he added disdainfully.

"Did your wife never write to you or seek to see you to explain?" I asked in amazement.

"She wrote," he said, "and the lawyer forwarded it; but I never read the letter; I would not reopen the wound; the cicatrix was painful enough; why should I let her torture me again?"

"But you can't tell anything from the act," I insisted; "one might kiss and nothing more."

He shrugged his shoulders, impatiently.

"You haven't followed my story with full sympathy," he said. . . . "Surely you know without my telling you that I went through all the tortures of hell. At first I wanted to go back and kill the Jew and when that madness left me the memory of her beauty and her kisses drove me crazy. She had made me feel more intensely than anyone: her body was always before me, in its slim beauty; I'd see it, touch it, get drunk with the odor of it. A thousand times I said to myself: 'I'll go back; what does it matter to me whom she kissed so long as she'll kiss me, give me the illusion of love.' My body ached for her, man; a thousand times my mouth parched and desire choked me.

"And my maimed, lost soul cried for her day and night incessantly. I was lonely always and missed her as the blind man misses his eyesight. . . . Time and again I found myself in the train, once at least I got to Vienna and then went back. . . . I could not face the ruins of such perfect happiness, such divine bliss. . . .

"Don't think I blamed her! No, I quickly got over that. She may have kissed him, I said to myself, for any one of a thousand reasons; the flesh is faithless in woman as in man; she may even have loved me best, nay, she must have loved me best, else why did she marry me and not him whom she had known all her life. . . .

"But the heart does not reason, my friend; it aches and contracts in agony, or it triumphs and grows big and joyful. My heart bled and my lifeblood drained away. Day and night I cried: 'Why? why? Oh my soul! Marie! why?' The pain choked me and I lived without living, without joy or hope or interest till gradually years later, away off there in China I found myself taking a faint interest in music but my heart was dead and my interest in life was no longer living, vivid, but mere curiosity. . . .

"They say that cells in the body can outlive the body's death for years; my music cells will outlive soul and body in me; but the little corpse-light of life is not strong enough to do any good; I'm finished. . . . Are you answered, my friend?"

"I understand," I said, "but nevertheless," I persisted, "it's your duty to write a great piece of really new music,

music that shall appeal to every human ear; think man of the fame to be won; immortal reputation as the Bahnbrecher, the Roadmaker to a new Kingdom of the Spirit; you owe a debt to Humanity; pay it first; your life's not your own."

"How often I've said the same thing to myself," he began, slowly; "if you only knew how much I grew in those happy years. I had divined nearly everything I learned later in China; the music of the future is clear to me from the tom-tom of the savage to—but I can't write, man; I can't; the love of my art is dead in me; she killed my very soul.

"All the music I've played here for you is old, old stuff; it has all been memory music, every note of it. You surely know that you must be alive, intensely alive, before you can create anything! It's the life in you that you impart; I'm dead: the heart is cold in me; the soul a corpse. I can do nothing worth the doing—"

He shook his head: "I can't. You will not understand; the bad alone survives in me. What good would it do to picture a madhouse or a wild beast's cage? Your Joachim was right; art is there to cheer, encourage, console, warn even if you will; but never to horrify and disgust and discourage. And I see nothing but beasts, lunatics, idiots; the posturing, gibbering apes are loathsome to me!"

"Thanks for the compliment," I exclaimed, laughing; "but you don't dislike Neumann or me, do you? Well, another concert or two and you'll find hundreds like us to love and admire you and our love will inspire you to do the new work."

He shook his head: "What an optimist you are! You see you had the knocks first, the training first that hardened you; I had the triumphs first that left me soft and weak."

"At any rate give yourself time," I pleaded; "do nothing hastily; don't go off at half-cock, as we Americans say;

another triumph or two will make a difference; you know the French proverb, '*l'appétit vient en mangeant*'—the appetite grows with eating."

He smiled, "I owe you that, at least I won't do anything till I must," and forced therewith to be content I went off to consult with Neumann whom I brought back with me to dinner.

The second concert was a far greater triumph than the first; all the best music-lovers in Vienna were there and prepared now to welcome a great master. As he stood bowing on the platform at the end and the audience cheered and cheered and the women even came up in crowds to the stage, I made my way to the side door that led behind the stage. As I got there a young woman addressed me: "Are you Herr—?" Then without waiting for an answer, "I am his wife; take me to him!"

"I would, so gladly," I exclaimed, "but is this the right moment?"

She looked at me with wide frightened hazel eyes: "What do you mean? I must see him, explain. . . . My God, speak man: will you take me to him?"

She was quivering with excitement; she caught my arm in her hands as if I were about to evade her; she was certainly very pretty; I tried to persuade her for his sake.

"I'll do whatever I can," I said impressively; "but now and here you won't get a chance of a quiet talk; he'll probably have left the place as he did last time before I can catch him; but he lives with me. I'll get you a good opportunity, Madame, where you can use all your persuasiveness. I want you to succeed and save him, I promise you—"

"Oh, now, now," she interrupted, "please, please, for God's sake. I've waited so long, all these weary years, please," and the tears poured down her cheeks.

"Come," I said, unable to resist, "we'll find him if we can," and hurriedly I took her through the passage to the

waiting room, but Hagedorn had "left two minutes before," as Neumann told me looking intently at my companion.

"Go to my rooms at once, Neumann," I cried, "and if
Hagedorn is there keep him till we come or keep with him
at least till you bring about a meeting. For the love of God
don't lose sight of him till we all meet. If you don't understand, please believe I have good reason and don't tell
Hagedorn I was with a lady; just say I must see him!
See?"

"I understand," replied Neumann, "I'm off, and if he's
not in your rooms I'll wait there for you. What a success,
eh?" And the next moment he was gone.

"Now," I said, "Madame, we can go quietly to my
place. Should we drive or walk; it's only ten minutes'
drive?"

"As you please," she replied quietly; so I took her outside and got into a fiacre with her and gave my address.

"Shall I explain to you?" she began as soon as we were
alone. "I feel that you know the story, know it perhaps
better than I do. Why did he leave me? Why didn't he answer my letters? It wasn't because of one kiss?"

"I fear it was," was my answer. "I'm not defending him
or accusing you; but that's what he says. He must have
always been an idealist!"

"That's why I loved him," she cried, "but good God!
how unjust, how cruel of him! I can hardly explain how it
happened; perhaps you won't understand. We women do
so much out of pity, for pity's sake.

"I had told Goldescu that his cynical way of talking
disgusted and pained me; it did him harm too; he was
growing coarser, worse, and I was so happy. I told him he
must stop it or I'd have to cease seeing him.

"He didn't speak for a little while and I thought I had
been hard on him.

"Then he began in a strange passionate voice:

" 'You blame me for being cynical: it's too much. I'm cynical because I was a fool, lost my chance. Are you stone-blind? I might have won you, was near it years ago and waited thinking you would come to me, waited too long and he won you in an hour, that Musiker! And now you blame me for being cynical—you! the cause of it! you!'

"I was thunderstruck, shaken.

" 'I'm sorry,' I muttered. We women are always sorry for giving love-pain!

" 'Don't be sorry,' he cried, 'I couldn't stand that. I never meant to tell you; don't be sorry; I'm the only one should grieve, but say you forgive me.'

" 'Of course I forgive you,' I cried.

" 'I'll try to be better. We'll never talk of it again,' he said. 'One kiss of forgiveness,' and before I thought he lifted my face and kissed me—a long kiss.

"As soon as I felt how he was kissing me I pulled away and started up hot with rage.

" 'A poor comedy,' I cried, 'but even you can only play it once with me,' and I went to the door; it was open.

"Vaguely I wondered why; after Goldescu had gone I wondered but then forgot all about it till I got that awful letter from the lawyer.

"I couldn't believe that; it seemed all too monstrous to me; it does now! Like a horrible nightmare turning sweet sleep to horror.

"A thousand times I cried: 'Why should he leave me?' Goldescu kissed me without my will; I was as if hypnotized; the next moment I stopped him; I've never seen him since; wouldn't see him; I loved no one but my husband, no one, ever! Oh! oh!" And again the tears drowned her face and voice.

I pitied her so that I could not help trying to console her: "Don't fear, please; it will all come right, it must"— the usual inanities.

When we got upstairs Neumann met us: "He's not been home yet, but he's sure to come before dinner. You'll not forget you're both dining with me; this lady too, if she'll come."

"We may be late," I said, "but we'll come if possible."

Neumann took the hint and left.

As soon as we were alone Madame Hagedorn began to fidget. "I feel misfortune in the air," she repeated. . . . "You know I feel sure if I can talk to him, I can convince him that my love never changed. And then I'll love him so, he'll have to love me again. Don't you think so?"

Then she began graming and grieving: "I've been so unhappy, and now so fearful; are you sure he's not been here; is this where he sleeps?" And she pointed to my sofa-bed.

"No, no," I replied, "he occupies the bedroom in there," and I motioned to the door.

"Let's go in and see if he's been in," she cried.

I went first and opened the door; the bed, the chairs, his clothes—all in the usual order. "You see," I said, turning to her, "he's not been here"; but even as I spoke she pointed to the head of the bed and there on the pillow was a sheet of paper pinned:

I took it and read:

I knew she was in the hall; I felt her presence; I saw her speaking to you; I fled.

It's no use, man. I will not renew the intolerable anguish; I dare not. I prefer to—Good-bye. You did all that could be done. . . . I forgive, but there is only one way to forget.

E. H.

A
CHINESE
STORY

IT WAS MY SECOND VISIT to Shanghai after a long interval.
I had only a vague idea of the old walled city, though the
European settlement seemed fairly familiar. But now the
old Chinese city drew me in spite of its gloomy, stinking
streets and swarming verminous life. What lay on the
other side? What was the soul of China, and that Chinese
civilization which speculated in transcendental philos-
ophies and practiced impressionist painting when Rome
was still mistress of the world? Could I get any glimpse of
the tantalizing mystery in spite of the veil of language?

An English student-interpreter put me on the way:
"There's a Pole here named Shimonski," he said, "who is
called in in every difficulty; they say he knows more about
China than the Chinks themselves: he'd be an ideal guide.
I'll send him to you tomorrow morning, if you'll be in."

I agreed gladly; but no Shimonski appeared next morning or the morning after, and the appointment was gradually blotted out of my memory by the rush of new and
strange experiences.

One morning I had been accosted in front of the hotel
by an old Chinaman, who talked to me with many genu-
flections in a tone and manner of profound humility.
While I was trying to understand his expressive face and
mimicry he suddenly flourished a large knife, evidently

not with any evil purpose, for as soon as I turned away, the knife disappeared. I went about the hotel trying to get the matter explained to me, and about eleven o'clock returned to my room.

To my astonishment a man was seated in my particular armchair at the table, smoking my cigarettes. He did not get up as I entered, so I said to him: "Have you not made some mistake?"

"I think not," he replied, in a quiet voice and excellent English. "I was told you wanted to see me."

"And your name?" I asked.

"My name is Shimonski," he replied, negligently knocking off the ash from his cigarette, and looking up at me.

"Oh!" I cried, "you are the guide whom Lawrence spoke of?"

He nodded merely. Rather interested by his casual way of taking the matter, I drew up a chair and sat down beside him.

Shimonski was tall, almost six feet in height, and spare of figure. He seemed about forty, but might have been five years more or less, for his whiskers and moustache and hair were all of that straw color in which grey hairs scarcely show. His features were very irregular, almost like a Tartar's—the forehead low, the straw-thatch growing down into it and making two bays, so to say; the eyes small and grey; the nose, the prominent feature, long and thin, pinched, indeed, on top, with very broad nostrils that vibrated with every emotion, and in anger grew quite white. The dominant expression of the face was sharp temper, inclined to suspicion. I was not pleasurably impressed.

"They tell me," I began, "that you know more about China than any foreigner."

"That would *not* be high praise," he answered quietly. "Here, as in India, the natives speak of the whites as savages, and with good reason."

"I wonder," I went on, "whether I could learn anything about China without knowing the language. All that I hear is so strange to me. I am told that all of the great mandarins and governors are appointed according to their literary achievements. I wonder how that works."

"Do you think it would be preferable," he asked sneeringly, "to have them appointed by money, as in America, or by snobbery, as in England?"

"You've got me there," I laughed. "I am prepared to admit that rulers everywhere are a poor lot, and I dare say they are no worse here than elsewhere."

"Better here," he retorted, "though not much; there is a good deal of human nature everywhere."

The man's way of talking interested me. He was evidently free of prejudice and used words scrupulously.

"You think I may learn something even without the language?"

He nodded.

"How much do you want to be my guide and teacher?" I asked.

"If I am to do you any good," he said, "it ought to be forty or fifty dollars a week."

"All right. Shall we begin from today or tomorrow?"

"As you like," he answered; "but I think you ought to give me a check now; not that I have any claim on it, but I want it." The remark was made in the air.

I could not associate cheating with this nonchalant, thoughtful person, so I wrote him a check for the larger amount and handed it to him. He put it in his pocket.

"How long are you going to stay in Shanghai?" he asked.

"Two or three months," I replied; "but I am not limited to time if there is anything of value to learn."

"That depends on you," he said, and his little eyes bored into mine. "Well, so long!" He turned abruptly and went.

As soon as I was alone I began to reproach myself for not asking him to explain the old Chinaman, but I told myself that it would be time enough next day.

But next day there was no Shimonski, nor the day after, nor the day after that.

One evening I spoke to an American merchant who had been in Shanghai twenty-odd years and asked him if he knew Shimonski.

"A queer fish," he replied.

"Is he honest?" I asked.

"Oh yes," said the merchant. "I say he is queer, because he lives like a Chink; his eyes are getting to look like a Chinaman's, don't you think? And you even see him in their dress."

A day or two later I was told that someone wanted to see me.

"Send him up to my room," I said. To my astonishment a little Chinese girl came in and gave me a slip of paper on which I read: "Please give bearer my week's money; I shall see you soon. Shimonski."

I hesitated. It seemed to me the height of insolence.

"Can you take me to Mr. Shimonski?" I said to the girl.

She shook her head: "He isn't in Shanghai."

"When did he give you this?" I asked.

"Before he went away, a week ago," she answered.

It was curious, but the man's personality was so impressive in its entire sincerity, in its absence of pose, that I wrote out a check and handed it to the girl. As she put out her hand to take it I noticed that her skin was lighter than the skin of the majority of Chinese women. "Maybe Shimonski's daughter," I said to myself.

A couple of days passed and I heard no more of the matter, but I was again accosted by the old Chinaman with the knife.

Then one afternoon the door opened and Shimonski came in.

"Good-day!" he said.

"So you have turned up at last," I replied.

"Yes. I had something to finish that took me out of town, but now I am at your service, and from tomorrow I think you will find me fairly punctual. I suppose you will be up about nine o'clock?"

I said I would, and the next moment, without a word of excuse or explanation, he had left the room.

The next morning at nine o'clock I was up and dressed. Again he came in without knocking. "Shall we go out?" he said.

I took up my stick and hat and went with him. At the door I was once more approached by the old Chinaman.

"What does he want?" I asked Shimonski. "He has bothered me three or four times."

Shimonski spoke to him and then turned to me.

"His proposal," he said, "is to kill himself any way you like for ten dollars!"

"Why should I want him to kill himself?" I asked.

Shimonski shrugged his shoulders. "He says he will do it according to the Japanese way, which is the most painful, or he will go across the street and cut his throat there, or do anything you please."

"What good would that do me?" I asked.

"Good?" said Shimonski carelessly. "I don't know; it would be an experience."

"One that I won't buy," I said. "What does he want ten dollars for?"

"He has an only daughter," said Shimonski, "and he can get her well married for that dowry."

The old Chinaman had stood listening to us with his head on one side, looking from face to face. He seemed so eager that I took out ten dollars and gave him the bill. He pressed it against his heart and then again took out the great knife and made remarks.

"Tell him to put that knife up," I said, "and go off to his daughter."

Shimonski said a few words and the Chinaman disappeared.

"What an extraordinary creature," I remarked, "to be willing to kill himself for so little."

"Life is cheap in China," said Shimonski; "they all recognize that life to the poor is worthless."

"Does that explain, I wonder, our shootings in western America?"

"Sure," replied Shimonski. "Where life is easy and pleasant it becomes precious."

"But men in western America are free," I went on.

"Nothing like so free as they are in China," snapped Shimonski.

"What do you mean?" I asked, in surprise.

"That old Chinaman could have killed himself in the street and no one would have interfered with him; some days would probably have elapsed before the corpse would have been taken away. No country in the world is so free as China."

"Really!" I cried.

He looked at me, smiling. "What countries did you think freest?" he asked.

"I have always thought England and America," I replied.

"Surely," he retorted, "you know that the Greeks and Dalmatians are infinitely freer. In England, it is true, there is a little sense of personal liberty; in America there is none: it has been completely lost. America has a small sense of equality; here there is no sense of equality; no sense at all, but an extraordinary sense of liberty. Freedom is a religion in China.

"I am taking you now to the execution of some pirates who were caught the other day at the mouth of the river," he went on, "that will teach you what we mean here by freedom," and he led the way over one of the bridges. In ten minutes we came to a sort of yard, at the other side of which was a poor-looking temple structure. We had been there only a few moments when there filed into the yard eighteen men, all with their arms tied tightly behind their backs; their legs were tied too—in fact so closely haltered that they could only totter with short steps.

In a little while the executioner appeared—a gigantic man from North China—the biggest Chinaman I had seen up to that time, six feet three or four inches in height, of superb breadth and strength. He was flourishing an enormous sword as he came to us; it was scimitar-shaped and fully an inch thick at the back: it must have weighed thirty pounds. When he spoke the pirates all knelt down and he stood in front of them and made a short speech, which Shimonski translated.

"He says that he is the greatest executioner in the world, and that if they will only keep quiet and push their heads well back and their chins up they will never know that death came to them nor feel the stroke. See, he is shaving hairs off his arm to show them how razor-sharp the sword is."

As the executioner stepped smiling toward the first man in the line I stared round me and noticed that half the wall looking onto the street had been broken down, but of the people who were passing not one even paused to look at the tragedy.

The executioner said a word or two to the first man and lifted his chin in the air with his hand. Then stepping to the side, with one slice, he cut off his head, that rolled in the mud. I was horrified; but again the executioner stepped in front and said a few words.

"What is he saying?" I gasped, with dry mouth.

"Simply asking them to notice how perfect the stroke

was; that the man has gone into the other world without knowing it. Look at his head; you will see the features are quite composed," Shimonski replied coolly.

Again and again and again the tragedy took place, accompanied each time by the boasting of the executioner. It was the fourth or fifth body that remained upright after the head had been sliced off, the poor torso spouting blood two feet high in a stream.

The executioner pointed with his sword to the body and said: "That's the way I do my work; all you have to do is to keep quiet, chin up, head back."

To my astonishment the remaining pirates nudged each other to look at the headless trunk, and laughed.

"I must go," I said to Shimonski. "I cannot stand this; that laughter and the cold cruelty are too horrible."

"It may be interesting," he said. "Wait."

But I could not wait, and hurried outside to get the wall between me and the ghastly spectacle. It was ten minutes before Shimonski rejoined me. "You might as well have waited," he said; "nothing happened."

"Do you call the murder of eighteen people nothing?"

"Nothing," repeated Shimonski, shrugging his shoulders. "Thousands die every day in China that no one cares about."

"Fancy," I said, "not one person outside even turned to look; in America there would have been a crowd."

"Yes," replied Shimonski, "you are interested in your neighbor; in China we mind our own business; that's all."

Chinese contempt for human life was made plain to me by this execution, but Shimonski seemed determined that I should learn something more about the judicial system in China, for the next time we went out he took me to a court.

One or two cases were decided, not by argument of any sort or an appeal to law, but simply by the sense of justice of the judge, a peculiar-looking little Chinaman, with eyes that were mere slits and a low monotonous voice that was, somehow or other, impressive.

The first few cases were decided with a sort of rough justice, I thought, and then came a more important case. A merchant, it seemed, was complaining of his manager or chief assistant. He was a stout, rather large man, very voluble. He declared that his assistant had recently married and was living in a better way than his salary justified. This excited his suspicion. He took a sort of inventory and found that certain silken garments were missing. He believed that his assistant had stolen and sold them and made use of the proceeds; how, otherwise, could he have got the money to live as he was living?

The complaint seemed to me absurd and unfounded, but the little mandarin on the bench said a word or two, which Shimonski translated: "The judge says he wants to hear the assistant."

So the assistant came forward, one of the finest-looking young Chinamen I had ever seen. His face was almost Caucasian, the eyes large and frank, and the expression honest and intelligent; he was, besides, a fine figure of a man, taller even than the merchant and broader, but carrying no fat. He showed no fear or anger, and told his tale quite simply. Shimonski translated for me as he went on:

"He says the accusation is absurd: if the merchant will take an inventory he will find that nothing has disappeared that has not been paid for; he has never taken any garment outside the shop; he makes much extra money by going to the European Hotel in the evening and carrying baggage to the steamer or doing anything they want him to do, and his wife, too, works."

Again and again he was interrupted by the merchant. When he had finished the judge said a few quiet words and Shimonski chuckled.

"What is it?" I asked; "surely he will dismiss the case."

"The judge asks him what became of the silken garments that the merchant says were in the shop. The judge is in favor of the merchant. The employee is too bold. We shall see some fun."

The young man answered the judge at somewhat greater length now and with much greater emphasis, and when interrupted by the merchant he turned on him and spoke indignantly. Again the judge peered through his slits of eyes and said something and there was a commotion in the court; two or three Chinese police went out by a side door.

"Now you will see something," whispered Shimonski excitedly. "This is getting interesting."

"What is it?" I asked.

"The judge is going to make him confess," said Shimonski. "You'll see."

A moment more and two policemen came back with the most curious-looking affair I had ever seen. It was a high pole, as thick as one's leg, with a very large basin-looking thing at the base, a bar stuck out horizontally at the top, with a pulley attached. In the basin was a huge cannonball of stone that must have weighed two or three hundredweight.

"What on earth is that thing for?" I asked.

"You'll see," replied Shimonski curtly, with gleaming eyes.

Again the mandarin on the bench said something in his slow, monotonous, quiet voice. Two or three others pulled the cannonball about six feet high by the rope. A policeman shoved the right foot of the young man into the basin and held it there. A word from the judge and the ball fell with a thud on the young man's foot and turned it into mere blood and pulp. I never heard such a cry as he uttered. I was fascinated with horror. "Good God!" I kept repeating. "Good God!"

I turned to Shimonski. He was smiling, with his eyes

fixed on the mandarin, who was speaking again, evidently addressing the young man, who was being held up by the policeman.

"What is he saying?" I asked.

"The judge is asking him if he remembers the silk robes now, and he says 'No. He can only repeat what he has said already.' "

The merchant came forward and even his face was white. He made some remark and Shimonski translated: "He says now he may be mistaken. Won't the honorable judge please let the young man go?"

For the first time the judge used a few short sentences: Shimonski translated: "He says that as the merchant had pleaded for the young man's life he may go, but he hopes the punishment will be a lesson to him to keep from stealing in the future."

The little old mandarin then got up and disappeared through a door at the back. The policemen took their hands off the young man, who pulled himself together and limped to the door, a long stream of blood pouring from his right leg to the floor.

"Good God!" I cried to Shimonski, "give the poor fellow some money and see if he cannot be carried home and his leg attended to."

"Why give him money?" asked Shimonski. "In a couple of hours he'll be dead. Why waste money on a corpse?"

"But can't they put a tourniquet on his leg," I said, "and stop the bleeding? He will be a cripple, but he may live."

"What good is life to a cripple?" replied Shimonski. "Give your money to people who are sound, if you want to give it."

"Let us get out of this," I cried, appalled. "I cannot stand your Chinese justice."

A day of two afterwards I cross-examined Shimonski about the matter. "Is there no appeal in such a case?" I asked. "The merchant evidently lied and the young man was murdered for nothing at all."

"No, no," said Shimonski; "he was impudent."

"Innocence," I retorted, "is always impudent."

"Wealth is the only thing in China that dares to be impudent," said Shimonski. "If you are independent you can be impudent; if you are not, you had better be respectful."

"So," I said, "this is the way your boasted liberty is bounded: freedom for the well-to-do; torture and untimely death for the poor."

Shimonski shrugged his shoulders. "As long as I am one of the well-to-do," he said, "I do not bother."

There was no doubt he took pleasure in cruelty, and when I asked him he admitted it quite coolly.

"You have a childish idea," he said, "that pleasure in life is only to be got from love and liking and such roots, but I think as much joy in life comes from gratified hatred, and there is keen pleasure in punishment that falls on another."

"Justice has nothing to do with it, then?" I asked.

"Nothing," he said. "You do not ask whether you deserve to be kissed or not; you take pleasure in the kiss. The wise man gets all the pleasure he can out of life."

"But can there be any pleasure in cruelty?" I asked.

"Of course," he replied with a sigh, as if tired of such foolish questions, "the very sharpest."

A little later he took me to another Chinese execution, but before I tell of it I want to say that his cruelty had begun to interest me. I wanted to find the reason for it, the explanation of it. After all, he couldn't have been born with that fiend's nature.

The second execution which Shimonski brought me to see is certainly an institution peculiar to China and throws a grim light on Chinese judicial proceedings. It, too, was in public, but this time a crowd had collected in the half-paved yard, where bloodstains could still be seen from the execution of the pirates.

Against the wall, underneath the temple, a wooden staging had been built, and the back of the staging was planked right up to the top of the wall. The executioner was a man of ordinary size, but of considerable muscular development, and he was stripped to the waist. He was abrupt in movement and vibrant with energy.

A large basket was at his feet and he had two assistants. It took them perhaps a quarter of an hour to tie up the criminal to big nails let in on the wooden hoarding at the back. When they had finished the victim was spread-eagled against this wooden background, but standing more or less at ease on his own feet, though he could not move his hands or head or limbs, because he was trussed like a fowl and tied everywhere to the hoarding like an advertisement. The victim was a man of perhaps forty years of age, but of an extraordinary emaciation; he looked more like a skeleton than a man. It appeared he had entered the house of a rich man to steal, and had been arrested after killing one of the policemen.

"Want drove him to it?" I remarked to Shimonski.

"Probably poverty," he replied: "he looks like it."

Shimonski was not as interested as usual. "They are not going through with it," he said disconsolately. "The man has some girl children and they have curried favor with a rich mandarin and I hear the executioner has been bought; if so, we shan't have much fun."

"Justice, then, can be bought in China?" I said.

Shimonski looked at me. "Justice is bought everywhere; sometimes with popular applause, as in America, sometimes with money, as in France, and sometimes with titles and snobbery, as in Great Britain; but everywhere justice is bought. In China money is the purchasing power. The Chinese are a matter-of-fact, realistic, sensible people."

Scarcely had he finished speaking when the executioner turned around and made a speech. Shimonski translated it for me. He began by saying: "In this basket at my feet are fifty knives. I do not know what is written on the handles. I pick them up and read, and act according to the instructions. It is all a lottery and our lives are at the mercy of our masters."

"Fifty knives!" I cried. "What on earth does he want fifty knives for?"

"You will see," said Shimonski. "Wait and see."

Suddenly one of the aides drew the cloth away from the basket with a flourish and immediately the executioner stooped down and picked a knife out of the basket: there was a label on the haft. He read it out: "Through the arm," and whirling round at once he pinned the man's left arm to the wood by driving the knife through it.

The victim did not utter a sound nor move, but his head bent further forward on his chest and his yellow face became grey; he appeared to be on the point of fainting. Another knife was taken out and read: "Through the shoulder," and it was thrown in the most marvelous way, just catching the skin on the shoulder. The grey face became livid, but not a sound.

The executioner lifted up the third knife and read: "Through the heart," and whirling round drove it through the heart of his victim. There was a roar of hatred and rage from the crowd, who evidently expected that the pleasant performance would be prolonged.

"I told you so," said Shimonski. "I heard the executioner had been paid; that is the proof; otherwise he would have shown off his skill, using every knife to the end, and the man would have been squealing before the tenth, like a rat whose legs have been cut off."

I left the ground while the executioner was still trying to tell the mob that he had simply to take the knife that came first; that he could not say what was on the label: in fact he was trying to justify himself as if he had been an Anglo-Saxon politician or profiteer.

"And can judges also be bought in China?" I asked Shimonski.

"Of course," he said; "but the price for judges is higher, and they are usually bought from above by the governors or the State."

"And for the three hundred and fifty millions of Chinamen," I said, "there is no justice and no law?"

"None," Shimonski answered. "But for the hundred and fifty thousand or so who can make some money and live independently China is the best country in the world. You can buy whatever you want in it and everything is very cheap. Did you ever get such good service before? Isn't the food excellent? the fish and chickens wonderful? the climate healthy? perfect freedom? What more can a man want?"

"The whole thing is a horror to me," I said. "What is there for the soul here?"

"Ah!" said Shimonski, "that is another question. You will find greater paintings in China than anywhere in the world—an art that grew and blossomed through two thousand years. Every school of painting imaginable can be found in China. Have you heard of the painter who said that it was no object of the artist to represent life or even to give you the effect life produced on you, which is the object of the modern European schools, but that the true aim of the great artist should be to represent the rhythm of life itself—not progress, that doesn't exist; but the ebb and flow, the movement and rhythm of life?

"In the same way our poets always try to give us new emotions, and the moderns want to catch the most evanescent feelings, the fancies that break through language and escape.

"Our vases and cups are the finest in the world: common household things with a glaze on them of priceless beauty. Carpets, too, we have which make all other carpets look like rags."

"I know," I cried. "I have admired turquoise blues and camel-hair effects. I think them wonderful."

"You will never know what a carpet is till you see an old Chinese carpet two or three hundred years old, for, unlike all other carpets, its beauty increases with age; as it gets worn down a gloss comes upon it that can only be compared to the bloom on a peach or grape. I could show you carpets three hundred years old that are as lovely as any picture—beautified, indeed, by the patine of the years, the unimaginable touch of Time."

"But the religion?" I asked. "Can there be any religion in a people where justice is bought and sold and cruelty is a passion?"

"Oh yes," replied Shimonski. "Man is a complex animal; he unites in himself many contradictions. The religion of China is the highest and most abstract in the world."

My memories of Shimonski are becoming unduly voluminous; I must bring them to an end.

I have dwelt on his delight in cruelty and on his originality of thought, for those were the qualities in him which excited my curiosity and admiration; naturally he possessed dozens of other virtues and vices, but these two in eminent degree. It was especially his epicurean pleasure in cruelty, his savoring it as a tidbit and dainty, that intrigued me, for after some months of acquaintanceship I found that the Chinese girl whom he sent to me as a messenger was an orphan whom he had picked up, educated and cared for. He had another girl in his house who looked after his clothes and books, though she was blind of one eye, and an old woman who cooked for them, and all three he had rescued out of pure pity, and they all adored him as a sort of god.

As I got to know and like him he grew more communicative. We went up country together that summer to see some old porcelain and on the journey he gave me the key of his strange nature. I'll try to tell the story as he told it, but without the interruptions and wanderings of his narrative.

One thing was peculiar in his confession. He never tried to justify himself or to moralize his conduct in any degree. He was certainly above good and evil, in his own opinion at least.

We had been away about a fortnight and had stopped for the night in a walled town, three hundred miles from Shanghai. He had been explaining to me how curiously free and independent these towns are in China. The Imperial Government, it appeared, sent down annually a requisition setting forth what amount the town would have to contribute in taxes to the Imperial revenue; but the method of taxation was left to the town itself.

I told him that the same municipal power existed all over Germany, and was one of the chief reasons why Germans could stand an extreme Imperial despotism, because in their village and town affairs they were their own masters.

He shrugged his shoulders indifferently. He had no great liking for the Teutonic races, he said; the Germans and English, and even the Americans, were all tarred with the same brush—a self-sufficient greed varnished with hypocritical righteousness or sentimentality which he thought ridiculous. He preferred the Latins to the Teutons, but reserved his special admiration for the Slavs and the Chinese. In China, he said, we have had the "general strike" for a thousand years now which you are only beginning to think of as a protest. If the Government does something we don't like, we all strike and the Government soon gives in. Despotism, like democracy, is only a word. . . .

It was a beautiful morning in early summer and a beautiful scene. The river ran through an ever-narrowing valley; the banks were thickly wooded and the trees were all blushing in the light, warm air of May.

Rounding one turn we came upon a strange procession—coolies in front carrying clothes and provisions, two or three palanquins, and more servants bringing up the rear. We asked what it was, or rather Shimonski asked, and was told that it was a girl being brought down to be wedded to a Chinese general in the town we had just left.

"My fate came to me like that," Shimonski remarked.

"Tell me about it," I said.

"It is ten years ago now," he began. "It was far up country I met just such a procession. A handsome youth was in charge of the bride, his sister; he told me he was taking her, as the loveliest girl in the whole province, to be wedded to the Governor of Szechuan, then the most powerful of provincial rulers. I was mildly interested and a little curious, so I told him where he ought to stop next and gave him various pieces of information he wanted; then I praised his looks and bearing just to get his confidence, so that when I said I'd like to see his sister, he took me to the palanquin at once and drew the curtain. Never have I seen anything so wonderful! Her eyes held me and fascinated me, and it was some time before I could throw off the enchantment enough to realize the different traits that constituted her exquisite loveliness.

"Oh, the flower face! Well was she named the Morning Glory. Her face had only enough of the Chinese type to give it a strangeness that enthralled. At first glance she might have passed for a Russian, only no Russian was ever so beautiful. How shall I describe her? When I have said her eyes were very large, a dark hazel in color, lit and warmed by golden points; when I've told of a straight nose and perfect oval of face and rose-leaf skin, and lips a little too full and ripe, I've said nothing. Other girls have these.

But her eyes, besides being beautiful, were nobly serious, with a brooding expression that came from depth of feeling; there was a question in them and an appeal and trust that enlightened the face to a smile; and then I saw the slender arm and the dimples at the elbow and the budding breasts, and my mouth grew dry as in a parching wind.

"Do you realize at length that in China we know more about beauty than any other people; we have studied it more curiously, more intimately than any other race. Have you ever noticed that our hawthorn jars are moulded after the curves of a woman's hips, and that the magical powder-blue vases are copies of the lines of some slight girl's body? The glaze itself has the smooth gloss of a child's flesh and the radiance on it is of our wonderment. I have shown you marvels in material things; you must just trust me when I tell you that this girl was perfection perfected, her body a rhythm, her face a flower. . . .

"I turned and went with them—made myself a guide and protector. Both the brother and sister trusted and liked me, and I did all I knew to increase their liking. I told them all sorts of strange stories: tales of heroes and fightings for the youth and of romantic love and despair for the girl. I ransacked my memories of Russian and Polish and German and French history, and I used to love to have their eyes fixed on me and feel her breath catch. . . .

"The halts for the midday meal grew longer and longer and our daily journeyings shorter, while they listened enthralled to my stories. I told of sinner and saint, of St. Elizabeth of Hungary and of Ninon de Lenclos of Paris, and she drank in everything I said.

"And always the youth wanted to learn and the girl to feel; but I think she grew even more quickly than he did. I remember telling him once of the great Chinese Emperor Shi Hwang-ti. Do you know the story? He came to the throne at thirteen and while still young abolished the feu-

dal system, divided China into provinces, built roads, ca-
nals, and at length the Great Wall. The feudal princes
revolted; writers and pedants held up to the admiration of
the people the heroes of feudal times, and the advantages
of the old, worn-out system. To break once and for all
with the past, the great emperor ordered the destruction of
all books having reference to the past history of the empire, and many scholars were put to death for disobedi-
ence to the 'edict.'

"I can still hear her sighing: 'What a pity a great man
could kill innocent people! Is no great man at once strong
and wise and gentle?' The divine sweet spirit of her!

"You don't know how wonderful our Chinese girls can
be," Shimonski went on, "but at least you realize now that
Chinese art is the finest in the world, and soon you will be
able to see that our old Chinese religion, too, is the highest
at once and most rational ever held by man. And when
you acknowledge this you may be ready to understand
that Chinese men and women are the noblest human creatures of whom Time holds any record.

"At any rate I would like you to believe that it is not the
blindness of passion makes me put this simple Manchu girl
higher than any other human being I have ever met. If I
am not utterly depraved it is because of her; whatever
good there is in me comes from her; my soul is merely an
emanation of her divine passion and pity. . . .

"But I must get on with my story. I had been with them
nearly a fortnight when one day the brother went away to
see a famous temple and I told the sister the story of
Jeanne d'Arc. It had a tremendous effect on her, an effect
I never anticipated. She grew paler and paler, and tears
fell from her eyes. When I told her of Jeanne's martyrdom
I expected her to break down weeping, but it had the contrary effect on her; her whole face was transfigured; and
when I told how Jeanne acknowledged that she had lost
her 'voices' through her own selfishness and her woman's

wish to do what her king desired, my girl's eyes glowed with enthusiasm and she exclaimed: 'What a great end! What a noble girl!'

"She fell silent while I told how the Catholic Church, centuries later, canonized Jeanne as a saint, and how she was loved and revered now wherever her story was known.

"Glory, as I called her always, got up from her couch and suddenly leaning forward took my head in her hands and kissed me on the lips.

" 'Thank you, thank you,' she cried, 'for the great story; it will be a part of my soul forever.'

"It was not passion with which I kissed her, for a great reverence was upon me and I was enthralled by her emotion; but afterwards passion woke in me, for I had held the round firm figure against my body, and the supple grace and litheness of it got into my blood and the desire of her shook me like a fever.

"What a day of days it was! Fate is sometimes good to us. The brother did not return and we spent the evening together, and when she rose to retire I kissed her hands, one after the other, for she was sacred to me; but she drew me to her and offered her lips and I put my arms around her. I kissed her and kissed till she pushed my head back gently, saying: 'Dear, you take my breath'; but really she had flushed crimson for the first time, I think. Conscious of her body, she had yielded for a moment to a man's passion.

"The days after went by on wings; her brother liked me so much that for a fortnight he did not notice the intimate terms we were on. But one evening he had said 'Goodnight,' and gone, but returned quickly and found me kissing her. She said simply; 'I love Shi,' and put her hand on his shoulder with a caress and left us.

" 'How will it end?' was all he said after a pause, and

then: 'I must leave it to you both. You,' he went on to me, 'will, I'm sure, think of her safety.'

"And I answered him that I would and told him the truth, that our caressings had all been innocent and I would not engage the future lightly; but even while reassuring him I knew that I had come to the extreme verge and uttermost limit of control, and was ripe for anything, with no more self-mastery than a child.

"Women, I often think, are far braver in such matters than men. Next day Glory wanted to know what we had decided, and walking beside her palanquin I told her we had arranged nothing; but he had left it to us. She nodded and said nothing.

"That day her brother did not stay with us after the midday meal, but made some excuse and went out, leaving us together, and at once, I don't know why, I took her in my arms and began kissing and caressing her. And she yielded to me; but in a moment her lips grew hot and she drew away.

" 'Have you really decided—at last?' she asked, and there was a challenge in that added 'at last' which stung me.

" 'For myself—yes,' I replied; 'but for you—how can I decide to bring you and him into danger?'

"The deep eyes held me, and without a word she put both her hands on my shoulders and studied me.

" 'Your Jeanne d'Arc,' she said after a moment, 'gave her life for her king. Do you think I am afraid? To lose you would make me afraid; with you I fear nothing in the world. I am proud you want me, happy you have chosen me, my man of men; with you I am content and my heart's at peace,' she added like a child, and gave her mouth.

" 'I want to have a talk with your brother first,' I said. 'We must get rid of all the servants and I must arrange to get you and myself to one of the treaty towns, where we shall be safe. But the risk is appalling and the chances of success small, for the Governor is as powerful as a god and the news of your beauty will have reached him.'

" 'Do men want beauty so much?' she asked. 'You know he has never seen me; he can't care much if he loses what he doesn't know.'

" 'You are wrong, you dear,' I cried. 'Men desire beauty more than anything, and you are so wonderful that he will have heard about you and be inordinately curious to see and possess you. Then for a strong man with power to miss something he desires, to lose it to an inferior is very bitter, and I'm afraid he'll do his uttermost against us.'

" 'Then take me,' she said, 'as long as I am yours and you are mine—me I mean,' she corrected, nestling to me; 'I am content, happy.'

"Ah! the sacred boldness of her whose law was love.

"There's one verse of your English poetry comes into my head when I think of her, and only one:

> "Teach me, only teach, Love;
>   As I ought
> I will speak thy speech, Love;
>   Think thy thought—
> Meet, if thou require it,
>   Both demands,
> Laying flesh and spirit
>   In thy hands!"

"It was Glory who showed me the heights of Chinese thought. Till I met her I believed that the practical teachings of Confucius and his rules of conduct constituted the religion of China. She introduced me to his master, Lao-tse, whom he called 'the old philosopher.' Confucius was a mere moralist, but Lao-tse was the deepest thinker who has yet arisen among men, and his religion is the earliest known to the Chinese as Buddhism is the latest.

"Lao-tse wrote his *Tâo-Teh-King* in the sixth century B.C. The title even is almost untranslatable, but may be called the *Way of Virtue*. No foreigner has ever yet grasped what the *Tâo* means, and even students are put off by apparent differences. Glory, however, was the daughter of a great thinker and she made the *Tâo* clear to me.

"Lao-tse went far beyond a belief in God or in man; the childish dualism of body and spirit, this world and the next, the Devil and God were ridiculous to him; both flesh and spirit seemed to him equally unimportant. What he saw was the unfolding of life, the mingling of life and death; the Becoming; and this perpetual Becoming is the rhythm of Life itself—the rhythm, mark you, and not the progress or development, the world of thought and deed and Being as it is in constant unfolding. That is the *Tâo*, and a study of it shows how to live in harmony with it. Glory had all the master's best sayings by heart and she taught me many of them.

" 'Those who are skilled in the *Tâo* do not dispute,' she said; 'but they know some things. They know "there is nothing softer than water," as Lao-tse said, "and yet nothing can resist it." They know that "he who inflicts death is as one who cuts wood; soon or late he cuts his own hands." They know that "trees and plants and men at birth are soft and easily bent, and at death hard and firm, and the sage therefore keeps the innocent softness of the child." They know that "when a people does not fear what it ought to fear, its great dread shall come upon it." They know that "the Sacred Way I call the *Tâo*, unlike the way of foolish men, diminishes where there is abundance and increases where there is deficiency." '

"Somehow or other her spirituality intensified my passion and gave me the sense that what was so far above ordinary life or ordinary thought must be enduring. But every now and then facts broke in and disturbed my dreaming.

"One day her brother said to me: 'We are within a fortnight's journey of the capital, you know, and though we may take a month over it, still—the Viceroy may send to meet us. And your passion is being talked of by the coolies. Even the *Tâo* prescribes foresight . . .' and he smiled.

"I was struck to the heart. Should we try to escape at once; there was no sense in drifting. I was like an opium-smoker, lost to everything but my exquisite dream-life. And how wonderful it was can never be told, for Glory was all sorts of women in one. At first a child, afraid that this or that might not please me; then so filled with joy when she found that whatever she did delighted me; shy now and now curious; frank as a boy, and wise as only a woman's love is wise.

"I went to her. 'What are we to do?' I cried. 'I am yours. Decide!'

" 'Is there a chance of escape?' she asked.

" 'Yes,' I replied; 'just a chance.'

" 'One week, one day with you is life to me,' she said; 'do you feel that too?'

" 'Sure,' I replied.

" 'Then let us try at once to escape,' she said. 'First of all let the coolies return today; pay them in full; content them without overdoing it: my brother will see to that. He will probably prefer to return himself and take up my father's business. Then you and I will go into the—appointed—whither you will.'

" 'Are you afraid?' I asked with shrinking heart.

" 'No, indeed,' she replied, smiling; 'but it is impossible, says Lao, to live long on the heights. Yet such life, even for a day, is better than years on low levels.'

"All was done as she had outlined.

"I planned to break to the west, for the frontier tribes there were in partial revolt, and it would take an army to get us; but this was only a blind. I intended to double back and get to the river, which leaves no trace, and if possible reach the sea before the chase grew close. Any foreign steamer, English or German, would then bring us easily to safety and a new life. After forty-eight hours of forced marching west and back we were on board a sampan on our way to happiness.

"But happiness was with us on the boat."

Shimonski paused: "Often I tell over to myself those golden hours, each one filled with its own joy, a delight in living and in memory. In that week I learned all a woman could give in passionate tenderness, and with what treasures of gaiety and courage she could crown her love.

"The moment we went on board, Glory took up her new part. European girls often make good wives and mothers; but she was an incomparable lover first and at the same time a companion of infinite variety. It was impossible to be dull or depressed in her company; she drew the best out of me and then declared that the wisest or wittiest sayings were all mine. She flattered me outrageously; but then who does not love to be praised by the woman he loves? The more I studied her body and face the more beautiful I thought her. She had no need to bind her feet, whether to make them look smaller or to increase the obsession of love by sedentary living; and the more I learned of her mind and spirit the more I had to admire her. She never pretended to be well-read, but she had been brought up by a wise father, who encouraged her to think for herself. She was astonishingly original in thought and ingenuous in feeling—a girl's body and a woman's soul. While loving me and telling me all sorts of things about China and her own bringing up, she managed all the time to watch the boatmen and make them her friends and protectors.

"Thanks to her mainly we hadn't a single hitch—no trouble with any of the towns or villages we passed through, no sign of any pursuit. As we neared the great harbor I allowed myself to hope, for I had planned to reach the port in the small hours of night, and knowing the Chinese ways I felt sure we should be able to evade even watchful eyes.

"Everything happened as I had foreseen; it was black night when we ran alongside the German mail steamer. I had already promised the men a large reward, so taking Glory in my arms for a long kiss I begged her to cry out if she saw anything suspicious, then ran up the ladder to see the German captain. He received me in bed, told me he would be glad to take my wife and myself as passengers, and I returned, knowing that Glory's beauty, if there was any difficulty, would be my best advocate.

"As I sprang on the deck of the sampan I was surprised not to see my love; but before I had time to think, I was struck down from behind, and remember nothing more till I awoke in a Chinese house, with Chinamen about me and a pair of Chinese eyes boring into my dull consciousness. In a moment or two I found I was cold and wet; they had probably thrown cold water over me to bring me to. And Glory! My hands and feet were bound. I was caught—but Glory? Glory! Could she possibly have escaped? If so, I'd pay for both gladly.

"I can hardly describe what followed. I soon realized that the mandarin watching me was the Governor. I lay on a sort of couch in the middle of a room, two men on each side, while he questioned me. He wanted to know whether the brother was in the plot. I said 'No. I had persuaded him I was coming straight through.'

"The Governor told me that if I lied he would torture me so that I should beg for death as a release. No bodily pain could have added to my misery and remorse.

"I grew to fear and hate his cold eyes. I thought we had

only one chance and I took it. I told him if he would give me Glory I'd serve him all my life as no man yet was ever served. I begged with all my soul. He told me he would give Glory to his servants before my eyes. . . .

"I don't remember much afterwards; it is like a dream in fever, half-reality, half-mists of pain. But one moment is clear; when she fainted I heard someone laugh. It was I. From that moment I lived for revenge.

"They tortured me too—did something to me they thought would give me a lingering death in agony, and threw me into the street. I crawled to a coolie's hut and got a girl to fetch me a German surgeon. A timely operation saved my life, and that same night I learned that Glory was dead.

"The rest's a long tale, but I can cut it short. I went to Peking and got a place in the household of the empress; in time she took a liking to me, and I thought and plotted and planned till at length she sent for the Governor and told him to come without a retinue.

"I had made my arrangements. He was taken outside the town, brought in by my servants, and bound in the cellar of a house I had bought. . . .

"He was a month dying.

"Every day I went to my duties at the palace; every evening and morning I spent an hour with those cold eyes. He used to beg me to kill him; that made me laugh. . . .

"In that month I learned the keen delight there is in torture.

"Do you know," Shimonski broke off, "I never see a punishment now or an execution without seeing that man in the place of the victim. His pain thrills me. What a month it was! I soon found out what parts of the body hurt the most when you tweaked off pieces with red-hot pincers. You'd never guess.

"He grew old in a week. . . . As I pulled his nails off, his hairs fell out. . . . With his tongue and teeth gone, his

beard turned white and the yellow skin of him shriveled as
I . . ."

I put up my hand to ward off more, and Shimonski
turned and went across the room muttering to himself.
"Glory, Glory!"

Had suffering turned his brain—or passion?

THE
TOM CAT
An Apologue

Johnny and his sister, Chrissie, lived in a small house in a row of other rabbit-houses, and behind was a great space walled in, where Johnny and Chrissie used to play. In one corner was an old tree-trunk which Johnny made into a forest inhabited by Indians and wild beasts, especially tigers; while Chrissie turned it into a throne room, with a Prince in shining raiment making love to a fair-haired girl.

On his way from school one day Johnny found a kitten which he brought home, intending to drown it in a bucket, just for the fun of seeing it try to swim; but Chrissie beat him and called him cruel and took it from him, and dried it and fed it with milk from a saucer, and claimed it as her own. And she took such care of it that it grew rapidly into a fine black cat, with the glossiest coat and brightest green eyes that were ever seen, and sometimes even Johnny laughed at the way it used to play, with its tail curved up over its back like a bow, making little sharp runs here and there without any sense.

But as it grew older it became graver, and one morning the children were together in an upper room and they saw the cat, which Chrissie called "Black Prince" from her history book, suddenly rise from the grass, make one or two quick steps across the gravel, and then spring upon the great high wall, and there "Black Prince" sat sunning himself and washing his face and combing out his whiskers.

Now, in the next house there was a great grey cat that the children had often noticed, and there it lay, in the center of its grass plot, blinking its eyes; but when it saw "Black Prince" upon the wall it rose slowly and swelled out to a great size and made one rush across, and sprang up the wall right at "Black Prince." Quicker than lightning "Black Prince" jumped off the wall into his own garden, and hid himself in the house.

"Oh, the dear!" said Chrissie, "how clever of him!"

"Beastly coward!" said Johnny, "I'd like to kick him. Look!" and there was the grey cat smoothing his hair in the sun after the exertion, and combing his whiskers.

A little while later "Black Prince" was missing all one evening, and Chrissie cried herself to sleep, and when she got up next day she was really ill with grief at the loss of her favorite; but about ten o'clock in the morning "Black Prince" suddenly appeared from goodness knows where, and he was a terrible sight. His coat was all ragged and dirty, and someone had thrown filthy water over him, and there was a long scar all down his shoulder, showing the red flesh, and his left ear was split, and his nose and forehead all torn; but Chrissie picked him up in her arms and laughed through her tears, and took him in and combed him, and washed him, and brushed him and fed him, and cared for him till in a day or two he was as sleek and fat as ever. The very next day when the sun was blazing down on the backs of the houses the children saw "Black Prince" walk quietly across the gravel path and spring upon the wall, and begin to sun himself in the heat, and the grey cat in the next garden rose at once and looked at him threateningly and then rushed across the walk and sprang up the wall; not directly at "Black Prince," this time, but some yards away. As the grey cat moved toward "Black Prince" he moved stiffly and swelled enormously and his back arched like a bow and all his fur went up on end, and he looked wicked and strong. "Black Prince" went on smoothing his hair and basking in the sun; but when the grey cat came quite close to him "Black Prince" rose up and looked him in the eye a moment or two and then, so to speak, shrugged his shoulders and sprang down into his own path and began to comb his whiskers out in his own place, and the grey cat sat upon the wall in pride of possession.

And it came to pass after this that "Black Prince" used to go out very often at night, and he always returned in the morning tired and thin; but never so dilapidated as after his first excursion; and the children wondered in vain where he had been and what he had been doing, Johnny declaring that he was a knight adventurer who did battle with his peers, and Chrissie believing that he was away seeking for his love. . . .

But one day the children were in the same upper story and "Black Prince" had returned after an absence of three or four days and had been fed up by Chrissie and cosseted for nearly a week, and was looking his very best, when he rose slowly and climbed the wall as before, and took his ease in the sun, and as before the vicious old grey cat rose up in his wrath and climbed upon the wall and came toward him with every hair on end, threatening death; but to the children's delight "Black Prince" no sooner saw him on the wall than he rose, too, and swelled visibly, and hooped his back, and all his bright black fur stood up on end, and he began to move along the wall toward the grey cat stiffly, and as the grey cat looked at him his heart turned to water, and his hair went down upon his back, and the curve died out, and he jumped back into his garden, and for a moment "Black Prince" looked as if he would follow him, but then he shrugged his shoulders, so to speak, and lay down upon the wall, and took his ease in the sunshine; and Johnny rejoiced in "Black Prince's" victory and praised him and was proud of him.

But forty years later Johnny having himself grown grey found a certain pathos in the grey cat's defeat; for then he knew by experience that age has to expect humiliation and defeat.

AFTERWORD
The Legend
of Frank Harris

By Elmer Gertz

ONE HUNDRED AND NINETEEN YEARS AGO, on February 14, 1856, James Thomas Harris, later known as Frank Harris, was born in Galway, Ireland. This simple assertion may be inaccurate in each of its particulars. We are not sure as to the year or place of Harris's birth, nor, indeed, of many other details of his life. This man, who supposedly told so much about himself in his very frank autobiography and other explicit writings, has created distrust and doubt in the minds of virtually all of his biographers and others. There have been at least six studies of him, and one that may be regarded as definitive is about to be published. There have been novels in which he is a principal character, plays, monographs, parodies of his style, innumerable essays, chapters in books, fugitive passages in countless works. There has never been a time since his life was at its apex when he was not the subject of controversy, discussion, curiosity. Just as he has written of his distinguished contemporaries, many of them have written of him. Bernard Shaw, whom he sometimes admired and often patronized and seldom understood, found him endlessly interesting as a kind of monster and had much to say of him over a long period of time. Harris's last book was about Shaw, and to this day there is much dispute as to how much of it is actually by Harris, how much by Shaw (who buried the traces), and how much by Frank Scully, a one-legged character of the French Riviera, where Harris lived in his latter years, who induced Harris to undertake the book for the money rather than the glory.

As one of the first biographers of Harris, I know at first-hand the monumental difficulties of researching or writing about him. Yet, I feel that the essential facts are pretty clear. Like many other lower-middle-class persons, ungainly in appearance, short in height, and lacking the aristocratic advantages of position and prospects, Harris compensated for these by drive, direction, and truculence, and a sense of adventure, a willingness to take chances. Brighter than those around him, and less encumbered by scruples, he was able to thrust himself forward almost from birth. As a youngster he ran off to America and emerged, strengthened and emboldened from all of the vicissitudes of the America of the post–Civil War years. He seems to have labored on the building of the Brooklyn Bridge in a menial capacity; at least, he seemed to have intimate knowledge of the horrors, such as "the bends," in working underground. He may have been in Chicago around the time of the Great Fire; at least, he was able to write of it with some intimate perception. He went West and became a cowboy. Then, meeting a bright and luminous and altogether extraordinary young man in Lawrence, Kansas, a professor of Greek at the State University, named Byron Smith, he was fired with the desire to become a scholar, a writer, a doer. He attended classes for a while; read law in the manner of the day and was admitted to the Kansas bar; he may even have practiced law. Nobody was sure as to what he did, openly or clandestinely, although rumors of a bizarre nature sprang up. Smith died as a young man. Any steadying influence that he might have had on Harris was lost, although forever afterward Harris cherished his memory. Magniloquently, he said that Smith lit the sacred fire in him. The most moving pages in *My Life and Loves* deal with Smith. Even the passages that may be in bad taste have an aura of love and worship about them.

There followed several years of wandering in Europe, learning at universities in Germany and perhaps elsewhere, making stabs at writing, teaching at a little college, lovemaking, and, above all, trying to make connections that would project him to the very top of the heap in a London that throbbed with all of the excitement of England in its greatest hours. He became known as one of the best Socialist speakers in Hyde Park. Then he was touted as a good prospect for Parliament and the Cabinet as a conservative. He was best described as a Tory Anarchist. He married a wealthy widow. He was still in his twenties when he became the editor of a London newspaper—some said he got the position through the wife of the proprietor. Scarcely older, he took over the editing of one of the most influential publications of its day, the *Fortnightly Review*, and was described as both brilliant and dangerous. Then he obtained control over the *Saturday Review* and made it one of the great legends of British literature. Later he sold it for a fancy price to some who did not share his views. Imagine a weekly magazine having as regular members of its staff Bernard Shaw, H. G. Wells, Max Beerbohm, Arthur Symons, Cunningham Graham, John Runciman, and others of like stature. Some of these men were at the very beginnings of their careers and felt that Harris had projected them into their high places. Some, particularly Shaw, remained grateful for more than a season. When later Harris came to write his autobiography, it sometimes appeared that at this great time he was interested in everything except literature. But, Tom Bell, his secretary during this great period, told me that Harris would not have walked across the street for any woman.

He was received into all of the great houses of England—"once," as his great friend and critic Oscar Wilde phrased it; but Wilde had also said that Shaw "has no enemies, and none of his friends like him." Wilde had need of much charity in this distressing time when what we know as Victorianism was in full flower. Harris defended Wilde before, during, and after his imprisonment, although he had no sympathy for Wilde's abnormality; and later wrote a celebrated life of Wilde, which is still the center of much controversy. All of the later biographers of Wilde devoted much space to telling why they disagreed with Harris; yet all of them leaned upon his work, and Wilde in a dedication to his play *An Ideal Husband* referred to Harris's "power and distinction as an artist," "his chivalry and nobility as a friend."

Harris had three great heroes—Shakespeare, Jesus, and himself, and not necessarily in that order. There can be no doubt that he read all of Shakespeare's plays and poems so often that they impressed themselves upon his memory, life, and style. He found himself differing almost violently with other students of Shakespeare, even when he borrowed from them. Inevitably, he wrote one major work on the subject, *The Man Shakespeare*, and other studies and a play as well. Just as the Wilde biographers have pecked at Harris, the Shakespeareans have been, if anything, more lividly bitter against him. They have accused Harris of making Shakespeare a man after the fashion of Harris himself—that is, a slave to passion. They have refused to believe that Shakespeare unlocked his heart, not alone in the sonnets, but in all that he wrote. They think of Shakespeare as being above his work. Harris sees him as a part of it. It is the great merit of Harris that his writings are like deeds—they stab, stimulate, anger, cajole. Everything bears his personal impress. It is a full-blooded man who has lived and written his stories, novels, essays, critiques.

If you do not like the man, you may not like his writings.

The truculent Harris was devoted to the gentle Jesus, and fancied himself as following in His footsteps. He was conscious of no blasphemy. He could criticize Shakespeare for being a snob and weak in some of his ways. But he could not dissect Jesus in any such frank and brutal fashion, whether in his stories or elsewhere. He was persuaded that the world would have to adopt the ways of Jesus if it were to survive; and one cannot say, really, that he is wrong. We have Christians of the pew and pulpit, but few who understand His meaning.

His worshipper, Harris, scarcely emulated the gentle Jesus in his daily life. He sought out every sort of experience, noble and ignoble. He consorted with the money changers, and sought to shortchange them. He dealt with the politicians, the nobility, the generals, the gamblers, even the chefs and maître d's. He served them for a price and was accused of blackmailing and defaming them. One result was his going to jail briefly, and into bankruptcy. Another was the enrichment of experience leading to his best stories, novels, contemporary portraits, journalism. He saw his punishment, not as flowing from his personal defects, but from the sins of England. He fled to America, at the outbreak of the First World War; wrote a book critical of England and somewhat sympathetic of Germany; gained control of a magazine, *Pearson's*, and made it a highly personal forum for a decade. Just as he had won the excessive devotion of gifted young men in his down-at-the-heels days in London, following his great *Saturday Review* period, he won the almost idolatrous support of other young people in America. Many of them felt that he was an authentic great man, suffering the wounds of neglect because of his qualities rather than his defects. There was, perhaps, some symbolism in his getting his clothes made at the shop run by Henry Miller's father. The young

Henry helped Harris to take off and put on his pants for fittings. Miller recalls that Harris was the first great man he ever met. Harris encouraged him.

In this period of his life his great medium was the contemporary portrait—what might be called a psychograph of a celebrated person. There were five volumes of these portraits. The first and most controversial had been published in England; the others in the United States. Harris professed to know all of the poets, philosophers, painters and politicians of his day, and to depict them as they were, whether great or lesser or a mixture of qualities. It was difficult for ordinary critics who had not lived Harris's ample life to believe that the man could know so many of the highly placed persons of several continents. Even some who knew the opportunities that had come to him questioned his portraits. Nobody, not even a parish priest, could be the recipient of so many confessions. His critics would have been better advised had they looked upon the portraits as the creative efforts of a born storyteller. His aim was to give verisimilitude, poetic truth, rather than factual accuracy in the fashion of census takers and statisticians. I learned this when I studied the antecedents of Harris's portrait of Richard Wagner. I tell about this elsewhere. Suffice it to say that the subjects of Harris's portraits at their best have a life that is more real than reality, and truer than the facts.

We see this in Harris's two superb novels, *The Bomb* and *Great Days*. The first mentioned is an account of the Haymarket tragedy in Chicago when some idealistic anarchists were unjustly hanged by a community more interested in repression than in curing social evils. The second, by way of contrast, deals with England and France in Napoleon's time. Both novels read like slices of the author's autobiography. It is as if Harris himself shared all of these historical experiences. He personalizes the impersonal; he makes what is outside one's ken as intimate as one's skin. He does this in his Shakespeare books, his Wilde biography, his *Contemporary Portraits*, his short stories, everything he writes. He is a part of everything he sees or imagines. The past becomes present. All become emanations of his spirit and drive.

Nobody knowing Harris would have imagined that he suffered from inhibition, the inability to express himself frankly. But he felt that he was prevented from speaking out with the utmost candor by the restraints imposed upon all creative writers by the Puritanical spirit of the Anglo-Saxon world. He believed that love, bodily love, was the greatest influence in life. Nobody could write of love if he were compelled to corset his women, conventionalizè his language, pay undue tribute to the grim and glum Mrs. Grundy. He dreamed of a time when he would set an example for all creative spirits by writing a completely true, completely undraped, autobiography. So, as old age was upon him, when his memory was somewhat dimmed and his style less distinguished than it had been, he wrote his several volumes of autobiography, the first one called *My Life and Loves*, and went abroad to print and market them. We who are now accustomed to Henry Miller, Philip Roth, Norman Mailer, and their ilk, cannot grasp the incredulity with which the conventional world read Harris's narrative of sexual escapades. The police were set upon anyone who dared sell the books. Several young men went to prison for distributing the work. Harris was afraid to return to our shores for a visit until I received assurances from the renowned lawyer, Clarence Darrow, that he would defend Harris if he were arrested. Even in France, Harris was summoned by the police, and left undisturbed only when the great literary masters joined in a manifesto in his behalf.

This had been Harris's experience several times in his life. When he was editor of the *Fortnightly Review*, a popular clergyman, the Reverend Newman Hall, led the pack against him because of the candor with which he depicted a love affair in his story, "A Modern Idyll." And when he wrote what we would now regard as an innocuous essay, called "Thoughts on Morals," the editor of the conventional journal, *The Spectator*, stormed against Harris for writing and *The English Review* for publishing not wholly orthodox observations on life. Outstanding English writers, some of whom did not care for Harris personally, joined in a statement supporting freedom of utterance, which *The Spectator* found unimpressive. When, in his first *Contemporary Portraits*, Harris wrote of Carlyle's confession of impotency and its adverse effect upon his sexually unsatisfied wife, Scottish moralists and others were shrill in their attacks upon him, at least one writing a little book to dispute him. Ironically, this book proved that Harris, as a young man, did know Carlyle, a result certainly not intended by the critic.

By the time Harris died in August 1931, in Nice, France, one could not be sure of his ultimate place in the world's literature. He often expressed himself as confident that he would one day be accepted as a master. He would intone: "We are immortal only when we die." Harris had far greater influence than has generally been recognized. D. H. Lawrence's *Lady Chatterley's Lover*, perhaps James Joyce's *Ulysses*, are products, in some degree, of Harris's influence; even more so the writings of Henry Miller and a flock of good and bad imitators. It is recognized that our literature was retarded in its growth by the baneful power and narrow vision of Bowdler, Victoria, Comstock, Sumner, and a host of like-minded censors here and abroad and their unnamed imitators in numerous villages. Sex was, in Lawrence's phrase, a dirty little secret. Harris's great virtue was that he refused to be confined by the secret and those who guarded it. He spoke out, and he has had many followers, some of whom do not know his name, and others who have denigrated him.

His influence on literary portraiture and biography has been both unrecognized and considerable. We think of Lytton Strachey as being the father of the modern biographical realism and candor, but Harris has an equal claim. Wittingly or unwittingly, his *Contemporary Portraits* and his life of Wilde, of the same genre, have affected all who write of living or historical characters. Shakespearean criticism and biography will never be as they were before Harris. Harris has taught us that the true portrait must deal with blemishes as well as virtues, the inner person as well as the outer, the naked ape no less than the draped social creature. The secret loves are as much the man as the public papers and parades.

The stories included in this volume suggest that Harris still has life as an artist. We told of them more fully in the Preface. But I am still not sure whether Harris will live as a writing man, rather than a literary legend. At his best he has qualities that transcend his subjects, his style, and his words. In my time and in an earlier day he was able to inspire many young readers into an almost rapturous love of the great creative spirits and all high endeavor. He made us feel that great poetry, although surrounded by poverty, was nobler and spiritually more rewarding than the worldly successes of the Rockefellers and Astors and their bloated retainers and apologists. He inspired us to go forth boldly into a crass world and to change it by our tilting into a regal sphere fit for saints and seers and singers. Sometimes, later, when we settled into realism, we scolded him for not himself living up to the best that he asked of us. But is that not foolish? It is enough if one ennobles others; it is too much to expect the singer to be like his song.